the Girl at the Window

Rowan Coleman lives with her husband and five children in a very full house in Hertfordshire. She juggles writing novels with raising her family. She longs to live at Ponden Hall.

To find out more about Rowan Coleman, visit her website at: www.rowancoleman.co.uk, Facebook or Twitter: @rowancoleman.

Also by Rowan Coleman:

The Summer of Impossible Things
Looking for Captain Poldark
The Other Sister
We Are All Made of Stars
The Memory Book
Runaway Wife
A Home for Broken Hearts
Lessons in Laughing Out Loud
The Baby Group
Woman Walks into a Bar
River Deep
After Ever After
Growing Up Twice
The Accidental Family
The Accidental Wife
The Accidental Mother

the Girl at the Window

Rowan Coleman

EBURY
PRESS

First published by Ebury Press in 2019

3 5 7 9 10 8 6 4 2

Ebury Press, an imprint of Ebury Publishing
20 Vauxhall Bridge Road,
London SW1V 2SA

 Penguin
Random House
UK

Ebury Press is part of the Penguin Random House group
of companies whose addresses can be found at
global.penguinrandomhouse.com

www.penguin.co.uk

A CIP catalogue record for this book is available from the British
Library

ISBN 9781785032462

Typeset in 10.1/16.9 pt ITC Galliard Std by
Integra Software Services Pvt. Ltd, Pondicherry

Printed and bound in Great Britain by Clays Ltd, Elcograf S.p.A.

Penguin Random House is committed to a sustainable future for
our business, our readers and our planet. This book is made from
Forest Stewardship Council® certified paper.

For Julie, Steve, Kizzy and Noah, and all the residents of Ponden Hall, past, present and future.

PART ONE

No coward soul is mine,
No trembler in the world's storm-troubled sphere:
I see Heaven's glories shine,
And Faith shines equal arming me from Fear.

Emily Brontë

PROLOGUE

There's a phone ringing, somewhere very far away.

'*Wake up, Tru. Wake up. Wake up, Trudy, wake up!*'

Abe. Hearing his voice I am instantly awake, turning to him at once. Unwilling to open my eyes just yet, I feel the weight of him sitting on the edge of our bed.

'What is it?' I murmur, reaching out for his familiar warmth. His long fine fingers that I am so used to being entwined in my mine ... my love, my husband, mine.

'I was dreaming about when I was a girl, the day that Dad died,' I tell him. 'It seemed so real, just as if I was there again ... It must have been the phone ringing that brought me out of it. But who's ringing at this time of night? It is night, right?'

'Tru, I'm so sorry.' Abe's whisper dissipates as my hand arrives on a cool and empty sheet.

'Abe?' My hand travels over an expanse of bed, searching, but he is just out of reach. 'Abraham?'

'*Wake up, Trudy, wake up.*'

'Tru, I'm so sorry, I love you,' he says very softly in my ear, close enough that I feel the heat of his breath on my neck. 'Don't forget that I love you – and nothing can change that. Not even this.'

'Abraham?'

'Mummy!' Will grabs my arms and shakes me.

'I'm awake.' Sleep makes every part of me as heavy as lead. 'I'm up. Wait, Daddy was just … Abe?'

But there is nothing but the empty space of his side of the bed. With a sharp pang I remember: Abe's not here. He's overseas; Peru this time. Using his training as a general surgeon, midway through a six-week-long aid mission.

'Can't you stay at home?' I'd begged him.

'You know why I can't,' he'd said.

'Mummy.' Will climbs into bed, skinny legs and freezing feet snaking in between mine. 'The phone woke me up; it's been ringing and ringing. And stopping and ringing again. Didn't you hear it?'

'I didn't.' Reaching out, I switch on a lamp.

The landline telephone is next to the bed. No one ever phones the landline. Will and I flinch as it begins to ring once more.

'Go on,' Will urges me, wide eyes and wide awake, like only an eight-year-old can be. 'It will be Daddy!'

I don't know why I'm so afraid to pick it up, but I am. I can hear distance on the line.

'Hello?'

'Is it Daddy?' Will reaches at once for the receiver. 'Let me talk!'

'In a minute.' Twisting away from him, waiting for the other voice on the end to speak one moment more before filling the silence with a gush of hopeful words. 'Abe? Can you hear me? I was just dreaming you were here. We miss you. Will is right here, say something!'

I half laugh and hear the desperation in my own voice echo back at me down the line. In the short, silent space that follows, I somehow know everything all at once.

'Ms Heaton?' It's not Abe that speaks; I knew it wouldn't be. It's not my beloved, my heart, my soulmate, my reason.

'Ms Heaton, I'm so sorry to have to tell you ...'

I watch Will's face as he watches mine. I see his face fall, and watch our whole world implode in the reflection in his eyes.

CHAPTER ONE

. . . .

Eight months later

'Here we are,' I say to Will, reaching for his hand as I climb out of the car, parked just down the road from the house. I inhale the landscape around me. Bathed in the last of the afternoon sun, it glows softly of coppers and golds, and it's just how I imagine it when I think of it, which is often: always different, always changing, always the same.

Ponden Hall is a house built with light.

It's a beacon, a lighthouse with no sight of the sea, pulsing in the dark and sending messages far and wide for the special few that can hear them.

'*You* can hear them, because you are a Heaton and we have always lived here since the first foundation stone was laid in 1540. Our ancestors made this place for you, and every Heaton there will ever be,' he would tell me, the reassurance of his hand heavy on my shoulder. 'They birthed the house out of the hillside.'

'Yer, Ma,' he'd say, lowering his voice, 'isn't a Heaton, so she can't see the lights. She only sees the shadows.'

Ma, who I haven't seen for all these years, is somewhere within those thick, ancient walls, with sixteen years of 'I told you so' waiting to greet me. So why am I here? Because Abe was lost without trace, and, although I didn't want to have to turn to her, at the same time there was only one place that I wanted to be: home. Months passed, hopes faded, money ran out ... and eventually I gave in to the call of the beacon. I'd run back to Ponden. It just so happened that Ma would be there, too.

Will scrambles past me, ignoring me, standing in the middle of the flat area of hardstanding, looking around him, trying to understand a landscape that is as unfamiliar to my little urban boy as the surface of Mars might be; more so, in his case.

For me, though, it's like breathing above water. Taking in a deep breath of clean, quiet air, tipping my face into the welcoming wind, it cools my heated cheeks with every passing whisper. The relief. The joy of arriving somewhere where even the air is a familiar friend. It's only because my son is standing next to me that I don't fling my arms open to embrace this place that I have missed, every single moment, for sixteen years.

'There's nothing here,' Will says, his body hunching up against the cold.

'What do you mean, nothing?' I look up and down the valley, hills billowing on either side of the flat, cool expanse of the reservoir and the sky reaching ever upwards. 'There's *everything* here.'

'I don't like it, I want to go home,' Will says, his voice very fragile and small. In the silence that comes afterwards there is the resounding absence of London traffic, and of school friends shouting his name, footballs clattering against the neighbour's fence. What he can't hear is the hum of our washing machine and the TV always on. Of Daddy laughing and talking too loud on the phone, the last human on earth who actually liked making phone calls. All the noises that Will has always known are silenced here.

'It is different here,' I say gently, lightly dropping my arm round his shoulder. 'It is, I know. But turn around and you'll see your house. The one that has always been yours, even before you were born.'

Gravel crunches under our feet as, ignoring the way he stiffens at my touch, I turn him around to look up the hillside at the house.

And there she is: my friend; my mother; my haven. I see her for the first time again at the exact same moment as Will. Dearest Ponden Hall, perched in the crook of the hillside, watching out for me, waiting for me to come home, arms outstretched.

The ancient walls are as solid and immovable as the rocky moor they are made from. The diamond-pane windows glint and wink, reflecting the cold bright blue of a cloudless October day. The tall drystone wall that encloses the garden is just about still standing, stones precariously balancing, one atop the other, just as they have for hundreds of years.

Oh, the relief to be here, to be safe, to be near somewhere that has always healed me.

Every Heaton knows that Ponden does have dark corners, deep shadows and lost stories caught within its history, fleeting shadows that are gone the moment you look at them. But every Heaton loves it nevertheless, and now it's Will's turn.

'I don't like it,' he says, eyes dark. 'It looks cold, and old, and full of spiders.'

All Will sees right now is a house without his father in it.

'I think you will love it; do you know why?'

Will looks up at me, his brown eyes full of tears that he is doing his best to contain. Slowly, he shakes his head.

'Because this house was built for you, five hundred years ago. Everyone who has ever lived in this house has been a Heaton, and nearly every boy that has lived here has been called Robert or William, just like you.'

'Really?' Will looks back at the house, and I hold my breath as his cold hand reaches unconsciously for mine, as it always used to before all this. 'But I'm a Heaton Jones.'

'You are,' I say. 'But you are a Heaton nevertheless, and this house will know you the moment you walk in through the door, I promise you. It will recognise you.'

'That sounds creepy, actually,' Wills says. He has a point, this little boy of a world of fitted kitchens and night lights.

'Not creepy, just different. You'll see.'

'But ...' Will stops as we walk up the hill towards the front door. 'What about Daddy? How will Daddy know that we are here?'

'He ...' I stop. Every expert I have spoken to since it happened said I had to be clear when talking to Will about the light aircraft crash. That I had to explain that, even though no trace could be found of the plane, or the people in it, we had to understand that Abe was most likely dead. That no one could survive, unaided and injured, in dense rainforest. Tell your son his father is never coming back, they said, that he will never see him again.

That is the only way for an eight-year-old to truly understand grief, they said. To be able to process, and eventually recover from, what's happened, even if there is no body, and no grave. Don't tell him his father has passed away, or gone to sleep. It sounds brutal and cruel, they said, the grief counsellors and the social workers, but in the end it's the right thing for him to be able to face it and recover. So that's what I did; I did what they told me to do for Will, even though it broke my heart.

And yet Will won't listen to me. He still believes that his father is alive, no matter what I say, and more than that, he is angry with me for not believing too.

'I left the address at the flat,' I tell him, which is true; I left a forwarding address. 'Besides, I lived here when I first met Daddy – I have lots of stories to tell you about that time. So Daddy knows, he knows where we are. He knows that if we're not at our flat, we'll be here.'

'Then why have I never visited here before?' Will asks me as we stop at the front door of Ponden Hall. That's a question I don't have the courage to answer right now. For a fraction of a second I hesitate by the gate set into the high garden wall, seeing it out of the corner of my eye, unwilling to look right at it, remembering what I saw there once, a long time ago. Lifting the latch on the old front door, I push it open.

'Hello,' I say to the house, 'this is my little boy, William. We're home.'

Light filters through the stained-glass window at the other end of the hall and dapples on the flags. The air inside is static and thick with dust; it smells like a museum, a long-forgotten, lost civilisation. Which is not like Ma and her fondness for lemon-scented disinfectant at all, constantly cleaning, in perpetual motion. But for someone like me, who has devoted their working life to exactly those sorts of institutions, it only adds to the homecoming.

'Mummy.' Will's voice waivers in the gloom; the only thing he has ever been afraid of is the dark. 'I want to go home.'

'It's OK, I promise. I promise you will like it once you get used to it.'

We follow the ever-so-gentle downward slope of the hall as it bends right, taking us down into the heart of the house. Firelight flickers under the door to the sitting room; there's the snuffle, snort and scratch of a dog's paw at the gap under the door.

This is it, then. The reunion. Half of me wonders if, after the archaic exchange of short, curt letters, sent second class, and half-heard messages relayed via Jean from Middle Farm's landline, if she has any idea that we are coming at all. But it's too late to turn back now.

'Ma?' I call out as I push open the door. 'Ma, we're here. We've arrived.'

'I can see that,' Ma's disembodied voice says. 'I've got eyes, don't I?'

CHAPTER TWO

At first the room, lit only by firelight and what's left of the afternoon sun, looks empty of any life except the elderly retriever, standing legs set, grumbling in a decidedly half-hearted fashion.

'Away with you, Mab,' Ma says, and my head turns towards her voice, lost as she is in the great dark recess of an elderly hooded leather porter's chair. The claws of her hands cover the ends of the cracked and worn armrests; stockinged legs ending in disintegrating slippers are set on the ground in the same stance as the dog she is talking to. 'Too late to get your knickers in a twist now, old girl.'

'Hey, girl.' Dropping to one knee, Will holds out his hand to Mab and her nose delicately investigates his fingertips, her tail thudding against the same sofa we have had since I was a little girl. Will folds down next to her, eyes lighting up as she pushes the dome of her head under his palm, leaning her unsteady weight into his. Seeing him relax, so do I, just a little.

Ma leans forward so at last I can see her face.

'You're older,' she says.

'So are you,' I reply, taking her in. Her once-thick blonde hair is now streaked with silver and, always delicate and as fine-boned as a wren, she is truly thin now: much too thin. In the firelight, every hollow and dip in her face is deepened, revealing the skull beneath her skin, making her look so much older than her fifty years. A sudden longing leaps into my chest and I realise that, despite everything that happened, I have missed her. Or missed having a mother, at least.

'And this is the boy.' As she gestures at Will, her eyes meet mine, unreadable. No cue as to how to proceed. 'This is William.'

'Will. He loves dogs,' I say, just to say something as I look round this familiar room where I grew up, longing to lose myself in nostalgia. The great hall, they called it long ago, though it is not so very great. The huge inglenook fireplace stands sentinel at one end, and at the other, the great dresser that has been in the house for almost as long as it has been built, elderly oak blackened by centuries of touch, standing floor to ceiling, so heavy it's bolted to the wall. When I was a little girl I used to think of it being like Pippi Longstocking's chest of treasures, always something miraculous to be found in every drawer or cupboard, whether it was meant for the hands of child or not; it was another place to go, another world to me. Ma talks about Mab, something about finding her starving in the back garden. Ma always had so much more kindness to offer animals than she did humans.

I half listen as Wills asks more about Mab, watching brand-new night unfurl against the stone window frame, the diamond-paned glass reflecting fragments of firelight into the room. Just visible, high in the ceiling, are the old metal hooks where pheasants and meat once hung, the ornately moulded Yorkshire plaster roses that decorate the very tops of the walls a sign that, at one time at least, the Heatons had gone up in the world. And beneath Ma's scattering of rugs, the flagstones that have always been there, only a little worn by so many thousands of pairs of feet crossing them day after day. For a moment I remember how I used to lay my cheek against the cool stone and close my eyes and think of all of those feet that had smoothed it away. I'd always thought of one pair, in particular, which had known my house almost as well as I did. I'd close my eyes and try to imagine Emily Brontë sitting at our table, leaning against our dresser, warming herself by the great smoky fire and walking again and again across the flagstones to the Ponden library that she loved so much. And as I lay there, I'd whisper my secrets to her, because when I was ten years old I couldn't think of anyone better equipped to keep them than the author of *Wuthering Heights*.

'Anyway, it's been nearly a decade since I took her in, ten years of just her and me. Old Mab here will be glad of new blood.' Ma draws herself up to standing and I realise that

I'm taller than her now. 'She's sick and tired of me, for the most part. Old bag of bones, I am; you can't even chew on me, can you, Mab?'

Mab is too lost in Will's ministrations to care what Ma says, her large paw braced on Will's shoulder as he rubs her tummy, setting her hind leg into a frenzy of agitation.

'So, William ...' Ma peers at him with something like apprehension. 'I'm your grandmother.'

Will looks up at her, blinking.

'I've already got one,' he says. 'Granny Unity. She's my dad's mum, and she lives in Putney.'

There had been several long talks about going to live with Unity after I realised I couldn't keep the flat on alone. I'd thought of it, me and Will in her big, sunny garden flat. She'd cook and nurture us, take care of us, shower us with the love and kindness that she always had, almost from the moment Abe first brought me home to her. So why weren't we there in her warm embrace, heads on her shoulder? She'd wept as we'd left this morning, and Will had twisted in his seat and pressed his hands against the rear-view window, crying for her.

'Don't take what's left of my boy away,' Unity had begged me last night. In the end, only the truth reassured her, as crazy as it sounded.

'I'm going back to the place where I first found him,' I told her. 'And I know it will be so much more difficult than if I stayed here with you, and I know it's hard to understand, but, somehow, I feel like he's there, waiting for me. It's not for ever, Unity, it's just something my heart needs to do.'

And that was the truth: I needed home. I needed Ponden more than I ever had, this one magical place in the whole of the world that healed any hurt, soothed any harm, just like a whispering mother. The absence of it had always been part of my life from the day I left, a background hum of longing, the other joys in my life blotting it out. But in the last few months it has called to me, singing out in the dark. It was the one place in the world where I felt I might know something like peace again, not only for myself, but for my son.

There was something else, too: there was Ma. I'd asked her to let me come home because I wanted to give Will a break from London life and a change of scene, and because I needed Ponden. I'd expected ... Honestly, I don't know what I expected, but it wasn't her swift acceptance. And the other reason I'd come back to Ponden was for Ma. Maybe Ponden could heal us, too.

'Well, now you've got two. I'm Granny Mariah,' Ma said to Will, bending stiffly forward, extending a hand towards him. 'I'm pleased to meet you, William. Did you know that every generation of Heaton men that have lived in this house has been called either Robert or William? Your grandfather, he was a Robert.'

'Yes.' Reluctantly, Will briefly shakes her hand. 'Mum just told me – and *I'm* not a Heaton, I'm a Heaton Jones.'

'You're a Heaton first,' Ma says, 'so you're a Heaton.'

'Ma ...' I wanted time, time to talk to her about how to talk to Will, how to handle him, but Ma always has her own agenda.

'I know who I am.' Will returns his attention to the dog, and Ma's expression is one of mild amusement.

'A Heaton first,' she mutters.

'Thank you,' I say quickly, before Ma can say something else to Will. 'Thanks for letting us come. I know it must be ... disrupting, after having the place to yourself for so long.'

'What else am I going to do?' Ma's eyes roam over my face, as if trying to discern any trace of the girl I once was. 'You're blood, after all. I made up your old room for you both; there's your old bed and a mattress. I don't sleep up there nowadays – roof's a wreck – but that room's OK if it don't rain. There's bread, cheese, butter, bacon in the pantry, if you're hungry.'

'*I'm* hungry,' Will says.

'You get settled, then. I'll make you a sandwich.' Ma pushes herself off from the table towards the door, and for a moment I'm worried she will topple.

'Ma, I can do it ...'

'You won't know where anything is.' Ma waves me away. 'Do as you're told and take your stuff up.'

'Right,' I say, and it's like being fifteen again, having to force myself to drag out every awkward word. 'I spoke to the electric people; they said the power will be back on today or tomorrow. You owed them quite a lot.'

It's not a subtle dig, to point out that I'm settling her debts for her with what meagre savings we have, but I can't stop myself saying it anyway.

'In the meantime ...' Ma gestures at three candle stumps, wicks blackened and broken and a battered box of matches.

Mab lifts her head off the floor in weary protest as Will stands up.

'Everyone says my dad is dead,' he says, looking at Ma. 'But he isn't, I know he isn't.'

'Fair dos,' Ma says, but Will isn't done.

'Granny Unity says you are a racist and that's why you didn't want Mum and Dad to get married. And if you are racist that means you hate me too, doesn't it?'

'Will ...' My instinct is to step in but it's the wrong one. I'm so proud of the stalwart line across his shoulders, the refusal to look away, his raised chin. My little boy, eight years old, and already there are ever more minutes of the day I can't make safe for him, battles that only he can fight – and worst of all, he's already used to it.

'Now then,' Ma says, 'the boy deserves a direct answer to a direct question.' She turns to Will, fixing him with her pale china-blue eyes. 'I never hated your dad. I thought he was a very fine man, just not the man for my daughter. I had my reasons. And your mum, she had hers. We fell out over it. But I can tell you this, Will, it had nothing to do with your dad being black. Nothing at all. I'm many things, but I ain't one of them, and if you ever meet one round here, I'll take my stick to them, do you hear me? I won't have that vile filth near me or you. You are my grandson, and you are welcome here. And there aren't that many that are. Just know that.'

'Mum *said* you weren't a racist,' Will says. 'She said you were just nasty. I wanted to check.'

'Happen I am nasty,' Ma replies, with a shrug that says, 'nothing more to add'. 'I can't help who I am, now can I? You can hate me for that if you like.'

This time it was Will's turn to shrug.

'You like dogs,' he says. 'Anyway, my dad's not dead. He's coming home, I know he is.'

'Happen you're right, son,' Ma says mildly. 'After a life living in this house I'm inclined to think that death isn't quite the dead end that everybody says it is.'

And for the first time since we left London, Will smiles.

Ponden 1654

Praise Be to His Greatness that delivered me to this Place that has given me shelter and food, and safety when I was lost and lived as one of the damned. Praise be to His Glorious name forever, for His salvation and for my friend and brother, Robert Heaton, who, so that he may not forget his own schooling, now denied to him, took to showing me my words and letters that I might know a little of the books that are kept within this great house.

These words I write are my gift to dear Robert, these words that I will gather here, in the glory and gratitude of my Lord God, that mark down the tales of our lives and how we are Blessed by His mercy to have come to one another over many great and wicked miles.

I was likely no more than nine years of age when I first came to Ponden Hall, though I was small and underfed, so may be older.

The war was two years won, but even so, soldiers still walked abroad the land, taking what they could with force and violence. Many folk starved, even in this great county of Yorkshire where so much is taken in tax and levies. Poor have no respite, no help but what the Parish may afford them, which is precious little. And so it happened that my own mother sold me on the roadside to my master and father, one Henry Casson, may God forgive her.

He who had once been a paid soldier from across the border did not make a kind father, rather he was a man most cruel and evil in his intent.

Long days we travelled, days when he called me sometimes daughter, sometimes dog. From house to house we'd go, and he'd take and steal in word and deed, with not a care for the harm he left after him. Until, after some very bloody trouble on the road, trouble which I dare not speak of, we came to this place, Henry Casson aware that the mistress was presumed a widow, her husband not returned from war. Here he contrived to stay.

On that first day I was much afraid of what he would do, trying to hide myself in the shadows and smoke that had gathered there as I watched him sitting at the great table, in the shadow of a towering dresser, talking with Mistress Anne Heaton. As before, he called himself my father, and me a motherless girl. He told her that she needed the protection of a strong man to care for her and her properties, make sure all is done that is right by her.

His voice could be very kind, when it had a need to be.

It was then that Robert Heaton first found me, cowering against the wall, and told me not to be afraid, that the maid, Betty, would have buttermilk in the kitchen for us.

'I am Robert Heaton, master of this house,' he told me on that day. 'I am twelve years of age and you are welcome in my home.'

The milk was warm and sweet, the fire good, and I praised His Glory for bringing me these moments of comfort. For all the days and nights that I had followed Casson, not knowing what else I might do but die, I had never troubled my master with disobedience. But on this day, seeing how this house was good, decent and God-fearing, I sought to go against Casson and warn Robert of the danger that sat up at his table.

'My name is Agnes; I do not know my age and that man is not my father,' I told him. 'I do know that he means to marry your Mother. He means to stay here forever or for as long as it will serve him.'

Even as I write this now, with my words so few and so clumsy, I see the great grief and loss in my Robert's face.

'Father went to the war and didn't return,' Robert told me, 'and Mother cannot manage alone.'

'She should try,' I told him, with every ounce of strength that a girl of so few years and such little import could muster. 'Tell her she should try.'

On that day Robert took my hand and promised me that as long as I stayed at Ponden Hall he would protect me from all harm. Dearest Lord, I bless You for the gift of his protection and care, and the words that are now becoming mine, even though I am only poor and low-born, and I vow that I shall only ever use them in the praise of Your Glorious Name.

And that my friendship and loyalty to Robert is such that it will never be broken or ended, but instead, an eternal loving regard that will endure for all time.

Agnes Casson, for I do not know what name was previously mine.

CHAPTER THREE

A creak on the floorboards, a breath against my cheek, the palm of Abe's hand smooth and warm on my back, the scent of him; for a few seconds I feel calm, and safe and then …

Opening my eyes, I stare hard at the curtainless window, concentrating on screwing back the grief tight inside my ribcage. Every morning it's the same, the shock and the loss renewed with every rising sun.

The last traces of the night sky, just visible through the laced vines of the ivy that has half overgrown the window, are ebbing away outside, evolving into a perfect royal blue. I've slept much later than I meant to, although I don't know how, on this worn-out carpet, with the loose boards creaking and shifting underneath me all night.

Will's small bed is empty; he must have gone to the bathroom. Peeling myself off of the floor is a laborious process, stiff muscles and mismatched bones sing out in complaint.

'Will? You OK?' I call out. The air seems to flinch around me, as if unused to hearing voices, and I sympathise. When I was a child I lived with silence for hours, sometimes; I relished it. As an adult I spend much of my time alone, with nothing but the sound of whispering books. Silence has been a companion, something that spins outwards from my own closed mouth, protecting me within its confines. Ma has been here alone for a long time, silent for a long time, and her silence has crept into every crevice of the house, muting it.

'Talk to me,' I whisper into the chill air. 'I miss you.'

And the room that was once my kingdom talks back, with a host of memories, each one clamouring to be heard. Once, long before I was born, this room was twice as wide and twice as long, a grand and important library, the finest for miles around, lined with bookcases that are still partially intact. But for all of my childhood this fragment of a lost room was mine and the books that lined the shelves my freedom. It's strange to see the place where I felt so happy, so warm and content, with fresh adult eyes. And so profoundly moving, feeling the echoes of that child all around me. Even if the sky-blue paint I chose to match the view outside my window is peeling, and a thick layer of sticky dust coats every surface, it's still just as magical to me – although I'll admit the gaping great hole in the ceiling almost succeeds in taking the shine off.

At some point, a deluge of water must have brought a large part of the plaster down, leaving a jagged black hole right above my head and, beyond that, a small, ragged gap in the roof tiles.

'No one's taken care of you for a long time.' I speak to Ponden as naturally as I always have, passing conversation with a dear friend. 'I'm sorry I've been gone so long, but I am back now. I'll fix things while I'm here, get you back on your feet again.'

Today, that feels possible.

Last night, as I lay under the hole in the ceiling, so bone-tired I could have slept on stone, I caught a glimpse of something glittering right up in the exposed eaves of the house. As my eyes adjusted to the deep velvet of the night, I realised it was a single star twinkling above my head, its light a traveller through time, making its way from somewhere deep in the galaxy over thousands, maybe millions, of years; the ghost of a star that might not even be burning any more, travelling all this way to be seen and remembered just by me. And I knew that, whatever might be waiting for me in the fathomless days ahead, it didn't seem so frightening because that light had travelled all this way with no expectation of being seen, and yet, in this small corner of the universe, my eyes were there to see it. And that gives me hope; it gives me hope that there are beautiful things that I cannot yet see, but which will one day reveal themselves to me. So I kept my eyes on it until sleep took me away, knowing that even though it's no longer visible in daylight, it is still there.

Getting up off of the floor, I wander about, unpacking some of our things, folding Will's clothes onto the bookshelves. I need a watertight place to keep my kit from the Lister James museum, where I had worked in the archives until ... until I had to take a break from preserving, tracking and recording every single item that was held there, old and new. I had an idea, half-baked, to search out all the old family documents, many of them stuffed into that great dresser downstairs, and make a proper Heaton archive out of decade upon decade of discarded admin. But that was before I saw the state of disrepair the house was in; it seemed I'd be spending my savings much quicker than I planned, but at least one day it would all be for Will.

Where was Will?

I call out his name once again, tugging open the stiff door and walking over to the bathroom. He isn't in there.

'Dear Ponden,' I say very politely, 'please tell me, what have you done with my son?'

At the end of the hallway, the oldest part of the house stands facing outwards, sentinel against the ages. A great stone lintel holds the original door that was made for it five hundred years ago in its gentle grip, and the door swings open, just enough to allow a slice of sunrise to cut through the gloom. Of course, this would be the room that an eight-year-old boy would hide in; it's the room with the ready-made den in it, after all, and Will would have no idea of the importance of that particular find, other than it invites adventure the moment you look at it.

'Will, are you hiding in there?'

A whirlwind of dust motes dance in its light like a shower of sparks as I open the door; wood creaks and whispers.

The room is exactly as I last remember seeing it, empty except for the infamous four-hundred-year-old box bed, the closeted bed, no less, that Emily Brontë wrote into *Wuthering Heights*, and the window she imagined the ghost of Cathrine Earnshaw's bloody hands smashing through, too. Today it looks more like the room you might find Sleeping Beauty in, the morning light cast into shades of green, filtered through the trees and vines that have grown up far too closely around the house, giving the room the feel of a silent glade in a leafy forest. The door to the bed is drawn shut and there is no sign of Will.

'Will?' I call his name. There's no reply, but I can sense him. Sense his movement and mood, so I tread very carefully. 'So, this room is pretty cool, right? This is the room that makes Ponden Hall really famous, because once, a long time ago, a very famous writer called Emily Brontë visited Ponden Hall all the time to use the library here. It's this room, and that bed you're in, that she describes in her novel, *Wuthering Heights*. So that's pretty cool, isn't it? To live in a famous house that people all over the world have visited, even if it's only in their imaginations.'

I wait, he waits. The room waits, watchful.

At last the door of the box bed slides open and Will's tousled head appears, his face creased with deep sleep.

'What am I doing in here?' he asks me, blinking. 'This isn't where I went to bed, is it?'

'Hmm,' I say. 'I think that means that Ponden likes you.'

'What do you mean?' Will shakes his sleepy head, blinking in the light. 'How did I get here?'

'Following your dreams, I suppose,' I tell him, climbing into the box bed alongside him. His breath has misted the deep, stone-set square window that the bed is built around, and I reach out to touch the family Bible that rests open on the windowsill. 'When we first moved into our London house you'd sleepwalk a little bit, but then you grew out of it. I guess that change of scene brought it back.'

'I don't like change,' Will says forlornly.

'Not even this bed?' Smiling, I press my palms against the dark wood. 'When I was a kid, this would be my ship, my flying saucer, my jet, my playhouse ...'

'It's just a bed. A stupid bed in a cupboard,' Will says. 'Why would anyone want to sleep in a cupboard?'

'Because, once upon a time, everything used to happen in one room: cooking, working, eating, sleeping ... It was a way to be private.'

'Yuck.' Will wrinkles his nose at the thought.

'Do you remember how I told you that Ponden is full of stories?' I ask him, brushing his long curls from his forehead. In the morning light his eyes are the purest green, deep as moss.

'Yes,' he replies. 'But I don't see how houses can be stories. Houses are buildings, not words.'

'Think of it as a bit like the Hubble telescope,' I say, falling back onto the mattress. After a moment Will stretches out by my side. 'This house is like a lens, or a perfectly polished mirror in a telescope. It sees very far back in time – and maybe even into the future. There are so many stories to be made up here, and adventures to be had. Some that happened years ago, and some that haven't happened yet, all of them just waiting for you.'

Will says nothing, his gaze tracking the roll of the clouds.

'This is a lot for you deal with,' I tell him. 'Don't think I don't know that. Thank you for sticking with me.'

'I feel better, actually,' Will says, turning to look at me.

'Do you?' I ask cautiously. 'How so?'

'Because I think Daddy will find us here. It's a shiny place.' He seems so certain that I feel it too, just for a moment. The beat of Abe's heart, the sound of his voice, the broad strength of his presence at my side. Everything sensible about me should disagree, of course, but it's still there, that tug at my heart that brought me home.

'Come on,' I say, kissing his warm skin as he squirms away. 'Let's get you wrapped up warm and find some breakfast, shall we?'

'Mummy ...?' Will rolls into my arms and I hold him close, my son, my heartbeat.

'Yes, little boy?' I say.

'You said you'd tell me the story of you and Daddy; you said you'd tell me about how you met here.'

'I did,' I say, releasing him to clamber out of the bed. 'It's a long story, Will.'

'Well,' he says, as I carry him out of the room and feel the door pushing itself shut under my hands, 'this seems like a house with more than the usual amount of time.'

Funny how he's only been here a few hours and he already understands this place exactly. It seems Ma was right: he's a true Heaton after all.

Tru and Abe

'I like the way you smile.'

Those were the first words Abe said to me. Not my smile, but the *way* I smiled.

I'd been watching him out the corner of my eye for the whole evening, me on one side of the bar, where I was only supposed to be collecting glasses, but serving pints anyway, him on the other, drinking them at a steady rate. His wasn't the loudest laugh, nor was he the funniest or best-looking of his friends. He was the only one who had this stillness, this sense of calm and a kind of unconscious choreography in every moment. I'd made up at least eleven stories about him – who he was, and what he did – before I ever spoke to him, and had settled at last on a mountaineer, a free climber who had once summited Everest. He had those kinds of hands, the kind that look elegant enough, and strong enough, to defy gravity and turn the world underneath them.

'Students,' Mick the landlord had murmured, blowing my story with one word that carried enough expression to relay exactly what he thought of such creatures, which wasn't very much all.

We didn't often see students out here on the edges of the moors, though there were two university towns just a few miles away. However, we got more than our fair share of travellers from all over the globe. Any typical evening we might have a Japanese group just come down from Top Withens, the most likely location for *Wuthering Heights*, or twin-anoraked couples, or any number of local people who treated the pub like an extension of their living rooms. Some might think a small country pub in the middle of nowhere would fall silent when a group of medical students entered, but not us. All human life passed through those doors at one time or another.

Although Mick never turned down money, he wasn't so fond of students, especially their shouts of laughter, for reasons that weren't exactly clear. Still, they kept spending, so he kept serving, and so did I.

'I like the way you smile,' Abe'd said, a little unsteady on his feet. High cheekbones, tall and a little thin, his smile had listed to one side, just like him.

'The *way* I smile?' I'd questioned him, leaning in close because his mates were singing at the top of their voices and he was slurring his words a bit.

'Yeah, sort of wonky and lots of teeth.'

I'd laughed, and he'd laughed – and then swayed, before finally tottering onto a barstool and settling like a leggy puppy.

'My head is spinning; I don't usually drink,' Abe had told me. 'We're supposed to be hiking for a charity thing. No one said anything about drinking. But suddenly, it's like "if you don't drink you aren't one of the lads".'

'Aren't you a bit old for peer pressure?' I'd laughed, pouring him a glass of water from the tap. 'Here, get this down you and I'll make you a coffee.'

'I'm studying medicine, you see,' he'd said, swaying perilously backwards on the stool and collapsing forward again, just in time. 'My name is Abraham. Abe, most people call me. I'm going to be a doctor.'

'Congratulations,' I'd said. 'I'm Trudy, Tru for short.'

'Doesn't that make you fancy me? The doctor thing?' he'd asked, gesturing at his mates who were whispering and giggling like kids. 'They said it would.'

'Takes a bit more than potential earning power,' I'd told him.

'Like what?' he'd asked.

'Like who's your favourite poet? Which work of art makes your cry, have you ever stood on the top of the moors and screamed at the sky, what do you think of *Wuthering Heights*, can you write music, do you believe in ghosts, do you dream about travelling to Mars, do you think you might have lived on this earth before?'

Abe had blinked at me and rested his forehead on the bar for a moment before focusing on me once again.

'You're one of those girls,' he'd said, after a moment. 'One of those *thinking* girls.'

'I'm not sure I know of any other kind,' I'd replied, which would have been more meaningful if I'd had a lot of friends at school, except I never did, because I'd made books and long-dead writers my friends.

'Why are you only working in a pub?' he'd asked, belligerent. 'You seem clever.'

'We can't all be doctors,' I'd said. 'And anyway, I'm still doing my A levels.'

'Oh.' He'd closed one eye. 'Want to come outside with me?'

'No,' I'd said. 'It's bloody freezing out there and I'm pretty sure you are going to throw up.'

'But still good-looking, right?' Abe had grinned at me then fallen off the stool.

'I think it's time you lot went home,' Mick had said then, easing his considerable girth out from behind the bar. 'Come on, lads, you don't want sore heads in the morning. I'm closing up now, anyway.'

There'd been protests and swearing and many more songs, but all in good cheer. I'd watched Abe as he'd stumbled out of the door, turning to look at me just as he was about to leave. 'I'm coming back tomorrow,' he'd promised. 'Not drunk ... To tell you I've fallen in love with you at first sight.'

'You do that,' I'd said, rolling my eyes at Mick.

Later, I'd walked home, even though Mick had offered me a lift, because I liked the quiet, the cold and the smell in the air after rain, earthy and rich, flavoured with red-tasting iron. That night as I'd walked by the reservoir, the moon was so bright it left a halo of light in its trail as it set behind the hills. The dark had been full of magic and promise, the kind of night where love at first sight could happen to someone, even if it wasn't me. I'd listened to the din of the insects singing in the dark and heard the hidden creatures moving in the undergrowth. Barn owls and bats had swooped and called overhead, and I was part of it, another wild creature under the stars.

And when I'd thought about what the student doctor had said to me in the pub, I'd felt like maybe life didn't have to be so lonely after all.

Then the next day there was a knock on the door. It was Mick.

'I'm not working, am I?' I said, reaching for my coat.

'No, but you don't have a bloody phone either,' he puffed, even though he'd driven his Land Rover right up to door. 'There's a bloody idiot in the car who won't leave until he sees you, and I wasn't just about to tell him where you live so ...'

He gestured at the car, and Abe was sitting inside, looking distinctly sheepish. He offered me a half-hearted wave.

I looked at Mick. 'So you drove him round to murder me instead?'

'Oh, bollocks.' Mick took his cap off, and ruffled what was left of his hair. 'Anyway, talk to him, will you? I'll hang about here, knock him on head if he seems like he might be a wrong 'un.'

'Who's there?' Ma called out from the kitchen.

'No one, Ma,' I call back. 'Just Mick about extra shifts. He says get a phone!'

'Don't set her on me,' Mick said, and he wasn't joking. Ma's tongue had been a local legend even then.

'I reckon you can go.' I looked at Abe. 'He looks harmless.'

'Murderers always do,' Mick said. 'Plus he told me he's training to be a surgeon and they're the worst kind for chopping up bodies and such.'

'If he tries anything, I'll shout for Ma.'

'But how will he get back?' Mick asked me.

'He's on a hiking trip, Mick. Reckon he'll find the way.'

'If you don't make your shift tonight because you're dead in a ditch, I'm going to be right peeved,' Mick told me very seriously. 'Pub's downwind: if you scream loud enough in the right direction we might hear you.'

Abe got out of the car and smiled, but before he could say a word I dragged him a few hundred yards up the hill, out of sight of the house, and kept walking. It soon became apparent that the hiking trip must have had a lot more to do with drinking than walking.

'Where are we going?' he asked, out of breath, struggling to keep up with me.

'My ma's nosey,' I said. 'Trust me, you aren't ready to meet her.'

'That is true.' Abe followed me up the track, like a great lolloping nerd.

'So, what do you want?' I stopped dead in the path, as soon as I thought we were as far enough away from the house to be out of the reach of Ma's radar.

He collected himself, and took a deep breath. 'I said I'd come back ...'

'You did,' I said.

'To tell you I'm in love with you.'

'That's bollocks,' I said.

'Maybe.' He grinned and shrugged. 'But I do like the way you smile, all lopsided and toothy, and your hair is all wild and tangled up and I like your blue eyes. Look, I'm sober now and I really fancy you and I'd like to see you again. A lot. I'm studying in Leeds, but it's easy to get over here, or you could get over to the city and ...'

I must have looked sceptical, because he hesitated, looking up at the storm that was gathering in the sky, ripples of grey spreading outwards with the slow menace of sudden heavy rain.

'OK, I know you're still at school, and I'm twenty-one. But that's cool, I'm not going to, you know, be weird.'

'You kind of already are,' I said.

'OK.' Abe immediately put his hands in his pockets, and studied the toes of his barely worn hiking boots. 'But would you write me a letter, then?' Abe asked me. 'You could just write to me.'

'Write to you? Like *letters*?' I thought of Charlotte Brontë's letters, of the hope, and joy and pain she'd poured into each one, and thought how wonderful it would be to have a living human being to write letters to. 'Really?'

'I was thinking emails, but sure, letters, why not? We can get to know each other and, if you like me, then maybe you'll let me come and see you again.'

'I'm strange,' I told him. 'I'm the loner at school. I like Victorian novels and being by myself.'

'Cool,' Abe said. 'I dissect dead people.'

'I like you more already.'

I was standing slightly higher than him on the incline, looking down at him, and every last bit of what was left of the sun lit up his face. I saw amber and gold in his brown eyes, copper and oak in his skin, and such sweetness and hope in the angle of his head and the fall of his hands that I found I wanted to hold him and kiss him right then.

'I can't write to you if I don't know your address, can I?' I said, because it didn't seem sensible to declare my feelings right then and there, not when I'd been doing such a good job of playing it cool.

'Oh shit, yeah.' He tapped his pockets. 'I don't ...'

'You write to me first. It's easy to remember: Trudy Heaton, Ponden Hall.'

'Really? OK, then. Yes, I will. I definitely will, Trudy Heaton of Ponden Hall.'

Then I kissed him, hard. Flung my arms around his neck, sending him staggering back a few steps and inhaled him, like he was the wind and the sky and all the sustenance

I'd ever need, and he kissed me back in exactly the same way. Sunbeams refracted behind my eyelids, red and green, lights going off, and I tasted the scent of his skin on the tip of my tongue, soap and salt. Before that moment my entire kissing history had been teeth, saliva and tongues. This was something so much greater than that: it felt like the curve of the earth to me. When I let him go, he blinked and shook his head as he looked at me.

'Sod it,' he said. 'I meant it when I said I was in love with you. I don't know why or how, but I am, and I don't even care if that freaks you out, I just have to say it.'

We'd stood there a moment longer, just looking. Just knowing that this was the beginning of something that would last forever, and even though I was just seventeen years old I wasn't afraid, or daunted. I was just sure.

'Don't go the way you came,' I told him, setting him on the footpath across the moor to Haworth. 'This way is longer but it doesn't go past the house. I don't want my ma knowing my business.'

'I'll write,' he said, walking past me backwards, up the path.

'I know,' I said.

The first letter came two days later.

CHAPTER FOUR

'So why *were* you so sure that new Granny Mariah wouldn't like Daddy?' Will asks as I finish telling him that story, while he spoons porridge into his mouth. As I'd talked, I'd filtered my words through my own memory in real time, crafting them into something fit for an eight-year-old.

The sight of him sitting at the kitchen table, bundled up in his duvet against the biting morning cold, his bobble hat pulled down so the brim sits just above his eyes, makes my heart smile. There is still no power, despite the promises of the electricity company, which means a walk up the hill to where there might be some signal to phone them later. And yet I still don't regret my decision to come home, despite the cold and discomfort. Sitting at this table that is as familiar as my own palm – with my son and bright morning sun flowing in through the two large kitchen windows, fighting its way through the vines of ivy that make rather picturesque picture frames – is enough of a salve to make it all worthwhile.

'Granny …' I try to come up a reason that would make sense to Will. 'Granny has always been the sort of person to tell everyone to mind their own business, while at exactly the same time sticking her nose in yours. At the beginning, I suppose, I just wanted to keep your daddy to myself for a while, because I'd never been in love before, or ever again, except that I am madly and crazily in love with you, of course.'

Will pulls a face. 'Yuck! That's so gross. But then what did Granny do to make you not talk to her until now?'

'That,' I said, 'is another story, Will. One I'll tell you in about ten years.'

'But—'

'Now then.' Ma comes into the kitchen, and even just woken she is all hard edges, her thick silver-blonde hair brushed smooth, dressing gown tight-knotted. Her skin has that particular ceramic glow you only get from washing your face in freezing water. Sensing me looking, she pulls her dressing gown a little tighter around herself, turning away from me as she lights the gas hob with a match, setting the kettle atop the flames.

'What happened in the night?' she asks, as if that is perfectly exchangeable with, 'did you sleep OK?'

'Nothing,' I say, avoiding her gaze. 'Just a bit strange for Will, waking up in a new place, I suppose. Why are you sleeping in a chair, Ma? Even if the roof upstairs is shot, you could put a bed in Dad's old study, or any of the other downstairs rooms.'

'No.' Ma shook her head. 'I like the chair, I like the fire. I like Mab on my feet, I like the sound of the John Heaton clock. Do you know, Will, that the motto on the clock face translates to "Remember to Die"? Besides ...' she smiles at Will '... your grandad's old office is where they used to lay out the dead, you know.'

'Cool.' Will's eyes widen with the ghoulish delight that only young children can truly know.

'I never once saw a ghost in there my whole life,' I say to Will.

'That just means you never saw 'em, not that they weren't there, girl,' Ma tells me. 'Anyway, I've got used to my ways. For a while, when you live alone, you go on living like you did for other people, and then one day you think, what the heck for? So I do as I please and it serves me well enough; bus into the village once a week to do my shop and that's me done. Besides, I don't go upstairs any more.'

'Why not?' I ask her.

'I just don't go upstairs any more,' she says again, in that way that has always meant the subject is closed.

'I'm still cold.' Will hugs Mab as she waddles to his side, engulfing her in his duvet so that only her snout is showing, enduring his affections with stoic good grace.

'You go into the living room with Mab,' Ma tells him. 'I got the fire going in there already and Mab'll keep you warm as toast.'

I watch Will go, his hand on Mab's collar, already making conversation with her before he's out the door.

Ma stands over a kettle on the range, taking a shawl that's she hung over the AGA and wrapping it around her like a cloak as she waits for the water to boil, looking so much older than she actually is. I never realised it until I left home, but 'kitchen' is hardly the right word for this basically equipped room that hasn't changed so very much in the last two hundred years. With the power off, even the thirty-year-old fridge has become a relic. I suppose it's something of a blessing that the cold keeps the milk and meat fresh at least, what little there is of it.

'You'll want tea,' Ma tells me and she's not wrong. 'Looks fine out there now, but those clouds mean business.'

Is this is how it's going to be, neither one of us talking about what happened, making small talk about the tea, dog, the weather and Will?

'Always were away with the fairies.' Ma snaps her fingers in front of my face. 'Still take sugar, I asked?'

'Yes.'

'Boy drink tea?'

'No, he's eight, Ma.'

'You drank tea when you were eight,' Ma reminds me.

'But I'm a Yorkshire girl, he's London.'

'That'd be a double skinny macchiato, then,' Ma says, and it's so absurd, coming out of her mouth, that I laugh.

'Where have you heard of those?'

'I'm not a nun, I know about the world,' Ma says. 'I have a flat white and a piece of Hummingbird cake in Cobbles and Clay on every second Wednesday and buy some books in Hatchard and Daughters. Do you think I've sat indoors moping since you walked out?'

'You know why I left.' I say it mildly, but it hangs in the air between us, like our icy breath.

Ma's glacial eyes hold mine.

'I know what I did,' she says, passing me tea, strong and sweet just as I used to drink it as a kid.

For a moment, the hurt threatens to rip out of me, but I swallow it hard and whole, wash it down with a swig of tea. 'You were wrong about us, do you at least admit that?'

'True enough,' Ma agrees. 'Trudy, the time will come when words will be said. But for now there's more pressing matters. You and the boy need to heal, you need to feel at home. Whatever you may think of me, you're my flesh and so is that child. You will always have a home here; it's yours more than it's mine, after all. And I need to say something; I know you won't like it, but it needs to be said.'

Ma goes to the window, pouring the water that's left in the kettle into the washing-up bowl. Beyond, the valley is utterly serene, a landscape immune to human cares. I wish I didn't know what she was going to say.

'He was here, you know? The night your Abraham went to his death.'

'Ma, I know how much you love your stories but you have to see that this isn't the time—'

'You saw him too, didn't you? No matter what you told the boy. The Gytrash.' Ma lowers her voice, glancing over her shoulder. '*Greybeard*. Him that's appeared before every Heaton family death for four hundred years. Maybe not like I did, but in your dreams. You did, didn't you?'

'No.' I shake my head. 'Ma, there was no other worldly being standing at the end of my bed warning me that my husband was going to die. Jesus, do you have any tact at all?'

Ma peers at me, just like when I was kid and she'd work out whether she thought I was lying or not. I turn away from her.

'Middle of the night, it was,' she goes on, relentless. 'Mab starts up growling and barking at the window, and she's too old and too weary to bark that much at anything any more, so when she does I pay her mind. I get up out of my chair and I look.' Her gaze slips back to that moment and I see the fear and disgust in her expression. 'And he's there, just a pane of glass between us, looking back at me. Eyes like black holes, but I know he sees me, I feel it in my bones like ... disease.'

'Ma!' I don't know how to reply to this voicing of our fear, our own and very particular truth. 'It was a dream, a nightmare. It's a legend, a story. It's not real. You heard about Abe and then you thought you remembered a dream, and in your head it all makes sense but it's – it's ghoulish, Ma, and it's cruel. I lost my husband, and not for one second do I want to think a curse in the shape of a demon came to claim him. Don't you understand that?'

The moment I've spoken the words I realise what a fool I am. I'm not the only widow standing in this room. And it wasn't Ma that saw Greybeard the day Dad died, it was me.

'What happened, that day, it was coincidence, Dad's stories and my imagination, Ma. At the time ... at the time I didn't understand why you were so angry with me for saying I saw him, but now I do. And I'm sorry, really I am.'

A one-sided conversation takes place behind her eyes, in the tiny muscles around her mouth, the way her fingers knit and twist, but none of it is spoken aloud.

'I'm not much longer for this world, Trudy,' Ma says. 'Maybe Greybeard was here for me.'

'You've been saying that since I was ten,' I tell her, with a small smile.

'Yes, but this time I mean it,' she says. 'I feel it, Trudy. Drawing in like a winter's evening.'

'You're still young, fifty is nothing! Anyway, you can't die yet, Ma,' I say very quietly. 'Not while we've got unfinished business.'

Ma doesn't speak. She doesn't look at me. Her hand reaches out for mine and she takes my fingers for the briefest of seconds, squeezing my fingers tightly between hers.

I know she is doing her best. It can't make up for everything that has happened between us, but in that one precise moment, it is enough.

Ponden Hall 1655

Praise Him and His mercy that a year has passed since I last had time, privacy and ink to test my words on paper, though I have had some use of chalk, stone walls as my paper, Robert my teacher, the sky my classroom.

Praise God that since I last wrote that which is private, I have not fallen ill, nor been injured, and no great harm has come to me. Though I am ashamed to see what ignorance was shown in my first writings, I am much improved now.

Praise His glorious name forever, for granting me a year of safety amongst Godley people, enough food and work to make my life a prayer to His greatness.

Much has changed since I first scratched out my letters, including myself. No longer a false daughter, now a servant, I lead an honest life and thank God that Casson didn't see fit to put me out or dispose of me as I have seen him dispose of some, but simply to forget he ever claimed I was his child. It may be that he no longer fears what I know of him. And Praise be that Mistress Casson, too, let the lie pass, and upon Robert's urging left me in the care of the maid, Betty, who is kind and pious, as much a mother to me as I have ever known.

I work hard, in the kitchen and the house.

Mistress Casson, as she must now be known, is kind to me. Though she herself be dealt much unkindness, she never lets it show beyond her chamber, and is always a good wife in every aspect.

Her life eased some after the birth of a boy that Casson named Henry also. The babe has all but supplanted Robert in this house, who no longer has lessons, or new clothes, nor the respect and position that ought to be afforded to him as the rightful Heir to Ponden Hall. Casson sacked his tutor and now he and I must creep into the library to steal books away that we might read them together in a place where we will not be discovered.

For all that, I am happy, thanks be to God, for Robert spends much of his time with Betty and I in the kitchen, and the three of us make light of what might else be dark, cheering each other with kind regard.

Above all, I thank God that now I am twelve years of age Casson has forgotten me, except to bring him ale and food, and light his fire.

When we may, Robert and I will take ourselves up to our favourite place, which is known about here as Ponden Kirk, and it is indeed a kind of church, made of rock and earth, but a prayer to God nonetheless. They say long ago, before the Lord came to this land, the old people would burn fires there and worship the old gods, side by side with the fairies, though those folk are seldom seen now, Praise Be. At the foot of the Kirk there is the marriage hole, and Betty says that if a maid does pass through she will be married within the year or never at all. We play here, as children may, and call it our castle. And when there is time we lie ourselves down on this great flat rock that protrudes from the hillside and into the air, and feel like we might be one with the sky and the birds and even closer to Our Lord, praise be.

Each day I must thank God for the friendship and brother I have found in Robert Heaton, who, despite the many cruelties that inflicted upon him, remains the kindest and dearest person I have ever known.

When circumstance will allow me to write again, I do not know. For a girl such as I to know words such as I do would be thought of as wicked and sinful by many, even dear Betty. I prayed on it myself, for many hours, and tried to keep from books and learning. Yet, would God fill my head with such thoughts and such talents if he did not want me to make use of them somehow?

Despite my claims previous, I have never shown my writings to Robert. I dare not. Not for fear that he would scorn me, or mock me, for it is Robert who gives me this gift, which I treasure above all else saving my Lord God.

I hesitate because I know not the right words, nor the order in which I may fully describe my heartfelt regard for him.

Agnes Heaton
Agnes Casson

CHAPTER FIVE

. . . .

'What happens next?' Will asks me, as he wriggles down further into my old bed, his toes seeking out the hot water bottle I'd tucked in there earlier.

Our day had been full, and so much more full of joy than I could have hoped for, the two of us following water-sodden footpaths that reflected fragmented pieces of the sky in footprint puddles, through the fields and across the moors leading directly to the sky.

And when we got home there was hot soup, fresh bread – and electric light at last. No central heating meant the house was still deathly cold the moment you stepped away from the fire or the AGA, but at least the immersion was working again. Of course, none of these things meant that Will wanted anything but stories by torchlight when he finally surrendered to bedtime.

An old blanket flung over our heads like a tent, the torch turning shadows upside down, we huddle around my childhood copy of *The Secret Garden,* the cracking of the stiffened spine, the grainy yellow pages releasing a torrent of memory as soon as I open them, as though a little part of my imagination had been absorbed into the paper alongside the ink that made the words.

'We'll have to wait until tomorrow night to find out,' I answer, gently closing the book and holding it to my chest. 'My eyes are too tired to read any more in this light.'

'No, with you and Daddy, I mean?' Will rolls onto his side to look at me. I can see myself reflected in his eyes, lost in his dark, dilated pupils. 'After you decided to be in love for ever.'

'Oh … We wrote to each other like we said we would,' I tell him. 'We wrote a *lot* of letters to each other, for weeks and weeks, actually. Months.'

'Like letters that came in the post?' Will has been more bemused by this antiquated piece of technology than anything else. 'You wrote them on paper and posted them and they didn't come until the next day?'

'If that,' I say and smile. 'I know it sounds crazy to you, but it was nice. It was … gentle and thoughtful, slow. We got to know each other, not just by what we said, but by our handwriting, the paper we chose. Sometimes Daddy would draw little things in the margins, or send me a pressed flower—'

'Gross,' Will says, but he is smiling. 'Have you still got the letters?'

'Yes, of course, all of them.' I don't tell him that they are in a shoebox in my overnight bag at the foot of the bed, the very first thing I packed. Mine to him, his to me, all tied up in a ribbon.

'Can I read them?' Will asks, and I think of that long, written courtship, so polite, so Victorian by design, each one either far too polite to be interesting or far too intense to be appropriate for an eight-year-old boy. How we danced around each other back then, Abe and I, writing about all the things that we loved, discovering each other's passion for ourselves; it was an evolution of a friendship almost before anything else. It wasn't that I didn't miss him, but I didn't want to see him because I *wanted* to miss him, which sounds like madness, but then, when I was not quite eighteen years old, I had this certainty that we had forever to get to know each other. Forever to think of kisses and desires, forever to always have each other's body as our own. It never occurred to me that the world around us might be the cause of our separation, whether I wanted it or not.

And yet I still wouldn't trade those letters for a more conventional romance. Each pen stroke was a stitch that hemmed us close together.

'You can read them when you are eighteen,' I say, which Will accepts based on the understanding that much of the universe would be open to him upon this mythical day.

'But why not phones? Because new Granny doesn't even have a land phone?'

'Partly. But also because letters are good for shy people. It meant that before Daddy and I met again we knew a lot about each other, and it was less frightening, because I knew what his favourite colour was—'

'Orange.' Will nods.

'And his dream pet ...'

'Rabbit,' Will says, giggling.

'His favourite food ...' I wait.

'Food!' Will bursts out laughing and I laugh too.

'And then spring came, and spring around here is just about as beautiful as anything can ever be. Snowdrops, and daffodils, primroses, sometimes violets if you know where to look for them. The trees full of pink and white blossom, and birds calling and nesting. The heather starts to come back, a deep, deep green that you know will later turn the whole moor purple and gold. You can have blue skies and snow side by side, and lambs in the field making a racket. You are going to love spring here, Will; I can't wait to show it to you, and I couldn't wait to show this place to Daddy either, so I asked him to come by.'

'And so what happened next?' Will persists.

'We met and kissed and kissed and kissed,' I say with a smile. 'For about a year.'

'Ugh.' Will pulls a face. 'Didn't you get bored? Or hungry? What about if you needed a pee?'

'Not literally one year,' I say, laughing. 'One day you will understand the appeal of kissing, and really, even though the kissing was very nice, that wasn't the best thing. The best thing was that we'd been a bit shy of each other, a bit scared; but after the second time we met, we never were again.'

'Why on earth would a great big tall man like Daddy be scared of you, though?' Will asks, incredulous.

'Daddy always used to say that it takes a lot of courage to be happy – do you remember him saying that?'

Will doesn't answer for a moment; he just rolls onto his back, looking at the dark gap in the ceiling, and I smile as I look as his face, seeing Abe in the planes of his cheeks and the almond shape of his eyes, even in the sweep of his hairline and seashell curl of his ear.

'I think it's true that you have to be brave to be happy,' Will says eventually. 'Because if you are happy, then you have to know that one day you might be sad too.'

'Daddy wouldn't want you to be sad,' I say, laying the back of my fingers against his cheek.

'Then he should hurry up and find us,' Will says. 'And I won't be sad any more.'

Closing my eyes, I remind myself what the experts said, that I have to explain everything to Will as clearly as I can, and I make myself say the words.

'Daddy isn't going to find us, darling. Daddy died.'

'No, he didn't.' Will turns his head to look at me, his eyes fierce with certainty. 'He *isn't* dead, I *know* he's coming home – and if you really loved him as much as you say you do, then you would know it too, and I just don't understand why you don't.'

'Will . . .' Back hunched, he drags the covers over his face, his small body trembling with stifled tears beneath them.

'Will, I went out there, I looked for him and—'

'But don't you see, Mummy?' he says, dragging the cover back, anger sparking in his eyes. 'If you don't believe as hard as I do, then maybe it won't work, maybe he won't be able to find us. So you *have* to believe, you *have* to, Mummy, you *have* to.'

'Then I do,' I say without hesitation. 'I *do* believe as much as you do. I was just too afraid to admit it before.'

There's a second of hesitation and then he's in my arms, his around my neck, and I breathe again.

'Don't be afraid to be happy.' Will holds me so tightly, the rapid thud of his heart matches mine. The damp of his tears dry on my neck and I know I shouldn't have said what I did, but what else could I say?

What mother could ever bear to refuse her child the gift of hope?

Tru and Abe

The true story of the second time that Abe and I met is that it wasn't at all like I expected.

Our letters had been so close that the words we wrote to one another were interlinked like chainmail, each new letter adding to the armour of us. Every page was so full of heat and longing that I'd had this idea that the moment we set eyes on one another we'd fall into each other's arms, to be swept away by passion.

I'd arranged to meet Abe outside the Parsonage, and as I stood there I wondered if Charlotte had ever stood in the same spot, wondering what it would be like to kissed by the man she longed for.

Summer was at its height, and for once it was a clear, warm day, so the footpaths were busy, bustling with tourists. It was almost certain that I would be seen, Tru Heaton with an unknown male of the species, but I was gambling on it not getting back to Ma.

I'd sat on the bench outside, and waited. When he came striding up the alley, I remembered his height, the breadth of his shoulders and the way that he moved. Looking at him took my breath away, and it was like every little bit of intimacy that we'd built between us in ink was washed away. Suddenly I was encased in shyness.

'Trudy?' He spoke my name as if he didn't recognise me, and perhaps he didn't, I worried. Perhaps he'd imagined an entirely different girl from the one who stood there now in ripped jeans and one of Dad's old shirts. In my letters I'd been bold, and brave, capricious and flirtatious. I'd painted myself in primary colours. Me in the flesh – average height, average build, average grey eyes, a sunburned nose and a cloud of curly brown hair that tended to frizz – was so much less than the versions I'd created on paper, that all at once I'd wanted to curl in on myself and vanish.

Nevertheless, I stood up to greet him and we hugged briefly, all wrong angles and hard edges, clashing without quite touching.

'I'm here, then.' Abe shoved his beautiful hands in his pockets.

'You are,' I said. 'I thought we'd go to the Falls, and then up to Top Withens.' Even as I said it I was regretting my words. That was an hour's walk at least, and here was this stranger, tall and dark, a veritable Heathcliff, and all I really wanted to do was to go home and read about being in love instead. It would have been so much easier.

'This is weird, isn't it?' Abe said after a few moments of us not talking, not quite looking at each other, and I loved him for it. 'Shall we just walk and wait for it not to be?'

Abe walked so much faster than me that I was out of breath trying to keep up with him, until he slowed, picking his way down the narrow rock path that lead to the deep, dark greens of the leafy valley that leads to Brontë Falls. A small party of walkers was already heading up the hill on the other side of the bridge and I knew that, on a day like today, it wouldn't be long before someone else appeared.

It had been my dream to bring him here to this place, to watch his face as he took in the wild beauty of it; heard the sound of the white water tumbling down the scar cut into the hillside, where the limestone boulders left by glaciers were scattered down the hill like pebbles that had been kicked there by a giant. Three slender sister silver birches on the bank peered into the water, their canopies nodding in the breeze as if they were agreeing with each other about how perfect the view was, and the persistent call of curlews echoed one another, minute by minute. I wanted him to love it as I loved him; I wanted him to love it as he loved me. Then, as we stood on the little stone bridge, water rushing under our feet, his fingers reached out towards me and my fingertips met his in return.

'We haven't said a word to each other,' Abe said, looking down into the bubbling, coppery water. 'It hasn't stopped being weird.'

'I know.' I didn't dare move for fear of breaking that slight contact. 'I thought it would be like ...'

'The letters,' he said. 'Me too, but it turns out that writing to you – it's not the same as standing next to you. Writing to you I'm funny and smart, thoughtful, deep and devastatingly attractive. But standing next to you, I'm – I'm trembling because you're near me, Tru. My knees have gone to jelly.'

'Abe, I—' I can't remember now what I thought I was going to say to him, but whatever it was the moment was lost as the clatter of chatter chimed around the corner, a group of women, laughing and talking, their conversation falling into silence as they passed us.

'Were you about to say I repulse you in real life?' Abe asked me. He looked at me then, his dark eyes searching my face so keenly that for a moment it was all I could do to simply return his gaze.

'Opposite, actually,' I said. 'That's the problem, *your* knees are like jelly and *I've* forgotten how to speak.'

'I want to be alone with you,' Abe told me just as the next group of walkers appeared.

I slotted my fingers into his and closed my eyes for a moment as I felt the friction of his palm against mine. And then I led him, step-by-step, moment-by-moment away from everywhere else.

We walked in silence again, for what seemed like a long time, but this time there was the connection between us. For no matter what rocks we had to climb, or walls we had to negotiate, some part of my body was constantly in contact with some part of him, and each time we touched it was like an unspoken promise, a tiny charge detonating.

Eventually, the footpath went one way, leading up to Top Withens, and that's where we left it, and I took him down, deeper into the shadowy cool of valley, tracing the banks of the stream until we came to a place where a thick copse of young trees tree sheltered us from view with their constantly moving canopy.

At the very last moment I let go of his hand to pick my way over the stones in the stream to the mossy bank on the other side, turning back to look at him. Instead of following me, he just stood there across the water, watching me.

'Are you coming?' I asked him. 'It's dry here.'

'I ...' He dropped his head. 'I never really wanted something as much as this before. I'm scared it will go wrong.'

'Well, I know. I'm the same. But it's just us, Abe. We're just the same people that we are when we write letters, and we've got all the time in the world to get it right, our whole lives to get it right ...'

I bit my lip, closing my eyes in horror. 'I don't mean ... I'm not saying that I want to get heavy or anything ... what I mean is ...'

When I looked up he was at my side.

'You're right,' he said, taking my hand in his. 'We've got our whole lives to get it right. We should start practising now ...'

What happened after that appears in my memory like a cloud of colours, a rainbow made up of endless, glorious hours of discovery.

If I close my eyes now I see burst of red and amber, I can still feel the residual heat of that day, the warmth of his mouth on my skin, the feel of his hips against mine, the thrill and the wonder of everything that was new and all that was familiar.

The deep, abiding miracle of falling in love.

CHAPTER SIX

There was a different quality to the cold when I woke up this morning. Sharper, somehow, than just the long sunless hours of the night. Will was already up and when, wrapped in my sleeping bag, I stepped outside my room, the temperature was a little milder, just enough to make me stop and think about the hole in the ceiling and the roof beyond. I was on my way to see if Will was in Cathy's room, when I heard his laughter from downstairs.

I stood at the top of the stairs, leaning in to listen, and it seemed to me the house was listening too, every one of its usual creaks and sighs silent as I heard Will's chatter. Of all the things I'd ever imagined it was certainly not Ma making Will laugh like the little boy he was. But his arrival in the house had stirred the still air, as I'd known it would. The next generation of Heatons had come home. Even in all this sadness it was something to feel glad of, from the heights of the rafters to the dankest depth of the cellar.

When I entered the living room, though, Will was alone, sitting on the rug next to the fire, a paper filled with a drawing at his feet, amongst an assortment of felt-tip pens. His eyes were full of laughter as he looked up at the windows, where the very scant traces of dawn were just beginning to ebb in through the overgrown foliage. The frayed edge of a memory tugged at me, a little bit like walking into the room and finding myself there.

'Oh, where's Granny?' I asked, looking around for the source of his amusement. He shrugged, and tucked his hands under Mab's solid body, hiding something.

'Who were you talking to, then?' I felt an uncertain smile hovering on my lips, and I was almost reminded of something ... something that fell just outside of my grasp.

'No one.' Will grinned conspiratorially. 'The cold woke me up so I came down here to draw by the fire. Granny said her back hurts and she was going to bake a cake.'

'A cake?'

Will nodded, and I got the distinct impression he was waiting for me to go so he could get on with his game.

'Do you like my drawing?' He handed it to me, and I stared for a few moments at a rather unprepossessing large undulating snake writhing in hurriedly scribbled green grass. Not his normal subject of planets or space stations, but it had been so long since he'd drawn anything at all that I loved it anyway.

'How marvellous,' I told him.

'Will you keep it safe?' he asked. 'Put it in a safe place?'

'I shall put it on Granny's fridge at once,' I promised him. 'And while I'm there, I'll make you some hot chocolate.'

The second I walked out of the room, Will burst into laughter again and I heard him say, 'She didn't see you.'

I find Ma bent over an old cracked mixing bowl, labouring with a wooden spoon. I discover a roll of masking tape in one of the drawers and tack up Will's drawing.

'I don't know what that is, but it brightens the place up,' Ma says, squinting at it.

'Are you baking at six a.m.?' I ask.

'Lad looks like he needs feeding up,' she says, without glancing up from her work. 'Skinny little thing. Vegetables and hummus and the like – it's all very well, but you need fat on your bones to get through a winter up here.'

'I've made an appointment with this historic buildings renovation expert called Marcus Ellis; he's going to come round and assess the house tomorrow.'

'Marcus Ellis?' Ma looks up at me. 'Sounds like an idiot.'

'His reputation says that he is the opposite of an idiot. And he grew up round here and knows Ponden, so he's the best call, I'd say. I know you won't like people in the house, Ma, but we have to save Ponden. She's falling to bits, and we can't let that happen. She's always taken care of us.'

'I know that.' Ma works the cake batter with a violent vigour, her other arm pinning the bowl to the table. 'It's been too much for me these last couple of years, since the … since I got that bit older. I did my best, on my own. But this place costs a lot. More than I got. More than you've got.'

'I know.' I pour a lukewarm cup of tea from the pot she's made, and sit down at the table to watch her. Outside, the earth is slowly bowing towards the sun, drawing wisps of colour into the expanse of night, revealing the grey-green of the trees, a hint of purple hillside glowing in the gloom. 'It's no one's fault.'

'You weren't here,' Ma says, pausing to glance at me. 'It were your fault.'

Eighteen years ago I'd have risen to greet that barb, just like she wanted me to. But this morning, in the kitchen still half filled with night, I let it pass along with the darkness.

'The point is, this house, it's more than just about us, Ma, it's about history. And the Brontës, and all the Heatons that have been, and all the ones to come. So we need to take care of it. Until Abe is officially ...' The words thicken in my mouth. The idea that I was about to say 'until Abe is officially declared dead', like it was some kind of inconvenient admin, makes me gag. 'Until Abe is found there is no insurance money, and I don't have much, but I started saving a little when Will was born. And I think I have enough for the roof. And if we get Cathy's room up to scratch then we can let people come and visit it for a pound.' Ma spoons cake batter into two tins, and the smell tastes of Sunday tea and *Songs of Praise*. 'Maybe you could make cream teas for visitors and then we could charge them ten pounds?'

'Strangers tramping in and out all day. Tourists. *Southerners*,' Ma says, growling. 'How many cream teas would have to get served to make any money?'

'I don't know Ma, it's just a thought, a start,' I say. 'All the farming land was sold off years ago – not that you or I would know what to do with it if it hadn't been. We've got this great big house, and we'll lose it if we don't find a way to make it work. Probably a southerner'll buy it. And we will be the Heatons that lost the house, after almost five hundred years. I don't want that, and neither do you. We might not see eye to eye over some things, but we both love Ponden.'

'It were never really my house,' Ma says, pausing for a moment, taking in the emerging view. 'But I did my best.'

As I sit there, I think about reaching out for her hand, making amends, building bridges, but try as I might I can't make my leaden fingers move from the table top. I'd thought that maybe the anger had drained away, that after all these years and the birth of my son, it had ebbed into nothing. But it's still here, burning bright and hard in the centre of my chest, together with its twin, the same insistent question: why didn't my mother ever love me?

'I'll do as I see fit then,' I say, and I leave her to her baking.

Now the winter axis is almost complete and night is due again. I spend the day in Cathy's room. Washing the windows clean, sweeping away the cobwebs, and even vacuuming the carpet I'm planning to rip, out, just because it had to be at least 50 per cent dust. Once it's done, I turn around in the centre of the room to take it all in, all the time captured there, unable to resist lying on the half-cleaned carpet to enjoy the simple quiet.

Beams of ancient oak – forked branches still intact – vault above me, keeping the high ceiling up, no matter what weather the last half century has flung at them. The lower beams are braced against the stalwart walls, reinforced at some time with great black iron bolts. A jigsaw puzzle of repair and renewal – evidence of dozens of pairs of caring, careful custodian hands. Three stone-framed windows gather in all the last light of the day, turning the space into a prism of sorts, refracting and reflecting the whole of the glory of the moors and concentrating the essence of all that outside beauty inside this one place. I feel what I have always felt when I am here: that I'm walking amongst giants and navigating the clouds.

No one has ever slept in this room, not as long as I've been alive, anyway, and I've never thought to ask why because it seems obvious: it's already occupied by all the life that already lived here.

The light bulb flickers as a gust of wind pipes down the chimney and blows ash into the room, along with a blast of freezing air. I shudder suddenly, seeing myself from above, at the windows, peering in.

There's still more work to do before I can rest; I need to get this carpet up before Marcus Ellis arrives first thing.

Plunging the elderly box-cutter knife I found in the kitchen drawer into the worn blue wool, I drag it in stuttering starts and stops through the brittle material, and dust, mould and rotten bits of rubber are flung upwards. I hack and saw at the carpet, finally freeing a chunk, and the secret subterranean world between it and the floorboards I'm excavating is finally uncovered, and the discovery makes this archivist smile.

When I look at what lies beneath, I realise why there is always a faint whisper and crackle accompanying every footstep in this room. The boards have been lined with newspapers, layer upon layer of them, by the looks of it, yellowing but dry and intact, which I suppose must be good news when it comes to the state of the boards beneath.

Sheet by sheet, I begin to rip them out. Red-topped tabloids, mostly – that's what Dad was into: footballers and Page Three girls – but my hands stop tearing, my heart stops beating, as I come across a half-finished crossword.

I'm looking at Dad's handwritten scribbles in the margin. They speak in a whisper, a long-distance hello from a lazy sunny day thirty years ago, welcoming me home. Carefully, I cut this hidden fragment of him out, holding it for a few minutes in the palm of my hand, before going to my room to unpack one of the acid-free cardboard folders I brought from London. There can't be a better place to start my Heaton archive than with this fragile fragment of my dad, a tiny second of his life caught in biro forever. Dad used to make me laugh like no one else could, tell a story like no other man alive. These marks he made, they are him. Waiting here, woven into the house like so many Heatons before.

Carefully, now, I peel back layer upon layer of paper. Under that I find sheets of patterned, mismatched lino. Carefully, I cut that away – and the first thing I see is the face of Lily Cove, a sweet young woman I know very well.

She is one of Ponden's ghosts, after all.

CHAPTER SEVEN

'Parachutist Killed – terrible death of a young woman' reads the headline of the *Lincolnshire Chronicle* dated 16 June 1906, and there is Lily Cove, a grainy image of a dark-haired, dark-eyed girl, full of grit, jaw set in determination.

One Halloween, when I was about nine, Dad took me down into the back field to show me the place were Lily met her death.

I can still smell the sharp scent of wood smoke in the air and taste the mist coming up off the reservoir, filling the hedgerows and ditches with pockets of fog. I could have felt frightened, but I didn't, because I was with Dad, and wherever Dad was, I felt safe.

Halloween was my favourite tradition at Ponden Hall, because it really was just ours. No one ever came round our way trick or treating, and there was no one for us to call on for miles around, so Dad make a fire in the back garden and we'd toast marshmallows and he'd tell me ghost stories.

Not of vague and dimly imagined dark, dark woods, or generic abandoned empty houses, though. His ghost stories would also be my ghost stories, because every single one of them belonged to the house. Every death, every tragic accident or brutal murder, was part of my Heaton inheritance.

'June 1906,' Dad had told me, his torch up-lighting his face. 'At that time there was a fashion up and down the country for scantily clad young ladies to ascend high into the air on a trapeze attached to a hot air balloon and then parachute down to earth, delighting the crowds below with their daring and a flash of their thighs!'

'Ugh, Daddy!' I'd giggled and Dad had waggled his eyebrows like he always did when he was making dad jokes.

'Our tragic heroine, young Lily Cove, had been booked to appear at the Haworth Gala, but on the day the weather meant she could not ascend. And yet, to be paid, she had to perform, so on this fateful day, with just a few bystanders watching, and the mayor and her manager, Lily went up anyway.'

'Poor Lily,' I'd whispered, and even though I knew the end of the story, still I had hoped for a happy ending.

'A sudden change in the weather saw her being blown off course,' Dad had continued, enjoying hamming it up. 'She was carried away from Haworth and towards Ponden Hall so fast they had to chase her in the milk cart.'

'She was so afraid,' I'd said, and Dad hadn't argued with me; we'd both known it was true.

'No one knows why she cut herself out of her parachute harness and plummeted to her death, head first,' Dad had said, shaking his head sadly. 'Though they did say she was terrified of drowning and might have thought the parachute was going to take her into the water. Either way, if Lily Cove hadn't sealed her own fate, she would have landed safely on land instead of becoming the crumpled and bloody mess they found folded into the ground of our backyard, on this very spot. They carried her into the house and laid her out on the kitchen table, and it was there, on the very same table you eat your breakfast at, with her insides pulverised and every bone broken, that she breathed her last, tragic breath.'

Dad had leaned towards me, close enough that I could see the fire dancing in his eyes. 'And they do say, that on quiet nights like this one, if you listen very carefully, you can hear her terrified screams echoing across the reservoir.'

We'd sat there for a moment, with just the sound of the trees bending in the dark and the crackling of the fire, listening for poor dead Lily Cove, when Dad had suddenly gone, 'Boo!' and I'd shrieked, and then laughed so hard I couldn't breathe. But as our laughter had died away, the strangest thing had happened, something I'll never forget: we'd heard a bird calling in the night, shrill and high, a repetitive, plaintive call, unlike anything I'd ever heard before, echoing like a misplaced apparition.

'What's that?' I'd asked Dad, wide-eyed. He'd shaken his head and spent the next few months trying to identify the call, with no success.

Lily never made an appearance that Halloween night.

But then, as now, I didn't need there to be an apparition for me to believe that she was still here; it seems obvious and logical to me that a trace of her remains. That the atoms of energy that had once made her into the kind of fearless girl she was would still exist at Ponden, along with all the other lives that had passed through here, along with Dad's and, one day, mine.

Because Ponden Hall is a kind living time capsule, retaining just a fraction of every moment that there has ever been, and every moment there will ever be, constantly looping and retelling every single story written within its walls, refracting each one back into this present moment, making it *every* moment.

It's that which makes the silence seems so alive, that makes the stillness full of energy, makes me look at this photograph of long-gone Lily Cove and sense her moving in the air around me, as much a part of the fabric of the house as the limestone that built it and the floorboards under my knees.

Carefully, I lift her photograph out and put her away with Dad's crossword, feeling some small satisfaction at the idea that these remnants of them have been keeping each other company.

A few more minutes of hard labour, careful tearing and cutting, saving anything that looks interesting, and at last I am down to the bare pitched-pine boards, broad and strong. Although I'm no expert, they look sound to me.

Kneeling on all fours, I run my hands over the ancient wood, made of trees that were probably several hundred years old when they were felled, so much time running through every grain and knot. So many feet would have walked over them; every Ponden Heaton that's there's been, that's for sure, and Emily Brontë, too, when she came into this room to read by the fire ... probably her siblings as well.

Folding over onto my side, I lay my cheek on the wood, giving in to my exhaustion, seeking out the different shades of ruby-red and amber embedded in the wood, feeling for each fingerprint swirl and loop in the grain. Running my hand along the grooves where the boards meet, a great sense of warmth and peace trickles through me and I know that, if I close my eyes, I will fall asleep right here on the bare floorboards of this empty room and then—

Something jolts my eyes open.

Something rough and irregular under my palm catches my attention. It's hardly more than the breadth of my finger and yet ... Sitting up, I can make out markings on the wood, but it's more than just scratches or wear and tear. They have shape and purpose. Scrambling up, I reach for my torch and search out my magnifying glass, holding it over the marking – and catch my breath.

It's a word. Four letters scratched into the wood, letters so small that you would never see them if you weren't almost nose-to-nose with the floor.

Four tiny letters that remind me of something I've seen somewhere before and which spell out one word.

Look.

CHAPTER EIGHT

Heart racing, I crouch on all fours and peer into the narrow gap between the boards that the word is etched along and, yes, *yes*, there is something there, a wedge of wood, maybe?

Grazing it with my little finger, it feels smooth to the touch, though. Maybe leather?

Reaching for my box of gear, I find my long tweezers and shine the torch deep into the crack. I am barely conscious of the constant thrum of wind dropping suddenly, and then the utter stillness, the sense of being watched.

Lying on my stomach, I slowly ease the packet out, one excruciating millimetre at a time, until it is released.

This thing, this curious, dull object that has been hidden for so long, seems to absorb my torchlight. Turning it around I can see it is made of thin leather that has been tightly folded into a packet that would fit in the palm of my hand.

Retrieving my book pillow from my kit – a specially made beanbag designed to support old and fragile documents – I place the object on it.

The leather looks very old, greying and ingrained with black. It's secured with a tightly knotted cord; possibly it's also leather, but so stiffened with age and dirt it's hard to tell.

I know I should wait for daylight, but my heart is fluttering with excitement and I don't care that I am breaking protocol. Whatever this is, it's been waiting to be discovered for so long that to make it wait another moment seems unimaginable.

How long it takes me to painstakingly ease apart the knotted cord, I don't know, but time doesn't seem to matter very much. I know the night is darkening outside and that the moon is rising.

Far away I can hear Will's voice and Mab's bark, and somewhere in my chest I am still aware of that constant sense of loss and longing for Abe.

But just for now, however long now is, all of those things are pushed far away and I am lost in discovery. Using a stainless steel spatula, I encourage the leather to fall open along its fold lines, careful not to stress it with any sudden movements until, at last, the two pieces of writing, one folded inside the other, are revealed.

The papers are from two distinct ages, centuries apart; I can tell that right away from the quality of the paper and the style of the handwriting.

Once each layer of leather and paper is sufficiently unfurled, I lay them side by side.

'Oh dear God!' I can hear the amazement, the thrill and excitement, in my own voice, as if someone else has spoken the words aloud.

I *know* the handwriting on the second piece of paper. And as I look at it I know what the letters etched into the floorboard reminded me of. A sloping 'E', carved into a table.

I know this handwriting as if it is my own, because it belongs to someone I've loved since I was old enough to know her name, someone whose every last detail of their left-behind life has become as familiar to me as my own.

This handwriting belongs to Emily Brontë.

PART TWO

O God within my breast,
Almighty, ever-present Deity!
Life – that in me hast rest,
As I – Undying Life – have power in Thee!

Emily Brontë

Tru and Abe

Those first months, it felt like summer lasted for half a year. We'd hide away, deep in the heather and bracken, under the dapple of the sparse beech trees, allowed to grow tall and straight only by the good grace of the sheltering valley. When we were together there, under the arc of the sky, it felt as if we were part of the earth itself, making new discoveries of each other every time we met. If I close my eyes I can still feel it, the scratch of the gorse on the bare skin of my back, the scrape of Abe's cheek on my thighs, the tiny constellation bruises left by the rocks we rolled over, the way his fingers would encircle my wrists, not in dominance, but completion. When we were joined together, with the wind all around us, beetles crawling over our bare toes, we became infinite. Me, him, the earth, the air, the sound of the water collapsing down the mountainside and the iron-rich scent of the soil so strong you could taste it with every kiss.

That was all I'd wanted, then. I'd yearned and ached for his body and the ground underneath it, just as hard. It had been Abe who'd wanted more, who'd taken me once to his flat in Leeds and out for coffee with Unity, who'd fretted about my age and low expectations from life, but who'd been kind and hopeful, too. It had been Abe who, on meeting me at our usual places, had asked me to show him around the inside of the Brontë home.

I'd hesitated, worried he'd ruin everything by not loving the sisters like I did. My young and tender heart had kept the piece of it devoted to the Brontë sisters back, locking it away for safekeeping so that, at least, remained only mine.

It was only after I'd been fully satisfied that Abe had truly understood how wondrous the sisters were, how they'd defied every expectation of their age to set the world on fire, that I had let him into their home.

So that when he'd stood behind me in small, roped-off area, looking at the table they'd sat and written at, I'd known he'd understood that this wasn't just a room, that wasn't just furniture. To me it was a kind of temple.

'They were so fearless – and because of that courage, some of the greatest stories ever told were made *here*. Isn't that magical? Draw in a deep breath and you're breathing *them* in. Think about that.'

Abe had nodded and listened as I'd led him from room to room, never looking at him, telling him every little thing I knew about the Brontës and every relic on display, until half a dozen more people were following us around, listening too. And when we were finally outside again, in the dreamily warm afternoon, I'd realised I'd had been so nervous, more nervous even than if I'd been taking him home to meet Ma.

'Thank you,' Abe had said as we'd walked down Main Street towards his bus stop. 'I really enjoyed that.'

'Don't be sarcastic,' I'd said, laughing.

'I'm not,' he'd said, taking my hand. 'If you'd asked me a year ago about the Brontë sisters, I'd have thought about three boring women, who'd written three boring old books. You opened a door for me into something really wonderful – and watching you talk about them, all this knowledge and excitement pouring out of you? It's beautiful. *You're* beautiful.'

'Shut up,' I'd said, but I was grinning anyway.

'I wonder if I could have the same effect on you if I described the study of the central nervous system?'

'Maybe you could.' And I'd laughed. 'Although I learn quite a lot about my central nervous system just being around you. Do you have to go now? We could find a place—'

'Wait, don't distract me for a minute.' Abe had removed my hands from his chest. 'I need to say this. I've been meaning to, and now I realise exactly how much.'

'Say what?' I'd become suddenly nervous.

'You are so smart, Tru. Your A levels are coming up, but you haven't applied to any universities yet. You don't even talk about it, and I guess I want to know: why not?'

'I don't know,' I'd said and shrugged. 'We're not a family that goes to university, I suppose. Besides, I like my life like it is, and anyway, I don't know what I want to do when I grow up. I might not even need a degree to do it, so what's the rush?'

'The rush is that your life won't always be like it is now,' Abe had said, pulling me to a stop on the cobbles. He'd tried to meet my eye, but I'd refused, looking past his shoulder to the mosaic of people in their summer colours and patterns rising up the steep incline after me.

'All right, Dad,' I'd said. 'Loads of people take a year out.'

'A year out to travel,' Abe reminded me. 'Not a year out to stay at home and work part-time in a pub. Look, it's up to you, but everything I know about you, listening to the way you talked in there, there's so much more in the world to know and understand, to discover. You'd love university life; you'd love meeting new people, discovering more of the world. And you are worth so much more than ...'

He'd trailed off, perhaps seeing the frown that had set between my eyebrows.

'My life is worth a lot to me,' I'd told him. 'It might not be big or grand or ambitious, and I'm not going to learn how to save a life like you are. But I love this place, and I love my home, and Ma is ... well, I'm all she's got. And I have you. I've got everything I need.'

Abe had looked away from me, digging his hands into his pockets. I couldn't understand how what I'd said had had that effect.

'I do have you, don't I?' I'd asked him uncertainly. 'Or are you ashamed of me?'

'It's just ... you and me ... it won't work if ... it can't be like that,' he'd stumbled over every word.

'Like what?' I'd asked, laughing, but he hadn't smiled in return. 'Like what, Abe?'

'I love you, Tru, but I won't be one of the reasons you don't do something with your life.'

'What are you talking about? What I do is nothing to do with you, and I *am* doing something – *this* is something.'

'Something more, Tru. You could do a whole lot more if you just let yourself be free of who you expect to be. Who cares if Heatons have lived at Ponden Hall for five hundred years, or if that was the house you were born in? It doesn't mean it has to be the house you die in. There's a whole world out there, so much more for you to find.'

'Can you hear yourself?' I'd asked him. 'You're talking to me like I'm a child who doesn't know anything.'

'Because sometimes you act like a child!'

I don't know what he'd said after that, because I'd turned on my heel and marched back up the street, hearing him calling my name, waiting for him to arrive at my side, to have come running after me. But he hadn't. I wouldn't let myself look until I'd reached the top of the hill, and when I had, he wasn't there any more.

'Trudy Heaton.' I'd stopped dead at the sound of my name being spoken by Erica Sadler from the art shop. She was a woman who loved to talk. 'Lover's tiff, is it?'

'No,' I'd said, trying to walk on, but she'd spoken again.

'I've seen you about with your young man. Where's he from?'

'Leeds,' I'd said, crossing my arms.

'Originally, I mean.'

'Putney,' I'd told her, daring her to ask me again.

'Oh, well, I bet your Ma likes him, does she?'

'Loves him,' I'd said. 'He's the apple of her eye.'

'Just don't let young love get in the way of your exams, OK?' Erica Sadler had laughed then, and I'd smiled as I'd watched her go on her way. But I'd known that sometime, before the end of today, Ma would find out about Abe because Erica Sadler wouldn't be able to wait to see the look on Ma's face when she delivered the news.

And no matter what that old bag Erica Sadler might think, it wouldn't be the colour of Abe's skin that would upset Ma.

No, it would be that I'd kept something so important a secret from her, that I'd taken something special and made it mine alone.

And it would mean that I didn't belong to her any more, that I never really would again, and I'd known – I had always known – how much she would hate that, how much it would kill her to let me be free.

I could have gone home then, gone to find her and see her and explain before Erica Sadler got into her Honda Civic and dropped in, telling Ma she was just passing.

I could have, but I hadn't. Instead, I'd taken the long way home, letting the summer sun burn the backs of my arms and make my head swim as I'd walked up to Top Withens, picking my way in and out of walkers, until I was alone with the wind and the clouds at last.

It wasn't until I was on my way down the steep and rocky descent and almost home that it had occurred to me that it wasn't that I didn't want a life outside of the one that I knew, it was just that I didn't know of anything else that I wanted more.

I'd known that if I stayed where I was, in this place, I'd be content.

But, for the first time in my seventeen years, I'd wondered if content was enough. If it was, it wasn't going to matter for very much longer, because when I got home Ma was waiting for me and Abe had been right. Nothing stays the same forever.

CHAPTER NINE

'You must be Trudy Heaton?'

Marcus Ellis catches me pacing up and down outside the house, caught between watching Will and Mab play an approximation of fetch and glancing up at the window of my bedroom, where yesterday's find is carefully concealed in a box folder.

Moments after I had realised, or thought I'd realised, what I was looking at, Will had arrived in the room, filling it with his kinetic energy, and the clocks had started ticking again.

'Mummy, it's nearly ten o' clock and I haven't gone to bed!' he'd told me, his eyes shiny from too much screen time. 'Gran says she's had enough of my goings-on for one day and to come and fetch you.'

'Oh, Will, sorry.' I'd looked again at the words on the page before they'd floated and merged, and I'd realised how exhausted I was, not just from this one day of work, but from months and months of just keeping going. 'I took up the carpet from this room, though; what do you think?'

Will, who had tipped into the kind of frenetic overtiredness that only children can truly achieve, had delighted at the sound of his bare feet on the boards as he'd run around and around and around, while I'd safely delivered the papers to a cardboard folder.

'Careful, Will.' I'd forced myself back into reality, like dragging myself out of a vivid dream. 'We haven't had the surveyor in to look at the floor yet!'

'What does he need to know, apart from that it's a floor?' Will had asked me, laughing and flapping his arms as if he were about to take off. With trembling hands I'd slid the folder, along with the leather square, into the box with Dad and Lily Cove.

Had I really seen what I thought I had? Perhaps it was exhaustion or even hope, filling in the unknown with the impossible because I needed something, anything, to hold on to.

'Can we have more *Secret Garden*?' Will had asked. 'I like it.'

'Did you eat?' I'd asked him, appalled with myself for not knowing.

'Yes, jam sandwich and cake,' Will had told me.

'Then extra teeth cleaning and bed – and stories,' I'd said, feeling the shame of wanting so badly to look again at what I had found above putting my son to bed. I'd pushed the box file onto the highest bookshelf in my bedroom, shutting the bookcase door, and pulled myself out of that bubble and into the now. I'd laughed as he'd made faces at me while he brushed his teeth, and watched the top of his head as he'd burrowed into my side as I'd read. I'd waited as he'd fallen asleep in my arms, his head on my chest, and I'd said a prayer to the star that rose into the precise position above the hole in the roof, thanking God for my son who refused to give up hoping and laughing and living, until, at last, I'd slept too. And for the first time in months the night flew by in an instant, without a single dream, and when I'd woken, still dressed in yesterday's clothes, I'd felt as if my body and mind had really rested.

Now, as the sound of his voice, high and happy, is carried away across the hills along with the scuttling leaves and any last traces of summer, the papers remain unread.

Last night I was desperate to know if I really might have come across something new that had been penned by Emily; now I'm afraid to look again and discover that it isn't.

'Trudy Heaton?' He says my name again and I smile automatically, extending my hand.

'I am, and you must be Marcus Ellis.'

He is archetypal country money; fair, thinning hair, pale-skinned, blue eyes, waxed jacket and jeans that look brand new – exactly the kind of person that Ma hates on sight. But then again, when he looks at me he'll see an unkempt woman, wearing yesterday's clothes, covered with dust and with cobwebs in her hair, so I shouldn't be so quick to judge.

Marcus grins and nods, and he can't stop looking at the house behind him, like he's desperate to get in. I think I like him.

'And this is … ? He smiles at Will, who ignores him.

'My son, Will, and Mab, my mum's dog.'

'*My* dog,' Will says, without looking at either of us.

'Will, come and say hello, please,' I prompt him firmly, but Marcus shakes his head.

'It's fine,' he says. 'What self-respecting kid wants to make conversation with an adult? I know I barely do, and I'm nearly forty.'

'I like to think I brought him up to have good manners,' I say, loud enough for Will to hear, dropping my voice to add, 'But he's dealing with a lot of change, right now, so thanks for cutting him some slack.'

'Can I stay out here and play with Mab?' Will asks.

'Yes, but go into the garden, not on the track, OK?'

'OK.' Will gestures enthusiastically to Mab to follow him and, after a moment, she heaves a shuddering sigh and waddles after him.

'I have to tell you I've been dying to get inside this building for years,' Marcus tells me, his eyes sweeping every surface as I lead him inside. 'Brontë mania rather runs in our family; Dad walked me past this house when I was a kid, at least two dozen times, and told me the actual *Wuthering Heights* box bed was inside. Once, back then, I even sneaked inside to try and get a look, but this terrifying woman threw me out on my ear.'

'Oh, that will've been Ma,' I say, unconsciously lowering my voice as I lead him inside. 'You broke into my house?'

'Well, not exactly; the door was open.'

He pauses as we step in through the front door and a huge grin spreads across his face, compelling me to return his delighted smile.

'This is going to be wonderful,' he says, his eyes alight. 'Very ancient buildings have a way of talking to you that means you have to stop and listen and work out what they want to tell you, don't you think? So many secrets waiting to be uncovered.'

'I've always thought that, too,' I say. 'Actually, I've always talked to Ponden since I was little; it feels impolite not to.'

I stop outside the kitchen where I can hear Ma banging around with the Sainsbury's delivery and hope that my demeanour is enough of a signal to Marcus that it's best that we don't attract Ma's attention just yet.

Perhaps remembering the woman who threw him out once before, he's quiet as he follows me up the stairs and along the hallway to where I open the door into Cathy's room for him, watching with interest as he walks in. He laughs with sheer delight, and that makes me laugh too.

'I can't believe I'm actually standing here,' he says. 'I've known about this room for years, since I was a schoolkid. My dad was a collector and dealer in rare and antique books – my family has been for generations, in fact – and of course it was the law that I had to have read all of the Brontës' books by the time I was twelve. When he told me about this room, and that window here, I was desperate to see the place that inspired that scene in *Wuthering Heights*. It might have been one of the reasons I got into renovation, and a couple of time I tried to offer my services here, but never got any uptake. Now I'm here and ... it's magical, Trudy. It's astounding.'

I watch his face as he walks into the middle of the room, slowly turning around, taking in each beam and block of stone, seeing his smile deepen.

'This is incredible,' he says. 'And the box bed! The box bed is a treasure. I can't believe I'm looking at it at last. May I?' Nodding, I watch as he walks over to it rather hesitantly, before resting his hand on the dark wood, sliding the door open. I hear his breath suck in sharply as he sees the small, square window.

'Amazing. It's like stepping into the novel. And it looks entirely original, too.'

'It's great to meet someone who feels the same way about this place as I do,' I tell him on impulse. 'Ponden is quite choosey about who she likes and who she doesn't. I have a feeling you are just her type.'

'Well, she is certainly mine.' Marcus turns to smile at me, and the warmth in his eyes is reassuring. A sudden impulse to rush and grab my finds to show him almost overtakes me; I know he'd almost certainly feel the exact same excitement and thrill about them as I do if I were to share them with him. But something stops me, something like a hand on my shoulder, an unexpected sense of caution and a strong urge to keep my treasure as secret as it has been for at least two hundred years. I'm the only person in the whole world who knows it exists. There's power in that.

'We must have both grown up around here at the same time,' I say, 'but I don't remember you from school?'

'No, I was sent away to school.' Marcus's smile fades just a little. 'My father thought it would be more character-forming and all that. I hope you don't mind, but I looked you up and discovered that you used to work at the Lister James Museum in London. I visited there last summer – it's an incredible place. The hall of death masks was unexpectedly moving.'

'That's how I feel about it,' I say. 'Funny, because most of our visitors have nightmares about it afterwards; they don't understand how familiar Victorians were with death.'

Marcus takes an iPad from his briefcase.

'So, what I need to do is to make an initial assessment, which will be based on historical dating and structural integrity. Whatever we can save that is original we will, and we'll also know exactly how to renovate and repair anything we can't save in a way that will please English Heritage. It will take me most of the day to complete the whole of the sixteenth-century wing and then, once I've compiled all the data I need, I will write a report and then we can talk about the cost and the requirements of a Grade II star listed renovation and—'

The sharp sound of a frightened cry darts in through the open window. It's Will.

CHAPTER TEN

I explode into the outdoors, and tumble into the wide grey sky. My feet hit the stony ground and I run, breathless, racing towards the sound of Will crying, long grass tufts and dips under my socks, whipping and grabbing at my ankles. I run like someone who knows that the worst can happen, does happen – full of fear and expectation.

My little boy is lying under the great old oak, curled into a foetal position, sobbing and rocking his way into the soft earth. Mab stands over him, like a bridge, four paws planted firmly on either side of his skinny torso, guarding him from further harm. Only when I'm near does she move aside.

'Oh baby, what happened, what happened? Can you move this, and this?' I run my hand over his limbs, searching for any obvious injury as I gather him into my arms.

Finally his cries subside. One shoe lies a few feet from us, turned on its side, his face is buried in my neck.

'I was in the tree, climbing it like you said you used to, and I – I fell out of it.'

'Oh baby,' I say, pressing the back of my hand against his hot cheek. 'I bet that was frightening.'

'It was a shock more than anything,' he says, parroting back at me a phrase I've spoken to him a hundred times before.

'So, where does it hurt?' I ask. 'Arms? Legs? Head?'

'Ankle,' Will says. 'Only a bit. Maybe so much that I might not be able to go to school tomorrow?'

This takes me aback. I study him, as his chin dips. Did he … ? He wouldn't have … not just to get out of starting a new school, would he? Am I that out of tune with his worries and fears?

'Hello, there,' Marcus greets us as he walks across the field and Will scowls as he settles down in the wet grass, not seeming to care about staining his pristine jeans.

'Now, I know a thing or two about first aid; I'm in the Territorial Army – well, it's the Army Reserve, now – so do you mind if I look you over?'

'Do you have a gun?' Will asks.

'I do.' Marcus answers him very seriously. 'But not because of the Reserve. I shoot for a hobby, so I have a couple. Can I check you out?'

'Do you shoot animals?' Will narrows his eyes.

'No, never.' Marcus smiles. 'Just targets. Now, can you wiggle your fingers?'

Will obliges.

'Toes?'

Will's toes ripple under his socks.

'OK, I'm just going to test the range of movement in your ankles and knees, arms and wrists, OK?'

One by one, as he tests each joint, Will calms further, observing Marcus with naked curiosity. I have to admit, I feel the same, watching this well-spoken, well-dressed man kneel in the boggy grass, his fine fair hair falling into his eyes; there's a familiarity about his sense of certainty that tugs at the centre of my chest – and then I realise, though he couldn't look more different from Abe, he reminds me of him. His manner and quiet assurance are as soothing as balm. The flash of recognition hurts so much it takes my breath away, and it takes a concerted effort to fold away the desire to just lie down with my face in the soil and cry.

'Which branch were you in, mate?' Marcus asks, looking up at the tree.

Without thinking, Will stands up and points to a lowish branch.

'Must have been scary,' Marcus says. 'But at least you had a soft landing. I think you're OK.'

'Will you show me your guns?' Will asks.

'I don't have them on me,' Marcus says, and laughs. 'I keep them locked away.'

'Come on,' I say, collecting Will's shoe. 'Let's get you inside. How about a movie on the sofa, and I'll make you a sandwich.'

Will makes a point of hopping ahead, one hand on Mab's collar, as we head back towards the house. I look up at the window of the room I was just in and see the window blinking back at me, patiently waiting.

'Thank you,' I say to Marcus as Will hops into the house. 'For checking him over. My husband is a doctor—'

'Oh, then you didn't really need me wading in, did you?' Marcus says with a smile. 'Is he at work? You could give him a call?'

'He's ...' I sigh; it never gets any easier. 'I thought everyone knew.'

'Knew what?' Marcus turns to look at me.

'He's missing, after a plane crash eight months ago. What I mean to say is that he's dead. He is dead. His body hasn't been recovered, but ... he is dead. There is no chance he could be alive and so ... well, and so ...'

'Oh Christ.' Marcus stops. 'Trudy, I'm so sorry.'

'Me too,' I say. 'I'm sorry, this is so awkward for you. I thought someone in the village would have told you. Or you would have just known, somehow. It doesn't normally take long for word to get round Haworth.'

'No.' Marcus's smile is sweet and sad. 'No. But I'm not really in on the local grapevine. My ex-wife was; she worked at the Parsonage and always knew everything that was going on, but not me. Sometimes I think I'm just a natural outsider. But in this case, I wish I'd known; I'd have been more ... well, more something.'

'You've been very kind,' I say, looking at my knotted hands.

'Who is this?' Ma stands in the doorway, barring Marcus's entrance. 'What did you do to my grandson?'

'Mrs Heaton? You won't remember me, but we met before, a long time ago. I'm Marcus Ellis, here to survey the sixteenth-century part of the house before we begin phase one of the renovation work.' Marcus presents the same smile and extended hand as he did to me and Ma looks at him like he's something she just trod in.

'I don't give a rat's arse who you are, I never said you could come in my house.'

'Ma, I told you I'd arranged for Marcus to visit,' I say, quietly. 'Something needs to be done, remember?' I glance back at Marcus, who is looking distinctly uncomfortable. 'It has to happen whether you like it or not; I need to make sure Will has some security in his life and Ponden is it. It's a special place, Ma; it needs looking after and I really don't understand why you are against it.'

'I—' Ma shakes her head. 'I'm not discussing it with him here. I just want to wait, that's all. I have my reasons.'

'Then can you check Will?' I ask her. 'He was shaken up when he fell out of the tree.'

'He fell out of a tree? Dear God, lass, why didn't you tell me?'

I rub my hands over my face as she hurries inside.

'Sorry.' I look at Marcus from between my fingers.

'I normally make a better impression on mothers,' Marcus says.

'That's Ma for you.' I smile. 'She'd die before admitting she's wrong.'

Will is lying on the sofa, blanketed by Mab, his chin on the top of her head, hands tucked under her ears, eyes fixed on a movie on my laptop. I can hear Ma banging around in the kitchen, complaining to her pots and pans.

'How are you feeling?' I ask Will, sitting next to him.

'Good,' he says.

'No headache, no sickness?'

He shakes his head.

'Will, before, when you said you might be too hurt to start school tomorrow?'

'I might be,' he says, twisting to look at me. 'I might be in shock.'

'Look,' I say, 'I know it's weird starting a new school, so far from home, halfway through term ... You must feel really worried, but you can tell me if you do.'

Will regards me for a long, sombre moment.

'I don't want to go to school tomorrow,' he says. 'Or ever. I don't want to go to school around here. What if I'm the only kid that looks like me? What if everyone hates me? Can't I just stay at home until it's time to go back to London? Or, you know, in Australia, some kids are taught over a two-way radio. Couldn't I do that? Like with Skype or something? Miss Andrews wouldn't mind, I bet, if we ask her. I could be a head in a laptop on my desk.'

He smiles at the idea.

'I wish it could be like that,' I tell him gently. 'I wish we hadn't had to go through so much change in the last few months, baby, but—'

'I'm not a baby!' He squirms away from me. 'And I don't want to go to school here, in this place.'

'Why not?' I ask him. 'After a day or so you'll like it, make new friends, join some clubs. I bet they have a football team.'

'I don't like football, and everything is different. And I don't want any more different. Not yet. I'm not ready for more new things, Mummy. Maybe, when Daddy gets here … Can't I just say at home until Daddy gets here?'

'Will …' I pull him into the crook of my arm. 'This is so hard, so much harder for you, and I keep forgetting that. This place was my whole life when I was your age, and I suppose I thought you'd see it the way that I did. When I think about it, the way you must see it, then I suppose it might seem a bit lonely out here, a bit scary but—'

'It's not Ponden,' Will says. 'I like Ponden. It's everything outside I don't like.'

'I know you miss your friends, and your bed, and everything you knew. So do I, darling.'

'I miss Daddy.' Will looks at me. 'I miss Daddy and I don't want to do anything new until he comes back. I don't want him to think that we were just getting used to life without him, Mummy; that will make him sad.

So can I just not do anything else new, Mummy, please? *Please*? I'll read books, lots of books, and eat salad and tidy up, I promise. *Please* let me stay with you.'

'Darling, there is honestly nothing more I would like than for it to be just me and you, every day. I want to stay still too, but – but we can't, Will. We have to do the things that we would always do; we have to be brave and keep going, keep trying, until it doesn't feel like trying any more.'

'So I have to go to school?' Will seems to shrink in my arms and I hold him even closer.

'I tell you what; will you just see what it's like?' I ask him. 'Daddy would want you to see what it was like, wouldn't he? Like he always said, if you don't climb the mountain or get in a rocket to the moon, you'll never know what its like to be on top of the mountain or walking on the moon.'

'But Daddy isn't here yet ...' Will' voice is very small, very quiet.

'He is,' I say. 'He's always with us. When I look at you, I can see him. His heart and courage, that smile that made everyone fall for him. I can see him in you. When I look at you, you give me courage.'

Will looks at me. 'Are you scared, Mummy?'

'A little bit,' I say.

'Of the bad things outside?'

It's such a strange thing to say that I laugh a little.

'No. I'm scared of always feeling so sad inside, of missing Daddy so much that I don't see and feel all the things that are still good, like you.'

'I'll go to school tomorrow,' Will says. 'I'll see what it's like.'

'You're a good boy,' I tell him. 'And tomorrow the sun will be out and everything will seem better. I expect falling out of the tree took it out of you a bit, and I don't blame you.'

Will turns towards me a little so that I can see one eye.

'I didn't fall out of the tree,' he whispers, as if he's worried about being overheard. 'I was pushed. The bad one pushed me.'

Ponden 1655

Dear Lord our Saviour, please forgive my sins, for I have committed theft. This night, while Casson was drinking with his cronies, I crept into his study and took sheets of paper, and more ink. Lord God, I had to do it, for otherwise none will ever know of the horrors done by this man, for there is only Robert and I to record them. My letters improve daily, and I burn with such a longing to form every thought on paper that I cannot contain myself, even if it is the Devil that tempts me. Dear God, forgive me and keep me safe from evil, but how can knowledge be a sin, Lord, if my heart and intentions are pure?

Every day Casson seeks to push Robert out of his own home, and take what is his. But I shall make a record here of the crimes I know that he has committed and when the time comes, I shall present them to the justice, even though it may be my life is forfeit, for there were times when I was his accomplice.

For though I am but a female, and lowly born, I am no coward. Nor will I stand by and see another life ruined by he that ruined mine. My soul burns in fury at the injustice he metes out on good people, and I will not let him have peace as long as I am strong enough to stand on my two feet.

Often, Robert sits in the old Porter's chair in the hall, hiding in the shadow of the hood, and listens to what Casson has to say. The more ale that passes his lips, the looser they become. When I am able, I crawl in next to him and we listen together, twined up like a brace of grouse.

This very evening, parading his infant as if it were a prize animal, we heard Casson say, 'We don't need more hungry mouths, now I have a babe to feed. We don't need more dead weight, and it's time that boy made his own way in the world. Or any way, as long as it is far from here.'

And there was much laughing and shouts of agreement, for the men that Casson calls his friends are all in his employ and they know who to grovel to.

I held Robert's hand, and sought out his gaze and saw such sadness and anger there, and I feared he would do something that would get him beat.

'Are you afraid?' I said to him.

Robert replied, 'If Ma dies that bastard would see me soon dispatched after her.' He peered into the hall, where the baby still shrieked, and the men still laughed.

'Perhaps he will let the babe fall,' I said. May God forgive me, but Robert is a much purer and more devout soul than mine.

'Tis not the baby's fault the father is a demon,' he said.

I spoke to him of my greatest fear, that soon I will be made to leave Ponden Hall. How I'd dreamed that I was lost in paradise, as green and as beautiful as Eden, and how I had been cast out into a great churning river to drown, red-painted demon faces watching me as I was lost in the fierce brown water. I draw the face here, or a little like it, at least.

Robert held me very close and very firm to his bosom and said to me, 'Ponden Hall is your home and so it always shall be. I say it is, and I am this house's master. I shall never let you leave me, Agnes, for if you do, all hope will die.'

Never have I felt at once so happy and so full of fear, afraid of what thoughts and desires stirred in my heart, pray forgive me Dear Lord our Saviour. And Robert spoke once again, his eyes fixed on mine so that I would know each word was a vow.

'I would die for you, Agnes.'

'And I'd kill for you, Robert.'

No more words were spoken, no more were needed. When Robert left me at last, I stole this paper and ink and I do not feel sorry for it, for there are now so many words in my head that I could fill a library with everything I wish to express.

Agnes, aged 12 or thereabouts

CHAPTER ELEVEN

Night falls, and I wait for Ponden to quiet, for Ma's radio to stop blaring, and Will's breaths to steady and deepen.

Tonight, as I kissed his forehead a gentle goodnight, Mab crept up the stairs, and positioned herself across the door with a groan. The first time she's ever done this since we arrived. It could be that she and Will had bonded more, or that she senses he's anxious about tomorrow.

'What do you know, Mab?' I asked her and her amber eyes regarded me solemnly. 'I'd love to know what you know, but you'll keep an eye on him, won't you?'

She settled her great head onto her paws, her eyes still fixed on mine as I pushed the door to a close, and I took that as a yes.

Will said he was pushed out of that tree. He was adamant about it, though when I tried to get him to tell me who or what the 'bad one' is, he clammed up, refusing even to look at me.

And yet there wasn't anyone else in the garden; I know that for sure, because I would have seen them. There was no one in the lane, or anywhere. But when I went over it all with him, he insisted that he was forcibly dislodged. He felt a hand shove him in the small of his back, he said.

So I went out to look at the tree, just before it got dark. The afternoon absence of sunlight had left a metallic-hard chill in the air and the garden was quiet, even of birdsong, just the sound and suck of the damp ground underfoot.

The branches of the tree were covered in moss, every inch of trunk and branch furred with a deep green, as often so much of this landscape is perpetually steeped in water, whether it rises from below or falls from above. After a deluge of rain in the morning it would have been slippery to stand on and a firm gust of wind might have felt like a shove.

But he was so sure, so very sure that he was pushed and tonight is the night that Mab's decided to take up the position of sentinel outside his room.

Now, taking the box file out of the bookcase, I tuck it under my arm, opening the bedroom door. Mab looks up at me and then into the room where Will is sleeping.

'Go on, then,' I say, and at once she goes inside and clambers up onto the bed, curling herself into the concave space made by his sleeping form, and I'm reassured as I see his arm curl around her middle. It's good to know that she is there, keeping watch over him, an elderly guardian angel, and I know that no other creature could be as diligent and loyal as her.

For a moment I listen at the top of the stairs, for any sounds of life downstairs. There is nothing but the creaking of old timbers, and the rush of the air over rickety roof tiles. Walking into Cathy's room, I cross over to the window to take one last look at the tree Will was climbing when he fell. I can barely see it now, just a dark web of branches reaching into the sky.

When I was little, Dad had told me about the Ponden Child, never seen but often heard, which sounded like a very small child crying and scratching at the windows as if it were trying to get in.

'No one knows the name of the poor soul,' Dad had explained. 'Just the sound of a poor lost child crying for its mother, scratching to come in.'

'I've never heard it,' I'd said, my eyes fixing just above his shoulder.

'So,' Dad had said then, 'tell me about your friend, the girl who you play with up here sometimes.'

And that's when it comes back to me, that's what I was trying to remember when I found Will laughing and talking in an empty room. I'd had an imaginary friend myself once.

It comes flooding back now, how I'd spend hours in my room, playing with the dollhouse, talking to her, laughing, listening as she told me stories. It hadn't been until Dad asked me that question that I realised the girl might not be real.

'It's just a game,' I'd said to Dad, noticing her standing in the corner of the room, waiting for him to leave. 'I just made her up, Daddy.'

'OK.' Dad had looked relieved as he'd smoothed the hair back from my face and kissed me, just as tonight I had kissed Will in that same room, in that same bed. 'Don't make friends with the dead, lass,' he'd told me. 'Don't want them to get so attached to you they want you with them always.'

Sixteen years apart from here and I'd forgotten how much Dad had talked about ghosts as if they were as commonplace as clouds, but that was often the way around here: talk of the Gytrash and the barghest as if they were as real as the sheep in the fields, and the story that the fairy folk only left when the industrial revolution moved in. Long enough ago to be a fairy tale, but recent enough for a glimmer of those old ways to still flicker just within living memory, passed down from child to child. You grow up and all the magic seeps away, that's how I always saw it, but not Dad. Dad believed in magic until the day he died.

So, it's with him in mind that I turn around, searching every corner of the empty room.

'Is there anyone here?' I ask out loud, and I am surprised at how my gut contracts. I hold my breath as my skin prickles and bumps, but there is no reply. No bump in the night, no ghostly sigh. There is nothing but that which there always is here: centuries of existence. And now that I am alone at last, I have a chance to look at a little bit of the mosaic that I discovered yesterday, and see if it really could be what I hope it is.

CHAPTER TWELVE

At last I can let the contents of this box occupy my head once again, although there is a part of me that doesn't want to open it, that doesn't want to discover that, on closer examination, it was a trick of the light that made me believe what I saw might change literary history for good.

My hands are trembling; I feel the reverberation in my fingers as I carefully set out everything I need. It's only been a few weeks since I left the museum for good, but I've missed it, this feeling of anticipation as I bring a little piece of history to light.

Since Abe was lost there has never been any room in my head for anything except getting from day to day, somehow. Not until this secret, waiting here always throughout the whole of my life, just for me.

Is it wrong to feel such joy that it is *mine*, my discovery? Because yes, it belongs to the house, but then again, so do I. So this is mine, and I am Ponden's. And this is mine.

Once again, I carefully unfurl the papers, laying them side by side, and simply allow myself to see, before I really look. For, whoever wrote these words, here is evidence of someone long gone, someone who breathed and loved and laughed and wept, and whatever these papers contain, even if it's mundane, that is thrill enough for me.

That connection, that stretching back, one hand to another, life to life, age to age, linked only with memory and objects, and sometimes, very rarely, both.

What I'm looking at has always been meant for me. And it is a conviction so strange and yet so strong that no amount of sensible thinking will chase it away. Still I hold back from looking, from reading, from knowing, until I have everything ready.

Although we have the power back on, there is still no phone signal or Wi-Fi at Ponden, so I return to my books and biographies, opening the pages at the illustrations of the few surviving diary papers of Emily Brontë, her letters and sketches, the reproductions of which are not nearly as good quality as they should be to make a comparison, but for the moment they are all I have to go by. I look at the chaotic, sprawling hand as it races down the paper, framing a sketch of a thin and pitiful-looking girl, and then speeds around the corner at the edge of the paper, at a forty-five degree angle, the letters becoming ever smaller and more illegible.

It looks like something Emily might have written; it looks like her hurried, impatient hand. It looks just like it. Still, it could be a prank, a tribute. If I'd thought of this when I was twelve or thirteen, I definitely would have made my own Emily Brontë diary papers and hidden them in the room she used to read in.

The moment of truth: I position my lamp right over the paper, hold the magnifying glass over it, and begin to read. And the moment I do, a voice as clear as a striking bell leaps into my mind.

August 1848

Charlotte and Anne are at home and I have come to Ponden alone. It took me an age to get Robert to leave me be to read, for he always wishes me to talk to him about nothing of consequence, as if I have any care for his poor efforts at poetry and drawing. He is a good friend, and gentle. Even so, I'd wish him much less present when I come to Ponden to read. Eventually I scowled and ignored him away and was left alone at last, which is when I came across these three diary papers, dated almost two hundred years since, found within the pages of Du Bartas: His Divine Weekes and Workes. A book which, in itself more than two hundred years old, lends credence to the dates of the papers.

I do believe that none have laid eyes on them for centuries. There will be more, because I hear her, the girl who wrote this. If I listen very carefully, I can hear her voice in the creak of the boards or the breath of the wind. There are a thousand books in the library at Ponden, and many of them have only been opened by me, these last

several years or more, so I will search them all for more
of her words, mindful that they must be dated before 1660.
For here is a story waiting to be told. EJB 1848

It's her! I feel it in my bones: I know it. I've read every one of the few words left behind in her own hand, and I recognise it. I look around the quiet room, as if there might be someone here to share the news with and, in the middle of this disbelief, this joy, how I long to run and find Abe and tell him what I've discovered. I can see how he would smile, how his eyes would light up. This grief, this joy entwined in one moment of certainty. This handwriting belongs to Emily Brontë, I'm sure of it. Of course, I need to take it to the experts, to the Parsonage, but I know that it is her and *I* found it. I found a piece of her that no one else has ever seen, and this might be the most remarkable moment of my professional life, the most triumphant and important moment of my career. Slowly, I right myself, and read it again, tears and smiles all silent, and I long to touch it with my bare hands, but I don't. Instead, I move the light across to the other three sheets of paper that Emily felt so entranced by, and some need to handle them makes me pick one up, as fragile as it is. I hold it in my ungloved hands, feeling the brush of the thick, aged paper and I wonder who touched it first, who touched it last.

It's feather-light, but heavy with memory and touch, saturated with DNA and being. It's one moment in time unfurling into another, colliding history into the present and making them one. It's beautiful.

The handwriting is archaic but clear, the paper covered not only in words but drawings, one image repeated again and again, a fearsome-looking face, half of it shaded dark, the twist of something that could be a vine or a wreath, or a river she has dreamed about or simply a seventeenth-century doodle that borders the page. And there is one word, written so heavily that the ink has blotted on the page, and underscored with several slashes of the nib that have cut right through the paper. The blood thickens in my veins as I read, for I see here a name that has haunted the Heatons for centuries, a name that still makes us pause and throw salt over our shoulder.

Henry Casson

The bulb over my head flickers and blinks out.

CHAPTER THIRTEEN

I sit very still in the dark, the room moving and whispering around me; I breathed in the second the light went out, and have yet to breathe out. Outside the window the moon is bright, and distant car headlights track across the wall behind me. I am suddenly intensely alert, each sense tuned to every molecule in the air; to taste, sound, movement.

There is a creak of a board at my back, and yes, the sound of a long breath, a sigh that I feel finish on the back of my neck.

Mab appears in the doorway, growling. In the scant silver light I can make out her ears pressed back against her head, her tail between her leg, the glow of her eyes fixed on a spot just above my head.

There's no fear – that is the most curious thing I understand at this moment. I am not afraid of seeing something, it's almost … almost more that I am afraid of there being nothing there.

Slowly, so slowly, I turn my head and look over my shoulder.

The light buzzes on, flooding the room so fast with artificial yellow that I'm not sure if what I glimpsed for just a fraction of a second was made up of moonlight and imagination or not, but whatever created it, she was there, if barely.

A young woman, as thin as a wisp, bathed in red, looking right into my eyes, though she had no eyes of her own.

I recognise her.

I played with her when I was a girl.

Tru and Abe

On the day of my eighteenth birthday, Abe and I had been
together for ten months. We'd finished exams, and I had
finished with school for good. I had a place waiting for me
to study English at Leeds, but for now there was just the
end of the summer and us. When I went to meet Abe from
the bus that morning it was a perfect day, a faultless blue sky
presiding over the sun-drenched countryside.

Ma had made my favourite chocolate cake for when we
got home, and when I'd met Abe from the bus he'd carried
a huge bunch of fat pink roses and his backpack had chinked
with bottles of cheap champagne. Together we'd walk the
now-familiar route home, the heat of the sun on the back
of our necks, dust in the air. The purple of the heather had
faded in the heat of a long, dry summer, and the hills were
covered in shades of gold. When we'd come to the path that
would take us back to Ponden, Abe had hesitated.

'I don't want to share you yet,' he'd said, and we'd kissed,
standing on the crossroads. I remember how I'd let my
whole self fall into him with every kiss, every touch. Rather
than becoming increasingly familiar, each new embrace
ignited fresh emotions, stitching us closer still, so much a
part of one another that he became me, I became him.

'I don't want to go home, either,' I'd said. He'd stashed
his backpack in a hedgerow, and we'd walked hand in hand
along the path to Top Withens, that cuts its way through

the deep heather, reinforced here and there with great slabs of stone, a twisted and gnarled moss-covered tree standing guard where once the gatepost would have been. And as we'd walked, I'd thought of all the people who had trodden that path, including Emily herself, who would have looked across at the rise and fall of the hills, and caught her breath in the wind, and I'd imagined that all of this wildness and grandeur was everything she knew about love. It was so hot … perhaps that's why the path was empty, or perhaps it was because, as it felt to me, that the moors were waiting there, just for us, on that afternoon, as the heat built in the air. We'd walked slowly, in silence, fingertips touching. Hot skin leaned into hotter air and I'd felt the sweat trickle down my back, the powdery earth crumble underfoot, and still we'd walked until we'd come to the derelict farmhouse that inspired the location of *Wuthering Heights*. A merlin hawk had hovered in the air and some desiccated roses had been laid in the window of the farmhouse. There'd been almost no wind as we'd sat in the shade of a hardy little hawthorn tree, branches stretching outwards, its growth distorted by decades of the prevailing wind.

We'd stayed there a while, without the need to talk, just letting the landscape speak for us in the rise and fall of the land, the billowing bank of white clouds, the wind drawing patterns in the heather.

And then he'd taken my hand and we'd made the walk the rest of the way to Ponden Kirk, and we'd stood on the stone for the longest time, hand in hand, shoulder to shoulder, each of us trying to work out how to say what we must.

'I was reading about the Kirk,' Abe had whispered into my ear.

'Were you? Why?' I'd said, smiling.

'Did you know that there is a long tunnel that runs right though the base of the kirk and if we climb down to the bottom there is a rock there called a marriage stone?'

'Yes, of course!' I'd said, laughing. 'Girls used to believe that if they crawled through it they'd be married within a year. Some still do.'

'In recent times, yes,' Abe had said. 'But long ago, in ancient times, it was a place of marriage. A rebirth, a crawl through the rock as two people, to be reborn as one.'

'Really?' I'd smiled into his gentle eyes. 'Sounds a bit icky.'

'Come through the rock with me?' Abe had asked, laughing, leading back to where we could make our descent down the steep hillside. 'Come through the rock with me, Tru.'

'Why?' I'd broken my hand from his, feeling a sense of unease as I'd neared the edge. 'Why?'

'Why do you think?' His smile had been as bright as the warmest sun. 'Because I want to marry you, Trudy Heaton.'

'I want to marry you, too,' I'd said. 'But I have to tell you something first … pretty soon I wouldn't fit through the marriage hole. I'm pregnant, Abe.'

The joy in his eyes, the certainty. He'd pulled me into a long hug.

'Then I want to marry both of you,' he'd whispered into my hair.

All fear had gone away when I'd taken his hand, as we'd half climbed and half slid down the hillside to the base of the rock. It should have felt silly – it should have been stupid and ungainly – but once I was there, peering into the marriage hole, a long square tunnel that bisects the rock, once my hands were joined with the stone, I'd felt a thousand hopeful hearts, the weight of belief and tradition, older almost than the rocks themselves, and it had seemed right.

So Abe and I had climbed through the marriage rock, me first, he following after, collapsing onto the soft hillside. Lying side by side, hand in hand, he'd pulled a tiny sprig of bright-red scarlet pimpernel from the rock and laid it in my hand. I'd looked at the miniature treasure, the first time I'd ever seen this strange little flower blooming here, amongst the heather, cotton grass and sundew.

'We're married now, under the eyes of this rock,' Abe had said. 'Trudy, will you marry me under the eyes of the law, too? I can't promise I won't get things wrong, won't hurt you or make mistakes, because I'm only a man. But I will never mean to. I'm a man that loves you, and every day I'll do my best to deserve you and be a good father to our child.'

The sky had been filled with cloud, vaulting above us like the ceiling of the Sistine Chapel, and I'd felt that, if I reached out, I could touch heaven.

'I'll marry you,' I'd told Abe. 'Yes, I'll marry you.'

CHAPTER FOURTEEN

Bright sunshine, after a deluge of rain at dawn, turns the trees golden against a pewter sky, and the streets look fresh and new as I walk with Will down to his school.

There's a dreamlike sense to our walk, and I see the village around me through two sets of eyes: mine, who knows every brick and stone here, and his, to whom it must all seem so peculiar. How strange it must be to the little boy who took a London bus to school every day to walk the streets of a town that tumbles away down the hillside, surrounded by nothing but air and a fortress of hills.

Will doesn't hold my hand – of course not. But he keeps his step in time with mine, his eyes fixed on the pavement.

Earlier, as he ate breakfast, I walked into Cathy's room and stood right in the middle, in the slant of sunlight that dappled on the floor. In my bag, in their folder, the pieces of paper were waiting. My plan was to take them to the Parsonage, to get the eyes of the experts on the writing and confirm that it really was Emily's.

But two things gave me pause.

Emily had seemed certain that there was more of Agnes's story to be found, and that might mean that there could be other places around Ponden where she had hidden papers and notes to herself; and if there was more of her to find, I wanted it to be me who found it. And that meant before any further work was done on the house, which might risk losing it forever. Emily had been a reluctant author; she'd fought against Charlotte's determination to publish her poems, and we can only guess how she felt about the reviews of *Wuthering Heights* that she'd kept. Reviews that spoke of her great genius and her wild, uncouth brutality, reviews that wondered how a woman could ever conceive of a novel so full of evil and cruelty.

For her to want to keep those clippings, they must have affected her. But she never wanted that scrutiny, never needed that recognition in the way her older sister did, so it wouldn't be impossible to imagine that she might have kept something secret, something just for herself ... perhaps even the second novel that she had planned to begin.

And then there was Agnes. Her story. And a glimpse of something that I couldn't quite understand. That a girl of her age and social standing was writing and recording her life in the mid-seventeenth century was remarkable in itself. If she hid her papers in the library's books, and if that's where they'd remained, then they were lost forever, because the contents of the library were sold in 1898, the year when the Ponden Heatons almost lost their home. But if Emily had found them first, if she'd concealed more fragments around my house, then there was an unprecedented piece of history waiting to be discovered in my home.

And they belong to me; they are mine. I *need* them to be mine, so I am carrying two precious, potentially priceless finds in my bag as I walk beside Will, still uncertain about what to do next.

Now Will's steps are slowing, his chin dropping ever closer to his chest as we draw nearer to school, until eventually he comes to a standstill outside the old apothecary.

'What's up there?' He points towards the alley that runs past the church.

'That's the Parsonage where the Brontë sisters used to live,' I say. 'Remember I was telling you how they used to come to Ponden to read books? And how, when I was a bit older than you, I fell in love with them?'

'But how can you love someone you've never met,' Will asks, 'someone you never knew?'

He allows me to take his hand and we cross the street, climbing the steps outside the church until we see the windows of the Parsonage, watching through the trees, drifts of bright leaves banking up around the gravestones.

'Because I believe that people are more than blood and bone,' I say to him, once we are in full sight of the house. 'I think people are deeds and ideas. They are thoughts and love and kindness and cruelty. They are energy, Will. And what do we know about energy?'

'It can't be destroyed, only transformed,' Will says.

'So when people live as powerfully as they are able to, with as much joy and passion and commitment as possible, then even after they die you can still feel the after-effects of the life that they lived; you can still know them, and love them for what they left behind. All the ideas and words, feelings and images are caught up in the pages of a book, like the flowers we pressed last summer, remember?'

'So, a bit like the radiation waves left over from the big bang?' Will looks up at me.

'Yes, exactly like that.' I smile. 'You know, Emily read whatever she could get her hands on. I think she would have loved all the books you love about physics and space.'

'Will you take me there soon?' Will asks, and I try my best not to look too thrilled.

'Yeah, sure,' I say. 'Now, how about school?'

'Which way is home from here?' Will asks me, squinting at the horizon, which is covered in houses.

'Well, if you keep walking in a straight line past the Parsonage you come to the same footpath that we walked along for a little bit the other day. Follow that, turn right at the Brontë Falls, and that leads all the way back home.'

'I meant our *real* home,' he says. 'Our flat. Which way is that?'

'It's a very long way in that direction, I think.' I point vaguely southward. 'But Ponden is our home too, Will. It's always been a home to Heatons, and you are a Heaton, after all.'

'A Heaton Jones,' he reminds me. 'And anyway, what does it matter what name I have?'

'It matters,' I say, 'because it says who you came from and where you are going to. And today that means school.'

It's a modern building, surrounded by trees, with ceiling-to-floor windows that are covered in handmade decorations. I remember a childhood of sunny afternoons, sitting cross-legged on the story mat while the teacher read to us; remember best friends and imaginary ponies that I galloped round the playground. It was a happy time for me and I want it to be a happy time for Will. Perhaps it would never be as happy as it had been before – he'd learned too young how fragile life was, that those he thought invincible were not, and learning that at any time life can strip away a layer of happiness that never truly returns. But all I want for my son is for him to find a way to be as happy as he possibly can be, convince him that I will do all in my power to protect him from further hurt. That it is OK to breathe out again.

'I'm not ready.' Will suddenly grabs my hand, his voice trembling. 'I don't want go in, Mummy, please don't make me.'

The words, the tone, the squeeze of his fingers strike home hard into my heart. He crams into me, pressing his face into my stomach, his arms reaching around me, and I hold him in return.

'Will, my baby—'

'I need more time, I need more time,' he says, sobbing. 'This is too much. I don't want to go to school. And they shouldn't make me, should they?'

He looks up at me with his eyes full of tears, and nothing else matters but the need to take him somewhere safe and hide us both away from the world, where we can curl around the pain of all that we have lost.

'Come on,' I say, but before we can leave we are stopped in our tracks.

'You must be Will,' says a kind female voice.

We turn back and see a woman in her late fifties, shoulder-length silver hair, a smile made brighter by bold pink lipstick.

'I'm Mrs Rose, your teacher. We've all been looking forward to meeting you so much, Will. Do you want to come in with me?'

'We were just thinking that perhaps we might leave it until next week,' I say, aware of Will disappearing into the fold of my coat.

'Yes, of course, if that's what you want – but then you'll miss our pumpkin painting, and this afternoon we are going to make working rockets from plastic bottles and baking soda.'

Half of Will's face emerges as he looks at her.

'Then we'll be talking about the solar system, and I hope I get it right, Will, because I know hardly anything about the solar system.'

Mrs Rose has read the letter that I wrote her, a letter about the things Will loves, the passions and obsessions he loses himself in when he wants a direct flight to the stars, away from what has happened to our family. She's read it and she understands, and I am profoundly grateful.

Will comes out from behind me and looks at Mrs Rose for a moment.

'I suppose I could help you with that,' he says quietly.

'Would you?' Mrs Rose's smile is full of kindness as she offers him her hand. 'That would be wonderful.'

'OK.' He takes her hand and looks back at me.

'I'll be here to pick you up,' I say.

He nods and doesn't quite smile, and I mouth a thank you to Mrs Rose as she leads him away. Letting him go pulls me inside out, but perhaps this might be the beginning of that new kind of happy. The best kind of happy you can have after you have learnt, too young, the secrets of life and death.

CHAPTER FIFTEEN

'Trudy?' I turn towards a familiar voice, to Marcus walking briskly down the hill towards me, smiling broadly. 'What luck! I'm so glad to see you. I thought I'd better leave discreetly the other day so as not to rile your mother too much, and I didn't have a chance to talk over my findings with you. But I've written up my report, so do you have a moment to go over it?'

His eyes are bright and excited, full of pleasure at the prospect, and I find his enthusiasm a welcome distraction.

'Um, yes, I suppose I do,' I say, releasing my clenched fingers one by one.

'Are you OK?' Marcus sees the colour in my face. 'Oh, you were taking Will to school today, weren't you? That must have been hard for you both, a big step.'

For a moment I look away, waiting for my composure to return.

'There's a big part of you that always wants to keep your children with you, close by your side, where you can protect them from harm,' I say then.

'How about a cup of tea?' Marcus's voice is kind, his smile gentle. When I was sad, Abe would sing to me, badly. But it always made me laugh. I miss him so much, right now …

'One thing we're not short of around here are tea rooms and very good cake,' Marcus prompts me again, and I hold on hard to my tears.

I'm grateful as I follow him to the café, grateful for the lives of others going on around me, for the sweet-scented steamy windows of a tea room, and the balm of buttercream icing. Each thing, in its way, a reminder that somehow, after the worse has happened, we still must go on.

'It really is remarkable,' Marcus says, as he pours us tea, my cup first and then his, 'the whole of the original sixteenth-century part of the house is in an *incredibly* good state of repair. I mean, almost 100 per cent intact and original, except for the roof – and that looks like it's only been replaced once. I can't tell you how incredibly rare that is, Trudy, especially for a building in such an exposed position; it's almost like she regenerates herself.'

The pleasure in his open face is reviving, his smile the smile of a man who has just found his long-lost love.

'It's as if time hasn't moved in that part of the house at the same rate as the rest of it – which, as you know, is in a terrible state of repair. It's so rare and so interesting that, with your permission, I want to carry out some tests – humidity, materials used, how they've been treated, that sort of thing – it's a bit like a bog corpse that's been beautifully preserved by an accident of nature, and I'm desperate to know what that accident is. Would that be OK?'

'Yes, but would you mind if it wasn't right away? There's so much upheaval in Will's life, and I think I forgot that what is a homecoming for me isn't for him. Can we wait until he's settled? Besides, there is so much stuff that I need to sift through and clear out.'

'Of course.' Marcus smiles, but he doesn't do a very good job at hiding his disappointment. 'Do tell me if you find any hidden first editions in all that junk; I'm a rare editions collector, you know. OK, so tomorrow I'll come and survey the later parts of the house, and if you don't want work to begin right away I can call in some favours to make sure it will see you through winter. Make good the roof at least, get some scaffolding and tarpaulin up; how does that sound?'

'That sounds really good, thank you,' I say, feeling bad for shutting down the thrill that Ponden had given him. 'I'm sorry to delay your work a bit, but you know, seeing how much you love my house means a lot. I really only want people who care about it as much as I do to be part of it, and I can see that you do.'

'I do, Trudy.' Marcus smiles at me. 'I really do. But even for me, humans come before houses. And you and your son are two of the nicest humans I've met for a while, so I want to help as much as I can. You know, I was thinking that if you opened Ponden up as a B & B, the Brontë fans from around the world would queue up to sleep in that box bed. I know I would.'

'Ma would have conniptions,' I say, almost smiling. 'But maybe. Maybe one day. So my house, or part of it at least, is a bit of miracle? How strange. But I'm not surprised, you know. I've always thought of her as a living thing.'

'What an incredibly wonderful description.' Marcus's eyes shine with joy and I have to look away. Abe would get a similar look in his eye about a new trip overseas, a particular kind of thrill when he thought about the places he'd see, the people he'd help. I'd see the light of adventure in his eyes and know that I was going to lose him for a little while, but that I had to let him go, because if I didn't, I'd lose the man that he'd become forever. The man that always wanted to make the world a little better tomorrow than it was yesterday.

What I can't bear to think of now is that, when he left on that last trip, I'm not sure I even really looked up from the book I was reading to say goodbye. I think I might just have tilted my head to receive his kiss, so certain was I of the bond between us, so used to the way it would unravel and lengthen as he travelled, sure that it would never break, a cord from my heart to his. I was so sure he would always be able to find his way back to me. So sure – and so wrong.

'Trudy,' Marcus speaks my name with a particular kind of softness. 'I know we hardly know each other, but I'd have to be blind not to see what you are going through. I'm not sure I can help you, but I can listen if you need to talk.'

I study his face for a moment, taking in his open features, and all I can think is how much I wish it was Abe's face I was looking at, his dark amber eyes meeting mine, his hand reaching for me.

'I'm fine,' I say to Marcus with some effort, though it's clearly not true, and I see I've hurt him a little, pushing away his gesture of friendship. But there is something I need to talk to someone about, that glimpse of something I saw last night. 'I mean, I think I saw a ghost last night but apart from that, I'm fine.'

'A ghost?' Marcus's eyebrows lift.

'Not really. Not an apparition, more of an impression, a feeling that I could see. Does that sound mad?'

'Not at all. Our minds play tricks on us all the time.' Marcus smiles. 'You're in an old house; there's centuries of folklore that your imagination is ready to plug right into. Add in tiredness, emotional state ...'

'You're right.' I smile. 'Besides, I lived in that house for half my life, so two ghost sightings hardly amounts to evidence of a haunting.'

'Two?'

I hesitate, a deep-seated discomfort making me queasy. I've only ever told this story to one other person in my whole life, and she hated me for it.

'Do you know about the Gytrash, Marcus – the grey-bearded man that foreshadows the death of a Heaton?'

Marcus nods enthusiastically. 'Yes, I read about it first in that book by Halliwell Sutcliffe, and then in an account told by the man who claimed to have exorcised his spirit away.'

'Really? Where did you see that?' I lean forward a little. 'That account was in the Ponden Library, but it was lost when the library was sold and I've never seen another copy.'

'Now I think about it, I'm not sure.' Marcus looks perplexed. 'I suppose it must have been online – I'll try and find the source for you.'

'Well, the exorcist didn't do a good enough job,' I tell him. 'Because I've seen Greybeard myself. On the day that my dad died, standing at the garden gate. I was only ten and Dad had told me all the Ponden ghost stories except for that one. Ma said later that it was the only one that scared him.'

'Do you mean you dreamed seeing him, or imagined it?' Marcus leans a little closer to me.

'I mean I saw him.'

The moment I recall the memory it is there, the feeling of the sun on my neck, the tickle of the mossy grass against my bare legs, my collie dog, Myrtle, lying next to me in the grass. 'It was a warm day and I was playing with my dog in the front garden when I felt eyes on me. I looked round, and there was man with a grey beard who seemed to be *all* grey – skin and clothes – except for his eyes. They were as black as coal and, on that blazing hot afternoon, I felt cold to my bones. The wind fell silent, the birds stopped singing. There was just him.' I shudder, the memory passing over me like a shadow. 'I shut my eyes and screamed for Ma, but by the time she got to me and I opened my eyes again, he'd gone. At first Ma thought I'd been hurt or that someone had tried to take me, but when I told her what I'd seen she hit me harder than she ever had before or since. Within the hour they'd found Dad in a field, dead of a heart attack. She knew, you see, what it meant to see Greybeard. But I didn't. I didn't know anything about the legend until that day.'

I wait for Marcus to laugh, or make an excuse to leave, but he doesn't. He's quiet and thoughtful as I say, 'But if there *is* something else, something that stays on after death, why don't the people I love and miss ever visit me?'

'There are no such thing as ghosts,' Marcus says, but his voice is kind. 'I'm so sorry you've lost people you love. But you know, even if you hadn't been told the story of Greybeard, it is still possible that you knew it on some level; maybe it was talked about while you were a baby, or you overheard a conversation you thought you'd forgotten. Sometimes a person can look back on the most traumatic moments of their life and fill them with false memories that seem completely real. It's your brain trying to make sense out of something senseless. When Celia ... when my ex-wife left me, it used to make me feel better to think that she had died, because that way I could mourn her without hurt or anger, let her go peacefully and naturally. It took me more than a year to accept that she went to France to live with another man and have his children, when she never wanted to have kids with me.'

'I'd give anything to think of Abe alive and well somewhere,' I say quietly. 'Even if it meant he didn't love me any more.'

'Of course; and I understood that, eventually. I saw that the way she hurt me didn't diminish how much I'd loved her, how much, even then, I didn't truly wish ill on her.'

We are silent for a moment, and in the quiet I think perhaps there might be a chance of friendship here, and that chance gives me a little rush of something like optimism.

'If you think about it, maybe that's why you remember seeing Greybeard. As frightening as it is, it makes a kind of sense of the senseless if it feels like fate.'

'Thank you,' I say, 'for letting me talk and not running away. I feel ... reassured.'

'You are far too interesting for me to want to run away from you.' Marcus pours more tea. 'And besides, I am hopelessly in love with your house.'

Oh Dear Lord please forgive me. Oh Lord, please have mercy on my soul. Oh Lord, please Dear Merciful Saviour, I beg you to show me clemency, for what I have done is the worst sin that a Christian maid can commit and yet I did it willingly, Lord, happily, with a heart full of joy.

Henry Casson beat Robert this morn. Robert stood against him, seeing how his mother was once again broken, this time almost to the point of death, and how that John Casson's own blood cowered and screamed when his father came near. Robert is not yet as big as Casson, nor as strong, and though he has the heart of the people with him, Casson holds them in his sway for they are terrible afraid of him. But on this day Robert challenged Casson's command and he was struck, most forcibly, knocked into the mud. He did not cower, but rose again, was struck again, rose again and was struck again, and this did happen more than ten times, perhaps more than twenty; I do not know, in truth. Betty held me back in the kitchen and did not let me go to Robert until he was stone cold and so still I feared him dead. As soon as Casson rode out with his henchmen, I ran to Robert, as did Betty, and we bathed him by the fire, and tended his wounds where we might, Betty putting some of her own ointment into his cuts, made from the honey from the bee boles and heather from the moor. And it shames me to write it, Dear Lord my Saviour, please forgive me, but I must be truthful in this confession: as I looked on dear Robert lying there, and saw the rise and fall of his chest, the muscles in his arms and chest, and his dear sweet fair face, topped with golden curls, I felt a longing so strong and so pure, to put my lips on his, and my body on his, and to touch him in every place, and for him to touch me in return. Oh Dear God, Dear God, will you ever forgive me such wickedness?

Later Robert woke and Betty found him a mended shirt, and he was in a great state of agitation and fury and Hell bent on finding his tormentor and attacking him. Betty feared for his safety and so did I. She bade me take him up onto the moors as we did when we were children, even telling me to take a horse from the stable. With me at his helm, Robert rode us high onto the moors to our favourite place, our castle at Ponden Kirk, and there we rested, and though it was cold, the sky was as bright and beautiful as is all the creation of the Lord Our God, amen.

'I should not care to live without you,' Robert whispered to me as we lay on the rock, and oh how my heart sang to hear such words. 'I should not care to take another breath if it wasn't to know that I will see your face again on the morrow. I know now that you are more than a sister, more than a friend to me. You are my dearest love. Agnes ... Agnes, will you come with me to the fairy cave, and tell the sky that you are my wife?'

And he took me down the steep hillside at Ponden Kirk, though I was afraid that I might fall, and he showed me the long dark hole in the rock that I had heard the other maids at Ponden call the fairy cave, and where, on the eve of the Solstice, some did come here to be married the old way.

ROWAN COLEMAN

I was afraid of your wrath, Dear Lord, but the day was warm and kind as I followed Robert through the hole and, when we reached the other side, he threaded wild flowers in my hair, and kissed me and held my hands to his heart and called me his dear, beloved wife.

Dear God, oh Lord, I cannot write here what I felt because before that moment I had never known a second of pure happiness and joy, just slight glimpses of it here and there. And then, in an instant, I was transformed into the happiest soul that ever lived. I lay there on the rock, and Robert leaned over me, the sun making a halo of his hair, and I have never seen a more beautiful mortal thing. Indeed, in that moment he might have been an angel.

'Let me kiss you, Agnes,' he begged me, and I did let him kiss me. And Oh Lord, Dear God, Forgive me, I was lost in pleasure. I let his hands uncover my flesh to the cold wind, as my hands discovered anew that which they had always known and longed for.

'We are already married,' Robert whispered to me, 'you and I. We are man and wife in our hearts and souls and under God. Here is our church, these kisses are our vows.' And Dear Lord, Dear Lord, I let him lie with me as man should only lie with his wife and it was a terrible, terrible sin which will only be cleansed on the day we stand before a man of God and take our oaths as we should have.

It was a terrible, terrible sin. Oh Dear Lord, my Saviour, please forgive me.

It was a terrible sin. And it was Glorious.

Agnes Heaton, for now that is my proper name

CHAPTER SIXTEEN

A wide-load lorry, following its satnav through narrow lanes, delays me and I'm the last parent in the playground, jogging in with bright cheeks and sweaty hair. I can feel the eyes of the other parents on me, and I shoot them a shy smile. If I was willing to look up, look around and say hello, I might well see someone I know, someone I used to go to school with, but my desire not to make small talk with people I don't know is only outweighed by my eagerness to see Will again.

Children in a kaleidoscope of coats pour out the door into the arms of mum or dad, talking, running, skipping and shouting. Pasta-shape collages are handed over and there is still no Will.

It's only when Mrs Rose comes out of the school holding his coat, anxiety etched into her expression, that my heart drops like a stone.

'Where is he?' I ask her as I hurry over.

'He was here a few minutes ago,' she said. 'I saw him as I sent them out to get their coats on. He'd had a good afternoon and ... Mrs Heaton Jones, I'm sorry, I've lost him.'

'What do you mean, you've lost him?' I ask her, the words emerging as my mind races a thousand miles ahead.

'I'm sure he is around here somewhere – I'll check the loos again. Come in with me.'

We hurry into the empty classroom after searching the loos, then out into the corridor, the hall – and there's no trace of him anywhere.

Then I remember our conversation that morning, when he asked me the way home. I was late, just a minute or two late but maybe he didn't see me and maybe he panicked. And suddenly I know exactly which way he'd be heading.

My exit from the school is a blur of dark windows and electric light, voices echoing down empty corridors, glimpses of reflected faces, and then I am out, into the cold air, filling my lungs with the cold air, forcing my thighs to keep pumping up the steep gradient of the main street, tumbling up the steps past the church, finally, finally onto the great expanse of the moor, a great black bulk of land against the dark-blue sky rising up all around me.

Now there is only the sound of my breaths coming shallow and fast, my feet grinding against wet, stone-filled mud.

If he was trying to get back to me, then he would have come this way. I told him it led to Ponden, and while it's not the home he wants, it's where he knew I'd be.

What I didn't tell him was the walk was not a straight-forward one. That you have to make sure you take the right turn, or follow the right footpath so as not to get lost in the middle of the moor; and even if you know the way, it would take most adults over an hour. My poor Will – if he was sad, if he was upset and alone and he didn't know who to talk to, or who to ask, and he wanted to come home, of course he'd come this way. He'd come this way looking for me.

He wasn't ready for school, I knew that. I could see it as clearly as day and he told me as much. He didn't want to go, and I took him anyway.

My legs are weary, but I don't stop, can't stop. If I can just keep up this pace for long enough, I'll find him, I'll see him; any moment now he will be there. But the path that follows up to the crest of the hill is empty, and the path that leads down in the dark is impossible to discern.

'Will!' I call out. 'Will! Are you there?'

There is no reply but the wind in the restless trees and the distant hum of cars. I can hear the cry of curlews carried on the wind, but I can't see anyone. I have never felt so alone as in this moment, have never felt so much despair, not even in the chaos and heat of Lima, when I realised I wasn't going to be able to find my husband.

And then I see a light.

It could be car headlights, but unlike those I see tracking along the valley in the far distance, it is closer and static. It could be fool's fire, the local name for the will-o'-the-wisp, the naturally occurring lights that come from the build-up of methane on the marshy ground of moors, once famed for leading travellers off the beaten path to their doom. But I was lucky enough to see those lights when I was a little girl, and this is different.

'*Look*.'

I think the word, and as I think it, I hear it, and know that it hasn't come from me. Before I realise what I'm doing, I find myself running towards the light without a second of doubt in my mind, not knowing or caring who spoke the word because I need to believe it. So I run as hard as I can, towards the constant calling of something I don't understand, but trust.

At last I turn into a lane, made into a narrow valley by the high sides of the fields on either side. On the other side of a barbed-wire fence there's an old, derelict house, a sign saying 'Danger Don't Enter' just about readable in the gloom. Nevertheless, it could look like shelter to a lost little boy. And just inside the gaping dark mouth of a glassless window, that same light glows once again and the wind drops as I hear the sound of a bird calling. It's a sound I've only ever heard once before in my life, on the Halloween night as Dad was telling me the tale of Lily Cove. The call seems to be coming from within the house, beckoning me in. And then it falls silent.

The barbed wire bites into my palms as I pull it apart and clamber through, snagging my coat and my jeans, hearing a rip in the fabric, and feeling one in my skin. Will is here. I can feel him, the spark of him glowing brightly against the night, huddled in the dark.

'Will?' I do my best to keep my voice low and calm. 'Will, it's OK, Mummy's here and I'm so sorry I left you.'

'Mummy?' His voice comes from another room, deeper within the wreckage and I scramble through the branches of a dead tree that once erupted though the flagstone floor, to see him curled against a wall.

'Will.' Gathering him up with my hand I hold him hard against me, hard enough to feel the race of his heart beat in time with mine, to feel his breath on my cheek. 'I'm so sorry, so sorry, Will. What happened? Were you trying to get back to Ponden?'

'You weren't there,' he says, his voice as slight as a breath in the dark. 'I looked but you weren't there, and I was worried I'd lost you, too. I don't like it. I want my house, and my bed and my toys. And I want my daddy. I want him, and he's not here and I don't know where he is, but I know he isn't *here*. I thought that if I got really lost, out here in the dark, and called for him, then he'd come. I thought he'd have to ... but he didn't. Daddy didn't come to save me, you did.'

'Oh Will ...' I let him cry against me, his cheek against mine.

'You must have felt so scared in here,' I say.

'No,' Will shoots back, and I believe him.

'You weren't scared in this creepy old Scooby-Doo house in the middle of nowhere in the dark?' I smile, and see his eyes shine in return.

'No, I wasn't, I felt safe here. For while, in the dark, I was scared. It was far and I didn't know the way. But then it was like I wasn't alone, and the sign said keep out, but I thought, if I wait here, Mummy will come. So I did.'

'Well, it's not safe. It could fall down on our heads any minute and you are a very silly boy, coming out here on your own in the middle of nowhere but ...' I reach for his face, cupping his cheek in my hand. '... you're safe now, I've got you.'

'I'm sorry, Mummy.' Will's head burrows into the curve of my neck.

'And I'm sorry I let you down.'

'Do I have to go to school tomorrow?'

'Not tomorrow, no,' I say. 'But someday soon, Will. They don't let you be an astrophysicist until you've done Year Four at school.'

'OK,' Will says. 'Thank you for finding me, Mummy.'

'Of course,' I said. 'I'd never stop looking for you, baby.'

Will is quiet for a moment, and outside the window I can hear the shouts of searchers and see the beams of torchlight tracking across the night sky.

'But you stopped looking for Daddy,' Will whispers, just before the torches are trained on us. 'Why did you stop looking for Daddy, Mummy?'

Tru and Abe

We'd left it another month before we told our parents about my pregnancy. Enough time to find a place in Leeds to share, for me to talk to the university. Four perfect weeks of happiness when we could just plan our lives as if no one else had a say in them.

When the time came to break the news we had taken the train down to London first. Nearly three long hours of nerves and scarcely a word spoken, holding hands tightly on the tube to Putney, my whole body clenched protectively around the life within.

At first Unity had kissed me and welcomed me, and Abe's dad, Sam, had shaken my hand and kissed me on each cheek. Behind them tea was laid out on the dining-room table, and a bottle of wine stood in a chiller.

And then Unity had taken a step back from me as she'd held my hand and had looked me up and down.

'Well, Trudy,' she'd said, her smiling fading fast, 'you didn't tell me you were expecting.'

Of course there had been tears and arguments. Unity had cried and Samuel had taken Abe out for a long walk, while I'd sat on the edge sofa and looked out of the window, the whole of London marching towards me, tangling my fingers in knots. For a moment it had felt like I couldn't breathe.

'He's going to finish his studies,' Unity had said to me. 'He's worked so hard.'

'I know.' I'd turned to her. 'I've worked hard, too. And I'm going to take my degree. It might take longer, but I am. And we're going to love our baby, so much.'

She'd shaken her head, looking down at her hands for a long moment.

'I can see how happy you make him,' she'd said. 'And I won't say I don't think you are fools, but I'd rather be with you than against you. So, don't look so worried; you're my daughter too, now, and you're carrying my grandchild. So you've got me now, I'm in your life forever.'

When Abe and his dad had returned we'd eaten, and laughed, and I'd looked at a thousand photos of Abe growing up and it had felt so good to be in the middle of that family, to feel part of something bigger than just me.

But I'd known it wouldn't be like that when we told Ma.

Abe had borrowed a car and driven over to Ponden where I was waiting for him. He had brought her tulips, the old-fashioned kind you see in the paintings of Dutch masters, with different colours and frilly petals, the kind that she loved.

'No.' Ma had shaken her head just once when I'd told her what we planned. 'No.'

'Ma, I'm not asking you.' I'd stopped myself, and smiled, hopeful, pleading. 'Abe and I are getting married in Leeds town hall a month from today. I'd really like you to be there, like his mum and dad will be. We are so, so happy; happy about getting married and happy about the baby.' I'd taken a hesitant step towards her. 'Please, Ma, can't you be happy too? It would make me so happy if you were.'

She'd looked at the flowers she was still holding and tossed them in the sink, still in their brown paper wrapper.

'You're too young, you bloody idiot,' Ma had said. 'You're barely more than a child. What do you know about the world? Who have you loved outside of your bloody books? If you think Heathcliff is your dream man you got a lot of growing up to do, and as for you ...' She'd turned to Abe. 'She's always had her head stuck in the clouds, but you, you're going to be a doctor.'

'Mrs Heaton, we aren't the first people to get married young, to have a child young. It's not all stories of doom and gloom. We both want the best for each other, for our child. And I love your daughter.'

'If you loved her, if you really did, you would wait.' It had been Ma's turn to plead. 'Wait until she's finished university, until *you* have, for God's sake, until you've got a job, then, if you still want to get married, that's the time. That's the time to have a baby, not now!'

'Well, the baby's happening,' I'd told her, reaching for Abe's hand. 'It will be a January baby.'

'It's not like when I was kid. You don't have to get married, you don't have to have a baby because of one mistake. You don't have parents forcing you into something you don't want. You have a choice, Trudy.'

'I know,' I'd said. 'This is the choice I'm making, Ma, I'm choosing Abe and our baby.'

'Mrs Heaton . . .' Abe had extended his hand in placation. 'I know how it looks. Don't think we haven't heard the same from my mum and dad; they think it's too soon, that we'll regret it. But I told them what I'm telling you: Trudy is the woman that I love, the woman I want to make happy, the woman I will stand by for the rest of our lives and I will be such a good father to our child – and they are willing to support us.'

Ma had leaned her flour-covered hands on the table, a strand of her silvery blonde hair falling down over her eyes.

'You two,' she'd said, cold as first frost, 'don't know what love is. You think it's grand speeches? You think it's sex? It's got nothing to do with that, not really. It's hard work, compromise, accepting what you cannot change. You aren't ready for that, Trudy Heaton. You never have been – and take it from me, if you rush into this you'll find yourself with a husband that doesn't love you and a baby *you* don't—'

If I'd been listening then, really listening, maybe I would have been ready for what happened next. But I hadn't been listening to Ma; I'd been full of heat and fire and I'd just wanted to be heard.

'How dare you try and tell me about love?' I'd barked a laugh. 'I don't think you've ever loved anyone, Ma. You treated Dad like a stranger and me like an inconvenience.' Turning my back on her, I'd looked out of the window, down the hill to where the two sides of the valley met, longing to be on the other side of that horizon, far away from her, and still travelling. 'You've always hated me, Ma, you made that pretty clear. Normal mothers love their kids, they're proud of them. They spend time with them, they are affectionate, they comfort them when their father has died ... You were never there for me. Even after Dad died, the most "love" you ever showed me was to pour me a cup of tea. I tell you who doesn't know anything about love, Ma: it's you. You are a frigid, spiteful, bitter old woman who's jealous of her own daughter. You were jealous because Dad loved me more than he loved you, and now you're jealous because I have Abe and I'm happy – happy now I can get away from you.'

'Trudy, that's not fair,' Abe had said, but I'd shaken his steadying hand off my arm, my eyes fixed on her.

'What's not fair is having a mother who never showed me a bit of affection.'

'Then if you won't listen to me, listen to yourself,' Ma had said. 'I was a teenager when I married your dad. I was knocked-up too. He didn't want to marry me, but my dad was an old-fashioned man, and he wasn't going to give me the choices I'm giving you. So we got married, and we tried, me and your dad. Or rather, I tried. Your dad was bored with me before you were even born, and when you were born ... well, all you did was cry every time I picked you up. I was so tired, so lonely. And I waited to love you, to feel what everyone said I would, but it didn't happen. It ruined my life to be forced into marriage and motherhood then, just like it'll ruined yours. After that, everything I did was about this house, or your dad or you. Never about me. I didn't want a baby, it wasn't the right time for me, like it's not the right time for you. I didn't want you, Trudy, don't you see that? I didn't want you, and I couldn't love you and you've grown up hating me because I couldn't be the mother you needed.'

I didn't say anything, I didn't have to. I'd grabbed my bag, taken the keys out of my pocket and dropped them on top of the tulips. And I'd left. I'd walked out of the front door and hadn't stopped walking until a few minutes later when Abe had pulled up in the car he'd rented and I'd gotten in. It had started raining as Ma had hammered on the car window, but I hadn't heard anything she'd said.

There weren't any words spoken for maybe twenty minutes; we'd driven though Haworth and were on our way to Leeds when Abe's hand had reached over to hold mine.

'I love you, Tru,' he'd said. 'Your mum, she's a very unhappy woman, but I'm sure she didn't mean what she said. If she didn't love you, she wouldn't have been trying to stop you from leaving, would she?'

'She meant it, all right,' I'd told him, keeping my eyes focused ahead.

'Well, *I* love you. I love you and I swear to God that I will never stop loving you, not for one single second. Not until the day I die – no, not even then. You will always have my love, hear me?'

I hadn't needed to say anything in return, not out loud. I'd squeezed his fingers and watched the countryside slip behind me into the past.

I'd made up my mind I was done with her. That I wouldn't go back to Ponden until she was gone. It was another sixteen years until I saw Ma again.

Sixteen years between then and the day my husband's plane went down.

CHAPTER SEVENTEEN

Somehow Ma knows; she is standing waiting for us in the middle of the track, holding a candle in a lantern. For a moment, I see her dark figure there, cut out against the last of the twilight, and catch my breath, expecting Greybeard, but then the flame flickers against the shadows of her face and all I see is worry.

'You're late, what happened?' she asks as we tramp up the last few feet to Ponden.

Exhausted, Will walks past her, still wrapped in my coat, and into the house.

'Well?' Ma asks again, looking at me as Will disappears inside. Downstairs, every light is blazing, casting squares and rectangle-shaped beams of light into the dark. I see my little boy collapse onto the sofa, and Mab climbing on top of him. He buries his face in her ears and he winds his arms around her shoulders as she leans into him. I thought I had lost him, and the thought hasn't gone yet; it still nags at me, fraying my edges like a nightmare I haven't woken up from yet. My heart can't quite believe what my eyes are telling me; I can't quite believe that he's safe.

'Mum, we need to get a phone line in, as soon we can. He was gone, and no one could reach me. That's not OK.'

'Fancied bunking off, did he?' Ma asks, ignoring my demands, and for the first time I really look at her, standing in the square of electric light. Despite her tone she looks gaunt with worry.

'He ran away. Lost and homesick, and I let him down, Ma. I failed him, I didn't bring his dad home and I wasn't there when he needed me.'

I almost say, 'Like you were never there for me' but I see her reddened eyes and bite my tongue.

'He's safe, and that's all that matters,' Ma says. 'You've got second chances, lass. You've got time to make it right.'

'I don't know ... Oh Ma, I'm so sad.' I stand there, hot tears on cold skin, my shoulders shaking, and Ma stands firm in front of me. She doesn't make a move to touch me, but she doesn't leave either.

'Come in, lass,' she says not unkindly. 'You're making a show of yourself. Come in and we'll make a nice cup of tea, hey?'

Taking my shoulders, Ma guides me into the kitchen.

'I want to be with Will,' I tell her, but she guides me into a chair.

'I think he just needs a minute to sort himself out,' she says. 'Mab's got her eye on him.'

*

Feeling useless, I fold down on a rickety chair and stare into the dark outside the window.

'Feels like the end of the world, I expect.' Ma fills the kettle from the tap, the rush of water pinging against the copper.

'It is the end of the world, Ma,' I tell her. 'It has been since that phone call telling me Abe's plane went down. I never used to think what it would be like to just get through a single day without being terrified. And now that's what it's always like, all the time, and there's no fix. I can't fix it for him, and that's the worst of it.'

'No *quick* fix,' Ma says. 'But one day you will make it right for him. And you're in the right place for it. Ponden will heal you. For a little while, when me and your dad were first married ...' She smiles as she looks around the room. 'This place was always full of love and light. And now you're home, you'll make it shine again, both you and the lad will.'

'Ma, what happened to you and Dad?' I ask slowly. 'Why did you stop being happy?'

'It's hard to be happy when the man you love don't love you back,' Ma says. She doesn't flinch; she never does when it comes to the truth. 'You and the boy will find a way through this. It will take time, but you will; I have faith in you, Trudy.'

'Do you?' I look up at her. 'Why? Why now?'

'Because you are like your dad; he weren't one to stay down for long. Because I was wrong, wrong about you and

Abe, and about me. And how much I loved you, girl. And I'm sorry.'

I don't look at her. I'm afraid to say anything in case I somehow startle this moment and chase it away. I don't know how to answer, so instead I just talk, because talking to my mum is the one thing I haven't been able to do in such a long time and I'm hungry for it.

'I'm terrified that one day my son will wake up and see how much I let him down. He's already so angry with me.'

'I know.' Ma touches her hand to my shoulder. 'Give him time. I've been a stubborn woman my whole life, but these days ... these days, I don't believe there is a rift that love cannot mend with enough time and patience. There isn't a mistake, or a hurt, that cannot be healed simply by saying you're sorry and meaning it.'

I look up at her.

'Do you really believe that?'

'I hope for it,' she says. 'Have you tried it yet, saying sorry to the boy?'

I shake my head. I haven't said sorry for failing him. Because I made him a promise that I knew in my heart I couldn't keep. I promised to bring his dad home. The day after the news came through, I booked a flight. I looked my son in the eye and I told him I would find his father. And I failed. I lost faith, I lost hope. I stopped looking. I lost his father.

And maybe he will never forgive me for that.

1658

Calamity has befallen me. I am far from Robert and know not if he lives or dies. Thank The Lord that I do still have some of my precious paper and a little ink that I borrowed from the good Reverend of Haworth, though he does not know yet that it is lent.

This is how it came about. Robert and I were so joyous happy in our love and our union that we took every secret minute that we could to be together and fulfil our vows and promises of love.

Perhaps our smiles were too glad, our eyes too full of longing, and flushed cheeks and crumpled skirts did little to hide our regard for each other. Even that being so, I know the house servants, especially dear Betty, would not have betrayed us to Casson. But someone did.

Robert had been sent out to the tenant farmers to collect the rents and hear complaints. When night drew in I awaited his return, watching for his lantern along the long road that leads up to the Hall. As I saw that small sun glowing in the gloom, I knew it was my love come home. Though it was perilous cold I concealed myself in the garden gateway, pressed dark into the shadows, and waited while the horses were stabled and the carts put away. Then Robert came past as I knew he would, and I held fast to him and pulled him to me, so that he yelped like a maid.

The house was quiet or seemed it. There in the shadows Robert and I welcomed one another with kisses and such delight that we were lost in one another and unaware of danger.

Casson dragged me from Robert's arms and flung me into the mud, striking me hard across the face and splitting my lip. He flew at Robert, and they fought, the whole house, Betty, Mistress Casson, John, all coming out to see how Casson raised his hand to Robert again and again, for although Robert is now seventeen, Casson is practised in violence and Robert is not. And I was so afraid, for I have seen Henry Casson murder a man with my own eyes, and I feared that he might do so again.

The words, the foul and ungodly words he spoke to Robert, who he called a bastard, and a heathen cur, not fit for Christian life. And me he called a whore, and a witch. Robert lay bloody on the floor, no one daring to go to him for fear of angering Casson. The fiend grabbed my hair and marched me down the lane and told me I was cast out of Ponden Hall and told me that I may never cross the threshold there ever again and expect to survive. Last I saw of my beloved was Casson dragging him into the house, the mistress screaming, and all was done.

It took me several minutes to find the resolve to stand, as the pain in my ribs and face was most severe. Finally, I went to the back door, thinking Betty would hide me, or at least give me my cloak and shoes. But Casson was there in the kitchen and no sign of Robert. I watched through the window as he towered over Betty, his fist in her face, and did not need to hear what was said to know how he threatened her. All these years, since I outgrew my usefulness, he must have wanted rid of me, keeping me on only because he had no choice. To put me out on such a night as that, with bare feet and thin clothes, would kill me, and he knew it.

There was little that could be done, so I stole down to the bee boles, where the hives are stored and honey collected. There was a little shelter to be had, the bees being now quiet for the winter. I dare not move a bole, for fear of angering the slumbering creatures, so I gathered what branches, moss and heather I might and covered myself with a thick blanket of plants, as if I were lying down to die in my own grave. I prayed all night to God our Saviour to deliver me from this evil, this murderer. The sin that I have committed is of not having spoken up of what I knew. First too afraid of Casson's wrath, and then afraid that Robert would cast me out for allowing such a foul man to take over his family. But I have not sinned, not in my heart or soul. Robert and I are good and pious people who only do what is right. And yet it is Henry Casson who prospers, Henry Casson who abuses, beats, threatens and kills those who should be respected and loved, and I pray to God to show me why such men are not punished as they should be. I do not know if it was the branches or a deep and furious anger that kept me alive that night, only that I saw the dawn rise, and when I went out to the lane, I saw Betty looking for me. She had a basket, my cloak and shoes, some food. She sent me to stay with her brother, a weaver, in Haworth, and it is there I am now, ever grateful for her kindness.

If there were but a way to tell the truth of Casson's most odious Sin against the commandments of Our Lord, without losing my Robert, then I would tell it aloud, and then Henry Casson, Constable of Haworth, would find himself on the end of the rope.

But I may not speak of it. I may not ever say what I know, for how can I when my heart is in the hands of the son of the man he murdered?

CHAPTER EIGHTEEN

. . . .

'Where's Ma?' I ask Will, who's curled up under Mab, staring into the fire.

'She said she'd gone to talk to some bees ...' Will wrinkled his nose up. 'I'm tired; can I go to bed? Can Mab come too?'

'Of course.' I sit down and stroke Mab's silky ears.

For a split-second, Kodak-coloured moment, I see Mum telling the bees that Dad had died, laying them out a plate of funeral food, and leaving a glass of honey wine balanced in the grass.

'Don't you touch that,' she'd told me when she'd spied me watching her. 'If we don't honour the bees, they'll come for one of us next, maybe even you.'

'I put a shepherd's pie in the oven,' I tell him. 'You must be hungry.'

'I'm too tired to eat,' he says. 'I just want to go to sleep.'

'OK,' I say, careful not to fuss too much. 'Can we just talk a little bit first?'

He shrugs again and sighs, settling his face into Mab's fur.

'I only want to say I am sorry. So sorry about everything you have been through. The worst thing has happened. Everything you are feeling, everything you are thinking, I get it, I understand. It all makes perfect sense, to feel the way you do. I promise you that I will keep working until I've made a life for us that you feel safe in.'

He sucks in his lower lip and chews on it for a moment, before turning to look at me.

'Are you sure you looked as hard as you could for Daddy?'

I'm silent for a moment, because although this is a question I have asked myself again and again, I still don't have an answer.

'When I got to the camp that Daddy had been working in, I saw all the miles and miles of rainforest they needed to search. They had an idea of where the plane might have gone down, but it was impossible to look for him on foot, and from the air, the canopy was so thick that they had to look very closely for any sign of a crash. The official search plane looked for two weeks. Then me and the families of the other people on the plane, we found pilots and paid them to look again and again. There was always one of us on the plane, too. I went up several times. When you were up, it was like flying over an ocean of trees, so thick and deep you hardly saw the forest floor, all this green only separated by the great bend of the river. But still we looked and looked, hoping for a glimpse of something. Me and another lady, whose son was on the plane, we chartered a boat that took us downriver to as close to where they thought the plane went down as we could, and it was so hot and damp, it was like breathing in steam. For a week, our guides took us into the forest. We could hardly see more than a few feet in front of us at any time, but we looked as much as we could. And the noise … the rainforest is a very noisy place.' I hesitate, remembering the feeling of defeat and exhaustion I'd felt when I'd boarded my flight back to the UK. As the plane ascended I'd stared out of the window until we'd banked up through the clouds, still looking until the land was out of sight. 'Will, I think I *did* look as hard as I could for Daddy. I think I did. I tried my best.'

'Daddy will come home,' Will says after a moment. 'I know he will.'

Closing my eyes for a moment, I think of that light on the moor, soft and slight, that led me to Will's hiding place.

'I love Daddy so much, Will,' I tell him. 'Wherever he is, that doesn't change. And he loves us too, he will always love us, and I think … I think we will always know that, always feel it. I think I felt it tonight, felt him looking out for us. He's lost – but not to us. Do you see what I mean? We will always have him.'

Will is quiet, and he shakes his head.

'I don't think that was Daddy.' He speaks just above a whisper.

'What do you mean? Don't think what was Daddy?'

'Who helped us in the dark.'

'Who do you think it was?'

'It's just …' He hesitates, as if he might get into trouble for speaking up. 'She told me there was danger, she said it wasn't safe. That Greybeard was coming.'

'Don't listen to her!' I sit up, instantly furious. 'She's got no right to tell you to keep secrets from me. Granny is a very silly old woman.'

Will shakes his head and his hand reaches out and steals into mine.

'Not Granny,' he whispers, leaning in very close to me. 'The girl who sits at the end of my bed and tells me stories when you are asleep. You used to know her when you were my age; the red girl. She says the bad one is coming.'

CHAPTER NINETEEN

Will sleeps and I watch him for a while, my back against the bookshelves. I watch the sweep of his lashes, the rise and fall of his arm tracking the rise and fall of Mab's steady breathing. It's impossible to translate how I feel about him into coherent thoughts. The adrenalin of fearing him lost has begun to ebb away, leaving me trembling with exhaustion.

Lying there watching him, I know that there will be no scenario where I lose him, because I simply won't allow it. I'll defy God and the Devil to always keep him safe. His is a life that I will never, never give up on; that is the only certain thing I have ever been sure of.

As small and as vulnerable as he is, he is brave. And as sad as he is, he is hopeful. I have always thought of him as invincible, but this girl he is talking about, dreaming about – imagining. This isn't like him, to see figures in shadows, or hear voices where there are none. Is this his grief, his fear, manifesting itself? Or is it something more? I have never told him about my imaginary friend or Greybeard. If Ma has ...

I try hard to remember the imaginary girl I used to play with when I was small. In my mind's eyes she is another version of me at that age, a mirror image I invented to feel less isolated. Try as I might, I can't picture her. I think of her and I see the colour red, like a flame, always moving around her. It can't be the same girl, of course it can't, and yet ...

Very slowly, very quietly, I ease myself to my feet, opening one of the doors of the bookcase, to find the cold white pale face of one of Ma's old china dolls staring back at me.

Cursing under my breath as her blank black eyes stare right through me, I move her to one side, taking out a handful of fat paperbacks. Stacking them up to prop the bedroom door open, I return downstairs.

Ma is already in her chair. She has drawn it a little closer to the warmth of the fire, and all I can see of her is her bed socks and her hands on the armrests.

'Are you warm enough?' I ask her, building the fire once again.

'Your pie is in the kitchen, still warm.'

'Oh, I forgot about that. I'm not really hungry.'

Ma is silent; she doesn't want to talk any more, but there are questions I need to ask her.

'Ma, do you remember my imaginary friend?'

She doesn't answer. Seconds pass and I watch the new logs slowly begin to glow and catch fire.

'Ma? Do you remember her? There was a time when I used to play with her all the time, and Dad got a bit worried about me?'

'I don't know,' Ma says. 'I don't remember.'

'Will just told me that there's a girl that sits on the end of his bed and tells him stories. He said she told him the bad one is coming.'

Ma sits forward in her chair, her face emerging out of the dark.

'Did she say when?'

This isn't the response I was expecting.

'No ... Today was hard,' I say. 'You were worried.'

'I don't suppose I've a right to be,' Ma says. 'The older I get, the more I realise what I have lost. The boy, he's the first person I've met in a long time who ... cares for me.'

'Ma ...' I try to find words to counter her, but in the end she is right. I left her alone for sixteen years.

'I shouldn't worry too much,' she says. 'He's got a lot on his plate. And kids, they feel things deeper than we do, see the world like it really is, before their minds get hardened and set and there's no room for fairies any more. And as sure as eggs is eggs, death will come back to Ponden some day.'

'So you think he has made friends with a ghost, then? You think I did? Is that what you're saying?'

Ma simply shrugs.

'Who? The Ponden Child?' I ask, feeling the night creep into my bones.

'No, the child can't get in,' Ma says. 'Poor little wretch is trapped out there all alone. I don't know who she is. But there was no sign of her after you left until the day you came back. There's something in you she is attracted to, and Will as well, I suppose.'

'Ma, you're kind of freaking me out. I mean, these are just stories; you get that, right?'

Ma shakes her head. 'You asked me what I thought and I told you. Pay me no mind if you don't like what I've got to say.'

Drawing a little closer to the fire, I watch the flames leap and repeat, and try to make sense of this feeling of disquiet. We've lost so much, all of us at Ponden. We've all lost so much that we are raw to touch; even the air around us hurts sometimes. It has to be that which makes the shadows grow longer, the imaginations of a half-asleep child become solid, the stories of a woman who has lived alone for so long. That's all it is, that's all it is . . .

What I need to do is make amends, find a path between Ma and me that we can both navigate somehow, even after all the hurt we inflicted on one another.

'Ma, when I was taking the carpet out of Cathy's room I found something incredible . . . I haven't told anyone about it yet because it's so amazing, but I want to tell you.'

'What is it, lass?'

A crash sounds from above with such force it shakes the dust from the ceiling, sending cracks shooting through the plasterwork. And then the sound of something like footsteps running, *pounding*, follows at once, across the ceiling and then down the walls and through the room.

'Will!' Racing up the stairs I charge into the dark that waits at the top and stop dead in my tracks.

The bedroom door is shut, the books that were acting as a doorstop flung in different directions along the length of the hallway.

A furious barking starts on the other side of the door, high-pitched and insistent. I can hear Mab frantically scratching at the door, desperate to be out. Grabbing the latch, I try to open the door, but it's jammed, as if someone is pushing against it from the other side.

'Will!' I call out. 'What's going on? Open the door! Open the door!'

'Help me!' The call is so full of anguish, it hardly sounds like him. Pain explodes into my shoulder as I run hard against the door, but it holds firm.

'Please, dear God, help me!' His voice is so twisted with pain and fright it is unrecognisable, morphing into a language that I have never heard before stopping midway through a phrase or word.

'I'm coming, I'm coming, Will!' I shout, charging at the door again, my eyes widening as it swings open of its own accord a second before I would have made contact.

Mab shoots out past me and down the stairs, and I tumble into the room, sprawling on the carpet. For just a few seconds I think I hear a baby's plaintive cry, somewhere in the room or outside? But it fades almost at once, so quickly I'm not sure I heard it at all. My eyes adjust to the light and I push myself up to check my son.

He is sleeping peacefully in bed, his covers undisturbed, and when I rest my cheek on his chest his breathing is even, and his face is dry of tears. The room is perfectly still, utterly peaceful.

And then I see the only thing that is out of place, the china doll I shut back behind the bookshelf door. Now she is sitting on the end of Will's bed, watching me.

'What's happening?' Ma calls breathlessly from the bottom of the stairs. 'Is he OK?'

With some effort I scoop Will up in his blanket and carry him, still slumbering, downstairs. He doesn't wake once as I tuck him onto the sofa. Ma turns her chair to face him.

'He was asleep when I got in,' I whisper, watching his face in the firelight. 'But the door was jammed. I couldn't get in and I thought I heard—'

'Crying out,' Ma says. 'You did, *I* did. I heard a scream, too. And I heard the footsteps, the crash … And I heard a baby crying … you heard it too, didn't you?' Ma's thin face is as pale as dawn snow.

'I heard it too, Ma,' I say. 'It could have been that he had a nightmare and came out of it before I reached him. Maybe we heard farm cats fighting, or foxes calling.'

'But it weren't that, were it, Tru,' Ma says, looking up at the ceiling.

'No,' I say. 'No, Ma, it weren't that.'

And there is a name that comes to mind. The name of a girl whose story is only just coming to light after centuries of obscurity. Agnes.

PART THREE

There let thy bleeding branch atone
For every torturing tear.
Shall my young sins, my sins alone,
Be everlasting here?

Emily Brontë

CHAPTER TWENTY

Ma sits at the table, looking at the pieces of paper side by side, listening as I tell her how I discovered them.

'You found those here? Down the floorboards, under that old carpet?'

I nod. 'Yes, and I think they've been there at least a hundred years, judging by the last layers of papers that I found, and very easily many more. Was there ever any talk of this girl, Agnes? Anything in the family stories? I'm sure Dad never mentioned her to me.'

Ma thinks for a moment.

'Your dad talked to you more about this stuff than me,' she says. 'I always felt a Heaton by marriage isn't really a Heaton.'

I watch as, sitting with her hands in her lap, she peers at the extracts but doesn't attempt to touch them, or even lean in a little closer to see them.

'That's not true, Ma,' I say softly. 'Dad was always trying to include you in things. You never wanted to ... be with us.'

Ma looks at me, and I'm surprised to see the hurt in her eyes.

'That's how you remember it?' she asks me.

'That's how it was, when I think about my life here as a child. There was me and Dad, or there was me. You were always in another room.'

'It felt like you *wanted* me in another room. You two were so close and I was ... cut off, I suppose. I built a wall around myself when things got bad with your dad, but I never meant to shut you out, too.' She lowers her gaze to the papers again. 'And you think that might really be by Emily Brontë?'

'Yes,' I say. 'I think it really might be. I *know* it is.'

'That'd pay for the renovations,' Ma says.

'It's worth so much more than money,' I tell her. 'It's something new. Something we've never seen before. And I think there might be more hidden in the house – I just need to look for it.'

'Well then,' Ma says, 'Will can be with me tomorrow. This morning I went up to Jean's and she let me use her phone to call some telephone companies to come and survey us and see how long it'd take to get a line in here. They thought it should be easy enough. They say if they can get a phone line in they can get TV and that Internet too. Coming in the afternoon. Will can be with me and Mab; I've got books and I found a load of scrap paper he can draw on, and he said he wanted me to watch a film with him on that laptop computer. I'll keep him safe while you look for more. It's important, what you've found, lass. It means something.'

'I don't think we should tell anyone else about this yet,' I say. 'I don't want strangers here until we are ready.'

Ma nods. 'At last you are seeing things my way.'

'The night I found this, I thought I saw something. Just for a second. A figure out of the corner of my eye, there and then gone.' I hesitate. 'It's not the first time I've felt something at Ponden. This has always been a house of feelings – but this was ... I thought it was probably a trick of tired eyes but after what happened earlier, I'm not so sure.'

'It wouldn't be the first time.' Ma's voice is tight. 'You saw Greybeard.'

'I thought I did,' I say. 'But I was just a kid ...'

'You've come home after a long time away,' Ma says. Her voice is tense, but beneath is a kind of gentleness and it takes me off guard 'You are almost like a ghost yourself, a memory become flesh. You've come home full of grief and anger, with a child who feels the same way. Everything you feel here, hear or see, even what happened earlier ... it's nothing to be afraid of, nothing that can hurt you. It's like when the wind blows and all the branches in the forest bend in the same direction. Your loss and pain, Will's too, it chimes with all the other losses there have ever been, here at Ponden, and they echo back at you, answering your cries.' Ma sit back in her chair, looking suddenly bone-weary and I take a moment to process her words. I've never heard her speak like that before, like she understands this house, like she understands me.

'It's just … Ghosts, Ma, I can't believe in ghosts. Emotions that linger, atmospheres … but I'm sure there's a logical explanation for what happened. Tiles falling off the roof, maybe … .'

'There *is* a logical explanation,' Ma says. 'Ghosts.'

'So, if you're right, then what do we now?' I ask, not quite able to believe the conversation we are having.

'Nowt.' Ma shrugs her narrow shoulders. 'Well, not nowt. I think we should all sleep together until the spirits have calmed down again, Will on the sofa, you bring your sleeping bag down. And you need to search the house for more treasure. That roof ain't going to pay for itself.'

'The girl that Will says he talks to says that the bad one is coming. She was trying to warn him.' I shake my head. 'Kids say things all the time, but he was so adamant, Ma.'

'The thing you have to remember,' Ma says, 'is that spirits don't see the world like the living do. They don't see time like us; the past and the present and the future happens all around them at the same time. The danger might have been from when she was alive, or another ghost in the house. Greybeard, waiting for another Heaton to die. Danger is coming, has come, will come – it's all the same to them, because they are always caught in the worst moment they have ever lived, over and over again. And not even really them, just what's left behind, ripples of emotion, that sometimes reach out into this world too.'

Carefully I pick up the papers and slide them back into their folder.

'I didn't know you were an expert on the paranormal,' I say.

'I've been the only living soul in this house for a very long time,' Ma says, turning her hollow gaze to meet mine. 'But not the only soul.'

1658

I thank you, O God, Our most Righteous Saviour for your guidance, for since coming into this new situation, I have prayed as hard as I might, visiting the church every day, morning and night, and now I feel sure of my purpose. My purpose is simply to make what is ungodly godly, what is sinful, pure. To bring my heart's husband to God's house and make our marriage vows before a man of God, for there is no reason to delay any longer.

Betty's brother Timothy and his wife are kind, good Christian people, to take me in even though vile stories of what happened between Robert and I now spread over the hills as fast as cotton weed. They do not mark any word but Betty's and she is still my champion, Praise God. I have little to give them in return for their charity, in truth, except labour that they do not need. Now I am free of Casson for good, I will not wait a moment longer than I have to to begin my life as Mrs Heaton before the whole world.

But first I needed to see my Robert, for it has been five long days, and I have not had a word, nor have I dared venture anywhere near Ponden Hall. Betty has sent no further word either, and my heart is full of dread, but still, with God's good guidance, I knew what I had to do, and so last night I set off to visit him as soon as the sun was set.

Betty near enough dropped dead in her shoes when she saw me creeping into the kitchen and did chastise me most strongly for frightening her, and also for coming anywhere near, while Casson is still threatening to have me hung like the witch he claims I am. Dear Lord, protect me from his sin.

I said to Betty I am no witch. Would that I were and I'd curse them all. And Betty hushed me and crossed herself, and hushed me again. I asked her where my Robert was, and if he was very badly beaten, and she told me that since that night, and for all day and all night, Casson had kept Robert locked in the cellar, and such fury and indignation filled my mouth that Betty had to hush me and cross herself again.

I begged her to give me the keys so that I might free him and we might be on our way.

'I cannot,' Betty told me. 'I do not have the key. And besides, if I'm caught helping you then I'll be next without a roof over my head.'

And I was chastened then, knowing that if I were discovered with Betty I would bring much hardship down on her, and she has only ever shown me kindness and charity. Still, she took pity on me, instructing me to creep down the cellar stairs and see if Robert would hear me through the cellar door, though she made me promise to whisper only and keep myself invisible in the shadows.

I was not afraid, though I should have been, for to be caught would be very grave for me, but I felt that I was protected, cloaked in the Lord's Light that shieldeth those that are doing right.

I called Robert's name through the door as quietly as I could – and no answer came. A great terror gripped me. Was he dead, down there?

'Oh, Robert, answer me!' I called, this time too loud, but, Praise God, it was only my beloved that answered me.

'Agnes? His voice was faint but it was there.

'He says I am a witch, and you are to be sent away,' I told him. 'I need to free you and then we can be married at once and no one will ever be able to tear us apart.'

Robert's voice was weak, and worse, meek. He told me he was too badly injured to run with me, too badly injured even to stand.

'Then I will help you,' I told him. 'I will hold you up straight and be strong enough for us both, Robert, I swear it. I will steal a key and take you away from here.'

But Robert would not allow it. He told me to go back to Haworth and find work, to wait for him to heal and get strong, and then at last we will be married.

'I swear it, Agnes,' he told me. 'He'll let me out of here on the morrow if I'll agree to his plans, and the moment I am fit I will come and find you and we will leave together, I swear it. For my soul is yours and yours is mine. I will love you until my death and beyond. You are my heart, my wife before God. Go, before he finds you, and wait for me.'

I did as he asked and returned to Timothy's to wait as directed by my God and my Husband. I pray only that my wait will not be long now, for my heart yearns to be near its twin once more.

Agnes Heaton

CHAPTER TWENTY-ONE

Sitting on the floor in Cathy's room, I look, my eyes scanning every surface, searching for some obvious hiding place, somewhere Emily might have concealed more of her notes, more of Agnes's story.

Downstairs I can hear Ma and Will talking, her tones muted, his bright as a knife blade.

When he woke this morning, Will seemed cheerful and rested, as if all the drama of yesterday had blown away in the morning breeze. I watched him carefully as he slathered his toast with too much butter, and I couldn't detect any of that distress, that almost-fear that I'd seen in him last night. He didn't mention a girl that told him stories or any of the happenings that Ma and I experienced last night. I had let her talk of spirits get to me by the light of the fire. This morning it's so much easier to believe it was the wind, the house creaking and settling, a pair of farm cats scrapping. The bright sunlight dappling on the table top makes any one of those ideas seem so much more likely, so much easier to believe.

After Will finished eating, Ma gave him a pile of Dad's old *National Geographic* magazines, some ancient glue and a selection of empty packaging that she'd been saving for God only knows what – this moment, perhaps. Will's eyes lit up as she set the haul down in front of him with a baked-bean tin full of coloured pencil stubs that I think used to be mine, and together they sat at the long table, talking, cutting, sticking. Watching them for a while, I noticed Ma's smile as she listened to Will, her clear pleasure in following his thoughts, of simply being near him.

One of the magazines slid to the floor with a plop and Ma groaned as she bent to scoop it up.

'Hidden tribes of the Amazon,' Ma read aloud, as a girl covered in tribal art smiled up at me, half her face painted white, and half red. 'Imagine that, Will, living away from all technology, none of your Internet or your phones, lad.'

'That's just like living here,' Will replied.

Listening to them laugh together, I made my way upstairs.

I always thought Ma never wanted to be close to me and Dad, at least that's how I remember it. But what if Dad was the one who pushed her away, shut her out in the cold? What if it was *me* that marginalised her? Something tight tugs at my centre, and I get a glimpse, just a slight insight, into a life of unbearable sadness and loneliness. And all those years after he died, when we did everything we could to hurt one another, was there a moment when we were pulled so far apart that every last bond between us was broken? I can't remember it, but there must have been one.

Now Cathy's room feels utterly benign, peaceful and flooded with morning warmth. It would so easy to lie down on the welcoming boards and watch the sky pass by outside the window, just like I used to when I was little.

Instead, I look.

I can't see an obvious place where more papers might be concealed, and to be honest, although I had to check, I didn't expect it to be that easy. After all, I would never have found the secret package if I hadn't had my cheek to the floor, my fingers grazing the floorboards. The only way to thoroughly check this room is to repeat that intimacy with every inch of floor, walls and beams.

Crawling over to one corner, I start to search every floorboard, fingertips running over and probing each surface, every knot and groove. Working my way methodically up and down and along the floor, I scrutinise every detail until I think I see words made out of scratches, and treasures jammed into fissures, that simply are not there. When I meet the wall opposite from where I started I have discovered nothing new, unable even to find again the letters that first pointed me towards the hidden treasure.

Next I run my fingers over the walls, searching in webbed crevices and ancient boltholes. Crouching down, I shine my torch into the murk of the chimney breast, steeling myself against the creep of many spindled legs as I push my way through thick dust and sticky threads to search as deep inside as I am able. Nothing. Shuddering, I brush the remnants of desiccated insects out of my hair and off my face, and turn to the box bed. Bolted into the wall, it stands there in the corner, and somehow it feels as if it is waiting for me, beckoning me. When I was very little, in that dimly distant period of my very early childhood, when all I really remember is sunshine and the taste of strawberry ice cream off a silver spoon, I was scared of this bed. It was like a great crouching monster biding its time, and I used to worry that if I got too close to it, it would eat me up. Something I had forgotten entirely until just now, as I eyeball it. It seems to stare right back at me, but as ancient and as infamous as it is, I'm not going to be defeated by furniture.

Sliding open the door, I climb inside, refraining from shutting myself in. Outside the tiny square window, set deep into the stone, the morning has grown steely grey and ominous. The hum of the wind vibrating against the glass plays steadily as I search every surface, every panel, lifting the elderly mattress to check the cavities beneath. Diligently, I explore every etched scratch and notch in the wood, and all I find is dirt and dust, the detritus of a thousand lives and deaths.

Pausing for a moment, I press my palm against the cold glass and feel it shift and brace against the air, remembering myself running across the field outside with my long hair streaming in the wind behind me, socks round my ankles, laughing and talking to ... to who? For so much of my life there was never anyone else there.

Maybe the girl that used to be me is a ghost here, too.

'If you are here, show me something.' I say the words as I get out of the bed and instantly regret it, every muscle clenching, arms wrapping around me, afraid that I will be answered when the last thing I want is a reply. The ever-present wind courses around the exterior of the house and the boards sigh under my feet. I have the strangest sensation of ... something ... like a word about to be spoken on an inward breath. And then nothing at all, but a sudden drop in my spirits, a deep, abiding sense of hopelessness and a very sudden need to be outside, tipping my face upwards to a rain-laden sky to taste the very first drops on my tongue.

And a bitter truth hits me like a falling tree.

I didn't look for Abe the way that I should have. I didn't cover every inch of terrain where he might be, I didn't look in the places where no one would expect. I let grief defeat me and I gave up. From the moment Abe and I met, I fought to be with him, until he was lost deep in the rainforest. I lost hope, then, when I needed it most of all. I lost hope ... Nearly a year has passed and I know, I know he must be dead, but he is still there, somewhere amongst the trees; he is there, all alone, on the other side of the world, waiting for me to find him.

A sliver of silver light escapes from the dense cloud and bounces off the box-bed window. For a moment, the confluence of light and shadow creates an illusion of a face looking back at me as I stand in the garden. When I turn around to look down the valley, a rainbow arcs across the reservoir and suddenly I know something new, as if a voice, just this moment, whispered it to me.

The fight is never lost if you have the courage to keep fighting.

CHAPTER TWENTY-TWO

'Thank you for coming in.' Mrs Rose smiles at me. 'When you called to say that you were delaying Will's start with us for a few more days, we understood, of course, and I'm so sorry for what happened. I thought it was only right to show you the footage of Will leaving school.'

'I appreciate that, but I feel that it was my fault; I brought him too soon and he just wasn't ready,' I tell her as she leads me into an empty staffroom, a laptop open on a table.

'Every day after drop-off, our caretaker, Mrs Bennett, locks the gates,' Mrs Rose explains as she offers me a chair at the table. 'We know that sometimes children get ideas into their heads, and we keep a close eye on them, all of the time. And of course we take the threat of someone coming onto school premises very seriously. I called the register after lunch and Will was present, and I saw him a few minutes later in the home corner, reading, before I began some work with one of the other children. He wasn't mixing, but he seemed content. Both myself and my teaching assistant checked in with him throughout the afternoon, and she remembers him waving at someone through the window.

She thought it must be you, but it could equally have been a squirrel – you know how kids are. But then we saw this ...'

Mrs Rose turns the laptop to face me. There is a freeze-framed image of the school gates.

'We wondered who this person might be?' She points to a fuzzy image of a person, haloed by a peculiar glare of red light, even though the footage is black and white. 'If they are a friend of Will's, someone he might have seen and followed?'

Mrs Rose presses play and there seems to be a jump from one frame to the next, and a figure that could be male or female looking through the gate directly into Will's class. Two frames later and the image is gone.

'Was that even a person, or just a trick of the light?' I ask.

'Keep watching,' Mrs Rose tells me. A few seconds later I see Will open the gate, look up the hill, and begin walking out of shot.

'The time shows Will opening the front gate and walking out of school at a quarter to three – but I am certain I saw him with my own eyes, just as they were putting their coats on. At three twenty-five the caretaker went out to open the gates and she swears that the gate was padlocked, and the footage seems to show her unlocking it, though we can't be sure ... The truth is, we aren't yet sure how he got out so easily.'

Reaching out, I rewind the footage and freeze on the image of Will's face looking up the hill. He's smiling.

*

I hear the sound of the gates being locked behind me and I take a moment, walking down the hill towards the park, taking refuge among the neatly ordered flower beds, even though they are dormant now, leaves scattered across the grass like bright sparks. I'm trying to pinpoint this sense of unease that has taken up residence in my gut. There is sadness there, of course, the deep and pervading loss of Abe that I can never imagine receding. And there is worry – for my son, for my mother, for my home that is slowly falling apart, for myself. There's this thrill, at finding the Emily paper and Agnes's diary and the promise of something incredible, all swirling around, scattering any emotional stability I might have found to the wind. The honest truth is, I don't know if I am coming or going, and I have a son who talks to invisible girls and a mother who believes in ghosts.

There might have been something on the video, but it's much more likely to have been an anomaly, a flash of light, directly on the camera; maybe an insect. How Will got through a locked gate, I don't know, but he is a resourceful boy and he reads a lot. I have to be careful, in this state, not to fall into a fairy tale of my own making. Ma might be willing to talk of ghosts and omens, and maybe Will needs a fantastical friend right now, but not me. My job is to keep a grip on reality, to keep my feet on the ground and my focus on my son, and to search the house for more evidence of Emily and Agnes. Real evidence, of real people who lived and breathed, not spirits, not ghosts, not wraiths that come in the night. And I need to find a way to get back to Peru, and for that to happen, I need a job. I need to focus on practical issues. When my son looks at me, he has to see a woman who is in control of both our lives, who is keeping his world as safe as it can be, not seeing phantoms in every shadow.

The world seems to settle and solidify around me as I walk back to the car and I feel a sense of purpose. I had thought I came back to Ponden because I had no choice, but that isn't true. I came back because it's my home, because I love it; and I knew, somehow, that it would be here that I'd be able to find a sure-footed path through life once again.

Taking my phone out of my pocket, I find Marcus Ellis number. I need to ask him about fixing a tarpaulin over the roof before the worst of the weather sets in.

'Trudy?' He answers on the first ring.

'Marcus, hi! I was just wondering if I could ... oh!' As I walk into the car park he turns the corner, almost walking into me, and we laugh, my cheeks flushing.

'Hello, what a strange coincidence,' I say, pocketing my phone.

'Not that strange in this place,' he responds, laughing. 'Sometimes I meet myself going. Anyway, I was going to drive over with the costings report this morning, then I saw your car, so I was going to ring you but you beat me to it.'

He hands me an A4 brown envelope and then, with his hands free, looks rather lost; he shoves them in his pockets, adding to his rather sweet, dishevelled-schoolboy demeanour.

'I hope it's not presumptuous, but I wanted to ask you about my roof,' I begin, feeling a little awkward to be reminding him of his offer. 'You know you mentioned helping us weatherproof it?'

'Oh yes!' Marcus says and nods. 'Yes, so sorry, Trudy, I meant to tell you, I have a team coming out tomorrow; should only take half a day at most.'

'Oh great, will you send me a bill or …?'

'No, no bill – plenty of local builders owe me favours.'

'I can't let you do that, Marcus. I have some savings, so please, let me know what I owe you.'

'How about a walk?' he says with a smile.

'A walk?' I shake my head no.

'Well, it's such a lovely day; sun's out, air's fresh after the rain. How about we go for a stroll up onto the moor, before the last of the autumn colour is gone for good?'

I look regretfully at the car and think of Will waiting at home, of all the other places I haven't looked for more of Emily yet. And deeper still, under all that surface reluctance, is something more. Going for a walk with a man who isn't Abe, treading the same paths we once walked hand in hand, looking at the same views without him? I don't want to go – and I don't know how to say no.

'I can see you're reluctant,' Marcus concedes. 'It really is just that I might be able to offer you some employment and I didn't want to discuss it in a car park.'

'A job?' I say, unable to imagine what I might be able to do for a restoration building company. 'I've only got an hour left on the car, though.'

'I'll make sure you're back in time, I promise.' For a moment I expect him to offer me his arm, in that slightly off-kilter, mannered way of his. But instead he walks on, a little haltingly, and we take a series of mismatched steps until at last we find some kind of uncomfortable rhythm as we go up behind the Parsonage, up onto the top of the moor; and it's true that with every step I feel a little lighter, as if I'm leaving everything heavy in my heart in the valley.

'How are you managing, Trudy?' Marcus asks me after a few minutes of silence. 'Sorry, stupid question, probably.'

'Honestly, I don't really know how to answer that question,' I say, turning my face into the cold air. 'We are doing OK, me, Ma and Will. Finding our feet, I suppose, in a world without Abe. A job would help.'

Marcus smiles ruefully at the not-so-gentle reminder.

'I'm hoping you can help me sort out my library. A few years ago I inherited – well, a couple of thousand books, I'd say at a guess, from my father, who inherited a few from his, and so on and so on, and they were kept in storage until my house was built. I've now got them shelved in my library but I have no idea what is in the collection.'

'Really?' He's got me interested.

'You remember I told you I looked you up? Well, imagine my excitement when I discovered that you were an archivist.'

'That's not something that gets many people excited,' I say.

'Well, an archivist is exactly what I need. It honestly feels like fate, Trudy. After my wife and I divorced I renovated a house for myself, a totally burned-out Edwardian manor called Castle Ellis. It's hard to describe to someone who hasn't seen it, but anyway, it's my dream house. I built it just for me, and part of my dream was to have an amazing library to house the collection. I suppose I could have just sold them on, but there's something about books, don't you think? So personal. I couldn't quite bear to. If you would take a look at them, assess the time it would take and your fee to archive and collate the collection, I'd be eternally grateful.'

'Of course,' I say, half laughing. 'It's my dream job to organise a library from scratch! However, I need time for Will, and for Ponden ...' I'm careful not to mention the papers I have found. 'So it would be kind of ad hoc hours, but if you are OK with that, then yes, thank you, yes!'

'Really?' His eyes light up. 'I can't wait to show you the library. Sometimes I take dates back there, but you know, if you aren't a book person it's just a big room. I've been dying to share it with someone who will love it. This is going to be great.'

'Marcus, I hardly know you and you've been so kind to me,' I say. 'I'm grateful.'

'*I'm* grateful,' he replies. 'I get to work on a house I've always been fascinated with, and to finally have all my books curated. And more than that: make a friend.'

He offers me his hand and I shake it, sealing the deal.

'Come out to my house,' Marcus says, smiling as we begin to walk back to the car. 'How about tonight? I'll make you dinner. I have this state-of-the-art kitchen that I barely use, but I do know how to heat pizzas. And bring Will; I have a games room, and proper ramparts like a castle – he'll love it. We can eat, you can have a look at my library, and Will and I can play the latest Mario Kart.'

'Thank you,' I say. 'Yes, that'd be great.'

'Right, we'd better get you back to your car,' he says, and turning on our heels we head back the way we came. I look over my shoulder once, at the path that stretches away behind me, with a vague sensation that there is someone else on the path behind us. But there is nothing but a sky that is now full of the promise of thunder.

CHAPTER TWENTY-THREE

Ma had not liked the idea of us going out.

Night is already crowding in around the house as we get ready to leave, and the chill in the air seeps in through the leaky windows and doors.

'You'd think you'd have had enough of going out,' she complains as she buttons up Will's jacket, winding his scarf around his neck and tucking it in. 'Only yesterday you lost your son, and now you're gadding off, spending an evening with *that* man.'

'I didn't lose Will, Ma,' I tell her, with emphasis. 'And Marcus is a nice man; he loves this house. He loves it and *understands* it. You should be pleased it's him that's working on it. He's local and he's offered me some work, and I need work. We can't live off of my savings forever.'

'But if your *discovery* is authentic,' she lowers her voice, 'well, that'll be worth a pretty penny.'

'Ma, if it *is* authentic, I would never sell it. I'd lend it to the Parsonage and lecture about it, but I couldn't sell it, not ever! It's a part of Emily, in this house, in *our* house. It belongs to Ponden.'

Ma stares at me as if I'm mad, and I suppose I am, but that scrap of paper is about so much more than money to me; still, although she bristles, Ma doesn't bite back.

'Do I have to come?' Will complains, scuffing his feet in the gravel. 'I'm tired, and I want to stay with Mab. And Granny.'

Ma twists her mouth wryly and kisses the top of his head.

'Prefers dogs to people,' she says. 'Boy takes after me.'

It would be better to let him stay, I suppose; he's exhausted after yesterday, but the truth is that I want him by my side.

'Marcus has a games room,' I say, 'Internet and a huge screen. He's even got a PlayStation.' Will's internal struggle is completed pretty quickly.

'But why can't we take Mab with us?' he asks, adding a fraction too late, 'And Granny?'

'Because we're not invited.' Ma makes a face at Will, who grins in return. 'And anyway, you can tell a man that dresses like that wouldn't welcome a smelly old girl in his house. It'll be all white rugs and glass and *art*.'

'You shouldn't talk about yourself that way, Ma.' I risk a joke and am rewarded with a small smile from Ma and a guffaw from Will. 'Anyway, you'll be glad to have the place to yourself for an hour or two, won't you?'

'Suppose I've gotten used to having company here,' Ma says, wrapping her thin arms around herself and shuddering.

Without thinking, I put my arms around her and hold her small, brittle frame. 'We won't be late,' I promise.

'Drive carefully,' Ma calls after me.

I see her in the rear-view mirror, her tiny frame in the great doorway as we pull away. I pretend I don't see the shadow that passes behind her, the flicker of light that comes on in the upstairs room, the midnight-dark cloud that gathers overhead.

I pull the car to a stop at the top of the drive, as it wends its way down towards Castle Ellis, just to catch my breath. Marcus wasn't exaggerating when he said it was best first viewed at night.

'It looks like a spaceship coming out of a castle,' Will says, leaning forward in his seat, his interest in the evening suddenly invigorated.

And he's not wrong. Most of the original building is a ruin, a good portion of it still burned and blackened. All that remains is a faux medieval turret and part of the wing that supports it, blind stone windows shining with the electric light radiating out from inner construction. For in amidst the skeleton of the old building, an incredible modernist glass structure soars upwards, at least three floors high, with very solid walls, and it seems as if each room is ablaze with light, illuminating not just the bones of the old house, but the grounds it sits in, the sweeping drive and terraced gardens, now broken and crumbling, like a long-forgotten Camelot.

'Want to go and look inside?' I ask Will over my shoulder.

'Yeah,' he says, eyes shining. I put the car into gear and we head down into the natural dip in the landscape where the house is situated, descending until the stars are blotted out by the hulk of the land. I grin at Will as I pull up on the gravel drive where a huge fountain sits, illuminated by floodlight. A great decorative stone bowl, its weight is supported by four huge dogs, each staring outwards, forever on guard.

'This is quite something, isn't it?' I say to Will, opening the car door for him.

'I like it,' Will says. 'I want to go up the tower.'

The front door is from the old house, a huge high Gothic affair of carved oak, set with deep iron hinges and a sturdy lock. Best of all, as far as Will is concerned, is the great cast-iron door knocker, made in the image of the fountain's dogs' heads, the ring of the knocker held between this one's clenched teeth.

Standing on his tiptoes, Will grabs the knocker, cheerfully thundering it against the wood, and we both grin at the booming echo it makes.

I'm half expecting the door to creak slowly open to reveal a hunchbacked butler, but it's Marcus who opens it, wearing a white shirt tucked into the kind of pristine deep-blue jeans that Ma would despise.

'Welcome, Heatons,' he says, standing aside to reveal a glass connecting corridor that leads into the main part of the modern house. 'Will.'

He offers Will, who takes it very solemnly, a hand.

'Hello,' Will says. 'Mum says you have a PlayStation.'

'Will!' I laugh then, and so does Marcus.

'Follow me, Will,' he says, and we obey, our heads craned upwards at the spectacle of light around us.

'Your electricity bill must be huge,' I say, looking up at the floodlit interior of the old ruin as he leads us into a great glass hall.

'Well, all the glass I used is state-of-the-art solar glass that harvests the heat of the sun, which contributes more towards the bills than you might think, in Yorkshire; also, the house is insulated to the highest standard, and I installed a geothermal heat pump that makes use of the Earth's heat, so it's almost eco-passive.'

'Really, that's amazing,' I say. 'It's ... Well, I've never seen anything like it.'

'Thank you,' he says and smiles proudly, as though I'm complimenting his baby. 'It's not the only one of its kind, but I like to think it's the best. It was quite a feat to get planning permission for it, as you can imagine, but in the end, this was the best option for the original building. During the Second World War explosives were stored here, and an accident set off a catastrophic fire. Building an independent dwelling inside the shell – along with my turret, of course – was the best way to preserve it.'

'I'm honestly speechless' I say, as Will's hand steals into mine and we enter a huge, internal central courtyard.

'That fireplace ...' Marcus gestures at a beautifully tiled and arched Arts and Crafts era fireplace '... that's left from the original building, and the central staircase was rebuilt using as much original stone as possible. What do you think of it, Will?'

'Mum says you have Wi-Fi,' Will states.

'Indeed I do. Would you like to see the cinema and games room?' Marcus asks.

'Yeah!' Will's eyes shine and he hops and skips behind Marcus as he leads us deeper into the house, opening the door and standing aside to let Will get the full impact of the wonderland he is about to enter.

Will yelps for joy as he runs into the room, spinning around while he takes in three old-fashioned arcade games, which are lined up against the wall, and a huge screen with various games consoles at its foot, the controllers resting on a series of brightly coloured bean bags. The back wall of the room is made of rough brick and dark-wood panelling that Marcus must have saved from the original building. Through the slanted glass ceiling, the dark silhouette of the turret peers down at us.

'In his defence, he has been very deprived of technology,' I say, looking up at Marcus, who is smiling fondly.

'It's a treat to have someone to share it with,' he responds. 'Will, do you want to come and see the library with us, or would you rather stay here and play?'

'Play!' Will picks up a controller like it's food presented to a starving man and flops happily into an oversize beanbag.

'Come this way ...' Marcus walks away, but I stop for a moment and look at my son, anxious about leaving him alone in any part of this great big building. Seeing my hesitation, Marcus says, 'Will, we'll be in the room right across the hall, OK? I'll leave the doors open, so shout if you need us.'

But Will is already lost in Mario Kart.

Following Marcus across the tiles, I can't stop looking up at the night, the moon perfectly framed by the glass.

'Are any of your rooms private or are they all made of glass?' I ask.

'Some of them are walled – bedrooms, bathrooms.' Marcus has one hand on a double door of light oak, carved with three-dimensional images of books. 'Most of the internal walls are traditional in construction because I want the house to feel cosy as well as light, and the bedrooms are designed to be private. But actually, the geography of the house, where it sits in this dip, means that it's pretty hard to pry into, even if you wanted to.'

'I'm glad. I was worried it would be like living in a fish tank,' I comment.

'There's no one out here to spy on me,' Marcus says. 'That's one of the reasons I like it. I guess at heart I'm a bit of an introvert and I like my own company a lot. Except ...' He grins at me, opening the door. 'Except I've long wished for a friend who would really appreciate this particular room. Trudy Heaton, may I present to you ... my library?'

There are very few times in my life that I've been really lost for words and this is one of them. Three stories of floor-to-ceiling bookshelves, all full to the brim with books, all kinds of books, but even from here I can tell that many of them are old, really old, and my palms itch to explore the parade of spines. There's a spiral staircase at each end, leading to railed landings for each floor; and, on each landing, ladders on runners grant access to every single one of what must be thousands of editions. The room is lit strategically and carefully to protect the ancient documents, and there are a series of long tables, lined with chairs, each with a reading lamp. He's built it as if it might always be full of at least a dozen scholars, not just one man and his very occasional guest. And then I get it; he's built a temple, and ideal, a prayer to literature. And I love it.

'Oh my God!' I gasp, just like Will did a few minutes ago. 'Oh my God, Marcus!'

'I thought you might like it.' Marcus is smiling. 'I've inherited so many books from previous generations that I have no real idea what's here. My father was a proper collector and Brontëite, and he also discovered some local records in amongst the family collection which he added to. I've been adding as well, in my own haphazard way, over the years, but I don't have much of a plan. I just look for books or records connected to the area, to the Brontës, and buy them. A lot of them were in storage for decades until I built this place. Still want the job?'

'I don't know what to say.' I gaze around me. 'Apart from yes, yes please.'

'That is excellent news.' Marcus grins, crossing his arms over his chest as he takes in his kingdom. 'I can't tell what a joy it is to have a guest who is properly wowed by my wow factor. An archivist, a Brontë lover, a genuine Ponden Heaton – you really are quite the find, Trudy.'

'I'm ... thank you.' I smile warmly at him. 'I'm interested in why you collect records, though – they're mostly terribly dry and dull.'

'I suppose it feels like collecting lives: lost histories, births, deaths and marriages, old photographs, inscribed books ... They all meant something to someone once. Someone has to curate them.'

'That's exactly how I feel,' I reply, and we share a moment of understanding, that little rush of warmth when you find a kindred spirit.

My eyes roam from shelf to shelf as he talks, seeing countless boxes waiting to be opened, wondering what might be in amongst them that could show us a glimpse of something long past or forgotten, help us to understand history or even change it.

'Months ago I ordered in all this conservation material, special cardboard boxes and folders and things, but it's still all unpacked, so ...'

'Marcus, you are my perfect man.' The words are out of my mouth before I have time to think about what I'm saying, and I see his eyes widen, his pink cheeks becoming ruddy. 'I mean … I only meant … I didn't mean. Oh crap.'

It feels like a slap, a punch in the chest, to have forgotten Abe, even for a moment long enough to say something so light-hearted and flirtatious. And suddenly I feel as if I should leave.

'Trudy.' Marcus stops me, his fingertips on my shoulder, just for a moment. 'It's fine, honestly. Don't be embarrassed, I know exactly what you meant. And if you are still keen to work on the library, then may I present you with this?' He unfurls his hand, and in the middle of it is a huge iron key.

I stare at the key, instantly wanting to pick it up and feel its cool heft in my hand.

'This is the front door key,' Marcus explains. 'It's largely symbolic, to be fair. The locks are controlled by a PIN pad, but even so, don't lose it, because there are only two and it would be a devil to get a new one cut. There's a security code too, on the back of this card. You'll need these to get in and I'm often away.'

'Thank you, Marcus,' I say, taking the key and the card. 'It means a lot to me that you're giving me this opportunity.'

'Don't thank me,' he says. 'It pleases me to think of you here. And you can bring Will with you, too; my games room is his whenever he wants it.'

'You are a very kind man,' I tell him.

'Oh, I don't know.' Marcus colours a little. 'It used to be that good manners and decency were something we took for granted. Kindness is a kind of politeness, don't you think?'

'I do,' I reply.

'Now, dinner. And after that I'll give you a tour. We can go right up to the turret, but I'm afraid it's structurally unsound on the top floors; however, we can have a wander on the ramparts.'

'That would be so wonderful,' I say, excitedly, as I look up at the fairy-tale turret and notice a light in the upmost window.

'There's a light up there?'

'Yes, I like to make the place looks as romantic as possible. No floor, but I put a light in that simulates a candle and it's controlled from here – look.' He shows me a great dashboard of switches concealed behind a carved wooden panel that controls the light and heat in each room, switching the turret light on and then off. 'Truth is, I'm a terrible show-off. Now let's see if we can prise your son away from that screen.'

CHAPTER TWENTY-FOUR

We are home by nine and, after a bath, Will climbs into his PJs in front of the fire while I make up his bed on the sofa, shoving a grumbling Mab off several times before I can complete it. Will doesn't ask me why, and I don't offer a reason, although I have one ready: it's raining steadily outside and when I went upstairs to collect his belongings there was a steady drip of water soaking into the carpet. I placed an old tin bucket under it that Ma had in the bathroom, presumably for such occasions.

We read, and he tells me how he wants to be the first man on Mars, and I tell him how much I'd miss him, but I'll let him go, though, because you need to be brave to make new discoveries and, anyway, I could come and visit on holiday.

It feels so precious, this particular closeness, the weight of his body leaning into mine, the way he plays with the rose gold chain his father gave me on our seventh wedding anniversary, which I always wear around my wrist. We dream and plan for a future with flying cars and cities on the moon. Maybe it's here, in these tight spaces between

Will and I, that I can truly feel Abe, feel him recreated by the two of us.

'Ma,' he says, 'you haven't told me any more about you and Dad for a long time. What happened next?'

I think about the first year of my marriage and I hold him a little closer.

'What happened is that we lived very, very happily until you came along, and then we lived even more happily, which, you know, was because you were there, too.'

It seems to satisfy him for now and I continue to hold him as he falls asleep, feeling the weight of his head on my chest, his complete ease and contentment.

And I remember my firstborn child.

Tru and Abe

Our flat was very small, a studio: one large room and a bathroom. It was all we could afford but I loved it. Even though it meant leaving my home behind, the space and shadows, the moors I knew so well, I loved it, because it was ours. I'd look out of the high window at the city beyond and see our future, mine, Abe and our baby's, and it was always bright.

The day it happened there was a storm brewing, no rain at first, just the building charge in the air. I'd been at uni all day, so I'd flopped onto the sofa and put my aching feet up as I'd waited for Abe to come home with pizza. I'd felt content, happy.

When Abe had come in, he was flustered.

'What happened to you?' I'd asked, my hand covering the pit of my abdomen where I'd felt the tiniest tug of pain.

'Some old tramp, off his face on something, stood in the doorway, wouldn't move, wouldn't let me past him. I mean, what could I do? I didn't want to hurt the poor bloke or call the cops on him, plus he stank like the grave, so I told him that if he wasn't gone in five minutes there'd be trouble.' I remember smiling at Abe's half-hearted threat. 'Luckily for me he was gone after I'd walked round the block, otherwise I'd have had to call my pregnant wife on him.'

'Pregnant wife ...' I'd smiled and he'd dropped the pizza on the table and put his arms around me.

And the pain again, deep inside, sharp enough for me to wince.

'What up?' Abe had asked me, concerned.

'Nothing,' I'd said and smiled, but I think at that moment I'd known. 'You get some plates, I need a wee.'

'You always need a wee these days,' Abe had called back, laughing.

That's when I'd found the blood.

She was so perfect, our little girl. Though she never drew a breath she lives on in my heart and she always will. Our Emilia.

In the weeks that followed I'd wanted my mum, wanted her so badly. But when I'd thought of how much I loved the child I'd lost before I even had her, I could only think of what Ma had said to me on the day that I'd left home. And I hadn't been able to bear the thought of seeing her face.

CHAPTER TWENTY-FIVE

* *

'Why don't you sleep down here too?' Ma asks once Will is tucked in, watching a movie on the laptop over Mab's head. 'All of us together. Won't be any fun for you in that leaky room – the drip, drip, drip all night drives you mad. And you know, there might be happenings.'

'I might, later,' I say. 'But I want to read for a bit, remember? There's a book I want to look for. I looked for it this afternoon but had no luck, so I'm going to look for it a bit more tonight.'

Ma stares at me blankly for a moment before she finally cottons on that I'm talking about the diary papers.

'Come get a cup of tea off me first,' Ma says. 'I'm making one.'

'I'm fine actually, I'll just—'

'Just come in the kitchen,' she orders, pointing at the door.

I wait until Will begins to nod and take the laptop off of him, watching as he rolls onto his side and falls effortlessly into a deep sleep.

'Watch him, you're in charge,' I tell Mab, who positions herself at his side, her head on his hip, her eyes slowly closing as she falls asleep beside him.

'Well, hopefully your noxious farts will ward off trouble,' I whisper as I leave.

In the kitchen, Ma has lit candles and turned off the strip lighting.

'Ma ...' I see an upturned glass in the centre of the kitchen table and some pieces of torn-up paper that she is busy writing letters on. 'What's all this?'

'Long time ago,' she says, her head bent over her work, 'when me and your dad were first married and you were a scrap of a thing, he thought it'd be a lark to have a medium here one Halloween. I said no, I were dead against it. No point in stirring up that which is at rest, I said, but your dad wanted it. And when he wanted something, he had a way of making it happen, wearing a person down until you just agreed to make him shut up.'

'You were newlyweds?' I say, under my breath.

'Yes, bit more than a year, I suppose. Anyway, he wanted to have a party and make a big thing of it. You know how he liked Halloween.'

Suddenly I see what she's about.

'Are you *serious*? You want us to have a séance?' I sit down at the table, watching as she adds the words YES and NO to her scraps. 'Ma? Come on, really?'

'We did it at the big table, back then,' Ma said. 'But I thought we'd better not disturb the boy.'

'Considerate of you,' I say. 'Ma, look, these things are nonsense. I know – I've studied the Victorian obsession with them, all smoke and mirrors, all of it. And anyway, even if it wasn't, what do you and me know about ... it?'

'You don't need to know anything, you just need to be ready,' Ma says, looking up at me, her eyes bright. 'I mean, you only had to look at that baggage Bob got in to know she was a charlatan but, well, your dad were happy, his friends were enjoying it, and I thought it were harmless enough. None of us were ready.'

'Ready for what?' I ask her cautiously.

'Marion Makepeace, that were her name.' Ma wrinkles her nose as she remembers. 'Stunk of knock-off perfume. She told us she was going to summon any spirits present. Bloody load of old cobblers, she had no idea what she were doing.'

'So then why?' I gesture at her *Blue Peter* Ouija board.

'It were rubbish, most of it,' Ma says as she moves the pieces of paper around the table until she is happy with how they are laid out. 'Someone here with an "E" in their name, died with lung or possibly heart problems – the usual sort of claptrap – but then, just towards the end something happened. The room got so cold, and suddenly this woman, ... one of your dad's guests ... started weeping, tears running down her face, and she didn't know why; she just said she felt such terrible grief. And Marion Makepeace was suddenly afraid. She stopped talking and was just staring and staring at the glass. It had started moving – and this time she wasn't touching it. I saw it with my own eyes and it spelt out one word: "Look." Old Marion shrieks and snatches up the glass but it flies out of her hand and smashes against the wall.'

'O . . . K.' I say the world very slowly. 'So she threw it?'

'No, it looked like it was ripped out of her hands. The silly cow ran out the house screaming, and your dad's mates laughed their heads off. They thought it was a great joke, old Bob up to his tricks, and your dad didn't deny it. They all stayed up late drinking, up till dawn, if I remember rightly, but when he did finally get into bed, I said, "How'd you make the glass do that, Bob?" And he looked at me straight and he said, "Don't ask me, love, I didn't have nothing to do with it."'

'Dad liked to spin a yarn,' I say, repressing a shudder.

'He did, and I forgot about it after that day until this day,' Ma says. 'And then, after last night's goings-on, I had a thought. What if it was *her* back then, lass? Your Agnes. What if she's been waiting all these years and no one's helped her. All these years feeling so heartbroken and alone – that's an awful thing to live with. To die with, too. So what if it's your Agnes?'

'She's not *my* Agnes, Ma,' I tell her softly, glimpsing just a little of her unseen life once more, feeling the tragedy of it. How could I have lived in this house with her for so much of my life and not understood her unhappiness? How could I have left her to it?

'She's part of the house and the house belongs to you, so ...' Ma puts two fingers of each hand on the glass and nods at me. 'Maybe she can tell us something.'

'What, like where Emily Brontë's second manuscript is?' My laugh is strained.

'Well, maybe,' Ma says, and she is serious. And whatever else I do now, I want to please her, and if this is it, so be it.

Reaching out, I place my fingertips on the glass.

Dead-end darkness crowds around the curtainless windows. When I look out, all I see is myself looking back at me. All around us the house stretches and sighs. There is something like a movement from upstairs, the sound of a door closing, an echo of footfall.

'Is there someone there?' Ma says, and I repress a giggle. She eyes me and I do my best to keep a straight face. The truth is, it isn't the idea that this is foolish that makes me want to laugh: it's the fear that it might not be.

'Agnes, are you there, love?' Ma tries again. 'Do you need our help?'

The glass doesn't move.

'Speak to us, love,' Ma says gently. 'Do you need help, Agnes? Are you afraid?'

There is a sudden tension, a long, silent note of anxiety that stretches out the air around us to breaking point. Catching my breath, I watch the candles flicker and almost gutter completely. For a second, there might be another figure reflected in the glass, but when I look again, there is nothing there.

And the glass doesn't move. We wait, and we wait, and it doesn't move.

'Well then,' Ma says, very quietly, 'I'm away to sleep.'

A surge of relief floods through me the moment I take my hand off the glass, the atmosphere of expectation dissipating as Ma turns on the electric light, which flickers and falters before it finally catches, filling the room with its cheerful artificial light.

'I know you think I'm a fool,' she says, looking at me as she is about to close the kitchen door behind her, 'but I'm an old woman; I have my fancies.'

'You really aren't even close to old; you know that the life span of the average woman hasn't been under fifty for about a hundred and fifty years right? And anyway, it's fine,' I say, getting up to fill the kettle. 'I'll clear up.'

'And you'll come sleep downstairs after you've … looked.'

'Yeah, I will,' I say, puzzled at her sudden desire to have me closer to her, puzzled and touched. 'Course I will, Ma.'

She closes the door behind her, and I search out a clean mug, pour boiling water onto a teabag, muttering to myself in a vague impression of my mother, 'Agnes, are you there, love?'

It's only when I turn back to the table to clear away the pieces of paper that I notice that the glass has moved. It's neatly positioned over one piece of paper.

The piece that says YES.

CHAPTER TWENTY-SIX

It's desperately dark at the top of the stairs.

The shadows seem to be full of intent, peering down at me as I take the bottom step. The urge to turn around and go back into the warm, cosy living room is strong, but if there are other parts of Agnes's story, other parts of Emily's hidden legacy concealed within Ponden Hall, I won't find them anywhere I feel safe.

As I reach the top, I flick the light switch on, but the hallway remains dark: except, that is, for the thin slice of light under the closed door to Cathy's room. Taking a deep breath, I think of Mab and her quiet, stoic determination to stay by Will's side earlier, and push the thought of that glass out of my head. Squaring my shoulders, I walk into the whispering dark, towards the slice of light, and let myself into the room. If she was there, in the kitchen, maybe she left something here for me, some kind of message.

The bulb casts its false light mercilessly into every corner – and there is nothing. I walk around the room, seeing the other self, outside in the dark, mirroring my every move, afraid to look too hard in case I catch my reflection out.

Returning to the hallway, I flick on my torch and consider all the other shut doors, the rooms and spaces I haven't been in yet. Everything to the left of my old room was built much later than this part of the house. It was here when Emily used to visit, but not when Agnes lived here, and it is possible that Emily hid whatever she discovered in the more recent part of the house. Cautiously, I open the door to the largest room with the high windows either side. This was probably where looms were once kept and cloth made on the premises. Now it's only full of night, and Ma's junk. Impossible to really search this room until I've cleared it, but anyway, it doesn't feel like this is the place that I'm meant to be looking in. For a room so full, it feels remarkably empty.

The room Ma once slept in feels the same way, and the two adjacent. Each time I open a door, it is like opening up a portal into my childhood; memories caught up in smells, remnants of peeling wallpaper and ragged curtains, spring vividly to life. The blue peacock paper that was once Ma's pride and joy, and the tiny roses on the curtains in the small bedroom that matched the quilt cover and was my nine-year-old self's idea of the epitome of interior design. It is like a badly curated museum of my own life, full of moments, but not of intent. Yes, that's what I'm searching out, and, even as I think it, I wonder if perhaps I'm falling into some kind of madness, running away from grief and into a ghost story where the people you love might be waiting to take your hand.

Returned to the hallway, I stand in the darkness, switch off my torch and lean into the night, closing my eyes, searching for some trace of Abe here; just a breath of him that might allow me to believe that I will see him. He is not here, but as I stand there, all fear and apprehension draining away through the soles of my feet, I know where I have to look. Of course, it's obvious: the place that Emily came here to visit ... the library.

My room.

CHAPTER TWENTY-SEVEN

As soon as I close the door behind me I know where to look.

In the very same place that I used to hide all of my secrets: the bookcases. They aren't as old as other parts of the house – they were installed in the eighteenth century – but they were here when Emily visited and she was familiar with every inch of them. What's more, this might have been one of the very few rooms where she was left alone for any length of time.

And only someone who had spent her childhood searching this room high and low for a cubbyhole to hold all her secrets would know that there were places at the ends of the shelves where you could remove the panelling to reveal the spaces behind – and the rough stone wall, full of gaps and hiding places, that lay beyond that.

Now the shelves are packed with unloved paperbacks gathering dust, and Ma's dolls, neatly laid out as if for their own funeral, porcelain hands folded over their chests. When I was little I hid all sorts of things down in there, posting into the dark the scented erasers I stole from the newsagents, or little notes I wrote to myself, without concerning myself with how difficult it would be to retrieve them. It was enough to know that they were somewhere safe.

Grabbing books by the armful, I throw them onto the bed, puffs of dust rising from the stripped mattress with every impact. Other than the noise of descending books, the house seems very quiet, now; it feels at rest.

No sound comes from downstairs, no creaks bend in the hallway, even the wind outside has dropped for once. I pause to listen and all I can hear is the ringing in my ears.

As I throw the last book on the bed, I have the unexpected impression of seeing myself from very far away, up amongst the dark clouds. A lone figure, framed in a little rectangle of yellow light in a very old house, isolated in the midst of the vast mass of the moor. Such a very small and fragile life, in such a great and powerful landscape.

How vulnerable it is possible to feel out here. How powerless a human being can become when faced with the full fury of nature, of heaven and Hell and nowhere to turn for help or shelter. It's such a strange and melancholy thought, unfurling in the mind as if someone else has thought it. And as I feel that sense of helplessness, I'm overcome with the certainty that this must be how Abe felt, if he was still alive after the plane came down. He must have been so badly hurt, and so afraid. And he would have known that, for hundreds of miles in every direction, there was nothing but thick rainforest, and no hope of being seen, no hope of being found and nothing to do but die.

A surge of terror sucks the breath out of my lungs and knocks me backwards onto the bed and the books. Now is not the time to let these thoughts, that fear, in, to think of him lost and alone and waiting for me, hoping for me as I got back on the plane home. Not now. I looked. I looked as much as I could; I stayed there for weeks, I did everything possible, everyone said so, and yet ... and yet ... and yet ...

Finally, the shelves are laid bare before me. The first thing I do is wiggle free the panel I discovered as a girl, pushing my fingers into the dark expanse as far as they will go, searching the rough stone. I find a little coil of paper, and when I bring it out, my fingers coated in webs, I remember what it is as soon as I see it: a red thumbprint, made from the blood of my thumb after I'd stuck a pin in it, thick at the top, fading away to nothing at the bottom. I'd drawn a face on it and underneath had written BLOOD SISTERS. Funny thing is, I don't remember who I was supposed to be blood sisters with – what friends I did have were far too squeamish for that.

I tuck it into my pocket and search again. More notes, a single sock, a plastic ring that must have meant a lot to me once, but nothing any more. Feeling along the panelling at the back I find another loose slat on the top shelf, longer this time, spanning the height of two shelves. Painstakingly, I rock it back and forth, pushing at it, and, when I have enough purchase, I gently tug until it finally comes loose, falling down into the darkness beyond with a rattling clatter.

When I shine my torch into it I am at the wrong angle to see much, but to remove any more of the shelving would mean blunt force, and I can't bring myself to do more damage than I already have. Testing my weight on the bottom shelf, I gingerly climb onto it, mentally apologising as I climb on the next shelf, feeling as though I might slip at any moment. Balancing the torch in my hand, I pull myself forward and peer into the gap. Sheened with spider webs, I see the same rough stonework that makes up the rest of this part of the house, filled with dark and countless places, perfect for hiding something special.

Stretching, I work the torch as high up as I can and then down, and just below my eye level I see it, a hole in the stone. A hole that that has been dug into the mortar, a hole that's just wide enough to fit a hand in. It's just a few inches below the gap; if I can get an arm in …

My hand snakes its way through the gap and bends awkwardly downwards as I press my body further into the shelves, feeling them bite into my breasts and stomach as I try to lever every millimetre I can out of my fingertips. Feeling my way down the cool stone, inch by inch, I finally reach the ragged opening around the hole, but only with my fingertips. Try as I might, I can't reach inside. It's impossible to search further.

And then.

My hand is caught, trapped as if in the grip of icy fingers as thin as bone. And as hard as I try to be free and pull away to be free and, it feels like skeletal fingers are gripping mine with crushing strength, dragging me deeper into the hole.

There's no oxygen.

I cannot breathe, pain sears into my lungs and every muscle. No thoughts will form, just panic, as I struggle to free myself. Feet are lifted away from the shelf, my shoulder socket is screaming with pain and I can hear my wrist crack as it twists, feel it begin to bruise and swell, something sharp and ragged biting into my flesh.

Then I am released.

Tumbling backwards onto the floor, I hear the dull clunk of bone on wood as my head hits the bed frame and feel the pain of circulation returning to my tightly clenched fist.

Mouth gaping, sucking in air, I stare up at the gap in the shelf.

An unblinking eye, wide and feverish, stares back at me.

And then it's gone.

CHAPTER TWENTY-EIGHT

Stumbling into the living room, I collapse into the armchair by the fire, snatching at each rapid, shallow breath until they gradually lengthen and steady.

My fists will not unclench. If I close my eyes I feel again the grasp of icy fingers burning my skin, see that eye staring back at me.

I rationalise. I was panicking, stuck, dragging my arm out of splintered wood, that's what happened. The eye: I hit my head pretty hard, the room swam for a moment, and now my head is pounding. I was scared, it was my mind playing tricks on me. I was so, so scared.

I still am.

With some effort I tune in to the steady sound of Will's breathing. He is sleeping, Ma is sleeping. Mab is curled up on her feet. Whatever happened it was a combination of adrenalin and imagination, that has to be it. Except, as my fingers loosen I become aware of an object in my damaged right hand. My fingers tremble as I force them open to see what is resting in my palm.

Another leather-bound package, exactly like the last.

Turning my face away from it, I look at the window, waiting for the dawn. And outside I hear the wind, the rain ... and intermingled, a howling that is so like the crying of an abandoned child it brings tears to my eyes.

It's going to be a very long night.

PART FOUR

Vain are the thousand creeds
That move men's hearts: unutterably vain;
Worthless as wither'd weeds,
Or idlest froth amid the boundless main,
To waken doubt in one
Holding so fast by Thine infinity;
So surely anchor'd on
The steadfast rock of immortality.

Emily Brontë

PART FOUR

Tru and Abe and Will

Abe had held the door open for me as I'd carried Will in, taking him to the window of the flat to show him the street below.

'You were born in London,' I'd told him, showing him the red bus as it trundled down our street. 'But really, you're a Yorkshireman; it's in your blood. One day, I'll take you home to the most beautiful countryside in the world.'

From the moment I'd held him, and he'd regarded me with his dark eyes, I was anchored, like I'd known him not only all of his life, but all of mine. And there was the curve of his cheek, the shell of his ear that I'd see in his sister. Which might have made me sad, but instead had given me great joy to know that, whenever I looked at my little boy and saw how he had grown, I'd be catching a glimpse of her, too.

Abe had fallen so hard for our son the moment that he'd held him in his arms, tears on his face, an expression full of wonder, a smile such as I'd never seen before, so full of love – and something more that I can't quite describe, apart from a kind of promise.

'Look at how handsome he is,' he'd said, showing me the screwed-up, swollen face of our beautiful new son.

'He is handsome,' I'd agreed, brushing my finger over his dark curls.

'And intelligent; you can tell by his expression,' Abe had said. 'That's the frown of a thinker. Maybe even a genius.'

'And precisely two hours old,' I'd reminded him, as he gently laid our little boy back my arms, and put his arms around both of us.

And then we were home, standing side by side, looking at the world outside the window with new eyes, as parents who needed to make it a better place.

'We're building a new world,' Abe had said, 'you and I.'

'A world just for us,' I'd smiled up at him. 'And sometimes your mother, who is on her way over right now.' Abe had half laughed and half frowned, and I'd known what he was going to say next.

'Now we are married, now that little William is here, don't you think it might be worth talking to your mother again, Tru? Give her another chance? You both said things that I'm sure you didn't mean ...'

I'd shaken my head. 'Our life is so good, right now. And he is so perfect. No, I'm not ready yet, Abe. I'll write to her and tell her about him, send a photo. But for now, you and me and Will ... it's everything. Just us three, and sometimes your mother. Let's have this time, just you and me and our baby, and the new world we are making for him.'

'I am going to make this a better world for you,' Abe had whispered to the top of Will's head. 'I promise. I'm going to make this a fairer, kinder, more equal world, in every way I can. So that you grow up knowing that what makes a man worthwhile isn't money or power or the colour of his skin, it's how he treats his fellow human beings, no matter who they are. That's the world you are going to grow up in, son; me and your mummy are going to make sure of that.'

After that golden moment there were times of struggle, of course there were; every life is one of peaks and troughs. Months of exhaustion, of barely making ends meet, snatching precious hours together in between passing our baby back and forth, trying to keep down two jobs.

When I think back on those early years, I think of them as the days when our family sailed on a stormy sea, with dangerous swells and unpredictable winds. But no matter how hard it became, we kept on course, we kept together – and we never stopped believing in the world we were making.

So when Will had turned two, when Abe had settled into the first year of his residency, and I'd taken up my degree again, when the sea had calmed and our family was still there, stronger than we had been before, more in love than we'd ever been, more experienced, more mature, ready for whatever came next.

I wonder, sometimes, how we did it all then, when we were so young, so overwhelmed and unprepared. And then, in the very middle of the night, in the darkest hour, I wonder if it was because, somehow, Abe and I knew the unknowable. We knew, somehow, that our time together wouldn't be nearly long enough.

CHAPTER TWENTY-NINE

Closing the door on Cathy's room I sit in the centre of the floor, laying my tools out around me. Here there is order and logic, reason and rationale. My wrist still stings and throbs, pocked with crescent-shaped cuts, and on the back of my head there is a sizeable lump. The further away I am from the incident, the more dreamlike it seems, the more unreal. And yet, those crescent-shaped cuts on the back of my hand, the bruises that mirror the shape of narrow fingers, the packet appearing in my hand … I didn't tell Ma about it; I didn't say anything. I have no idea how to explain what happened without sounding mad, so I return to the academic in me, the archivist. I do what I know while, outside, the workmen Marcus has sent put a tarpaulin over the leaking roof.

This package is a little bigger than the last one. A palm-sized rectangular shape, wrapped in leather and secured in the same way as the first.

Huddling on the floor, the cold still courses through me, even though I stayed up the whole night, stoking the fire, warming my hands at it, leaning into its heat. It's as if whatever it was that happened to me last night flooded my body with pure ice, that flowed into me, crystallising my blood, permeating every organ.

This morning, when I came back in here, I stopped outside my bedroom door, which was firmly closed. It took all my courage for me to push it open, revealing the water-blue morning that was filtering in around the thin curtains. The books lay on the bed, the bookcase door was open, and there was the gap at the back of the shelf. Swiftly, I pulled on two sweaters and wound a scarf around my neck, stuffing everything that belonged to Will and me into a suitcase and dragging it outside the room.

I still feel so cold ...

After the shock, the heart-exploding terror and the pain ebbs away, I am left with the cold – and a feeling of such hopelessness and desolation that I don't recognise as mine. Even though I have felt it, lived the pain and anguish of loss, even though I know it, recognise it, I also understand that I received this along with the package.

Painstakingly, I pick apart the knot, minutes slipping by as I work at it, teasing the brittle leather. Once it is done I use my spatula to gently open the leather, a little of which tears along the fold as it is unfurled. Within, there are four sheets. Two types of papers, two hands. Both of which I know: Emily and Agnes, two women separated by two hundred years, their words bound together and hidden for almost two hundred more. It's almost impossible to imagine, to appreciate how incredible this find is.

In a moment I will have to decide what to do next. But for now, there are only these words.

With great precision and care I set about unfolding the papers, setting the sheets in Agnes's hand to one side and positioning Emily's scrawled hand under my light. The first thing I see is a doodle sketch of that face again, half in shadow, an indication of a firm-set mouth, and then her words:

October 1848

I searched every one of the older books and found these pages only. Half the story at most. Where the rest is, or what it is, I cannot guess. It may be that it was never written, that Agnes Heaton never saw Robert again and that she died, young and poor, as so many do, as my dear brother did, as I yet may. When first I set my pen to paper in Wuthering Heights, I believed that I imagined all the cruelty in the world, conjured it onto the page, and set it there. I wrote all that I had seen, all that I had heard at Tabby's knee and here, from Robert and his family. All the dark tales of what the evil man will do to his fellow man. I sought to tell it all, to show the fury that lies in man's heart when he is betrayed. And yet, all that I could dream was as nothing to what is real. What has been done, and is done. I won't speak of this to another, but as I read these papers once again, I felt her standing with me, beside me and within me, and there was such a terrible cold all about me, a cold that is still with me, even as I sit before the fire. Such a cold and such a fury that I have never known. And such a fear of death … a fear that is mine own.

I think of my dead brother, his skin so pale, so frozen to the touch, and how he sought death, how he wished for it, welcoming it like a lover. All I know is that I wish to run from it. To <u>never</u> know its face. To never be that cold, lifeless thing that he was, devoid of soul. I <u>fear</u> death, I <u>fear</u> the oblivion and I fear the entrapment. To be nailed into a box, to rot to *dust and never again feel the cold air on my face or the rain in my hair? For heaven will not want me, and I will not want it. I fear it, and I feel it. I feel my own death deep inside me. I feel it wheeze and creak and rattle.*

But I refuse it. I won't die. I will <u>write</u> – for Agnes and for Emily Jane Brontë. I'll write so that Agnes's story will have an end, and that we will not die. I will hold hard against the dark.

Papa and Charlotte will most likely not let me come here again when they see how I am weakened now; they will want to call for doctors, but I will not see them. I do not wish for Charlotte or Anne to see what I write, for I know Charlotte will be worried that I am too brutish, coarse and male; but I must write what I am, and what I know, and if that is coarse and despicable, then so am I. I fear that if I leave these pages for Charlotte to find she will burn them. But Robert will help me – I have made him swear on the love he used to hold for me. I will post him my pages and he will conceal them for me at Ponden; he has sworn it, and none shall set eyes on them or know of them but he and me. And when I am recovered, and only then, I will retrieve them and send them to London and let the world make of it what it will.

For I will not die. I do not wish it. I do not wish for that cold box, the lid nailed down. EJB

Reading the words she has written, the first person, perhaps, to have ever read them, tears flow down my cheeks, as if I am her, as if I feel every ounce of pain and regret that she does.

Because I know that, within two months of writing these words, Emily had succumbed to tuberculosis. To read her thoughts, her hopes, to hold this paper, even with my gloved hands, when I know that she was the last person to touch it, is profoundly moving. All the fear and strangeness of the last few hours falls away when I look at it. The house chose *me*. It chose me to reveal its secrets to, and even though that terrifies me, it comforts me too.

The words are like nothing else that remains of Emily's writing, outside her novel and her poetry. All that remains of her voice is just fragments, hurriedly scrawled letters and diary papers that seem to belong to another person entirely from the one who wrote such searing verse, such an impactful novel. This changes everything, and it is beautiful and thrilling and heart-breaking all at once. Tenderly, I place it with the other papers, then turn to Agnes's story, and I see the scraps she wrote on, the paper she stole, how she had to scratch out her words with a makeshift nib, how, in every painstaking letter, she was willing to risk everything to write her tale down. I see the same story of a girl unfold that Emily did, low-born, seduced by the son of the house, cast out for her seduction; a story that has been lived a million times, by a million anonymous women lost to history, collateral damage in a world run by men.

This girl was a miracle, a faraway star that has been shining her light for centuries, waiting until now for it to be seen.

'Mummy?' Will pushes open the door, walking into the room. 'What's that stuff?'

'Treasure,' I say, holding my arms out to him.

'Doesn't look like treasure,' he says, falling into my lap. 'It looks like writing.'

He turns my face to his.

'Are you crying?'

'Not in a bad way,' I tell him. 'I'm crying because this treasure will mean so much to so many people, and I am the one who gets to give it to them.'

'Some writing?' Will looks dubious.

'Of course, words are the most precious treasure that we have,' I tell him. 'This person, she wrote these words four hundred years ago, and now, all these centuries later, I am able to hear her voice, right now, in this moment. There isn't another technology invented that allows feelings and thoughts to travel through time faster than the speed of light, is there?'

'I haven't invented it yet,' Will says. 'So what will you do with the treasure?'

I hesitate for a moment. What I want to do is hold it close. I want it to be mine, but that isn't why the house has revealed it to me. The house needs it to be seen.

'I'm going to show it to an expert,' I tell him. 'Experts are good at knowing exactly what to do.'

'Mummy?' He winds his arm around my neck and I feel the curl of his hair against my cheek. 'Are you afraid?'

'Me, afraid? No,' I tell him.

'She says to be afraid.'

I'm about to ask him who when I stop myself.

'Can you see her now?' I ask, and feel Will shake his head against mine.

'No, she only comes to me in dreams and she always walks in green, the greenest green. Last night she was covered in red, every part of her except her eyes. But I wasn't scared because I knew she was showing me something – I don't know what, but something. And she said that you shouldn't be afraid of her. That any child of Robert's needn't ever be afraid of her. But that you should be afraid of the bad one.'

Robert, my dad's name. I think Will knows that, but even so, even if his words are just the jumbled-up remnants of a scrambled-up dream, I feel better, somehow. The cold is receding.

Will hugs me once again, and I turn back to Agnes and her words, the echo of a dreamed warning, slip away unnoticed on the air.

CHAPTER THIRTY

Grace Fullerton smiles at me politely as she shows me into the Parsonage library, offering me a seat at a large table where I put down the box folder I've brought with me. I recognise her smile; it's the same one I used to give to people who would bring me artefacts they'd uncovered in elderly relatives' attics or understairs cupboards when I worked at the Lister James museum. They'd present me with boxes of letters, postcards or photographs of people that no one recognised any more. Items that seemed too personal, still covered in the residue of life, to just throw away but that no one knew what to do with. I always accepted whatever they gave me with exactly Grace's smile, and archived each item with just as much care as if it had been Queen Victoria's lost love letters. Even so, as central as each letter or trinket had been to one life once, now it was simply something to catalogue as one of many more lost memories. This find was nothing like those.

'A Ponden Hall Heaton.' Grace leans on the table. 'Please accept my apologies for staring at you, but I love the idea that you Heatons have lived there for five hundred years, and your relatives knew the Brontës. It's amazing. It's like that Kevin Bacon thing, six degrees of separation.' She laughs. 'And Ponden Hall is such an incredibly important building. I've always wanted to come and see that box bed.'

'Welcome,' I tell her, liking her at once. 'Come whenever you like. Well, maybe not just yet. We have a few ... disturbances to settle first.'

'I heard Mrs Heaton doesn't like visitors,' Grace says, nodding.

'Oh, Ma hates them. But the house loves them and so do I.'

'Forgive me, but Haworth is a small village, so I heard about your husband, and I was out with the others looking for your son the other day. I just wanted to say that ... I know that times must have been hard.'

'They have been. They are.' I'm caught off guard by her kindness, her willingness to talk head-on about what so many people I meet either ignore or refer to in oblique euphemisms. Instinctively, I trust her.

'Grace, while I've been getting the house ready, I've found some incredible things and I want to show them to you. I need someone with your level of Brontë expertise to look at them – but I also need to know that you will not discuss them with anyone outside of this room. Not yet.'

'Wow, did you find the lost manuscript of *Wuthering Heights*?' Grace jokes.

'Almost,' I say, and the look on her face is priceless.

*

'This is …' Grace stares at the papers. 'I mean this is … You have the newspapers with the dates on, which were covering the floor? They will help to establish provenance.'

'For the first packet, yes. There's a selection in the box folder, and the packaging and binding is in there, too.'

'I need to put this before expert eyes, get the paper dated and the ink. But if we can prove that Emily's note has been there for a least a hundred years, then … Bloody Hell, Trudy, this is *her*. I know it is, I feel it. I can see it's her – and it's the most wonderful thing I have ever set eyes on.'

'This is nothing like anything else she wrote in her correspondence,' I add. 'To get this glimpse of her … And it was in my house all along. I walked over it a thousand times.'

'This, this is Emily the writer.' Grace's eyes are glowing. 'Emily the poet. Not the bored girl, dashing off a thank you or playing with her sister. This is the real her, the private her. I suspect that there were once many more documents that showed us this side of Emily, but Charlotte got rid of them, trying to protect her sister's legacy.'

'So she was right to be afraid of Charlotte burning them, then?'

'Yes.' Grace nods firmly. 'Yes, I believe she was. Charlotte was terribly worried what people thought of Emily and, by extension, of her. She did her best to protect them both; if Charlotte had known there was a second manuscript … Oh, Trudy, this is huge.'

'It is, isn't it?' I can't stop grinning. 'And what about Agnes?'

'Huge!' Grace repeats herself. 'Women of Agnes's status didn't read or write or record their story; there is hardly anything like this, a few testimonies written by a scribe, perhaps. The only thing I can think of that compares is the autobiography of Mrs Thornton, written after the Civil War, but she was a woman of learning. This is simply remarkable – and that it was Emily who uncovered these pages, and Emily that wanted to write her story?' Grace can't speak for a few moments and I understand why. 'It means that the whole world will read Agnes's words now. She'll be famous.'

As I carefully put everything away, she asks me, 'What are you going to do with them?'

'I want to look for more, more of Emily and Agnes. I think, you see, that there is more of a story that needs to be told. Emily was ill, but she may have been able to write. Robert may have hidden more of her work somewhere in the house, and after she died he left it where it lay. After all, she made him swear that none but her would retrieve it. And as for Agnes ... she was in love with my ancestor. But I have never heard her name in any of the stories. I've heard the name Casson, the man who married a Heaton and then cast out her firstborn son, the Robert that she loved, forcing him to buy back his own inheritance, but not of Agnes.'

'It's likely that no one thought she mattered,' Grace says. 'But if you want to find out more about her, then there are a few church records that date back that far, held in Keighly now. Only they aren't originals – many were lost in a flood, I think – and, of course, someone like Agnes may not have an entry for their birth or death in the church records. It's not really my area of expertise.'

'Or mine,' I say. 'I'm much more used to spending my time with dead Victorians.'

'Trudy—' Grace smiles hesitantly '—what will you do with this find, once you've completed your research? There are private collectors who would pay a lot – and I mean a *lot* – of money for this.'

'I know,' I assure her. 'But I wouldn't do that. I want the world to own these words. But before that, I want to keep looking. This is a story that needs an ending. And until I find out what that was, it's a story that belongs to Ponden Hall alone.'

CHAPTER THIRTY-ONE

As I walk out of the Parsonage and into the sunlight, I look back up at what was once Emily's window and smile. Grey clouds pile up on one another on the horizon, but the last few minutes of a sunny hour cast a golden light on everything in its path, warm and reassuring; the last remnants of that terrifying touch have evaporated away. For a few hours I thought that the only answer had to be gathering up my son and running away, but Will made me see the opposite is true; Ponden is my haven, my protector, and I am the custodian of everything within it, including those who are not quite gone. If there is danger coming, then I want Will safe in the sanctuary that has always kept us safe.

As I walk past the graveyard, which is covered in coppery leaves, a beautiful cockerel, black and gold, catches my eye as he stands proudly amongst the headstones.

And I feel something like a focusing.

A cloud passing over the sun washes the colour out of the leaves and a chill sends prickles down my spine; in the distance, between the green and grey of the tumbledown graves, I hear a baby crying – and at once I feel that familiar tug in my chest. The cry is so plaintive, so lost, that tears sting my eyes. I can't see anyone, not a mother with a buggy, a father carrying a child in his arms. The graveyard is empty.

The cries grow louder and, as a swirl of dead leaves whips over the stones, I follow it, gripped by a sudden need to offer comfort. Searching for the source, I weave in and out of the trees, step over grave after grave; and then suddenly it stops abruptly. When it does, I long for it again, and it hits me, this awful thought: it was *my* lost baby crying, my little girl looking for me, searching for me. The tears come, hot and thick, and I am so overwhelmed with grief that I can't move, or speak. I can't breathe.

I hear the cries of crows again, the sound of schoolkids laughing in the alley, the leaves gusting around my feet. My face is wet with tears, and I can feel it, that tiny child's loss and desperation, as sharply as if it were my own. If I stay there for a moment longer I'm afraid I'll dig my hands into the soft, damp earth looking for a baby to hold.

As the sun returns, dappling through the leaves, I see the worn-out inscription on the stone at my feet.

CATHERINE BOLTON, INFANT
BORN 1658 DIED 1659
BELOVED DAUGHTER. GOD HAVE MERCY ON HER SOUL.

All the little lives that lie beneath my feet, so small they hardly mattered at all, except to those that lost them. So much love, so much heartbreak and loss in these few square feet. All at once I understand. There is only one force in the universe strong enough to tether a soul to the earth, constantly seeking and searching for that which is lost. Only the human heart can contain enough love – or enough hate – to keep on beating long after death.

There is only one love I know that will never be defeated, not by any foe. The love of a mother for her child. And I think of the Ponden Child, crying in the night to be let in and suddenly I understand everything. Agnes Heaton is a mother. A mother looking for her child.

CHAPTER THIRTY-TWO

When I get back, Ma is sitting at the dining-room table, and the sight of her takes me by surprise. She's brushed her long fair hair back from her face and pinned it into a bun on the back of her neck. And she's dressed, not in her usual dressing gown and slippers, but a blue polo-neck jumper that I think I remember her wearing when I was a child, and pair of jeans that are a little too big for her now. Still slippers on her feet, but she is dressed.

'Now then,' I say, 'what's the occasion?'

'No occasion,' Ma says. 'Just felt like it. How did you get on?'

'Good. Grace is great and she thinks they are genuine.'

'Of course they are.' Ma snorts her response.

'And how have things been here?'

'Peaceful.' Ma nods at Will, nose deep in *The Secret Garden*. 'He's been reading, and the house feels relaxed, like it's got something off its chest.'

'I need to find out more about Agnes.' I lower my voice. 'Dad liked to tell me stories, but he never showed me any records and there must be a lot of paperwork somewhere – tax records, staff wages. Maybe I can find a trace of her there.'

Ma shakes her head. 'What little we do have will be in your dad's office, I suppose. Everything else, centuries of family history, were more or less stolen with the contents of the library when your great-grandfather nearly lost it all. All those precious books – a Shakespeare First Folio, Aubudon's The Birds of America – gone, vanished into thin air.'

The story of the lost Ponden library was legendary, more heart-breaking to think of than ever, now, knowing what might have been hidden amongst the pages of the books. The family was down on its luck, the hall mortgaged up to the hilt, so everything worth anything was sold to placate debtors. A local schoolteacher came in and made an inventory of all the books in the library and realised that some of it was quite valuable. But when the house sale took place, the books, the most precious asset that Ponden had, all vanished into thin air, and though the teacher did his best to track them down, they were never found. Everything else went for a paltry sum, and there is no record to say where. It was only some years later, when the inventory came to light, that we realised how valuable some of the books were, including two worth millions. If Emily's manuscript was amongst those stolen books too ... it doesn't bear thinking about. I can only hope that Robert Heaton thought of a more original hiding place than Agnes had.

'I wish Dad was here to ask,' I mutter.

'I'm here to ask,' Ma says. 'You never really ask about me and your dad, but I'll tell you a secret. I was in love with this house before I was in love with him. History was my favourite subject at school, but in those days there weren't no talk of university, or jobs like yours. Not for a girl off a farm like me. I'd walk past Ponden and look up at the windows, and think about all the people that had looked out of them.' When she smiles, I capture a glimpse of her as she would have been then, more than thirty years ago. 'That's how I met your dad, who thought I was hanging around outside his house to meet him. He knew all the stories about Ponden, but I know plenty, too.'

She lowers her eyes and I realise she is right. Almost every day Will questions me, asks me about Abe, and how we met and our life together. I never asked Ma about how she met Dad, or why she married him. I've never asked her who she is, not really. It comes as something of a shock to realise that I don't know my mother at all.

'I'm sorry, Ma,' I say quietly. 'For everything.'

'I'm sorry too.' She doesn't look at me, only raises her shoulders a little in a half shrug. It's only a beginning, but it's something.

'Tell me what you know about Henry Casson,' I ask her, and this time I sense a tightening in the air, the peace she spoke of disrupted by ripples of tension. Ma does too; she folds her hands in her lap and straightens her back.

'It was the end of the Civil War; William Heaton, like many others around here, had been fined for refusing to pay the king for a knighthood at a time when all men who owned land worth forty pounds a year were required to, and he had fought for Cromwell. He should have come home, victorious, but in the final weeks of the war he was lost.'

'Killed in the war?' I ask her, thinking of Agnes's last pages. 'Or murdered?'

'No one knew for sure,' Ma says. 'No one saw him go down in battle and there was never a body recovered or a report of him being captured; even in them chaotic times that was rare. He simply disappeared, leaving his young wife and their son, Robert, to fend for themselves. And his will had gone missing too, so it was quite a to-do. Those were dangerous times, the years after the war. Soldiers still went from village to village, taking anything they wanted, and there was very little justice for ordinary folk. Anne Heaton must have decided she and her son Robert needed a protector, and so she married Casson and he soon had his feet under the table, his own baby in the crib, and the role of Constable that had always been taken by a Heaton. He cut Robert off from education and did his best to cut him off from his inheritance, too.'

Ma and I watch each other as the afternoon light that had been flooding the room is pushed into oblivion by the gathering dark. We only look at each other, keep our voices steady and light.

'But he didn't?'

'He didn't. There are varying stories. Some say Robert made his own fortune and then bought Ponden back from Casson, or Casson's son. Some say that one day Casson just vanished, like William Heaton had, and was never seen again.

There is a rumble that I first feel through the soles of my feet, and it builds. I see the long table begin to vibrate, and then the great dresser that has been standing against the wall almost since the house was built, trembles and shakes and, one by one, Ma's collection of cheese dishes and ornamental plates begin to teeter to the edge and topple off. Then all at once the house is still again.

'What happened?' Will asks.

'Big lorry outside,' Ma tells him, and utterly unperturbed, he returns to his book.

'Well, that cuts down on the dusting at least,' Ma says, and a giggle bubbles up from my gut and explodes into laughter.

'This house doesn't like that name,' I say.

'If there's anything to be found, it will be in your dad's office. But I haven't been in there ... not since you left. Be watchful.'

'Because it's where they used to lay out the dead?' I ask her, with a wry smile.

'Because your father didn't talk to me much about the old Ponden stories, but he did tell me once that it was the only room in this whole house that he had ever been frightened in.'

Dear God, please forgive me my sins, which are many. I deserve the series of calamities that have befallen me, O Lord, but please, please not this. To have my heart so cruelly ripped from my body, to have all hope crushed. It cannot be, Dear God my Saviour. It cannot be, I refuse to believe it.

I waited and waited at Timothy's house, helping where I could, with spinning yarn and keeping house, but the longer I waited for word from Betty or my Robert, the more that Timothy's wife, Mary, gave me long dark looks, and counted out her food as if she and he might starve with my extra mouth to feed. This, even though Betty sent baskets of produce that she had collected at Ponden. Baskets would come on the cart with the linen, but no news.

Then one night Mary turns to me and says, 'You may not stay here any longer, child. You'd do well to travel to Leeds and see what fortune you may make there.'

'I will go soon enough,' I assured her. 'But I must wait for news from Ponden.'

'You better had not wait much longer,' Mary said in return. 'You thicken at your waist and soon will thicken more, until your babe is born.'

O Lord, as certain as my heart is true, I did not guess that I might be with child. Though I was sick and thin, weary and tearful, I am so sick of heart I believed it symptoms of pining. But as she spoke, I knew she spoke the truth. And, O Lord, I have never been so afraid. I had to see Robert. I had to see him and know that he was still true to his word, that we will be married at once, and that, above all, the babe would be born within the love and Grace of God.

I had no choice but to return to Ponden, waiting until dark fell. I walked across the moors and there was no moon; it was black as all ink around me, but I felt no fear, knowing each pathway as if it were a friend. At last I saw the house, black against black, silent and asleep. At once my heart was full of hope and fear. Hope, yes, because it was comfort to see the only place that had been my home, and fear for what truths awaited me inside. What if Robert was dead? What if I was made widow before I was ever made wife?

The kitchen door was locked firm, the fire dead in the grate. I dared not knock for fear of waking the wrong person. Soon I came upon the open pantry window, small, but I was smaller, even though my belly is swollen with child.

I found Betty sleeping in her cubby by the kitchen and shook her awake, covering her mouth with my hand so that her screams might not wake the house.

At first Betty's face was full of fear, and then dread when she saw who had woken her, and then great sadness.

'Betty, is he dead? Is that what you would not tell me?' I asked her and she replied, 'Oh God, Oh God, not dead, dear girl, but gone. Master Robert has gone this week hence, sent to Ireland.'

All I could do was shake my head, no. No, no and still no.

'He rode out on his horse, with Casson at his side, and his trunk on a cart, and I thought sure he'd find a way to come for you,' she said. 'I see that he did not.'

I wept then, most bitterly, and thought that I might die there, for my heart raced and fluttered and I could not breathe. Somehow I told Betty my predicament and she gathered me into her arms, and rocked me against her bosom as if I were the babe, and for a moment at least my fear was quieted and I was at peace.

'Maid,' Betty said, 'it is not the first time that a young man has broken a girl's heart with pretty talk. I'll help you as much as I can. But you can't go back across the moor tonight. In the dawning, go back to Timothy and I will bring more news to you as soon as I am able.'

Dawn broke as I walked back across the moor, and I stopped on the cusp of the hill and saw how God painted the sky with such colours as I have never seen, and how the beauty of it made my heart and gut ache for the love that I cannot and will not believe that I have lost.

Dear Robert, it is I, your wife Agnes, mother to your babe. Dear Robert, come to me, come to me, come to me. Answer my prayer, for you are my Lord and I am your disciple. I cannot be saved without your grace.

Please, Dear God, help me!

Agnes Heaton, still

CHAPTER THIRTY-THREE

Dad's office is a large, square room, right under Cathy's room, as old and as integral to the original house as the room above. Two stone-framed windows flank the corner; there is a fireplace, stone flags on the floor. My hand hesitates on the age-pocked iron latch of the door. When I was little, I remember this room flooded with sunlight, the trees dancing outside the window, Dad's stuff everywhere, his desk covered in paperwork and books and all the random things he loved for a little while before moving on to the next thing. He let me sit at his desk while he worked and I drew, or played in the corner. Here we'd read together, laugh together. Here was a place that Ma hardly ever came. There's a very good reason I haven't visited this room since I came home, and it's not because of Ma's ominous warnings. It's because I half expect him to be waiting for me behind this ancient door.

The electric light isn't working, which is hardly a surprise. I could go back upstairs and fetch my phone or a torch, but I feel like if I do, the moment will pass, and I'll lose what resolve I have. So I strike a match to the candle Ma gave me.

Candlelight is surprisingly effective, but it gutters and flickers and makes the shadows dance. What I see is a time capsule, muted with layers of dust, garlanded with spiders' webs, but it is just as I remember it: piles of books, photos in frames, and, on the walls, as many old drawings, paintings, and photographs of Ponden through the ages that Dad could find. There's a selection of mismatched flat-pack bookshelves crammed full with books, boxes, files, objects. I have no idea what I'm looking for, or where it might be. Stepping into the room I leave the door open, reassured by the sound of Ma's radio, and process my candle around the room, hoping for a box marked 'Ponden Records'.

But that's far too organised for Dad, of course.

This is not a job that can be done by candlelight; I'll have to put it aside until daylight. Turning on my heel, a pain shoots through my toe and shin. Wincing, I see I've made contact with a wooden box sitting in the middle of the floor. How I didn't fall over it before I don't know, but crouching down, I run my hands over it, and there's no dust. Pushing it slightly to test its weight, I see dust underneath it, as if it has only just been placed there. I hear myself swallow as I try to lift the lid, but there's a small brass lock set into the wood and it's locked. It's impossible to know what's inside, so, placing the candle on a shelf, I pick the box up, all of its weight, I think, in the solid hardwood, rather than the contents. Just as I reach for the candle, it snuffs out.

Yes, I think, it's time to leave this room now – but I take the box with me.

Will is sleeping with his head on Ma's lap when I return next door, his book splayed open on the floor. One of her hands is resting lightly on the top of his, and the look on her face as she watches him, the tenderness and care … It's hard to know how to feel about that, when I don't remember her looking at me that way.

She smiles when she sees me in the doorway.

'He asked me to read to him,' she says softly. 'Drifted right off after only a couple of pages. Not sure what that says about the book, but I thought he must need it. Look at his lashes, long enough to sweep the gravel path.'

'I need a week in that room, but I picked this up for starters.' I set the box down on the floor and sink into the armchair.

'Ma, I know a lot about the history of this house, but hardly anything about my own family. Tell me what you remember about my grandparents.'

Ma checks Will, making sure he really is sound asleep.

'Bobby, your dad, were always the life and soul of every party; everyone loved him, even those that didn't want to. But his dad, Bill, he was a troubled man,' she says softly. 'He died years before I met your dad, but Bobby told me that when Bill were in the grip of the "black dog", he sucked the life and colour out of everyone. He said it were like his mood were *heavy*, somehow, like it had a weight that bore down on everyone, but most of all on him – like he was being crushed to death by sadness, that's how your dad put it. And then, one day they found him down by the reservoir. Shotgun wound to the head. Shooting accident, it said in the paper, and that's what the family told everyone, but—' Ma stops dead, biting her lip, her hand unconsciously covering Will's ear.

'What?' I ask her.

'Your dad told me he read it in his mum's diaries, years later. She wrote her thoughts down every day, and she wrote about what happened to Bill, and one thing stuck out.'

'Yes?' I prompt her.

'She wrote that days before the accident he told her he were going to die.'

'Because it was suicide?' I whisper the last word.

'Because – because she wrote in her diary that Bill'd seen him. Greybeard. That after Bill thought he saw him, he was frantic. Said he couldn't stand waiting for whatever it was that was going to end him, that he'd rather do it himself. And then, a few days later ...'

Ma and I fall silent for a moment or two.

'This is a self-fulfilling prophecy,' I say. 'The problem of growing up with the legend of a family curse. You see some old bloke with a beard and suddenly you're doomed.'

'Maybe,' Ma says tactfully.

'What about Dad's mum?' I ask her. 'Did you know her?'

'I never met her. She had cancer, ovaries. She must have had it a long time but they didn't know about it, and then suddenly it happened so quickly. Bobby was nineteen – it was right before I met him. I was sixteen.'

'You were so young,' I breathe, aware of the hypocrisy.

'He had this place, the land, a bit of money. Too young. It all happened too young, to him and to me. You can see, can't you, why I were so afraid for you?'

'I can,' I said. 'Tell me about your mum and dad, Ma? I don't know anything about them, a whole half of me that I know nothing about.'

Ma doesn't answer for a long time, her eyes dropping to Will's face, impossible to read.

'I'll tell you about my mum and dad,' she says. 'Dad worked in the mill down the lane when it still was one. Foreman, he was. He used to wear this long coat, like a doctor's coat, but brown, and he'd always have three yellow pencils in the pocket. And a tiny little brush moustache. I think the war did something to him, broke him a bit. He died of a heart attack just after I were married, no age at all. I have photos of him somewhere ...'

'Was he kind?' I ask her.

'Gentle as a lamb,' Ma says, smiling. 'As for my ma, she was pretty. So pretty, you never seen anyone like her, not in real life. She was like a film star, to me. Golden hair all down her back, periwinkle eyes. I adored her, trotted around after her everywhere. She were here a lot when your dad and I were first married, helping me get a grip on managing a place as big as this. We had ... we had some hard times here, and I wouldn't have got through them without her. She missed my dad something terrible and she died soon after you were born. I still miss her.'

'Can I ask you something?' I test the words carefully, sensing Ma stiffen, seeing the look of contentment fade away.

'What?' She is guarded.

'Do you love Will?' She smiles, and it is a smile made partly of relief that I have not asked the more difficult question.

'I do,' she says, with a small smile. 'He's an unexpected pleasure in my life; he gives me joy. Now, how about you put the kettle on?'

It's enough that she loves him, even if she has never shown me that kind of affection; it's enough that she loves my son.

No, it's almost enough.

CHAPTER THIRTY-FOUR

In the kitchen I try opening the box again, shoving an old meat skewer into the lock, but it isn't fine enough. It takes a straightened paperclip I find in the bottom of one of the many drawers of stuff, and several sweary minutes, but at last I'm in. There is a jumble of folded papers, some clearly recent, others thicker, creamier, older-looking.

I take a wodge out, spread them over the table. Birth certificates, a family tree, tax records ... Hastily I rifle though the pile and flick through what's left in the box. Interesting finds for a Heaton archive – the corner of a photograph catches my eye – but there is nothing obvious of Agnes or Emily here.

Where would Robert have hidden the papers that Emily sent him? Where would I find more of Agnes's story? Looking out into the autumn evening I see my reflection in the window, hollowed eyes looking back at me.

'Don't you have any ideas?' I ask myself, catching my breath on the thought as I see – at least, I think I see – another figure reflected in the window, at the very edge of my peripheral vision, as slight as my own reflection, a dappled palette of dark shadow and dim light that makes up something like a face, standing just behind me. I don't dare look right at the apparition; I'm afraid to. Afraid that if I do I will lose her.

'I want to help you, Agnes,' I say very softly, feeling crazy at exactly the same time as I utterly believe that there is something there. 'Show me how.'

For several long moments there is nothing but silence, deep and close. Staring ahead of me, I track the headlights of the cars on the distant road, flaring and merging, yellow into red. It takes a second for me to realise that one red orb remains static, glowing softly, with a light that is so low it might almost not be there; a little light like closing your eyes after looking too long at a naked bulb. The distant star hovers just for a few seconds by the back wall, and then it is gone and so is the light.

But it doesn't matter; now I know where to look next.

Tru and Abe

'But do you have to go?' I'd asked Abe.

We were sitting in our Finsbury Park flat, where we'd moved when Will had turned four, after I'd landed my job at the Liston James Museum. We had a two-bed place on the second floor of an old Georgian house. When you opened the window the traffic roared past, and sometimes there'd be drunken fights outside at night, but we were opposite the park, and when you were sitting on the sofa all you could see were the tops of the trees.

'Everything is good,' I'd continued, 'everything is just right. Will is happy in reception, I love my job, you love yours, and now … and now you're going to risk your life on the other side of the world?'

Abe had tipped his head to one side as he'd smiled at me, his arm around me, his fingertips grazing my shoulder.

'There are kids out there, children Will's age, who have no immunity to the diseases that the outside world is bringing in, who are seeing their home, their whole way of life, being ripped away around them, as they're herded into smaller and smaller territories. Kids just like Will. It's a few weeks of volunteering; I go out, I perform simple surgeries, help with the clinics, do a little bit of good, Tru.'

I'd rested my cheek on his bicep, inhaling the smell of him.

'Is it dangerous?' I'd asked. 'Peru?'

'No! It's all organised by the Red Cross, it's perfectly safe. I'll be away for a few weeks and then I'll be home – you'll barely notice the difference.'

'Of course I'll notice the difference – and so will he.' I'd turned to look at Will. 'We have hardly been apart since he was born. I'll *miss* you.'

'I'll miss you, too,' Abe had said, his mouth curling into that smile.

'So why not just be a normal person who doesn't go volunteering in rainforests and stay home?'

'Come on,' Abe had said, nudging me a little closer to him. 'Are you telling me you don't find handsome-activist-doctor me a little bit sexy?'

'I can't deny there is a certain frisson to it.' I'd smiled in return. 'You are a good man, Abe.'

'Somebody's got to be,' he'd said.

We spent the whole of that night on the sofa, with Will asleep next door, the window open a crack, the traffic noise rushing in, the sound of drunks tipping out of the pub, and we didn't sleep for one minute of it, not until the dawn crept in.

Abe went to Peru, and when he came back he was so happy, so full of energy at everything he had seen, everything he had done. He glowed with it, with a passion to do more. So when he said he was going to make it a regular thing, it never crossed my mind to try and talk him out of it. Why would it? I was so very proud of him.

CHAPTER THIRTY-FIVE

After several minutes of scrabbling in the cupboard under the stairs, I find a rickety little trowel, the rowan-wood handle almost entirely loose. Switching my phone torch on, I head out into the dark of the misty late afternoon. The scent of bonfires and rotting leaves mingles with the rich, irony tang of the earth and the salty edge of the stones, so strong in the damp air that I can taste it.

Out here, against the back wall of Ponden Hall, is the dead, half-rotten stump of an old pear tree. You would never know it was here; you'd never notice it if you didn't know to look. But I knew that Emily's Robert Heaton planted this pear tree as a sign of his love for her; it was one of the first stories that Dad told me when I was kid.

No one knows exactly why here at Ponden and not at the Parsonage – I always think it was to encourage her to visit more. There's no record of a reason other than that he loved her, but here it is, close to the wall and rotting in the ground, a fragment of a young man's heart enduring against two hundred years of neglect.

Robert Heaton planted it long before Emily was dying and secretly sending him papers, so it wouldn't be right beneath the roots, but somewhere nearby, something I'm glad of, because I don't want to be the one to destroy this humble little relic of first love.

In the narrow beam of torchlight I examine the surface as if, two hundred years later, I might find some signs of disturbance to point me towards a burial. But of course there are none.

Where, where would he have put it? The package would contain paper, more than likely, so I hope to God he sealed it in something watertight, sheltering it from the elements as much as possible, in a place where he would be able to find it again easily.

And then I realise the perfect place: in or up against the wall of the house.

I draw a direct line in the dirt from behind the stump of the pear until I hit the wall and then I begin to dig. In this part of the garden the wall extends at least one floor below ground level, forming the outer wall of the old coal cellar. The earth is heavy, solid with clay and chalk, and after only a few scoops I lose the handle of the trowel completely. Taking the blade in my hand, I continue to dig, feeling the underside of my nails clogging with damp earth.

Sweat begins to bead along my hairline, and my neck and shoulder are aching by the time the wall gives way and I dig out a cavity two stones wide that looks as deep as the width of the stones. Holding my breath, I shine my torch in; sure enough, right at the back of the gap I see a strongbox, metal and padlocked. For a moment I rest my head against the cool of the stone, until my heart rate gradually slows.

This could be it. This could be the end of Agnes's story. This could Emily's novel. The contents of this box could change history.

Taking a breath to brace myself for another encounter with a helping hand, I reach into the dark. The stone cavity is slick with damp and some kind of slimy growth, but no freezing fingers search me out as I struggle to get purchase around the box. My knuckles graze against the stone as I drag it out, and at last drop it into my lap.

It's disappointingly light. Taking a breath I stand up, cradling it in my arms; it could almost be empty. There's no sound of anything shifting or listing within. Standing in the square of light cast from the kitchen window, the iron padlock that secures the box in my hand, I realise I'm going to need a crowbar.

CHAPTER THIRTY-SIX

There are three sheets of papers in the strongbox, plastered to the bottom of the box with damp and mould.

Ma and I peer into the box to look at the papers, joined one to the other. Robert did his best. The box was almost airtight, but not quite enough. What's more, the fragments that are left here are almost certainly not all that was once secreted within. The top piece of paper, in Emily's hand, slighter, trembling on the page, tells me that.

Dear Robert

November 1848

This novel, in three volumes, shall be called The House at Scar Gill and you need not fear, for I have changed the name of your family from Heaton to Akhurst. I enclose the first volume. Only you would I trust these pages with. Keep them safe, dear friend, until I may retrieve them; the rest will follow soon, God willing. I thank you for the further pages you have found in Agnes's hand. Sometimes, in my delirium, I believe I hear her whispering her tale to me. I will

return them when I am done and this story is complete.
In truth, I know that none shall wish to publish a tale of
such violence and scandal, but it is the tale that I must
write. My sisters fuss over me day after day, and indeed
I am weak and ailing. But I am certain that if I can see
out the winter I will recover in the spring.

Yours, believe me,

EJB

There is a novel, or at least a completed first volume of a
novel, and Emily sent it here to Robert for safekeeping.
Sinking into the chair I try and take in the enormity of what
has been waiting in the wall of my house for more than 100
and fifty years. There *was* a second Emily Brontë novel, that
is now certain; that is a fact.

The House at Scar Gill.

It's such a huge shift in what we thought we knew about
the Brontës, such a huge addition, that all I can do is sit here
and let it sink in for a moment. And then there is more. Then
there is Emily. These must be some of her last words, and
they were words of hope and determination to survive. But
within a few weeks of writing this note she would be dead.

And then there is more of Agnes.

Beneath this there is a title page, the edge to the title
just visible behind her note, and beyond that, an almost-
destroyed page of Agnes's writing, just a few words at the
end of each line, barely readable. I can just about make out

'babe is born', 'Grace of God', 'hope and fear', 'Dear God, please help me!'

The words I thought I heard Will cry out in his room.

Agnes has discovered she is with child and unmarried; somehow I know it as certainly as I do my own name. She must have been so afraid. And what happened to her 'Dear Rob' – did he simply leave her and his child to their fate?

'What have you got there?' Ma asks, wrinkling her nose at the smell.

'More of Emily.' I turn the box around so that she can see inside. 'And the hint of there being even more, once. *The House at Scar Gill* – what a perfect title.' I rub my filthy hands over my face in frustration. 'What happened to it? Why would it be moved and the box put back?'

'Maybe them that moved it didn't want anyone to notice it was gone,' Ma says.

'You think someone else found out about it? Got to it first?'

'We don't know who was here at the house sale in 1898,' Ma says. 'It took place just after that Robert died and all of the family papers were supposed to have been burned, we don't know why, and only a few, the ones in that tin, were secretly saved. It's possible that the same person that found them knew about the true value of the books in the library, discovered something that Robert might have thought hidden.'

'Oh God, I can't bear it!' I sink down onto the nearest chair, looking at the meagre contents of the box. 'To have come so close and to find it stolen, destroyed or lost. Something so precious – it's too much.'

'It's not all gone, though.' Ma nods at the few sodden pages. 'You can save those words and now you know a lot that one else knew before.'

'You're right,' I say. 'I'm going to leave the box in the sitting room tonight. Don't touch anything, OK? Tomorrow I'll take it to Grace and start talks with the Parsonage about what to do next.'

'Did *she* show you where it was?' Ma asks as she leaves.

'It just suddenly seemed to make sense,' I say, still unwilling to admit what I half believe. 'Robert loved Emily, so of course he'd hide something important to her close to something that reminded him of her. And poor Agnes, pregnant and alone ...'

'No wonder her soul is trapped here.'

'Ma ...'

'She'd have gone on the street, most likely,' Ma continues. 'There was precious little charity back then. With no family, no father ... She might have left the child as a foundling, they might both have died of starvation ...'

'What next?' I say in some desperation. 'Now I've found a little I want to find the rest, I want to know what happened to Emily's novel, what happened to Agnes.'

'If she really wanted to be helpful, Agnes could just tell us,' Ma says, meeting my eyes. We stand there, perfectly still, neither one of us dropping the gaze of the other.

'I'm hungry now.' We both shriek and then laugh at Will, his face creased with sleep, his hair sticking up like fledgling feathers. 'What?' he says.

'I'll get tea on,' Ma says.

'I'll get out of these muddy clothes,' I reply.

'You know what you should do, lass?' Ma says. 'You should write a book about what you've found. It's your discovery and you know a lot about this subject. You got qualifications and that. You should write a book about it.'

I stop in the doorway, turning the idea over in my mind. 'I should, shouldn't I, Ma?'

'You should, lass.'

'Ma,' I say, 'do you really think ghosts are real?'

'Stranger things, lass,' Ma says. 'Stranger things.'

CHAPTER THIRTY-SEVEN

In the daylight, Castle Ellis looks completely different to the magical wonderland that Will and I first encountered. Autumnal mist, thickened by rain, weaves in and out of the spectral-looking rubble of what was once a formal tiered water garden, as we make our descent down the winding driveway.

Without the benefit of the floodlights, you can barely see the glass and steel structure in amongst the ruined façade, just glimpses of it, like a forlorn spirit struggling to free itself from the brick-built ruin it is entombed in. In daylight, the crumbling and overgrown gardens appear ethereal and lost, and all the mismatched, broken angles seem to add to an atmosphere of unease.

Looking up at the jagged remains of the original house clawing into the belly of the low sky, I realise that it is taking some effort on my part to battle back a sense of foreboding.

Perhaps I shouldn't have read up on Castle Ellis's history after my first visit. If I hadn't, I wouldn't have known that the castle had been completed in 1888, but the first owner had died before it was habitable. Or that the second owner and his eldest son died in a rail disaster just a few years later, both so disfigured by the catastrophic crash that no one is entirely sure who was buried in the family crypt. Or that, just a few days later, returning from his father's funeral, the second son died from lead poisoning, thought to have been brought about by the freshly applied interior paint.

Castle Ellis had remained largely uninhabited by the family after that, used only for day shooting parties, or the occasional festivity right up until it was torn apart by the explosives in the Second World War.

Unlike Ponden, Castle Ellis was a house that was almost never lived in, an empty shell even before it was a shell, a skeleton house that never had a soul.

But it does have the most beautiful library I have ever seen. That's something to focus on.

'Here we are,' I say cheerfully to Will, as we pull up. 'Our own personal castle for the day. Excited?'

He looks up at the blackened stone window frames, the shadows of long burned-out flames still licking at the walls.

'I don't like it as much today,' he said. 'It feels sad.'

He's put his finger on it at once, and I'm surprised that I didn't. It isn't menace or doom that laces the misty air around the house, but a kind of grief. And the two buildings coexist, not in harmony, as I'd first thought, but in a constant tension. One is the captor, the parasite feeding off the other, but I can't quite decide which is which.

'You'll like it fine once we're inside, and you're playing *Minecraft* on a full-size cinema screen,' I say. 'Want to put the key in the lock?'

Will brightens, weighing the huge key in his hand for a moment before loading it, with some difficulty, into the lock, turning it with both hands until we hear a satisfying clunk.

After tapping the entrance code into the covered keypad set into the stone, we both push the heavy door open, giggling at its ominous creak. As soon as we are inside we are faced with another control panel and, forgetting every instruction that Marcus gave me, I push on every single button with a sweep of my hand, watching the lights come on down the length of the corridor and throughout this bell jar of a house.

'Do you remember where the playroom is?' I ask my son, who suddenly has a skip in his step again. Will nods, running off across the polished stone floors, kicking his shoes off to skid round the corner in one seamless movement. How I can see Abe in him, the joy he takes in the things he loves. Catching up with him a few seconds later, I find him already ensconced on a beanbag, plugging himself into his virtual world.

'I'll be just over there,' I tell him, pointing across the hall. 'Please don't break anything.'

'OK, Ma!' he says, and my smile turns into a grin as I let myself into the library, the heady scent of books lifting my spirits. My random switching on of lights has lit only half the room, and try as I might I can't find a way to switch on the others, which leaves half of the room in shadow, made denser by the dark day outside. It hardly matters, though; the air is filled with the scent of very old books and the promise of discovery. Not Emily Brontë's undiscovered second novel, of course, but even so, the thought of it hums under my skin.

Very precisely, I set up my workstation right under a table lamp, and switch on all the other lamps that I can find.

As the rainfall increases, so does the noise it makes, and the house rattles with each drop that explodes on the glass before running down the angled surfaces in thick, syrupy sheets, making me feel almost like a fish in a tank, or, more accurately, swept out to sea.

'Focus,' I find myself saying into the watery grey room. 'You have work to do.'

Just the word *work*, and the idea of it, is enough to please me, and I find myself smiling as I look up at the seemingly endless shelves, heavy with mysterious titles. Where to begin? Logic says I should start at the bottom, but that seems too methodical, and if they aren't shelved in any order it doesn't really matter what order I start in, as long as I keep track. On the second landing I see some archive boxes and the deliciously irregular shelf-line of a row of very old-looking books. I'm going to start there.

For a moment I'm afraid that the height and apparent fragility of the balcony might prove too much, but after recent events I discover that it takes more than a Perspex walkway to shake me, especially with a reassuring wall of books at my back. Leaning on the railing and looking down at the floor, I see the tiles have been cut and laid to look like open books, each intersecting with its neighbour. This really is a perfect room; I couldn't have imagined it any better.

Although there are archive boxes on the shelf, tucked a little back is an ordinary box file filled to the brim with an array of papers, badly stored and poorly cared for, their bent and torn corners reaching out of the closed file in a bid to escape.

Taking my seat in the bright circle of safe light, I carefully open the box, tutting at the creased and crushed contents which talk to me at once, my heart singing in answer. At a glance, I can tell from the paper and the handwriting that the contents range over at least two hundred years. Two hundred years of probably just ordinary little bits of administration, bills of sale, letters of intent, records and accounts, but each one of them a crucial glimpse into the lives of those that came before, artefacts covered in the fingerprints of ghosts.

Glancing in the direction of the playroom through the open door, I see Will's frosted figure cheer himself as he wins a race, and set about losing myself in the box.

*

When I next look up, I'm not sure how long has passed, only that the cloud cover seems to have trebled into a thick mass, so black that it almost feels like night has crept up on me while I made my way through the box, separating documents into eras, pausing to read letters of condolences, or receipts from the pharmacist. I stop when I find an order for a mourning bracelet and, in the envelope, a quantity of human hair, dull blonde, tied neatly at one end with a pink ribbon. The order, carefully filled out, mentions a little girl of only four, but it is clear that it was never fulfilled. It makes me wonder how it found its way here, opened and saved, but never completed.

Shuddering, suddenly cold, a faint metallic crackle catches my attention. On the window nearest to me, little branches of frost are rapidly forming in the corners, a pattern that is being replicated across the great glass façade. I must have missed the button on the control panel for the underfloor heating, and the tips of my fingers and toes begin to ache with cold, when only a few minutes ago I felt warm.

I'll leave the papers here on the table and return to them tomorrow. Carefully wrapping each page in acid-free tissue paper, and storing them in one of four archive boxes I've set up, I'm about to replace the lid on the old box when I realise that there are only two items left. Both of them look so much older than the others, and somehow, when I see them, I know that they are meant for me. Glancing in the direction of the playroom, I can't make Will out precisely, but I can see the flickering lights of the screen; ten minutes more won't hurt.

Opening the first, a leather-bound ledger, I see the words *Parish Records Haworth Church* and the date, 1650–1670. At once I am struck by the neat, measured writing, each letter exquisitely formed with great care, knowing that one mistake would be set against the rest of the words on the page, each one detailing a moment of great meaning to the human beings whose names record their births, marriages, and, all too frequently, untimely deaths. These are some of the records that Grace said were thought lost in a fire; that they still exist is a really important find.

And the ledger covers the same year as the infant's grave I stood by at the Parsonage. Hovering my finger over the list of names, I look for hers. When I find it, my heart contracts.

Catherine Bolton, aged 1 year. Beaten to death.

The emotion that overwhelmed me at her gravestone, where I heard the cries of a lost child, now makes my knees buckle, and I sit down. Could it be that Catherine Bolton wasn't just a lost baby; could it be that she was Agnes's baby?

Catching my breath, the hairs rising along my arms, I read the entry again. And one word stands out as brutal as stone.

Beaten.

'Ma!' I hear Will call me. Pausing for a moment, I close the ledger and put it away. It seems like a good time and place to finish for the day, except that the final document, folded and bent in the bottom of the box, can't be left in such a poor state another moment. Carefully I extract it and smooth it out. It's a pamphlet cover page, the seventeenth-century equivalent of a tabloid newspaper, and the headline reads, 'Trial of Agnes Bolton for murder and infanticide by Witchery.'

I shudder against the cold as my finger hovers over the words, gradually understanding their full meaning, translating into modern English as I read.

This is *my* Agnes, somehow I know it. Bolton. Like the baby's name, and she stood accused of killing her own child. *Beaten.* Beaten to death.

Wind rattles against the glass, shadows creep under the tables, gathering in corners. And although it still falls with the same velocity as before, the rain is silent.

On this, the Third Day of October, 1660, Agnes Bolton, of this parish, also Ponden Hall, also unknown, was tried for the murder, by witchery, of her husband John Bolton and their child Catherine Bolton, who she did beat to death in service of Satan.

I stare at the name of my house, written so carefully into the page, a deep, lurching nausea seeping into my gut. Agnes stood accused of killing her baby.

A shadow creeps across the table, not a cloud passing over the sun because there has been no sun today. The shadow is in the room, and it's growing.

I'm unable to move; my feet won't peel themselves from the floor as the darkness obliterates the lights in the room where Will is. My breath mists as I breathe out, and the tiny tendrils of frost that had begun to form on the glass bloom, crackling into life.

Oh Agnes, what did you do?

And then, in one sharp, powerful shove, the chair I'm sitting on is shoved away from the desk, sliding me back several feet. In a second I'm standing, looking around me, wondering if it was me, did I push myself away from the awful words? Perhaps I did.

But then, it's almost as if I can hear her voice, the voice I've come to know in the words she so carefully etched onto paper. I hear her rage, hear it vibrate and hum in the silence, and I need to know: what happened to Agnes that led her to marry this John Bolton and lose her child so violently?

Imagine how it would feel to know you are about to die, found guilty of the murder of your own beloved baby; imagine the grief and fury, because in amongst all the pent-up fury and violent hate I felt just now, there was also love. A deep, abiding love – and the bottomless chasm of loss that only a mother could ever know.

'Mum! Mum! Mummy!' Will is calling me again, and this time there's an edge of fear to his voice. 'Mummy, I'm lost!'

I'm still trembling as I exit the library, still battling the feeling that something terrible has just happened. Closing the door behind me, on the other side of the frosted glass the light flickers and blink out.

'What's up, Will?' I make my voice bright as I walk into the games room but he isn't there. 'Will?'

'Mummy?' I hear his voice; it's muffled and there's a kind of echo to it. It's close, but he's nowhere to be seen.

'Will, are you hiding?' It's hard to keep the anxiety out of my voice. 'Where are you?'

The giant screen is still lit up, left as if in mid game – cars engaged in some kind of phantom race. Picking up a remote control I switch everything off, lifting the huge bean bags one by one, expecting to uncover him, giggling at his great game.

'Come on, Will, it's time to go!'

'Mummy? Mummy, are you there? Mummy, I don't know where I am and it's dark.'

Frustrated, I look around; there isn't anywhere else for him to hide in this room, no other furniture at all.

'Will?' I look up at the driving rain, the enclosing night, the shadow of the ruined turret peering down at me. 'Will, stop playing. Where are you?'

'I don't know where I am, Mummy.' I hear his voice, but it's fainter this time.

'Will, call out as loud as you can,' I tell him. But when his voice comes it is small and muffled, and sounds so very far away.

'Mummy, I'm scared!'

That's when I realise: he's trapped in the walls.

CHAPTER THIRTY-EIGHT

It's only now, in this moment, that I see that this house isn't as completely open and honest as it first appears, but is rather a maze of false starts and dead ends.

'Will!' I run to the flat, laminated panelling on the other side of the room. 'Will, what were you doing when you got lost?'

'Exploring,' Will says. 'And then I don't know what happened. It's dark and I can't get back.'

'It's OK, Will.' I struggle to keep my voice calm and light, to fight against the instinctive, lurching dread; hearing my child's disembodied voice echoing in the air, seeping into my voice. The obvious thing to do is to call Marcus, but of course, there's no signal out here and I have no idea where or if he has a landline, certainly not in this room anyway, and I can't leave Will alone. We have to figure this out between us.

Backing away from the wall I go and stand in the middle of the room.

'Will, can you see any light at all?'

'No, I can't see anything, Mummy.' I hear his voice tremble. The only thing my brave boy has ever been afraid of is total dark, and now he's imprisoned by it.

'Pretend your fingertips are your eyes, Will,' I say. 'What can you feel?'

'On – on one side I feel rough brick, old brick like the castle, and the other side smooth. I can't stretch my arms out wide that way. I can if I move to my side; then it feels like a long corridor. But I don't know and I'm scared to move, Mummy.'

'That's OK, darling, you are doing so well.'

I know the long back wall of the room is the only one that intersects with the old building, running along the wall that leads to the turret and the ramparts.

'OK, Will, I know whereabouts you are. I think there must be a hidden panel, like a secret door in Scooby Doo, that you accidentally triggered. So I want you bang on the smooth side of the wall, OK? Bang as hard as you can. Don't worry, Will, I'll get you out. I'll tear this whole place down, brick by brick, if I have to.'

'Mummy?' His voice is suddenly very small, his fear tangible. 'Mummy, it sounds like there is someone else in here with me. I hear breathing.'

Urgently, I run my hands over the smooth, white laminate panels, their vast expanse only disturbed by a few randomly placed, down-lit curved shelves that look like something out of a spaceship, which house games and

DVDs. There must be some hidden button, some secret movement that will unlock a concealed doorway.

'It's OK,' I call out, 'you're probably just hearing yourself, Will. Just stay right where you are, OK? I've nearly figured this out.'

'Mummy, hurry!' Will screams, and, tearing at the panelling, my nails crack and break – and then I see it, on a low bookshelf, a solitary model figure of Darth Vader. Of course, Will would want to pick that up. Diving for it, I try to, but it doesn't move, so I push it back – and hear a click. A door opens, just a centimetre, but it's enough.

'Will, I've found it, I'm coming!' I open the door, expecting to find him right there. But he is nowhere to be seen.

There is no narrow corridor between the castle wall and the room, just a modern-looking dimly lit lobby leading to the turret staircase.

'Will?' I hammer on the narrow section of wall that closes off the gap between the old building and the new. 'Will, can you hear me?'

There is only silence.

'Mummy!' I suddenly hear his shriek – and it's coming from up the steps.

I hear him running down towards me as I rush up to meet him, and then we are in each other's arms. He clings to me, and I lift him off his feet and run. Down the steps, out of that room, out of that house, into the grounds and finally into the car, leaving everything open behind me, just knowing that we need to be out. We need to be somewhere I can control.

Once we are in the car I lock the doors and look at my son. Taking his tear-streaked face in my hands, I examine him for injuries. He's covered in dirt, there are cobwebs in his hair and he is as pale as a ... he is very pale. But uninjured.

The rain drives down, the night closes in, and I hug him to me, holding him close, until eventually I feel the tensions ease in both our bodies.

'You're safe,' I tell myself as much as him. 'You are safe, Will, I've got you.'

'I don't know what happened,' Will says. 'I didn't like it, Mummy.'

'Me neither, Will. How did you get up the steps? Did you find a way out?'

'I don't know, I don't know. It just happened, it all just happened, and I don't like that place. Bad things happen in that place. I don't want to go back, Mummy.'

'You don't have to, not ever,' I promise him.

'Here, this is for you.' Will holds out his clenched fist.

'What is it?' I ask, even though, somehow, I already know.

Will unfurls his hand to show a crumpled sheet of paper. I don't need to smooth it out to know that it's covered with Agnes's hand.

*The world has ended this day. This day my life is no more, and
I am a ghost that walks and talks but feels no more, for God
has abandoned me, and I must pay for my sins with my own
happiness.*

*There is no sign of Robert, no word, no message. My stomach
swells under my skirts, and soon I will not be able to hide my
predicament. Betty has tried her best, searching out news of
Robert, but could find none, not even where he had been sent,
and now I am certain he must be dead by Casson's hand. I
know what he is capable of, and my love lies rotting in a bog.*

*And God forgive me, I went to the Kirk and stood on the
rock and prayed that I might have the strength to leap and
end my pain, dashing out my innards on the rocks below that
I may join my love forever. But how could I, when faced with
such beauty, decide to see it no more? It is a sin to take my own
life, but a greater sin to take the life of the innocent babe that
quickens in my womb. I have no hope, now, except this spark of
him that I will love until the day I die, Robert's child, who I
must suffer the greatest pain and humiliation to protect.*

*'He will have you,' Betty said. 'And what will you do else?
There'll be no work for you. No home with a bastard in your
arms. No end but to find your way to ill-gotten gains. You
could travel and claim to be a widow, but on what means? You
have nothing, Agnes, and a woman with nothing must
take what she is offered and he will have you.'*

John Bolton, the man she spoke of, is blacksmith in the village. Older than me by my life again, and a drunk. I see him on the street, leering at me as I walk by, and I know that look, for I have seen it in Casson's face. It is a look that likes to hurt.

At first I railed against the idea. I cannot, I cannot, I cannot. The thought of another touching me again, after Robert touched me and loved me, of another man to have dominion over my body and my life. I cannot, I cannot, I cannot.

But Betty spoke on.

'He'll put a roof over your head, Agnes, and feed you and feed your babe. He knows you are with child and will raise it as his. He needs a good worker and a willing maid.'

Still I wept and refused, for I am not yet even sixteen, and for my life, that had once known such tenderness and such joy, to be made the property of such a filthy, pawing man, filled me with dread.

'You have had your love, Agnes.' Betty was insistent. 'More love than some see in a lifetime. And what did it bring you but heartbreak and sorrow? He is gone, and he has not once in these long months sought you out.'

'Because he cannot, because he is dead,' I wept.

'Perhaps that is so, but what can we do, when the man that took him from us is the Constable and the law? There is no justice in this world for the likes of you and me, Agnes. All you can do now is find a way to live on for you and for Robert's child. Marry John Bolton.'

'I will hate him,' I swore.

'Then leave,' Betty told me. 'Go on the road and spin a yarn of a dead husband on the way and see how long you will survive, before the roaming soldiers take you and your child. And what if one day you have no choice but to sell your baby, as your mother sold you?'

What little hope I had, that precious spark I had guarded so closely, was snuffed out in that moment, and I lost my God, for I cannot hear him any more.

'Dear girl,' Betty said, 'Robert's gone. He left you behind, and you must understand that. That part of your life is dead, dead except for the life that clings on in your belly. That's all you will have of it now, and, dear God, it's precious and fragile enough as it is. So protect it and make your marriage. You tasted the honey, child. Now you must live with the sting of the bee.'

And so I said I will marry John Bolton.

'Praise be!' Betty kissed me. 'Work hard and pray hard and you may yet be saved.'

I did not speak further, for if I did I would have misspoken. I would have told Betty that I do wish to be saved. I wish to be close. Close to the man that has ruined me so that I may make him pay for all he has done to me.

Agnes, all I have that is truly mine is my name

CHAPTER THIRTY-NINE

Will talks all the way on the drive back to Ponden. Words pour out of him, as if he feels the sudden need to articulate every thought and feeling he has had since we lost Abe, or as if some invisible wall he had built around himself has crumbled to nothing. I listen and he talks as we navigate the steep and winding roads around Debden Bridge, rainwater running down the inclines in impromptu waterfalls, streaming across the road, only a thin barrier of drystone wall between us and the wooded ravine beyond. He takes me back to the time before the crash, not just of the plane, but of his life. He reminds me of the ways things used to be, the peace and tranquillity that Abe and I had found, the family we made, our life which was small and inconsequential and quiet, but full to the brim with such love that it meant the world to us.

We take the road over the top of the moor. Mist gathers in pockets, absorbing my headlights as the night meets the land and there is no horizon. Will talks about the day I told him his dad's plane had been lost, about those weeks after I left him, kissed him goodbye and flew to Peru. About the hours he spent with Granny Unity, not talking about anything, staring at the second hand on the clock so hard that it seemed to him it didn't move at all.

I slow the car down to barely twenty miles an hour as I take each hairpin bend, uncertain of what I might find waiting for me in the gloom, half expecting a white face to appear in the mist, a hand to reach through the glass and grab me, and still my son talks. He talks about the day I came home without Daddy, and that he couldn't believe it. Because Mummy always finds everything he's ever lost, the tiniest bit of Lego, the most beloved drawing; Mummy always finds it, but she couldn't find Daddy, and then he looks at me as we wait at a temporary traffic light, with no other traffic on the road.

'Mummy, I'm sorry.'

'You don't need to be sorry, Will.' I reach my hand out to him, his fingers still cold to the touch. 'What do you have to be sorry for, my darling boy?'

'I didn't think you looked hard enough for Daddy; I thought if you'd really looked properly, you'd have found him.'

The light changes to green but I don't drive. Instead, I put the car into neutral.

'But Will, I think you're right. I looked as hard as I could, then, at that time. But I wasn't strong; I was lost and afraid and it was a strange place and I – I didn't want to know what had happened to Daddy. Do you understand?'

Will nods.

'But I came home to be with you. I *needed* to be with you. So – so I think you're right. I didn't look as hard as I could have. And I realise that we need to know, Will. You and I, we need to know for sure what happened to Daddy. Even if it might hurt, even if it might be hard, we need to know. So I'm going to go back, as soon as I can. I'll go back and look again, and maybe it will take more than one trip, maybe it will take years, but I promise I won't stop looking, Will. I promise.'

'Really?' Will's eyes shine and I see something in his face I haven't seen for a long time. What happened at Castle Ellis, it terrified him. But it released him, too – I'm looking at the face of the little boy I knew before the world went dark.

'I promise,' I say.

'I love you, Mummy,' he says. 'You are the bravest person in the world.'

When he says it, I feel as though it might even be true.

And then there are no more words to be said as we make our way through the thick night of the wild moors. We don't need a moon to guide us home, because we have the light of Ponden shining on the hill, the kind of light you feel in your heart instead of seeing with your eyes. And we have the hope of a family that still seeks to understand what family means.

And, more than anything that ever was or ever will be, we have each other.

CHAPTER FORTY

I let Will run ahead of me, into the arms of Ponden and his granny, to tell her about his adventure, without a thought of stopping him, for as terrifying, as improbable, as his tale is, I know Ma will believe him.

The last thing I expected to find at Castle Ellis was Agnes. Not in the archives, not in the house. And what I felt there was different from my experience of her at Ponden, as if the house tempers her somehow. But at Castle Ellis I saw that centuries of disquiet create a powerful matrix of emotion, and that emotion can be overwhelming and dangerous. It's as if all the traces of pain and loss that make up the remains of Agnes that have always existed in the air around Ponden recognised those same emotions in me and galvanised around them, finding impetus, a kind of force to finish what for so long has been incomplete, a wave of energy that has engulfed me, searched me out because we both seek the same thing in this vast expanse of time.

We long for hope and we will not rest until we know that we have found some reason for it.

It's as if this trace of a human life, this revenant, isn't bound to the house, but to me. And we will be together until I set her free into the air again, her journey complete at last.

Did she come with me to Castle Ellis, and perhaps even direct me to that one box where I would find a relic of her, of her existence outside of her mind? This other paper, the packet that Will gave me, I don't know where it has come from; I can't explain it. Castle Ellis was built long after Emily died, completed in the year that Emily's Robert Heaton died; neither one of them would have hidden it in the walls behind the playroom, so why? Why then, and how?

All that I know is that something terrible happened to the hopeful, happy girl who scratched out her first words in secret that brought her to be tried for witchcraft and murder just a few years later. Some cruelty and injustice that I cannot imagine.

I do know that the worst of witch hysteria was over by the mid-seventeenth century. As a child, I was fascinated with the fate of the Pendle witches and the heated fervour and fear, neighbour rivalry and feuding, that led to the death of innocent women, women who were nothing more than wise, knowledgeable or outspoken.

Within forty years, when the same accusations were brought against Pendle women again, they were eventually acquitted, because attitudes, education and enlightenment had advanced so much. Before that, though, the word witch was attached to every kind of woman who transgressed outside of what was expected of them.

If Agnes was believed to be a killer, even if she was just a troublemaker, or merely an inconvenience, the fastest way to dispatch her would have been to call her a witch – murder within the law.

There is so much more I have to discover, connections I have to uncover, secret histories that must be revealed, but somehow I know that, if I can resolve this one long-lost and hidden story of a life that was invisible to history, then I will find a way to move on with mine.

Then I see Ma's face as she stands waiting for me in the doorway.

'Jean came down to say she'd had a call for you. From the embassy. She had a number to call, so I – I hope you don't mind, I went back with her and used her phone. I didn't want you to have to do it.'

'They found his body, didn't they?' I ask, feeling the earth crumble away beneath my feet.

'No.' Ma's pale-blue eyes meet mine as she holds my hands, her fingers tighten and I brace myself. 'A hiking party found the plane, or part of it. There were no bodies in the wreckage, but ... they say it looked unsurvivable, Trudy.'

Reflexively, my body braces for the wave of agony I know will break, but all I find is calm. Not acceptance, but something else, something that I can't explain in any other way but love.

I love my husband with such enduring strength that nothing will ever alter it. And he loves me the same way, I know it. More than that, I feel it; in every beat of my heart and firing synapses, he is there, his love is there still. It is real, it is present and it is alive. It is an indestructible love. No body means there is still hope: that's what Will would think, that's what I feel.

Look, the word that started all of this scratched into a floorboard two hundred years ago, is the word that stays with me. I will still look for him until we know, and this news just strengthens my resolve.

'Are you going to tell Will?' she asks me, and I nod.

'Yes,' I say. 'He needs to know everything there is to know, but I don't want you or anyone to talk about Abe as if he is dead. Not any more.'

'Trudy, are you sure? Wouldn't it be better to accept—'

'No.' I shake my head. 'No, Ma. Never give up, that's what Will and ...' I glance around the room '... this place has taught me. Never give up, for in time everything that was once secret will become known.'

'Well,' Ma says, nodding, 'you know best, I expect. Maybe after you've given it some time to sink in, you'll feel differently. You must be in shock.'

'No, I'm not in shock,' I say. 'I understand everything that has happened. But I have to go on, I have to. I promised

Will that I would never let him down again, and I won't. So, for now at least, I have to go on hoping and believing. What other choice is there? I'm not giving in to this.'

'Proper Yorkshire woman.' Ma's eyes are bright with unshed tears. 'I'll get tea on.'

After she's gone, I take the crumpled and badly damaged piece of writing from my bag and smooth it on my knee and read it, my heart aching for Agnes. This is the first part of her story we have discovered which had not been accompanied by a note from Emily. Perhaps Emily never found this note; perhaps that's why Agnes went to such lengths to press it into Will's hand, to make sure that every part of her story is told. But there is something else too, something else I can't fathom yet.

Tru and Abe

I can hear the wind talking to me as I head up to Ponden Kirk, see it write its messages in the long grass, the heather that trembles under its touch, the wild flowers bejewelled with early-morning dew.

It's cold as Hell and my heart is beating hard as I tackle the steepest part of the walk, but it feels cleansing to be out here, my hair tangled with weather, cheeks numb and ruddy. Out here I feel at home, on top of the world, at the centre of the universe, for this is *my* landscape, as uniquely mine as my own fingerprint or palm.

Right back when we first met, this was a special place for us. From opposite sides of Penistone we'd walk towards each other, each knowing that the other would be there, waiting on the Kirk.

Sometimes he'd be there before me, and how my heart would fly to see his long frame looking out down the valley, how my soul would swoop and soar with the kestrel. He'd turn to me and smile and, even on the darkest, coldest day, there would be heat.

As much as I loved it I'd always been a little afraid of the Kirk, the way the rock juts into thin air, nothing above or below but space. Even as a girl I'd had to force myself to step onto it, edging forwards to its end, with my hands and backside firmly attached to its surface. God knows how many thousands of years it had been there, that outcrop of rock, but still it felt to me always as if it could tumble at any second.

One time we met there stands out like a jewel in my memory. As soon as Abe had seen me coming, he'd leaped onto the great flat rock at once, feet planted wide, arms outstretched, calling 'Halleluiah' into the air, his voice echoing down the valley.

'What are you doing?' I'd asked, half charmed and half mortified, although there wasn't another soul to be seen for miles around.

'I don't know. Standing here made me want to cheer on God for such good work.' He'd turned to look at me, holding out his hand and beckoning me to join him. I'd shaken my head.

'I like having a hill under my feet,' I'd told him.

'But this is your place,' Abe had said, laughing. 'Yours and Cathy's and Heathcliff's place. You're my Cathy and I'm your Heathcliff, right?'

'I hope not,' I'd said. 'Cathy was a terrible cow, and Heathcliff was a stone-cold psycho.'

'Where's your sense of romance?' He'd pretended to be shocked. 'Won't you come and stand with me and we can do Kate Bush?'

'Um, I would rather jump off?' I'd said.

'Please.' Abe had dropped his voice, so that I had to take a few steps closer to be sure I'd heard him right. 'Come to me and let me kiss you.'

I go back to this moment again and again, reaching for it, holding it almost close enough to touch, so slow, so gentle. I'm looking into his eyes again, feeling his smile against my cheek. My body is melting into his, my heart bursting into flame.

It's not that Abe made me brave, brave enough to step out onto the Kirk and into his arms. It's just that, at this one moment, I knew exactly how much courage I already had, and I knew that there would be nothing in my life that could frighten me as much as the idea of losing him.

'I love you, Abe,' I say now, letting myself fall back into the heather, as I stare at the indifferent sky. 'I love you.'

The world doesn't care that one human has lost another they love. How much grief, how much sorrow like mine, is mirrored all around the world in just this one moment, and then repeated again and again in every moment after?

The world doesn't care, but I do. So I tell the sky how much I love Abe, and how I always will, and how I need to find out what happened to him.

And even if it doesn't care, it listens.

PART FIVE

With wide-embracing love
Thy Spirit animates eternal years,
Pervades and broods above,
Changes, sustains, dissolves, creates, and rears.

Emily Brontë

CHAPTER FORTY-ONE

Dad's office in daylight is peaceful, and though the day outside is dark and filled with rain, this is much more like the happy space I remember: a haven.

In the kitchen, Will and Ma are setting about baking a cake. Will and I had sat, our arms around each other, as I explained to him about the discovery of the plane wreck, and his small, serious face turned into my embrace. As he'd listened, then simply folded into me, Ma had set out her old mixing bowls, ancient wooden spoons, a rusty tin and all the ingredients required for a Victoria sponge.

'Now then,' she'd said to Will, as she'd walked into the room, 'I'm about baking a cake, and I'll need a helper for the stirring and the tasting. How about it, Will?'

'OK, Granny,' Will had said, peeling himself off my lap. But in the doorway he'd turned and said, 'We are still going to look, aren't we, Mummy?'

'We will never stop looking, I promise,' I'd replied. He'd nodded and gone, reassured.

I'd paused for a moment in the hallway before coming in here, listening to Ma pretending to be scandalised by some joke Will had played on her, and closed the door behind me.

Now the work begins ...

After several minutes of moving stuff around, I finally clear his old desk chair and lift the last box off of his desk. What I see hooks into my heart and pulls hard. A pen, resting on a notebook filled with his handwriting. A mug, full of the dust of decayed mould. A flattened photo frame of him and me manning the barbecue at the local summer fair, Dad with his beard in full flight, me gazing up at his face.

Grabbing the corner of my shirt, I roughly dust the old and battered leather chair and the desk, put the picture frame right, and slowly sit in the chair, letting my elbows rest in the dents where his once had, my fingers tracing the imprints worn away by his.

Setting down the wooden box in the space I'd cleared, I begin to look through it once again, to make sure I didn't miss anything.

Carefully, I set aside the documents that I remember seeing in that first brief search, birth and death certificates dating back two or three generations, including my grandfather's, his cause of death listed as 'Death by Misadventure'. And I do find something I missed in the first search, probably because it's a poor-quality photocopy – but it's a copy of the original catalogue of the 1898 library sale. For a few minutes I trace down column after column of titles, wondering at all the treasures we lost. Much of it was land law, farming practices, animal husbandry. But there were centuries-old books of prayer, poetry, illustrated books of wild flowers and their uses, and, of course, the legendary lost copy of Audubon's *The Birds of America*, one of the world's most valuable books, and a Shakespeare first folio, both worth many millions, all gone, lost and no one knows exactly where. At least there was no first edition of *Wuthering Heights* – but what if it was among these lost books that Emily's Robert Heaton hid the pages of *The House at Scar Gill*?

The thought of what might have been, so casually lost, makes my stomach churn, and I press on.

Underneath that are some late seventeenth-century documents relating to the hearth tax that existed then, and it's strange to see the signature of my long-gone ancestor, William Heaton, lying about how many hearths we had at Ponden so as to play less tax to the county.

Amongst them, the most important document when it comes to the family history. The administration of the goods of William Heaton were returned to his widow, Anne Casson, and on 22 February, Agnes's Robert Heaton buys back his rightful inheritance from Henry, ending his reign at Ponden Hall and returning it to the Heatons for good.

Somewhere in this legal administration, lost to history between the lines of archaic legal language, is the story of Agnes.

The room stirs around me, just a little. Furniture creaks and settles, dust rises and billows, and the shadows seem to draw a little closer. I lean into the silence, hoping to catch the whispering trace of a voice telling me what to do and where to look. Outside, the storm has turned the day slate-grey, and the room darkens as the rain drives down into the ground.

Strangely, it's right at the bottom of the box that I find the most recent items, and I take them out. I can almost see Dad carefully burying them under all the archaic paperwork, trusting that no one would delve too deeply. I can see at once why one of the items was buried.

The first is a photo of a woman in a swimming costume, blowing the photographer a kiss. I turn it over and there is a date written in Dad's handwriting. It is two years after Ma and Dad got married.

The second is a cassette tape, unmarked. Under the window is Dad's old stereo, and after a few minutes of plugging leads into mysterious-looking sockets, I switch it on and the speakers hum. I hesitate for a moment before I push the tape into the slot and press play.

'I'm saying this now, and then I'm never talking about it again.'

I start at the sound of his voice and realise the volume is turned right up. Pressing pause, I turn it down low enough not to heard outside of this room, and give myself a moment to adjust to the shock of hearing his voice again after so long. Oh Dad, you were not perfect, I see that now, but I loved you. After a moment I press play again.

'This is Bob Heaton, aged thirty-four, and I am of sound body and mind, sober as a judge. I have lived in this house a long time, and I know there's more to her than meets the eye, but tonight … I can't believe what I saw just now. I'm at my desk, working late, trying to make the books balance, and I hear a noise at the window, scratching, and I think it's a cat maybe, or the twigs on the trees. But then I hear this crying, like it's part of the wind, but not quite. It's a baby crying outside, some poor little lost mite. And I've heard about the Ponden Child and thought maybe this is where it comes from, this strange kind of a wind that whistles down the valley. So I get up and I go over to the window; I don't know why, because it's black as night out there, and nowt to see, or so I thought. And I'm standing at the window, listening to the crying sound, of the wind as I thought. And there it was, pressed hard against the glass, white as snow and so small. A hand, a tiny hand, a child's hand.' I hear him swallow, hear the tremble in his voice. 'And then it's gone, and the wind's dropped and I'm already wondering if I imagined it. But I saw it, it happened, and this is the proof.'

The tape keeps running, and it's empty of anything but static. Is Dad still there, in that room, that moment when he made that recording? Is that him I can hear shuffling around the office, putting things away? Straining to hear more, I put my ear to the speaker.

'*Trudy!*'

One word, my name spoken as clearly as it could be, and I am propelled back across the room. It sounded like Abe's voice!

A whip of lightening brightens the air for the briefest of moments, followed by a dark, grinding roll of thunder. Outside the window, through the dripping wet foliage, I can see the horse mount, and beyond that the five-bar gate that leads down to the Bee Boles stands open. The thunder explodes again, and I realise I can't remember a time when that gate has ever been unlocked. I don't know why, but as I leave the house and the rain drives down on the top of my head, I feel like I'm following that voice, Abe's voice.

CHAPTER FORTY-TWO

At Ponden, down the lane that leads to the water meadow that the stream runs through, there is a curious construction. As old as the oldest part of the house, known as the Bee Boles, it is shaped like an drunken 'L', a drystone building holding several deep compartments just big enough to have once contained handmade straw hives. Here, the Heatons of Ponden would house the wild bees that they had brought down off of the moor, making honey and mead and candles out of the bounty that those industrious little creatures provided. It's long since been overgrown with weeds and blackberries, but once it meant the world to the house and those that lived in it. It's a place that both Agnes and Robert would have been very familiar with.

The walk through the woods is slippery, my footprints filling with water the moment I lift my sodden boot, my soaked hair running in rivulets down my back, rainwater stinging in my eyes. At least the worst of the thunder has shifted beyond the horizon, the sound of the sky gradually dulling with distance. Making my way down the steepest part of a track, I reach out for a sapling. Finding no purchase in the slippery moss-covered trunk, I half slide, half fall the rest of the way and arrive in a silvery puddle whose water soaks right through my jeans.

This had better be a hunch worth following.

The boles look like the kind of ancient ruin you might find in the heart of a jungle, so covered in brambles and weeds that, if you didn't know that they were there, you might almost walk past them, mistaking them for one of the rock formations that make up the cliff at their back. Quite suddenly the rain stops. In a heartbeat, the air is fresh and clean, and a sliver of sunlight brings everything into sharp focus, a kaleidoscope of greens. For the briefest of moments I'm dazzled by the glare of something fiery red, like the flare of an old photograph, and then it's gone, and all I can hear is the rush of the swollen stream gushing towards the reservoir, and the heavy drops of the last of the rain filtering through the trees.

My hands are tangled and scratched by the brambles as I tug them out of the way, reaching into the strange little drystone bee dwellings one by one. Each dark cavern is choked with webs and creeping weeds, but nevertheless I search them for any hidden hiding space or cranny, trying not to think of the many-legged things tickling across the backs of my hands.

Out of the vast green Eden, there's a rush of cold wind, and a great force axes into me, knocking me off of my feet. Tumbling backwards, I slide into the long wet grass, the

Mab regards me with her liver-coloured eyes as if I am the most ridiculous thing that she has ever seen. Perhaps it's because I am smiling.

Out of nowhere, a thought that doesn't seem as if it belongs to me presents itself so clearly I find myself speaking it out loud.

'And now that which cannot be borne, must be borne. That which cannot be borne, must be.'

sky spinning overhead, all the breath knocked and of me. There's a moment before I can breathe in again, and in that moment, just above the ringing in my ears, I think I can hear someone weeping. Is it me? My fingers sink further and further into the boggy mud as I try to gain enough purchase to stand, looking around for whoever or whatever might have landed me to the floor like that. A short, sharp bark sounds and, twisting my head, I see Mab, four paws planted wide, teeth bared, eyes fixed on something in the woods. A flash of something in the foliage and then all is still again.

'Come here, Mab.' I reach for her. 'Come here, girl.'

Obligingly she ponders over, bracing herself as I grab hold of her collar and pull myself onto all fours, flinging my arm over her body, digging into the boggy earth with my left hand to finally push myself free of the sucking mud. Just as I do, my frozen fingertips touch something hard and even colder than I am. Releasing Mab, I dig at the mud, which pools with brown water as soon as I clear a handful away. The iron-scented earth paints my hands and forearms the colour of the hillside, but finally my fingers close around the buried object.

I hear my own groan of effort as I pull free of the ground, falling back onto my rear once again. An old, wide glass jar, covered in thick muck, rests in my lap. Using my sleeve, I smear as much of it away with my hands as I can and see something inside: folded pieces of paper.

3

CHAPTER FORTY-THREE

I can hear Ma in the living room, chatting to Will as he gets ready for bed, so I creep through the kitchen and upstairs to Cathy's room to break the seal on the jar.

The house waits patiently as I go to shower in the cold bathroom. Just as I am about to get in, I catch sight of my face in the mirror; the top half of my face is covered in mud, the lower half just spatters. Hesitantly, I reach out and touch the glass as I realise: I look like one of Agnes's doodled faces. I hurry to wash myself clean in almost freezing water, rapidly changing my clothes, still shuddering even once I'm dry and warmly dressed again. And when I am ready, I set out my equipment and take my position on the floor in the centre of the room, the box bed at my shoulder.

'Are we ready?' I ask the room.

I have no choice but to hack away at the wax seal, which has clearly been inexpertly reapplied at some point during its history, although it has done its job preserving the contents. Under that is what looks like pitch-soaked cloth, bound around the thick neck with twine. Eventually I set aside what I can save of the seal, and, tipping the jar up, let the rolled pages fall into my hands. My heart bursts the moment I see Emily's hand alongside Agnes's. And there is more, another note, two sentences scribbled onto a torn piece of paper.

> *This jar was placed here by I, Robert Heaton, in 1848 at the request of my love and true friend, Emily Jane Brontë. She never cared for me as I for her, but she held good faith in me and I have concealed her work as she bade, and it shall remain concealed for always now that she no longer walks this earth.*

Emily's Robert, my great-great-great-uncle who died unmarried, held this secret close to his heart until his very end ...

Separating out the papers, I focus on Emily's letter, noting how her hand is deteriorating, how the sentences roam across the paper with so little direction that it takes me a few minutes to make sense of the words. As I read, I can almost feel the pain in her chest that came with every breath she took, the fever on her brow, the weakness in her arms, and I want to weep for her stoic refusal to concede to her condition.

> *December*
>
> *Robert, I do not wish to fear death but I do.*
>
> *I fear it, and fight against it with every little ounce of strength I have, I shall <u>will</u> it away, Robert. There is little else that I can now write, and indeed, this story*

pours out of me as if it is being spoken to me by another, and I am simply a scribe.

Charlotte and Anne would wish me to rest more. Papa continues to press the need for a physician to visit which I refuse. I do not wish to rest. I wish for each last moment of my life to be full of living!

Take this second volume. Keep it not with the first, nor with my notes or Agnes's papers. Separate them, spread them far and wide so that they will not be discovered by any who will seek to destroy them. For they are me, Robert. And her. And she who is not yet born, perhaps. But they are not for the eyes of this age that will not recognise a woman's life as having any value.

I am so weak that holding a pen, seeing the words on the page, is often a trial, but I won't be halted until I am done.

But if I should fail, Robert, if death comes to take me before I am ready, then I wish you to know of the deepest gratitude and respect I have for you, dear friend, for the gentle love you have shown me when I have often been cold and haughty, cross and sullen.

I have never loved a man. I love the land, the moors and the sky, my dogs and my animals. I love this land that we live in, the imagination that sweeps me away to other worlds, and I like God well enough. I love my family dearly, but most of all I love life, Robert. I care for it as tenderly as if it were a lover. I wish that it

> *would not spurn me, now, for I do not wish to go. I do*
> *not wish to go. I shall not go.*
>
> *Never forget me*
> *Your EJB*

Underneath her signature she has sketched a copy of the face that appears again and again in Agnes's papers. To read of her fear, her refusal to admit what she knows is happening to her, is heart-breaking, and to see how she realised that what she was writing would not be understood, but that she was determined to write it anyway, sets my heart alight with admiration for her. How Robert must have loved her, never turning from her, no matter how many times she spurned him, never losing faith in how much he loved her, not until the day he died, or beyond. Though she would never love him, he never stopped loving her.

This is what I understand about love, now. Love isn't a transaction; it's not a quid pro quo. It's a force that goes far beyond that, a promise and a vow. It's a declaration that says 'I will always be at your side, even when you are far from mine. I will never leave you without an ally. I am yours.'

Not all my Heaton ancestors have been good. Some were drunks, some were cheats and liars, but this man – this man loved with honour, and there isn't very much more a person can do to make a mark on the world, no matter how tiny it is.

As for his ancestor, Agnes's Robert – did he leave his young lover to her fate or did he return for her? I move to her papers and read on.

It makes no odds what he does to me. I accept it silently, like a good wife, close my eyes and let my mind wander the moors, retracing the paths in the heather and the warm smooth rocks under my back when Robert and I lay together, so perfect in joy that I felt like our love was as much as part of the land as the earth and the rushing water as each other.

But every morning, while he still sleeps, I take the tincture that Betty showed me how to make, so that I may kill any seed of life he might have planted in me.

He will do what he will to me. And I will work to the bone for him, because he has given shelter to me and my babe, but I will not let him bring forth life from me. Life should be made from love, from purity and joy. Not from what he does to me, night after night.

Catherine is my only joy and she is joy enough for a lifetime. She has the look of her father, though none see it but me. And she has hair like mine, as bright as a flame. She is healthy and strong. We see many mothers in the village bury their babes, and all the while Catherine thrives, fattens and grows. Whenever she sees my eyes upon her she smiles in delight. On a Sunday after church, when he is in his cups, I have the greatest joy of taking her to the moors where she may meet her true father, in the clouds in the sky and the whispering wind. I set her down amongst the heather and let her roam, exploring each creature she might find, overturning rocks, discovering pleasure in every inch of mud. She is my delight, my heartbeat, my hope.

Robert is still gone. Betty says they have no word from him, or if they do it is never related to her. Perhaps she speaks the truth, or perhaps she seeks to spare me, imagining me settled and at peace, a wife now, a mother yoked by drudgery. Betty believes that is best, that is safe. But she doesn't know that whatever it is that is keeping Robert from me now, cannot forever resist the great force of our love. He will return to me, because he cannot do otherwise.

And when he does, Catherine and I will be waiting.

In the meantime I will take my tincture and watch my daughter grow, biding my time because I know my time will come.

CHAPTER FORTY-FOUR

Ma sits next to me and we read each sheet silently together, as Will sleeps on the sofa, wrapped in dog. I read a little quicker than her. Having read them once before, my eyes are more used to the old dialect and writing. Sometimes I pause to explain or interpret for her, but there is an unprecedented ease between us, a familiarity that I have never known before. How is it that I have never truly known this woman, my own mother, never really seen her as she is until now? She's been so lonely for so long, even when Dad was alive, even when I was growing up here, caught up in her stiff upper lip, so busy trying to make the best out of a bad situation that it became impossible for her to reach out for love. And I, who have known love as kind and as gentle as it can be, denied the same to her.

Of all the mysteries that seem to circulate in the air around me, this is one I can't fathom at all, and yet it is the one that has given me the greatest cause for hope. Slowly, as she reads, Ma's hand steals into mine and there is a small moment of close calm. A bonding.

Putting aside for one moment the wondrous find of more of Emily Brontë's words, Agnes's story is incredible. Not the details of it, perhaps – the number of vulnerable young women seduced and abandoned to fend for themselves throughout history must be impossible to count – but Agnes is extraordinary because she herself has told it.

Try as I might, I can't think of another story like this, not even the *Autobiography of Mrs Alice Thornton* that Grace mentioned. Alice, who lived around the same time as Agnes and not so far away, was an educated gentlewoman, compelled to write her life story in response to slanderous gossip. Her account of her trials and tribulations in the Civil War was remarkable enough. But that these journals, by a lowborn servant girl, exist seems almost impossible. She must have been a remarkable soul.

'Agnes ...' Ma says her name softly in the candlelight. 'That's not a name you'll find on the family tree. Poor lass.'

'Yes, I know. Somewhere in this house, or on Heaton land, is the rest of Agnes's story and perhaps Emily's retelling of it, or at least part of it. If we find it, we make the greatest literary discovery of our age; we give Emily her voice – and we'll finally know Agnes's story.'

'You say she led you to this?'

'Something led me to it, something more than coincidence. Maybe it's just that Ponden is in my blood, that I know it as well as any Heaton that has ever lived here, and we'd always choose the same places to hide our secrets. Or maybe she is there, in the lights, in the shadows ...' I think for a moment of my hand trapped in the broken bookcase panelling. 'In the dark.'

I nod and shrug at the same time, still finding it rather hard to admit to.

'In my heart, Ma? In my heart I feel like it's her. A mother – a mother who wants her baby back.'

'If it is her, couldn't you just get her to turn up the whole thing all at once and pop it on the table?' Ma asks a little mischievously, glancing expectantly at the table.

'I'm fairly sure that's not how it works,' I say with a small smile. 'But I do know that every other piece we have found has been in the house, or in the grounds. Well, almost every other piece. We simply have to take the house apart looking, Ma. Will you help me?'

'S'pose I'd better,' Ma says. 'You never could find your nose in front of your face as a kid.'

'Mums always find everything,' I say, thinking of Will's words. 'Ma ... I think I had to be grown and a mother myself to see how you struggled, to try and understand what you went through when I was a kid. These days there are names for those feelings, postnatal depression, grief. So many reasons why we might not have been close back then ...'

'Agnes.' Ma speaks across me, chewing at her thumb. Frowning deeply, she gets up and goes into the kitchen, coming back with a torch.

'What are you doing?' I ask her, knocked a little off balance by her change of subject.

'I've just remembered something,' she whispers. 'Follow me.'

'What about Will?'

'He'll be safe with Mab,' Ma says. 'That dog loves him like her own pup. Come on.'

Reluctantly, I follow her into the hallway, propping the door open with a single workman's boot that, as far as I can tell, has no partner. Ma opens up the understairs cupboard, which is full of all the things that have ever been put there and forgotten.

'Are you expecting to find Emily's second novel in some mismatched wellington boots?' I ask her as she tosses rubbish out behind her like some burrowing rodent.

'Don't just stand there, help me, you great lump,' Ma instructs as she unloads the contents into the hall. I can see the crescent of Will's head through the open door and so on I go, moving boxes.

'What are we looking for?' I ask her. 'You haven't got the rest of Emily's book tucked away in here, have you, but you forgot to mention it?'

'You'll see,' Ma says, infuriatingly, and when finally the little cavity is cleared, she bends and, with surprising strength, drags a sheet of wood, an old table top, perhaps, out of the cupboard, revealing the top of a flight of stairs.

'I thought the cellar was sealed up for good?' I say, my mouth dropping open.

'Yes,' Ma says, like this unveiling of a secret room in my house is no big deal. 'But your father did it, and he was never one to put his back into anything much. I made him do it when you were a toddler – I was worried about you falling down the steps. It used to be the meat store, when Agnes lived ... was alive. They'd butcher the animals down there, and hang the meat.'

'Dad sealed the cellar with a table top?' I peer down into the darkness.

'You gone soft in the head or summat? I just told you, didn't I?' Ma says, shaking her head. 'Anyway, I haven't been down here nigh on thirty years, but there is something here that I only remembered just now. Something you are going to want to see.' She shines her torch on the steep, uneven stone steps that seem to tilt forward, 'Perhaps you better go first; I'm not so sure of my legs as I used to be.'

'I'm living in a ghost story and I'm the one who gets to go down first into the cellar armed only with a torch?' I mutter. 'Great.'

And yet there is a sense of elation as I make my descent; a sense of excitement. I never had any idea that this subterranean room was still accessible, and the existence of a secret room is a childhood dream come true, almost like finding a snowy forest at the back of a wardrobe.

The steps are difficult to navigate, but there are only a few. Once at the bottom, I hold out a hand to Ma and guide her down to join me. Shining the torch around, a picture of the room builds up in strips of light. It's small, perhaps twelve square foot with an arching roof, and deep alcoves lined with shelves – and hundreds and hundreds of wide-necked glass bottles and jars, just like the one I brought back from the Bee Boles. As my light sweeps back and forth, I see stacks of dusty plates, the huge metal hooks that hang from the ceiling, and to my right, two thickly overgrown windows.

'How can I never have noticed that there were windows that lead to this room?'

'Don't suppose you'd notice them if you weren't looking,' she says. Each window is covered in thick ivy, parts of which have insinuated themselves through the gaps in the glass and wound their way inside, while a thick, furry moss covers the stone and tints the dirty glass an ancient green.

'Your dad never liked coming down here,' Ma said. 'I didn't mind it so much, and when we were first married we couldn't afford a fridge, so I kept the milk down here, and cheese and such. And one day I was sweeping it out, thinking of turning it into a pantry, when I found this.' She holds out her hand, demanding the torch in a gesture. Wordlessly, I hand it over. 'I remember thinking how strange it was, to find it here, so low down and so roughly hewn ...'

Ma shines the torch on the stone at the bottom of the wall and I bend down to see closer, tracing my hands along each letter, carved with great persistence into the hard stone, perhaps with a nail or another piece of stone. And it spells one word.

AGNES.

As I kneel on the floor, many legged creatures scuttle away from the light, a centipede crawls vertically away from me.

Seeing this simple epitaph here brings me closer to her than anything else – her diary papers, even her apparitions. Perhaps because it pins her to a place, a moment. Maybe even the worst moment of her short life. Here, if I place my fingers in the grooves that she carved out of the stone, grooves that it would have taken many hours, maybe even days to make, I know that I am where she was, and it's almost as if it's her fingertips that feel each rise and irregularity that signifies the very last traces of a life once lived. It is so very human.

'Oh my God,' I say, thinking of the cold and the dark and the fear, the loneliness. 'Do you think they kept her down here, Ma, before her trial? Ma, what if this was the place that she died?'

'It could be her that scratched her name in the stone, or it could have been Robert, I suppose. He were down here too, weren't he? But it's a link, isn't it? Proof that their story is real.'

Leaning on my elbows, I shine the light on the carved letters, too crudely carved to get a sense if it is Agnes's work or not. And then I see, faintly scratched into the stone, a face, the upper half shaded out, just like those I have seen before, drawn into both Agnes's papers and Emily's.

'This is Agnes,' I tell Ma, certain. 'She doodles this weird face thing over and over again. This is her, though I've never worked out what it means.'

The cellar door slams shut and Ma's torch blinks out. At exactly the same moment Mab explodes into ferocious barks, as if she is ten Rottweiler dogs instead of one aged retriever.

'Go,' Ma says, as I feel my way through the dark, soft and sticky insects giving way under my hands as I scramble up the steps, stumbling as I try to find the latch to let me out of the cupboard. Mab's barks becomes high-pitched, and when I finally find the latch I expect the door to offer me resistance, but it doesn't. Instead, I push it open and run into the sitting room where Mab has Marcus Ellis pinned into a corner, her gums drawn back in a ferocious snarl.

'The front door was open,' he says, not taking his eyes off the dog. 'I probably should have knocked?'

Will sits up and, sleepily, rubs his eyes. 'What's going on?'

'Hush now, Mab.' Ma appears behind me, a little out of breath, the torch operational once more. She points it at Marcus, shining it right into his eyes so that he squints.

'Away, Mab,' she says, and reluctantly the dog stands down, circling twice before sitting at Will's side, her eyes still fixed on Marcus.

'You surprised us.' I'm irritated by the way he's just walked into our home. 'I suppose none of us expected you at this time of night, least of all Mab.'

'It's only just gone nine,' Marcus protests.

'Well, we're country people.' Ma fixes him with her best death stare. 'Bed early and up with the larks, that's us.'

'I can see that.' Marcus looks at Will's makeshift sofa bed, and the pile of blankets in my chair, clearly thinking that we are a house full of a lunatics. 'It's just that I got home and all the lights were on and the front door was open. Your bag was still on the table in the library, Trudy, and it was like walking in on the *Marie Celeste* – I was worried that something had happened to you.'

'Oh my God.' I cover my mouth with my hand, my resentment evaporating in an instant. 'I'm so, so sorry. No, nothing bad happened ... unless you count my son finding his way through your secret door in the games room and getting a bit lost, so I was very flustered when I left and I apologise for leaving everything open.'

'Oh no.' Marcus looks mortified. 'I'm so sorry, Trudy, I should have told you about it. When the builders discovered it, I had them preserve it because I thought it was so much fun. I didn't think about Will finding it and going exploring. I underestimated you, hey, Will?'

''Spose,' Will says.

'It was a bit hairy for a moment, actually,' I say.

'As long as you are both OK?' Marcus looks from me to Will, avoiding making eye contact with Ma.

'Yeah, fine,' I say, uncertain of exactly why I wish he would go right away. It's hardly fair, especially when I did leave his house wide open, exposed to the elements or any passing burglar. 'Look, can I make you a cup of tea in the kitchen, while Will gets settled back to sleep? We're not sleeping upstairs at the moment because ... well, it's taking him a while to get used to this old place; he likes us to all be together.'

'Right.' Marcus accepts both that excuse and my offer or tea, even though Ma scowls at me as I lead him into the kitchen.

'So, did you find anything interesting in my priceless library before you ran away, leaving the door open?' Marcus asks me, as we wait for the whistle of the kettle.

'I am so, so sorry,' I repeat myself, idly wondering if the whisky in that bottle on the shelf that's been there since before Dad died would still be drinkable. 'Once we arrived home I got the news that they'd found part of the plane my husband was in when it crashed, and everything else went out of my head. I should have gone back, or called you at least.'

I turn back to him and muster a smile.

'Can you forgive me?'

'Oh, Trudy, I'm so sorry. Of course the last thing you were thinking about was me. And of course I forgive you. Can you forgive me and my house?'

'Your house is quite duplicitous,' I say, 'but of course I do. Nothing that happened was your fault.'

'Good.' Marcus smiles. 'Because where else am I going to find someone with your experience and qualifications to catalogue my library? Will you come back again tomorrow? I'll be there most of the day.'

'Yes,' I say, but my tone is uncertain. When I think about the castle, I feel a certain disquiet, something concrete and real that shouldn't be ignored. And yet ... what if there are other traces of Agnes or the Heatons concealed there? 'I should be able to. Can I let you know?'

'Of course.' He seems a little disappointed, and I suppose it must be lonely, the only living creature in that great glass edifice. 'Well, I'm back to Scotland on Monday, and then I'll be back by Thursday and I'll have some time off before we start work here.'

'Great,' I say, but even to me my enthusiasm sounds strained.

'This is such a wonderful old building,' he says, looking around the sitting room, reaching his hand up to touch one of the beams. 'I've been in love it with for such a long time. And to be part of its restoration? It's very special. It feels like a part of it belongs to me now ... Anyway, I'd better get back,' he says, ruffling his fair hair. 'See you soon, Tru.'

As I watch the brake lights of his car disappear down the lane, Ma comes and stands at my shoulder.

'He's a strange sort,' she says.

'He's kind; I like him,' I say, with a shrug.

'Funny, I've never met someone I'd like to flat-out punch in the mug as much.'

I can't help but laugh.

CHAPTER FORTY-FIVE

The morning wakes us gently, the first light of dawn rousing us at around seven thirty. Will rolls off of the sofa and into my arms on the floor, where I'd made a camp bed, burying his head in my pillow. I hold him, inhaling the scent of sleep in his hair and the sweetness of his breath.

Ma swears under her breath as she gets out of her chair, muttering, and she retreats into the kitchen to set the fire and wash and dress. As for me, I'm content just to lie here, to be in that moment with my son for as long as I can, and as I hold him, I think of Abe, and how gentle he was, always, from the first moment I kissed him, to the last day when he hugged me goodbye. There had been times in our twenty years of knowing each other that I hated him – times he hurt me, times we both despaired – but never once had he ever been cruel, or rough. And it strikes me that the fact that I have known someone in this world who has treated me with such care is a rare privilege.

If there could be just one more moment, just one more, to hold him, to feel his smile against my skin, to touch his dear face with my fingertips and thank him for every little joy he brought me, just one more moment, then … then … I stop myself, and look at Will, my hopeful son, his heart full of light. Not if, but when. Until I know exactly what happened to my husband I will always believe that there will be a when.

'Are you crying, Mummy?' Will's green eyes are watching me and he takes my face in his hands. 'You *are* crying.'

'Sorry.' I muster a smile for him. 'Not so much crying as leaking feelings.'

He winds his arms around my neck and pulls me closer.

'I miss him too, Mummy; I miss him so much. It's OK to cry, remember? You told me it was OK to cry and feel sad. But everything is going to be OK.'

He pats my back, just as I pat his when he is sad.

'You know, you are a lot like your daddy,' I tell him, inhaling the scent of his skin. 'Just as kind and clever and brave as him. I feel very lucky to be your mummy.'

'You *are* lucky,' Will says, pulling away from me so I can see his small smile.

'There's tea,' Ma says, shuffling into the living room. 'Toast, if you want it, or cake.'

'Cake for breakfast?' I half laugh.

'I want cake,' Will says, and in a moment he is gone, with Mab close at his heels.

'I been thinking.' Ma leans on the back of the sofa as she talks. 'If we've got to search the whole house, then we need to get the rest of the crap out of it and me and Will can make a start on that today.'

'This cake is great, Granny.' Will returns, talking as he munches. 'Your best yet.'

Ma spits on a hanky that she has retrieved from her sleeve and begins vigorously cleaning Will's horrified face.

'But what I was thinking,' she says, once she's released him, 'is that maybe you could take us all into town? We could do with a few bits to make the place feel more homely; what do you think, Will?'

'I want a telly,' Will says very seriously. 'And an Xbox.'

Which is why, a couple of hours later, Ma sits stiffly in the passenger seat, in an old emerald-green raincoat buttoned up to the neck, and a peach-coloured headscarf tied under her chin. Will and Mab are in the back, Will struggling to put a seat belt on the aged dog, who doesn't share his concern with road safety.

'Will, just put *your* belt on,' I say. 'Mab will be fine.'

'But if we crash she'll hit Granny in the back of the head with the force of an elephant!' Will told me. 'I saw it on YouTube.'

'I'll take my chances,' Ma says, glancing at me. 'Well, are you going to drive somewhere or are we going to sit here like lemons, freezing our knackers off?'

'Is "knackers" a rude word?' Will asks me as I pull off down the potholed little road.

'I'm not completely sure,' I say. 'Let's say yes to be on the safe side.'

'I want a telescope, too,' Will says. 'The stars are much clearer here than they used to be in London.'

'In Haworth you're more likely to get some lovely Brontë-themed cushions and a nice lampshade or two,' I tell him, but that doesn't seem to dampen his enthusiasm. Parking behind the Parsonage, I wait while Ma steps out of the car, taking a moment to straighten up.

'I'll take Mab to the pub where I'm meeting Grace,' I say. 'I'll see you in an hour. And Ma, please don't wave that bag of cash around too much.'

I watch them for a moment, my skinny, awkward mother, and my excited little boy, hopping at her side, and a rush of pleasure floods my chest. This is the best of us, I think. Ma and Will, making friends, is the best of what it means to be human. Making a family, when there was none. Forgiving, hoping, loving, despite it all.

Ma, me and Will. We may never be complete again, but still we have each other.

CHAPTER FORTY-SIX

Despite its fame – or infamy – for being the place that Branwell Brontë was most likely to get drunk in, the Black Bull is almost empty, and it's easy to find Grace, sitting in the window, her long brown hair braided over one shoulder, a deep-green sweater setting off her hazel eyes.

'Thank you for meeting me on your day off,' I say, after I've ordered a coffee and sat down. Mab, a little restless to not be with her boy, paces about and whimpers at the door.

'No problem at all.' Her eyes sparkle and she rubs her hands together. 'When you said what you'd found, I couldn't wait! Did you bring the ...' she glances around furtively '... items with you.'

'I did.' Taking the jar and the pages, each one now protected by a clear folder, out of my bag, I hand them to Grace. She reads them, transfixed.

'This is remarkable.' Grace reads the final page one last time and when she looks up at me there are tears in her eyes. 'This is incredible.'

'I couldn't wait to show it to you,' I say, smiling to see the light in her eyes. 'And I believe, more than ever, that Emily's

Robert Heaton hid the volumes, at least two, anyway, in the house – and, hopefully, the rest of Agnęs's story. My ma and I are clearing out all the other rooms to have a good look for them, and maybe, if we're lucky, she will show us where to look.'

'Pardon?' Grace's smile falters for a moment.

'I ... Oh.' I feel the heat in my cheeks as I cast about for something to say that doesn't make me sound insane to a normal person, or rather a person who isn't a Heaton. 'I mean ... Well, working up at the Parsonage, you must know how it is. I expect you get so immersed with the Brontë sisters that you feel like you know them. You must feel as if they are there with you, right? Because their words, the letters ... they all come off the page and *live*. I know it's silly and romantic, but that's how I feel about these pages. I see Emily and Agnes as if they are in the room with me, talking to me.'

'Oh yes, I totally understand that,' Grace agrees, nodding. 'I feel they are there with me, in the same room, peering over my shoulder to see what I'm up to.'

She laughs, and I laugh, but I'm not so sure it's a joking matter.

'So, as well as searching the house for the world's greatest-ever literary find, I'm going back to Castle Ellis to finish my work there for Marcus; that will take weeks, but perhaps I'll find something else about Agnes in the records. He has no idea what he has in that library and I'm sure he'd want to return the parish records to the church or a museum, once he knows.'

Grace is silent for a moment, then: 'I'm not so sure about that, to be honest.'

'Really?' I'm surprised at the expression that has frosted over her features. 'He seems like such a nice man, and so keen on local history and the Brontës. I'm sure he'd want anything of public interest to be available to … well, the public.'

'Sadly, that's not the case. Sometimes Marcus Ellis bids against the Parsonage for the things that we want, and prices us out. We lost one of the miniature books to him last year.'

'Really?' I sit back a little in my chair. 'That doesn't sound like Marcus.'

'Well, there are two schools of thought,' Grace says carefully. 'The more charitable of these is that when a collector becomes obsessed with something, they simply must have it, even if it means denying it to the public.'

'I didn't really get the impression that he was that keen a collector, more that he just wanted to fill his library,' I say thoughtfully. 'But to outbid the Parsonage seems … not very gentlemanly.'

'Precisely,' Grace says.

'So, what's the other reason that he might be buying up all this stuff?' I ask.

'Tax fraud.' Grace laughs, but there is little mirth in it. 'Personally, I think it has more to do with obsession, to be honest; he's got that look about him. You know what I mean? A bit fanatic.'

I burst out laughing and shake my head.

'There *is* something a little offbeat about him,' I say. 'But fanatical? I don't get that vibe at all.'

'Well, I expect you are right and I'm just being a cow.' Grace shifts uncomfortably in her seat. 'Look, just do me one favour, will you? Don't tell him about these finds. Not until you've completed your research and established the provenance, OK?'

'You know, it had never occurred to me to tell anyone, apart from Ma and you, I don't know why. But I promise not to talk about it to anyone else yet.'

Mab noses her muzzle under my hand, whimpering and pacing back towards the door, a clear instruction that I should be moving on now, thank you very much.

'Well, be ready,' Grace says, smiling now. 'Everything you've found so far is enough to change your life completely – there could be a book, an exhibition, a documentary – you might end up famous!'

'I don't know about famous,' I say. 'More than anything I just want to show the world what we've found, because isn't it wonderful? And isn't it miraculous that there are still treasures to be found, still stories waiting to be told. Knowing that feeds my hope.'

'You're right,' Grace says. 'These two women's voices were cut off too soon, and you will be able to make them heard again. That *is* a kind of magic.'

1659

Praise God! Praise God, for at last he has given me light in all this darkness and I see an end to my suffering. I am not allowed to go to Ponden, no matter how I might try. John does not know the true father of Catherine, but he suspects it might be one of the Ponden men, and has told me that the day I return to the hall will be the day he beats every last tooth from my head and I believe him. Even so, I would go back if I thought there was need, but there is not. Whenever she is able, Betty sends word with her brother, Timothy, to tell me she will meet me at Ponden Kirk, and whenever I am able, Cathy and I meet her there. She tells me what little news there is, and it is often the same. Mistress Casson hovers ever closer to her death and little John Casson grows but weakly, and in fear of his father, and there was no word of Robert until this day.

I went into the village to buy flour and saw the Ponden wagon bound for the clothier. I stopped dead in the street and stared at it, with Catherine's arms around my neck, and I knew not why. For I have seen it a dozen times or more in the last months and never given it a thought. But it was as if my heart could feel him near. So I went, almost as if in a trance, to the door of the merchant, and peered within. And there he was. My Robert.

This last long year had changed him much. Not the fair boy I last kissed, but a man, tall and broad and strong, stood there. A good coat on his back and sturdy shoes. A man who looked like a match for Casson.

My Robert, my Robert. And I knew that he must feel me, as I felt him. So I waited outside, though Catherine grew heavy, and at any moment John might stalk down the hill to search for me.

And sure enough, as he exited, holding his hat in his hands, Robert's eyes met mine at once. And I saw it there, burning as bright as the sun that never sets. I saw his love for me, and oh, how I thank thee God for bringing my Robert back. We did not speak; we could not, with all about to witness. But as he climbed back onto the wagon, his eyes never left me, nor Catherine. His gaze fixed hard upon us until the wagon rolled over the hill and he was gone.

Such joy, all at once. Such hope.

For what does a false marriage to a false man like John Bolton matter when a true marriage like Robert's and mine exists in the world? God brought him back to me for a reason, and in doing so has brought me back to God. I stole into the church and knelt and prayed for as long as Catherine slept, and as I left, searched out more paper and more ink, knowing that the story I began so long ago, as an ignorant servant girl, is far from over yet.

Agnes Heaton

PART SIX

Though earth and moon were gone,
And suns and universes ceased to be,
And Thou were left alone,
Every existence would exist in Thee.

Emily Brontë

CHAPTER FORTY-SEVEN

There's an uncanny silence blanketing Castle Ellis like new snow as I step out of the car. No wind, no birdsong, and even the crunch of my feet on the gravel seems muted. The great fountain hasn't run for a long time, but if it had, I get the distinct impression that the water would have flowed soundlessly today.

Marcus's car is not in the driveway, and that suits me. As unsettling as I find this strange, disjointed building, I feel a profound need to have his library, his archives, all to myself, to lose myself in an ocean of thought.

Unlocking the door, I push against it and walk through the glass corridor into the main house. That feeling I always have in Cathy's room, the feeling of eyes upon me, is strong, and I feel my steps slow and my movements become more mannered and self-conscious in response.

I'm surprised to see that Marcus has left all the lights on, and the heating, too, so the floor is warm under my feet as I slip off my boots. My socked feet make no sound on the tiles as I pad towards the library.

The first thing I notice is that the door to the games room stands open, and that the giant screen flickers white light across the floor. There are so many switches that I press at least ten before the flickering screen turns to black, and the room falls into wintery shadow. Being in the room where I lost my son makes me shudder, and I have to resist the urge to retreat. There really is no sign of a secret door in the wall and I can't decide if having something so hidden, within such a childlike room, is charming or slightly creepy.

Curiosity overrides reticence and I reach for the model, and the hidden door clicks open, revealing the lobby behind. As I walk into the small space, lights splutter on overhead, and I tense for a moment, before I realise they are motion activated. It's cold in here, and there's a feeling of an entrance somewhere above that is open to the elements, but it is alluring, the old spiral staircase, perfect for swordfights and rescuing maidens.

Slowly, my hand tracing the curve of the wall, I begin to climb the stairs that swirl all the way up to the turret. There is a vacant doorway where the first floor would once have been. Peering down, I see a drop of several feet, the bottom of the turret overgrown with ferns and grasses, creeping up the walls. When I look up, I see something I didn't expect.

Marcus told me there were no floors in the turret any more and, sure enough, the second and third floors are completely gone, but high up there's what looks like relatively new boarding across what would be the top floor.

So there *is* a room up there, after all. But why would he keep that a secret?

Somewhere above me the sound of a door slamming echoes down the spiral and I start, almost slipping into the empty space beyond the doorway, grabbing for the stone and pulling myself to safety. Footsteps are approaching.

Panicking, I scuttle back down the steps as lightly as I am able in my socked feet, pressing the door shut behind me as I skid across the playroom floor to the library door, reaching it just as Marcus emerges from the games room.

'Trudy?' He smiles as he sees me half in and half out of the library. 'How long have you been here?'

'I just arrived,' I say, trying to smile away the vague sense of unease that the sight of Marcus in his own home has inspired. 'You made me jump! Your car wasn't out front so I thought that you'd already left for Scotland.'

'Ah, no. I took it round the back to unload some firewood. Sorry I scared you.'

'Not at all. I love it here.' I glance into the library longingly.

'Come and have a cup of tea with me? I have half an hour to kill before I leave for the border.' He holds out a hand to me, and uncertain of what else I can possibly do, I take it, letting him lead me away from the books and to his kitchen.

*

'So, how are things?' Marcus pours me a perfect cup of clear Earl Grey as we sit at his polished counter.

'Things are … Well, you know.' I shrug and smile, squirming a little under his mild gaze, trying to square this man with the version Grace talked about. 'And you?'

Marcus sighs, staring into his mug.

'Honestly? I am so busy most of the time that I don't notice how solitary my life is. And then I have a day like yesterday, a whole day with nothing to do, and it hits me kind of hard, rattling around in this great big folly. What's it all for if there isn't anyone there to love you and care for you, hey?'

His grey eyes are heavy with sadness and I feel his loneliness sharply.

'I'm sorry,' I say, reaching my hand out across the black onyx counter. 'But you know, you must be one of Yorkshire's most eligible bachelors, with your amazing job and incredible house.'

He smiles and takes my fingers in his, pressing them lightly. 'I wish I'd met you in another life, Trudy.'

'I … oh.' I withdraw my hand, unable to meet his gaze.

'I'm sorry,' Marcus says. 'I never meant to actually say that out loud.'

'Look, maybe I should go …'

'No, don't.' He stands up as I do. 'Don't go. This house – at least, this library – feels as if it was meant for you, so please don't go. More than anything I want and value a friend in my life. So please don't go; in any case, I have to get going now, so it would be foolish of you to leave on my account.'

'If you're sure?' I say.

'Of course I am sure,' he replies.

For one excruciating moment I don't know what to do and so I hug him, and he hugs me back, and I feel sorry, because he is kind and lonely, and I can't bear to make him feel even more sad.

'I'll see you in a few days,' he says, smiling.

I stand in the hallway after he has closed the door. He's been nothing but sweet and understanding, and yet there is a kind of disquiet left in his wake, a deep unsettling. Shaking the feeling away, I turn on my heel and head for the library. At least you always know where you are with books.

CHAPTER FORTY-EIGHT

Alone in the library I switch on all the lights and stand under the towering shelves of books, gazing upwards at the mosaic of spines, each one a doorway to somewhere else in time.

The box with the fragment of pamphlet that I discovered on my last visit is still on the table. It's my first port of call as I check it once again, just in case I missed something, but there is nothing new.

If there are more traces of Agnes to be found amongst this vast array of books and papers, they will be impossible to find without sifting through every book and record, one by one, and that could take months.

There's no system to how this collection is displayed at all; the books were just put on the shelves in the order they came out of the boxes that Marcus had stored them in. If that's the way they went in, I have to assume they are displayed roughly in the order in which they were acquired.

It was instinct that led me to that first box, instinct perhaps driven by something more, but, either way, it worked, so let the Heaton in me decide where to look next.

Walking up to the first landing, I reach out with my left hand and, looking away from the books, run my fingers along the spines, looking for something, anything that will reach out in return. When my fingers uncover the heart-shaped dip that characterises an Ottoman binding, I pull out a dirty-red leather-bound book.

When I open the title page, I gasp in recognition. The volume is entitled *The Man of Mode: or Sir Fopling Flutter. A comedy*, and it was one of the books listed in the Ponden Library sale catalogue, dated 1735; I remember the title because it was so incongruous and silly. Holding my breath, I open it to its title page, and, sure enough, there is something I thought I would never set eyes on.

A Ponden Library bookplate. Black and white, block printed, a roughly hewn image of the house and the name Heaton inscribed below it.

This is one of the lost Ponden books, the books that were stolen from under our noses, and it's *here*, right here.

My heart picks up speed as I carefully turn the pages, looking for a sign of Emily or Agnes – and find nothing.

Wait! If the books were unpacked together then there is a chance that there are more Ponden books here, that some of them may have stayed together after they vanished from the house. There might be more languishing in this collection.

The rest of the world fades out of focus as I concentrate on the task in hand. One by one I take every book to the left and the right of *The Man of Mode* off of the shelf. Although it was only a few days since I was looking at the sale catalogue, I can remember very few of the actual titles, so I check every one and, sure enough, every third or fourth book is a Ponden Hall book, complete with bookplate.

The Art of Love by Ovid, dated 1647.

A New System of Modern Geography: OR, A Geographical, Historical and Commercial grammar, AND Present State of the Several Kingdoms of the World by William Guthrie, dated 1792.

The Arts of Logik and Rhetorick, partly taken from Bouhours, with new Reflections, &c. by John Oldmixon, 1728.

Collecting as many as I can comfortably carry, I take them down to the long reading table and lay them, face out, in long rows, repeating the task again and again, minutes turning into hours.

When I am done, I count two hundred and thirty-seven books. Not the entire library by any means, but a large chunk of it. Many of these books would have been on the shelves at Ponden when Agnes was teaching herself to read and write, and all were there until the day that Emily's Robert Heaton died.

The only two books that I can remember from the list that aren't here, though, are the First Folio and *The Birds of America*. It would have been quite a thrill to discover several millions of pounds worth of priceless books lying forgotten amongst this collection.

It's wrong, 100 and twenty years later, to feel so angry at seeing our stolen books here, uncared for and unrecognised, and yet I do. I can't believe that Marcus knew he had these in his library; if he had, he would have told me. And yet ... It seems like an impossible coincidence. That little thread of unease tightens in my chest once again, but no, I push it away. Right now, Marcus isn't here. It's just me and my books.

Slipping on my gloves, I sit down before the great pile of books and I begin to look between every page. As the light dips down beneath the hills, and the clock ticks on the wall, I move from one book to the next, knowing that Agnes would have turned the pages of these books, that Emily would have chosen them and taken them to sit in front of the fire in Cathy's bedroom with, pouring over every drop of knowledge she could glean. And I imagine those two women, who lived hundreds of years apart, yet who trod the same boards, touching the same pages, standing over my shoulder, watching me as I work, waiting a little impatiently.

Then, in the fraction of a second that passes before I pick it up, I know that I have found what I'm looking for: a very old book, its leather cover blackened by age and neglect. When I open it, despite my care, the title page flutters out onto the desk, a black-and-white woodcut print that proclaims the title, *Britain's Remembrancer*, along a great unfurling banner, beneath which ships sail on a stormy sea; and above, battles wage and cherubs fight, all presided over by representations of Truth and Justice. Beneath that the author, one George Wither, and the date, 1628.

With precise care I insert the title page back where it belongs, with half an idea of searching out a bookbinder to preserve it, before I remind myself that these books don't belong to the Heatons any more, which stings a little, I have to say. A little further examination of this philosophical and political book that seems to muse on the state of pre-Civil War Britain, and it's easy to see why the binding is coming apart so easily. It's not just because it's very old; it's because someone has cut away the endpapers, inserted something within, and glued it back with a larger piece of paper from another book altogether. My cotton-gloved fingers feel along the ridge in the paper, much thicker than it should be, and gently press down on the brittle glue, hoping that, perhaps, newer papers might just come away without me having to try and unstick it. No such luck.

Weighing the book in my hand, I agonise over what to do. If it still belonged to the Heatons I'd take a scalpel to these imposter endpapers, carefully separating them from the boards without hesitation. Old books are often rebound, and it's not so much the binding that matters, as the history that each incarnation provides. But this is not my book and I have no way of knowing if what's concealed under there has anything to do with Emily or Agnes. The only way to know is to look. And to look without asking Marcus's permission is wrong. Except … except he has no idea what is in his library. I could just take a peak and put it back and he would never know I'd looked.

One, two, three taps of my pen on the table top – and then I put it in my bag.

1659

I waited in the dark until the house was quite still. Cold bit at my cheeks and toes. I'd left my babe asleep with John Bolton, and left my house, and it might be discovered at any moment that I was not present, but still I had left because I had to see Robert. I had to lay my eyes and hands and lips on him once again.

Finally, all was silent. The dogs slept, the lights were snuffed out. Going roundabout I found the entrance at the kitchen open and old Keeper, Robert's hound, stretched out in front of the fire. He did not stir as I passed. Betty slept in her cubbyhole and I stopped for a moment to look on her, and wonder at why she had not got word to me that Robert was back. For almost all my life I have loved and trusted her, above all others, she being something like a mother to me, but on this one subject she has held back again and again. She supposes that now I am married to John Bolton I am no longer free, but she does not understand love, nor what it means for one soul to be cleaved to another in such a way as Robert's and mine. She seeks to protect me from harm, I don't doubt, but she injures me to keep me from my love.

Quiet as a ghost, as a spirit, I climbed the staircase of Ponden Hall, my frozen feet bare so that I may make no more sound than a whisper as I travel. At last, as I stood outside the room where he slept, my heart felt as if it might burst with feeling. Slowly, I approached the box bed, not wanting to startle him, searching in the dark for the door that closed it away.

When I opened the door, though, all happiness, all joy, all hope, died.

For before my eyes I saw Robert, sleeping peacefully, and alongside him another woman.

A great sense of shock and grief took hold of me, and I could not move my feet. This vision that I saw was so unlike what I had dreamed that I could not perceive that it was real. So I stood and stared, like a fool waiting to be caught, without a thought to what would become of me, or Catherine, should I be found in Robert's chamber, with no purpose or reason to be there.

It must have been that he felt me near, for Robert alone woke. Seeing me, he sat bolt upright, smothering a cry, and stared at me in return until he could understand that I was not a vision, that I was really present.

At once he leapt out of bed, and taking my arm, rushed me down and through the house and out of the front door, and in a great hurry, bore me down the path to the bee boles where it was perfectly dark.

He was the first to speak.

'Agnes.' He said my name and it was the most beautiful music I have ever heard, for I knew when he said it that he still loved me and not the woman in his bed.

'You are back,' I said. 'You never did come to claim me, Robert; you left me to marry another man to protect your child. That woman who lies with you ... who is she?' I asked, though my heart knew full well.

'Betty sent word to tell me you were married,' Robert whispered, his eyes never leaving me. 'I meant to come to you, but there was no escape. Casson wanted me gone. He rode with me himself and put me on a boat to Ireland. Once on board I had no way, no means, to return until he deemed it so. I thought you were lost to me forever, Agnes. And in truth, you are. So I – I married. Mary is a good and kind woman, sweet and deserving of a good husband.'

'I am deserving of a good husband,' I said to him. 'I, who you left with your child growing within. I, who was forced into marrying a man I cannot abide to give our daughter a roof and a name. You left me, and did not think of what would befall me while you were away.'

'Not true.' That is what he said, stepping ever closer to me. 'Not true! I thought of you with every waking breath and in every dream. I failed you, Agnes, I was weak and undeserving of you, but I love you still.'

He put his arms around me, his mouth on mine, and his hands all about me, in and out of my garments, and, so help me God, it was so sweet and so full of delight that it took me all that I had to stay his rovings and step away.

'We cannot,' I told him. 'Though you are my true husband, we can no longer lie with one another as you desire. It is against God's will.'

'Damn the God that keeps us apart,' Robert said with such force that I saw that he was no longer the boy that I had lost, but a man now.

'Would you lie with me, Robert?' I asked him.

'I would,' he replied.

'Then you and I must find a way to be rid of those that shackle us. We must find a way to be together, Man and Wife, as we should be.'

'What way is there that isn't murder?' Robert asked me, and I spoke no words for a long time. I weighed it carefully, that which I knew and had kept too close to myself for all these long years. I weighed the risk of revealing against the longing to have what should be mine by right.

'I know something about Henry Casson,' I told him. 'Something we may use to force him to help us. I have known it since I was a child and kept it safe my whole life for fear that he would murder me if I did not, but I am a frightened child no more, and, with you by my side, to protect me, I believe that what I know may hold sway over him. Something that he will wish to keep secret, knowing that I was witness to his dreadful deed. I fear him no longer, and I, with the knowledge I have, believe he may be willing to direct the church to dissolve your marriage to keep his own neck from the rope.'

'My wife, she has done nought to deserve this ...'

'I am your wife,' I said, with such fury and grief that he took me in his arms, and held me until I was still once more, though I fought against him.

'You are! You are my true wife.' He spoke the words again and again until at last I was calm. 'What do you know?' Robert asked me, and I could see that he was afraid.

'Before I tell you, swear to me that you love me, Robert. Swear to me that never again will you let Henry Casson or any other come between you and I and that you will do all that is necessary to put right what is wrong.'

'I swear it, Agnes.' He held me tight against him. 'I swear it on our child's life.'

'Henry Casson killed your father,' I said. 'He murdered him.'

He stared at me as though I were the Devil, face as white as the Lord on the Cross.

'I will kill him! He has taken everything from me. He has taken it all.'

'You need not kill him,' I told him. 'But you must break free of him and the shackles he has put on you. I will kill him, Robert. I will kill him.'

Then Robert was upon me, with such lust and such fury and passion as I have never known, and after many long months of loneliness and anguish we were as one again. As we lay in the grass, looking up at the moon, he turned to me and asked me when I discovered this crime, and how.

Twas only then I realised that he did not comprehend what I had said before.

'I have always known it, Robert,' I told him. 'I have always known, because I saw him do it with my very own eyes.'

'And you never spoke of it to me?' His voice was dark as midnight, and for a moment I was afraid of him.

'I could not,' I said. 'And you know why. I was so afraid of him, knowing that at any moment he might snuff out my life *in an instant and then you ... you were lost to me. If you do not love me now, then tell me and I will go back to Bolton and live the rest of the days of my miserable life under his fist. But tell me, Robert, if you love me no longer.'*

I'd held my breath, felt the terror of losing him again as sharp as a knife in my gut.

'But I do love you, Agnes,' he said. 'What am without you, but half a man? I believe you. I'll talk to Henry Casson, for what I say holds weight and he knows it.'

Now I wait for Robert to do his part, to go to Casson and command him to have his marriage dissolved if he wishes his sins to be held quiet. And I shall do mine. And all that I have wished for shall be mine at last. And perhaps God will cast me out of his heart for what we are willing to do. Even so, it is a price I am willing to pay for my love.

CHAPTER FORTY-NINE

'You well?' Ma asks me as I return.

'Quite well,' I reply, hesitant. 'Why?

'You're clutching your bag to your chest like you stole it,' she says, eyeing me up and down.

'I suppose I sort of did.' Taking the wrapped book out of the bag, I open it to the title page and rest it on the table. 'Look, Ma.'

'A Ponden book!' Ma bends as she peers at the bookplate, following each rise and fall of the design. 'You found one.'

'I found more than two hundred,' I said.

'He's the one that stole the Ponden books?' Ma scowls. 'I knew I didn't like him.'

'Well, hardly him personally, Ma, it was a hundred and twenty years ago they went missing. But yes, I would like to know how they got there. See, here where it bulges? This one has something hidden under the endpapers.'

'So you're going to have a look?' Ma nods encouragingly. 'Go on, then.'

'Well no, I need time and my tools and, strictly speaking, I'm vandalising someone else's property.'

'No, you ain't,' Ma says. 'Those books were stolen. Even if Mr Fancy Pants bought them off of someone, they still belong to us. It's the law, love. And the provenance is pretty clear, wouldn't you say?'

'Really?' I look down at the book. 'So this is a homecoming?'

'You want to get all those books and bring them back here,' Ma says. 'Me and Will finished clearing out the three small rooms, and I had a good look, best as I could, all round them, but I can't get down on the floor like you, so you'll want to check them too. I made a steak pie for dinner. Build you up a bit.'

'Where is Will?' I ask.

'In the bath. Mab's up there with him. Hopefully not in the bath, though she could do with one. We both of us got covered in muck and dust, so I thought I'd better wash him.'

'Right, I'll check on him,' I say.

'And then get opening up that book,' Ma says. 'You've got time. I'll shout you when dinner's ready.' She nods, leaning in a little closer. 'I want to talk to you, Tru, tell you something important.'

'OK,' I say, hesitantly. 'Are you OK, Ma?'

'I will be,' she says. 'Now, go on with you; check that Mab isn't in the tub with our boy.'

Will is dried and snug in his PJs and Mab is somewhat damp but very waggy-tailed as they head off downstairs to see what Ma is up to. Holding the book under my arm, I stand at the top of the stairs for a moment, closing my eyes, trying to read Ponden. Somehow, I thought I'd find Agnes's unhappiness in the atmosphere, that longing and cold isolation. But it's not Ponden that apparitions haunt, it's me. I don't know if it's Will, or how things are between Ma and I, but this house is as full of light and love and warmth as I remember it when I was a very little girl, playing hide-and-seek with my dad. Which means my son is safe, and it's up to me, and me alone, to conclude this story.

It makes the most sense to examine the book properly in Cathy's room. Here there is room to work, and the best light – at least if I sit right under the bulb. And besides, this place meant something to Agnes and Emily. Parts of both of their stories were written here.

Sitting cross-legged on the floor, I set out my book pillow, page-turner and scalpel.

Taking a deep breath, I wait a moment for my hand to stop trembling before opening the book to the backboard. Picking up my scalpel I immediately put it down again. What I'm about to do to this book is sacrilege, something I find deeply uncomfortable. What I should do is apply a special poultice to the glue that will dissolve it without damaging the paper, so that, very gradually, over a period of days, I will be able to peel the added paper away, and so preserve it as an important part of the book's history. I know that's what I should do, and I know how to do it – and yet there is no time for the care that this book deserves. I have to butcher it as gently as I can.

So I pick up the scalpel again, and this time I cut. Slowly and with precision, retaining as much of the paper as I am able, I cut it away. And revealed beneath it, folded neatly in half, are more pages of Agnes's writing and two further pages of the Ponden Witch Pamphlet. And something more, something written onto the backboard of the book itself.

With trembling hands I take the cheap and flimsy printed paper out and set it to one side, and then I see them. Underneath where the papers were stored are a series of simple hieroglyphs, inked onto the board.

An eye.

And ... and a thumbprint made in red ink, a face drawn into it. This image that returns again and again, from one age to another. Agnes draws it, Emily – I did as a little girl – and now Emily's Robert Heaton. It must be a part of Agnes's story, perhaps related to how she died, to how she feels. Perhaps she's been showing this to me my whole life, and to others for many lives before mine, waiting for someone to understand what it means.

Beneath it, one word; one word that seems to be embedded into the card rather than written.

Look.

CHAPTER FIFTY

Within these pages a true relation of the barbarous murders committed by Agnes Bolton upon the persons of her husband, John Bolton, and her infant daughter, Catherine Bolton, only one year of age. And how she did use poison upon her husband, saying he died a natural death and had his body buried, until upon the violent death of her child at her own hands it was brought up again, and it was found that he had been killed by the witch, who wished to sacrifice her husband, and even her child, to Satan, that she would be brought great riches and power beyond measure.

Written in Caution to all Graceless Persons.

How terrible it must have been for Agnes to lose her baby to a terrible end and then face this accusation. The legend of the tiny ghost child, its baby hands scratching at the window by the box bed, crying to be let in, feels suddenly viscerally real, and then I understand.

Agnes, wherever she is, is not with her child.

All that Agnes wants is that which any mother who loves her child would: she wants to comfort her baby, the Ponden child crying in the dark.

And there is something in the air, not a sound, or a movement, but *something*. Some disturbance in the atmosphere that is something like a great letting out of air, something like a sigh of loss and longing.

There are tears in my eyes, tears that don't belong to me as I turn to the next page.

On this day, 3 October, The Year of our Lord 1659, Mistress Agnes Bolton was tried before the Constable Henry Casson, with the charge of double murder by witchery. That she did poison her husband with Devil's brew and dash out the brains of her child as a sacrifice to the Devil. And that she did curse the neighbour's cow. And that she did wish the death of her former mistress, Anne Casson, and so it did happen. And that she did dance naked under the moon to seduce good local men into her thrall. And that she did seek to blight the health of all that had crossed her, including the young and godly wife of Master Robert Heaton, who she hated with a jealous rage.

At the trial Mistress Agnes Bolton did proclaim her innocence at every turn and shouted over every testimony, crying and claiming to mourn for her poor, pitiful child, but none put any stock in her wailings.

She was found guilty and sentenced to hang the next day.

And yet in the night-time the Devil did come to claim his own, and she was taken from the Black Bull Inn where she was locked away, and escaped. And many say they did see her on the Devil's back, flying away across the sky, shrieking and howling and laughing at her evil and fiendish devilments.

Beware Godly persons that do read this tale. The Ponden Witch is not found yet, and some say she still means to curse and kill all that crossed her from now until the end of time.

'You escaped?' I stand up, letting the delicate page fall to the floor. 'You escaped, Agnes? What happened next?'

Before dawn I went up onto the moor, with Catherine on my back, and looked in the places where I knew I would find what I wanted, their roots buried deep in the bracken. It was not the season for foxgloves, and the cold earth was hard as bone. On my knees, I dug down as deep as I could, clawing away clumps of frozen earth until I found the bulbs I sought, collecting many more than I needed, storing them in my apron. At home, as Bolton still slumbered, I took them out, turning them over and over again in my hands, as I weighed what I would do with them. Great pain would befall the man that ate them, sickness and vomiting, fever, and a feeling as if his racing heart would soon explode. A crushing like a mountain would be placed on his chest, a great fear, and terrifying visions, and then, finally, death. He would not be given a good end. As I thought on it, I knew well what I was about to do. And it came back to me that strange dream from long ago, when I was cast out of Eden. Only now I see Hell, hot as fury, with flames of bile green and devils waiting to torment me for eternity. I know that I will burn when I am dead. But to live even one day on this earth, with my husband and daughter at my side, will be worth a thousand years of pain.

The sun was rising as I banked the fire and prepared his breakfast, when he finally woke, and set out to work. It was a fine day, cold, but with a bright sky, and he was in good spirits. Let him have the day, I thought. Whatever he has done he at least deserves the day.

That night it was harder than I thought it would be to set his fate before him. John Bolton is a cruel man, and has never shown me any kindness, nor affection. Perhaps, if he had been a different sort of man, a more gentle one, we might have made something of a marriage. I might, in time, have forgotten or, at least, learned not to yearn for my Robert. But John was lost to drink and anger before I ever knew him. And a thin, red-haired woman, who bore the child of another was not to be the woman to change him, if there were ever any.

I cut the bulbs very fine, and added salt and strong herbs to the stew to cover the taste. And I thought what life might have been like for me and for John if fate had not marked us so cruelly. There might have been kindness and companionship, love and partnership. Church on a Sunday, and every day in between seeing our children prosper and grow. A small life, perhaps. An ordinary one. But one that might have made me happy. Before Casson ripped me from my mother and made me party to a murder. Before Robert showed me what love could be, and spoiled me for any other. Before I was forced to sacrifice my own body to a man that all but hates me to keep a roof over my baby's head and food in her mouth.

But to be the cause of his death? I thought my heart, as battered and bloody as it is, would be more hardened to the notion, but it was not. Not in that fateful hour as, in a rare, warm mood he settled Catherine on his lap as he sat before the fire and sang her lullabies.

I had to screw my courage to the sticking place, as it says in the book of Master Shakespeare's plays that resides in Ponden library. I knew I must either throw out the stew and accept the beating I would get for not giving my husband his meal, and hope one day for an ounce of contentment in this short and brutal life. Or feed John Bolton his dinner and free myself of that which keeps me from the man I love.

All I have ever wanted was to live. To live the life that I deserve. A life with hope, and light, and love. If I should have never tasted such delights, then perhaps this bleak existence, and my belief in God, would have seen me through.

But God is dead.

And now, so is my husband.

CHAPTER FIFTY-ONE

'What did you find?' Ma asks, long after dinner when we are full of pie and Will is dozing in front of the fire, his head on my lap.

'More than I can figure out right now, except ...' I glance at Ma, who has moved out of her hooded chair and is sitting by the fire in the armchair, stroking the top of Mab's head. 'Except I know that Agnes is – was – a mother who loved her child very much. So much that it's sustained some fragments of her existence for hundreds of years, waiting for the time when she can find a way back to her child again. And perhaps because of Will, or Abe, I am the one she has chosen to right those wrongs.'

'Heaton wrongs?' Ma half asks, half states with something of an air of inevitability.

'I'm not sure yet. Agnes's Robert truly loved her, I think, but getting her pregnant and disappearing certainly didn't help matters.'

'Them apples don't fall far from the tree,' Ma mutters, and I notice how her fingers are twisting and turning in amongst each other, knotting with anxiety.

'Were the Ponden Heatons always thought of as a bad lot, Ma?' I ask her, hoping to lead her a little closer to what it is that she needs to say.

'Well, they borrowed and they never repaid, took land and kept it, drank likes fishes, spent money like it was water. Old Patrick Brontë blamed Branwell's addictions on their bad influence, they say. Don't suppose they were bad as such, more just rough. Country people, who sometimes had a lot and sometimes didn't, and weren't too fussed about how they changed their fortunes for the better. But there were poets amongst them, musicians and storytellers – your dad fancied himself as a bit of one of those. And Emily's Robert – he was a gentle soul, they say, and kind.'

She falls silent, and I listen to the sound of the fire, watching the logs as they burn from the inside, turning each one into a lantern.

'You don't have to say sorry, you know,' I say at last. 'For the way things have been with us. Dad and I were close, and I can see that you felt pushed out. It must have been hard, if things weren't so great between you and Dad that—'

'Trudy,' Ma interrupts me, 'I married your dad when I was very young. I thought I loved him, and he was handsome and funny and there was this house! Back then it seemed like a dream to me, everything sorted. I wanted to be his wife, fill this house with children. I thought we'd have this long and happy life together, but it wasn't to be.'

'Because Dad had affairs.'

'How do you know?' she asks.

'I found a letter from another woman in the tin. Someone called Janice.'

'She wasn't the first, or the last,' Ma says. 'Your dad was a good man, and a good father. But not a good husband. I don't suppose it was all his fault – we got married far too young and he'd had no idea what he wanted from life when he chose me.'

'Oh Ma ...'

'I should have left him, I expect, but I was pregnant with you, and I loved this house. I thought, maybe when you were born, he'd come back to me, but even that wasn't fair. By that time all I wanted was you.'

I don't speak. I just wait as the fire cracks and sparks, and Will breathes, and there is nothing but warmth and peace at Ponden.

'But when they put you in my arms I felt nothing. Nothing at all, Trudy. I tried to love you, I tried so hard. I took good care of you, best I could. I was never cruel; I fed you, clothed you. I was a good mother to you in every way except one. I never loved you, not the way they said I should ...'

Closing my eyes, I'm not sure what I expect to feel; anger and despair? Rejection and hurt? But it's something else entirely. It's relief. Everything makes sense now, and that is an incredible burden lifted.

'... Until now,' Ma says. 'When you walked back into the house that day, the moment I set eyes on you, after all those years, love came rushing in and knocked me off my feet. Girl, I love you so much. I think I always loved you – I just couldn't let myself feel it until that day. Can you forgive me?' she says, and her voice is barely more than a whisper.

'Ma.' Reaching out, I take her hand in mine and then, after a moment, kneel, before wrapping my arms around her. 'You took me in, me and my son when we needed to come home; after everything, you took us in and loved us. I love you, Ma, and there is nothing to forgive – we are only human, we all do our best.'

'There's something else. I've been meaning to say something ...'

'What it is it, Ma?' I hold her hand, and smile.

'Nowt.' Ma cups my cheek in her hand, and I see tears in her eyes. 'Just that I am so glad you are home, lass. I'm so glad you are home.'

Rain poured down as we put him in the ground, the same grave as where his mother, father, their lost babes, and his first wife and their dead infant lay, now almost ten boxes deep. A powerful wind came with it as the Parson made his prayers, snatching away his words as if it would not have the Bible read in this wild place. Bowling down the naked hill it came, tearing at my shawl where I had bound Catherine close against my breast; she cried and screamed and struggled, my strong girl, and I hoped the rain made enough tears for me.

I had laid out his body with something like care, washing him and wrapping him a good new shroud, covering his face against any that might see the terrible look of pain that still racked it. His brother had come, and the Parson, and said prayers over him as he lay there on our trestle table. Mark Bolton told me I might stay at the Smithy until he sells it on, or takes it over, whichever suited him best. Had I been a real bride to John Bolton, I might have asked where was my wife's portion, but I remained silent. What I had done, I had done to gain my freedom, not monies or properties, and the moment that Robert was free too, I'd have no need to fear for myself or Catherine ever again in that regard.

So I'd stood on the hill and watched as they crammed his box in on top of the other rotting boxes, and covered it with the sodden, acrid mud that made this place stink of death. Finally they laid the tombstone back, and John's name was added, very small, near the bottom, to conserve space for the next to be brought there. I thought, as I watched, that at least now it would never be me or my Catherine jammed into that vile hole, afforded no comfort, not even in death.

There was no money for a wake, though his brother did bring a keg of ale to the house, and some sat about drinking and talking of him, until it was late and at last I had the room to myself. Strange how I felt, no guilt, no remorse, and yet I had murdered a man. At the time I felt calm, at peace. And now I feel it again. I almost feel a great indifference to the terrible evil that I have wrought, and though I know that I should fear the flames of Hell, I do not. For I will never leave this earth, not even in death. I am more bound to the earth and the stinking mud than John Bolton in his grave. If Hell comes to claim me, I will refuse to go.

But then, past midnight, all the calm was ripped away by hate.

There came a knock at the door, and I ran to it, hoping it would be my Robert, who must surely have heard of John Bolton's death these past days, but who had not made himself known to me as yet. But it was not Robert that bent his head as he came across my threshold. It was Henry Casson.

If I had not known fear before, I knew it then. For his eyes burned with a terrible fury, and I knew that Robert must have told him of the secret I planned to use against him, though I could not think why, because it would surely put me in danger of his wrath.

'You were expecting another?' Casson said, looking at me with such loathing and disgust that I longed to crawl out of my own skin, remembering how badly he had used me, and hated me as he had done it. 'You will be disappointed. You are not the only one made widow in these last few hours. Mistress Casson herself passed last night, and her son and his wife remain at her side in Christian prayer.'

'Mistress Casson, dead?' I managed to speak, mindful of Catherine slumbering in her crib, afraid that if she stirred or woke he would harm her. 'Sickness?'

'She was weak, aye,' Casson said. 'The ague took her in the night.'

'Poor Robert.' The words were but whispered on my lips, and yet he must have discerned them for he struck me hard enough to dash me to the floor.

'And what of your poor husband, Mistress Bolton?' Casson stood over me, as if to strike me again. 'Did you really think in your stupid, addled brain that killing him would win you your love back? Robert came to me and told me of what you knew. A secret that was supposed to remain between you and I, and the only reason I have allowed you to continue to live all these years is because you are nothing, your life means nothing, your words ... nothing. You foolish child, how do you think that naming me the murderer of his father frees him of his wife? He is not like you and I, Agnes. He will not kill to get what he wants – he doesn't have the stomach for it.'

All the time he had been talking I had inched away from him, leading him as far from Catherine's crib as I could. My mind was engaged in furious thought, searching for a way to turn this situation to my advantage.

'You are the Constable, you are the law,' I told him. 'You could say that Robert and I were married in secret, a marriage which has only just come to light. You could produce papers, have the marriage annulled, and send the bride back to where she came from. And in return, Robert and I will keep silent on your evil, if you leave Ponden Hall and do not return.'

Casson laughed, spittle gathering in his mouth, as he grabbed me by the neck of my gown, pulling me up to him.

'You overstep yourself, Mistress Bolton. You were but a useless, starving child when I bought you. I gave you what little life you have and you should be grateful to me. You have kept my secret all these years, and in return I will keep yours, if you take your brat and be seen no more in these parts.'

'No! I shall not go!' Such rage as I had never known overcame me, and every kick and punch and mauling that Casson and any other man had ever subjected my woman's body to fuelled me with strength that felt beyond my possession. I pushed him away from me, with all my might, and this time it was he that stumbled.

'No, I will not go and I will not be silent,' I said. 'My husband died of sickness, and he was buried before a man of God, nothing more. But mark me, I will tell all your secrets,

Henry Casson. I will tell them all how you cut William Heaton's throat and threw him in the bog, still alive, to bleed and drown. And maybe you are Constable and I am nothing but a poor widow, but who do you think they will really believe, when they talk amongst themselves by the firelight at night? Half of them think you did it already – they've just been too afraid of you to say aught. But I am not afraid of you, Henry Casson. There is nothing that you can do to me that will make me so.' I had not realised it, but with every word I took a step nearer to him until we were but a hair's breadth apart.

'Don't you see that Robert doesn't want you, or your bastard any more?' he spat at me. 'For God's sake, Agnes, I am giving you a chance to have a life away from this place and the evil that has been done to you in it. Go now, and you may have a chance.'

'There is but one person whose word I will listen to on the thoughts and feelings of Robert Heaton, and that is Robert Heaton,' I told him. 'And how dare you mention God to me. You and I have nothing to do with God, Henry. We have not since you made me your mistress before I was ten years old. Give me what is owed to me, give me Robert, and you can keep the rest. He is all that I want.'

Catherine had begun to mewl, just then, and Casson's eyes went to her crib. A terrible, murderous look came over his face.

'I shall make sure you get what you deserve, Agnes,' he said to me. 'You may be sure of that.'

And then he was gone.

My hands tremble as I write this, remembering snatching Catherine up, remember her slumbering so sweetly on my shoulder. Perhaps, I'd thought then, we should do as Casson commanded and go, vanish into the dark to keep us safe from his wrath. And yet ... And yet I __had__ to believe that Robert would come to my aid, that he loved me still as he'd vowed he always would. For if that one last thing that I held to be true and good was corrupt, then life had no value.

Then had come the noise outside the door and for a moment my heart had leaped. Then it opened and all became horror ...

I do not care what happens to me now. My Catherine is dead, murdered most dreadfully, and they have dragged me here to the crypt to keep me prisoner until they hang me. And I do not care. My baby, my baby! He took my girl from me, beat her, beat her, and ... I cannot write more. These may be the last words that I ever write. They may kill me, but I will not die. Not until I have seen my child avenged.

CHAPTER FIFTY-TWO

'Now what?' I hear Ma's voice faintly in the background as I stand in the middle of the large upstairs room. This room had been our final hope for finding the last of the lost papers.

As soon as we'd moved the last of the furniture out, into the hallway, I'd gone to the old barn to look for tools. It had been something of a shock to walk into the rickety, leaky construction and realise that it probably hadn't been touched since the day Dad last left it.

His old anorak hung on the back of a battered kitchen chair, and reaching into the nearest pocket I'd found a mint wrapped in plastic. In an instant I was sitting on Dad's knee as he drove the tractor, sucking on one of the mints he always kept on him.

For a moment I'd stood in the shadows, noticing his mug balanced on his workbench next to a chewed biro. There's so little to tell me anything of the man I loved so much, and when I thought about it, I realised that though I might have loved him, I certainly didn't know him. I only knew a version of him, the version that played games, made jokes, told ghost stories. The man that had affairs, that cheated on Ma when she was pregnant: I didn't know *him*. And I'm glad I didn't. Perhaps the greatest act of love that Ma could have ever shown me was to continue to hide that side of Dad from me, to let me hero worship him and suffer the consequences of my constant comparison.

Going to his tool rack I'd selected a couple of hammers, some longs nails and a crowbar, and when I'd shut the door on the old barn it had felt as if I was shutting in a chapter of my life that had hurt once, but could no longer harm me. I was healed, and it was Ma who had done it.

We'd taken the floorboards up one by one, replacing them in turn. There were a few discoveries to be made. Under one already loose floorboard, we'd found a battered Matchbox Aston Martin DBR5, the James Bond car, some plastic soldiers and a reel of string that looked as if they might have been hidden there by Dad when he was a kid. After examining the treasure for a moment, I'd put them back where they had been and Ma had handed me the nails as I'd returned the board home. There had been a lot of dust and some signs of woodworm, but no trace of Agnes or Emily's books.

'Tru, now what?' Ma asks me again. 'You sure you checked the Peat Loft properly?'

'Yes,' I tell her, 'I've been over every inch and there was nothing.'

I'd been so hopeful about the Peat Loft. It was an older building, made one with the rest of Ponden when the middle part had been built to join the older parts together.

This humble little building had played an important part in the lives of the Brontë sisters, perhaps even saving their lives. In September 1824, the Crow Hill Bog suddenly burst with a violence that made the ground tremble all around Haworth, causing a tidal wave of earth and mud, some seven foot high, to thunder towards the young Brontë children as they were out walking with their maid. In terror they had fled up the steps of the Peat Loft and taken shelter there as the river of earth tumbled past them. Full of nooks and crannies, deep recesses in ancient stones, some of which were carved with gargoyles faces, it seemed like the exact place where Robert might hide something so important to Emily, but I had found nothing, not even a trace of something, or a hint that something might once have been there.

'Then Emily's book ain't here, or more of poor Agnes's story,' Ma said. 'Maybe when Emily died, Robert was true to his word and burnt it. Or if he loved her as much as the Heaton legend says, maybe he had it buried with him. We could go and dig up his grave in the middle of night and check.'

'Yes, it's not that overlooked, the New Cemetery,' I say thoughtfully.

'Trudy, I were joking.' Ma's eyes widen.

'So was I,' I say, although I wasn't entirely. The idea of coming this far and not finding *The House at Scar Gill* is almost too much to bear. Somehow it feels to me as if all of my future fate rests on the discovery; if I can find something that was so lost no one else in the world knew of its existence, then I can find anything. I can find Abe.

I can't give up now, I just can't.

'He buried the strongbox in the garden,' I say. 'And a jar by the Bee Boles, so it's more than possible that the novel is hidden somewhere on the land.'

'Back then, when Robert died,' Ma reminds me, 'the Heatons owned hundreds of acres. He could have buried it anywhere out there, and we'll never be able to find it.'

'No,' I say and shake my head, 'that's not how this ends. It can't. After all of this, after everything we have discovered and experienced, if I don't find Emily's novel, or what happened to Agnes, then … then I've let them both down.'

Ma walks over to my side, putting her hand on my shoulder as we look around the sunlit room. Outside the open window I can hear Will in the garden, teaching Mab tricks.

'That's the last thing you've done. Maybe it's enough that you've uncovered her story, and the notes you've found from Emily and Robert. The title page, Trudy – that's going to change the Brontë world. I know it's not the whole novel, but it's more than anyone has ever dreamed of, and Agnes is part of that too; people will know that there was this scrap of a kid that fought everything that life did to her to tell her story. That's not letting either of them down.'

'Maybe.' I feel my shoulders slump, the adrenalin of the chase that has kept me on my feet for the last few days seeping away. And then I think of Will, and my promise to him. Never give up hope.

'Robert might have hidden more in the Ponden books. I only went through a little over half of them, Ma. I need to go back to Castle Ellis and check the rest, and the rest of the library. I'm sure there will be more there, and maybe even the location of the novel. If I find nothing there, then … well, then I'll think again.'

'I know you aren't going to rest until you've done everything you can,' Ma says.

'Well, if Agnes hasn't rested for four hundred years, a couple of hours more won't hurt me, will it? Can you keep an eye on Will?'

'Yes, of course. And you come back safe.'

'It's a library, Ma,' I say, mentally crossing my fingers, 'Officially the least perilous place on earth.'

Putting my phone on speaker and resting it on my lap, I call Marcus as I start the short drive to Castle Ellis. He picks up on the second ring.

'Ah, Trudy,' he says, speaking up when he hears the sound of the car engine in the background. 'I wondered what happened to you. I looked in the library and it looked as if you were in the middle of something, but I haven't seen you for a few days.'

'I know, I'm sorry.' I make sure I sound bright and light-hearted. 'I got caught up in the big clear-out at the house, trying to get it ready for the work being done. Actually, I was wondering if it was OK to come over now for a few hours?'

'Oh, not really,' Marcus says, his voice cutting out for a moment.

'Oh … OK, then,' I falter, not sure what to say next. 'Marcus, are you there?'

'Only because I'm not there. I'm on my way back to Cumbria, restoring a house built by two weird old Victorian sisters. Not nearly as lovely as Ponden, but interesting. But of course, feel free to go over. I might see you if you are there in a few hours?'

'Hope so!' I say. 'OK, take care. Bye!'

It's a bright afternoon, the trees aflame with every possible autumnal colour. Flurries and showers of jewel-like leaves fall across the windscreen and there's something crystallising in the cold, clear air, something that tells me that something is about to happen. One way or another, I will uncover the secrets still held hostage in Marcus's library.

CHAPTER FIFTY-THREE

As I let myself into Castle Ellis, the daylight is slowly dwindling. Still, the glass rooms are bathed in a rose-gold warmth. The house is silent and tranquil as I walk through the building to the library; there is no sound at all.

It occurs to me, as I walk around Marcus's home, that there is very little of his personal stamp here. Everything is beautiful, utterly tasteful; but there is nothing at all that tells me what he likes, what makes him feel comfortable and safe. Despite the modernist structure, all the antiques are of the highest quality, each pieced picked out to complement its modern surroundings perfectly.

And then, at the very heart of the house, the square hallway from which both the library and the games room lead off, everything changes. I never really stopped to look before, but here, in this rare private space, I see a little bit of the things that really matter to Marcus.

Both the worn black Victorian sofa in the hall at the bottom of the central staircase, and the silk-covered upright piano that stands opposite it, are exact replicas of furniture from the Brontë Parsonage. More than that, they are items specific to Emily.

The sofa is the identical twin of the one that she died on, where she wrote her last-ever words, perhaps including *The House at Scar Gill*. The piano is a copy of the one that she played. Above it, is what I can only describe as a forgery of her portrait by her brother Branwell, painted in 1833. But what a forgery! Every crack in the canvas, every missing flake of deteriorated paint, has been reproduced so accurately that if I didn't know the original was in the National Portrait Gallery I might think that this was it.

Grace wasn't wrong when she said that Marcus was an obsessive collector, especially, it seems, when it came to Emily. The money and time that must have gone into these items represent a considerable investment, and maybe that's why I don't see any Brontë books on the shelves in the library. Perhaps Marcus keeps them locked away in his secret attic room, a gilded prison for the true loves of his life.

For a moment I stand outside the games room, then pushing the door open, I look at the blank, panelled wall and think of the staircase that leads behind it to the room at the top. I'd love to see inside that room.

But for now I have to focus on the matter in hand.

Leaving Emily's portrait behind, I let myself into the library.

My books, because I do think of the Ponden Books as mine, are just as I left them, the note I wrote, asking for them not to be moved, still in place. I'm fairly sure I left the neatly tucked-away chair pulled out, but still, it's hardly surprising that, if Marcus was in here, he straightened his own chair. He's not the sort of man to leave anything out of place.

The right-hand edge of my note was aligned with the first of the remaining Ponden books that I hadn't examined for signs of Agnes, the last ones of the collection which, judging by the titles, would be as dry as a mouthful of dust to read. Long-outdated property law, seasonal almanacs, political treatises, all of which seem to me to be the very last place that Agnes or Robert would hide something so important and so full of life as her story, whether told by her or Emily. And yet, maybe it was the least-looked-at volumes that would make the best hiding places.

As the sun warms the back of my neck, I pick up *The Rise and Progress of Religion in the Soul: illustrated in a Course of Serious and Practical Addresses* and begin.

Despite their subject matter, each book I look through is a genuine treasure.

So often, from the feel of the leather, you can almost make out the fingerprints of a hundred readers pressed one over the other into the patina of the bindings. The scent of these elderly books is something else too; a little acrid, a little like smoke and old ink. And the feel of the paper – the irregular pages are thick and oh-so-slightly tacky to the touch, every page turn leaving its mark.

Trapped within every page is a lost world, captured moments from ages past that hardly mean a thing to modern life, with ideas and concepts so alien to our own that we might as well be reading words written by aliens. And yet, only within the pages of books like these and others rare and special, can we find what cannot be found elsewhere: the exact contents of the minds of people who lived hundreds of years ago. Each book is a miracle to me, deserving of study and love, and I mourn the loss of every one of the Ponden volumes as I set them back down on the table, even the most humble and dull. This was a collection of books that defined a family, that illustrated their lives, their needs, their interests, for generations, and now they are imprisoned here, in a place where no one cares for them or the people that once handled them. Nobody but me.

Painstakingly, I study each one for traces of Agnes or Robert, and move on from one to the other in turn, until the last traces of the afternoon have turned into evening and I have run out of books.

I was so certain that I'd find something here.

Sitting back in my chair, I tune myself into the air, into my own Heaton blood as it pounds in my ears, searching for traces of Agnes. But there is nothing. It is possible that there are other Ponden books in that great wall of pages that rises above me, but to check every single volume will take days, which means coming back here time and time again, and inevitably seeing Marcus with all the jangling discomfort that brings. I can't give up, I won't, but I have to resign myself to the fact that I won't find an ending to this story today and it stings more than I expected it to.

Sighing, I sweep my tools into my bag, and switch off the library lights. Then, just as I'm about to leave, I hear the faintest of noises in the games room. Is Marcus back? Pushing the door open, I see that the secret panel is ajar, and as I stand on the other side of the room, the motion-activated lights splutter on.

Biting my lip, I drop my bag by the door and go over to the entrance; after the light of the lobby the spiral steps are dark and very cold.

'Marcus?' I call a little hesitantly. 'Marcus, are you up there?'

I wait for a response, but there is nothing except the flow of the wind over vacant window frames.

'Oh, what Hell, I'm only looking,' I say aloud, launching myself through and onto the icy steps. 'It's not like I'm robbing the place.'

I expect more lights to come on as I walk up the spiral steps, but it seems there are none, and after a few steps the light in the lobby turns off. It seems to take an age until gradually my vision adjusts to the dark and I see the lighter stone of the steps glowing faintly ahead of me, a starlit cut-out arc of sky showing through the window at the twist of the spiral above me.

My phone is still in my bag on the other side of the room, so I can't use its light to guide me. I could go and fetch it, I suppose, but if I turn back now, I don't think I'll have the courage to come this far again. So on I go, taking each step one at a time, feeling my way along the constant curve of the inner wall. Twice I pass a treacherously open doorway leading to nothing but thin air and a deep drop, and then at last I'm standing outside the top-floor door, and this landing is lit by an emergency light and the faint glow of a keypad lock.

The appearance of the door does nothing to dissuade me from the idea that this room is a kind of safe. Made out of what appears to be thick steel, it has been tailor-made to fit the Gothic arched entrance.

Leaning against the wall, I examine the keypad, as if simply looking at it might give me some clues. How many attempts will it let me have before setting off an alarm? One can't do too much harm, surely, so I try putting in the code that Marcus gave me for the front door. I'm not surprised when it doesn't work. What would Marcus use? I don't know how old he is, so guessing his birthday isn't an option. If he is obsessed by Emily Brontë, then perhaps it's *her* birthday; but that seems a bit obvious. And then I think of that black sofa downstairs in the hall, and suddenly I know exactly which date he will have chosen: the date of her death, 19 December 1848.

I key in 191248 and at once I hear a clunk deep within the mechanism of the door. Taking hold of the steel handle, I press it down. And the door swings open.

Inside is a world of wonders.

CHAPTER FIFTY-FOUR

This time it's me who is activating the lights as I enter, especially designed museum-quality lights, too, bright enough to clearly display the artefacts that are on show in the series of specially made glass cases that follows the curve of the turret room, but with a low UV band to minimise damage to the documents. There is also a state-of-the-art humidity control unit on the wall, a temperature gauge and a non-water-based sprinkler system. I haven't seen a better equipped room anywhere in any museum I've ever worked in. So what has Marcus Ellis got locked away in here?

I'm holding my breath as I go over to the first cabinet. Inside is a first edition of *Wuthering Heights*, of which less than two hundred copies were printed. In monetary terms it's worth tens of thousands of pounds – one sold to a private collector over ten years ago for £114,000, maybe even this one. But when it comes to its real value, it is priceless to someone like me, who would willingly give their right arm to own such a thing.

Also contained within the cabinet, resting on its own bespoke plinth, is a loop of hair plaited into a bracelet and ended with a silver clasp. Though it is lighter than shown in her portrait, I'm sure that it is Emily's hair, and to be so close to this remnant of her moves me much more that I could have imagined. As I lightly rest my fingers on the cabinet lid, it shifts just a fraction under my fingers, and I realise it's not locked.

Why would it be, when this room is so secure? I lift the lid, hesitating for a moment before I pick up the bracelet and hold it in my hand, feeling both guilty and thrilled at the same time. It seems morbid and ghoulish to us, in this twenty-first century world, to keep such personal relics close by, but not to the Victorians. They loved to live with reminders of their lost loved ones, from woven hair to post-mortem photographs, and so it seems does Marcus Ellis. Gently laying it back on its velvet pillow, I close the lid and move to the next cabinet.

None of this feels real; it's like walking through my very own dream, caught up in a bubble of fantasy where there is only me and these books. I catch my breath as I see one of the items I've been searching for, even though I didn't know it until I set eyes on it. It's a letter from Emily, a letter to my great-great-uncle, Robert Heaton.

19 December 1848

Dear Robert, it is done.

Here is the third volume of The House at Scar Gill. I have asked for a doctor to be sent for, now I have laid my pen down. For I am weary.

You know all my wishes, you are a true friend.
EJB

So short and so frail, the words almost seem to tremble off the page, but now at least I know that Emily finished her novel, and I am certain that it was the will to complete it that kept her alive for so long, for this note was written on the day that she died.

There is something more to consider, too. Marcus Ellis *knows* about *The House at Scar Gill.* For how long he's known I can't be sure, but I'm certain this letter was discovered in one of the Ponden books that have been in his family since 1898. Perhaps he's known since he was a teenager, trying to steal into the house behind Ma's back to search the box bed, but certainly he knew before he took such an interest in me and my house. He wanted access to Ponden so that he could look for Emily's hidden novel, I'm sure of it. My stomach lurches at the thought that he might have already found parts of it, and the idea that something so important might be kept prisoner here is almost as unbearable as knowing that it could be lost forever.

Under Emily's letter is a note written by Robert; I recognise his hand at once. He has painstakingly copied out Emily's last poem, 'No Coward's Soul Is Mine', written just before she died, and at the very end added his own line.

'For it will always be you as long as I live and long after.'

Poor Robert, suffering so deeply from a love that would never be requited, not in life, not in death. And yet he never failed her, never let her down. He was true to the last. After all, it was only after his death that these fragments, concealed in his library, were stolen away.

Pulling myself out of the moment, I rush to check the other cabinets for signs of Agnes or *The House at Scar Gill* – and can't believe what I see.

In the first cabinet I see a Shakespeare's First Folio.

My heart almost stops as I lift the book and turn it to the title page. On the opposite page to a line portrait of the bard, and the words *Mr WILLIAM SHAKESPEARES COMEDIES, HISTORIES, & TRAGEDIES. Published according to the True Original Copies*, pasted just under the famous message 'To the Reader', lies a Ponden bookplate.

This is the Heaton First Folio that I am holding in my hands. I close my eyes for a moment to feel the weight of it, to consider that I am holding around £3.5 million worth of book in my hands. I place it back and move to the next cabinet. This one is bigger, presenting its contents face out, and I recognise it at once. John James Audubon's *The Birds of America*, one of the rarest and most precious books on the planet. Double Elephant sized in paper terms, it stands at around three feet tall, resplendent and in incredible condition, staring out of the glass at me. I don't need to touch it to know it is the Ponden edition; of course it is. When this book was published in 1838 it cost £1,000, a small fortune back then, but my ancestors, in one of the family's wealthier times, snapped one up at once, and kept it, largely unread, it looks like, until it was stolen from them.

Rather than feeling angry or bitter, laying eyes on something that was thought of so permanently and irrevocably lost, spurs me on. There are more mysteries waiting to see the light of day, waiting to be solved.

In the other cabinets there are more treasures, but none that belong to me: Charlotte Brontë's signature in a guest book, some envelopes and letters with her handwriting, a pair of minuscule slippers, Anne's stockings, and, in its own small case, one of the miniature books they made as children.

I stop for a moment and look at it, my heart caught up in its every dimension.

These were the first things that captured my heart in their thrall when I was a child, these tiny books, just like the ones I made at home. And now there's one here, close enough to hold in the palm of my hand. This is what he took away from the public, what he shut away from the eyes of other ten-year-old kids who might have seen it and been transformed. And now I know why I don't feel at ease around Marcus Ellis. He wants to keep all this beauty and brilliance to himself; he wants to imprison it. And if he treats books this way, God knows how he treats the people in his life.

There are two cases left, and I gasp at the sight of a Gutenberg Bible. This incredibly rare, fifteenth-century book was the first of its kind, the first to be printed using movable metal type, and I have never seen one with my own eyes before. I can't fathom how much Marcus must have paid to have acquired this. And then something occurs to me: early last year a rare books' storage unit was broken into, and a Gutenberg was one of the books stolen. It was widely publicised that the copy had a tear along its third page, the information released to warn buyers off from purchasing stolen goods. Instinct makes me look, and sure enough, there is the tear – a photograph of this page was spread so widely across the media and the Internet that I recognise it at once. A collector, Marcus would have *known* he was buying a stolen item. But that's what a true collector does; if they can't find something they want the right way, they will find it any way they can. Because it's not about what the desired object is, it's all about owning it.

The next case is empty, and I'm glad it is when I see a small brass plaque already fitted to it, reading *The House at Scar Gill*.

He hasn't found Emily's secret second novel before me.

At the end of the room is a roll-top desk, and above it, a framed family tree, with Marcus's name solitary at the bottom. A curious sensation of expectation rises as I walk towards it. Resting my finger on the glass, I trace his line backwards through the generations, and right at the top of the family tree sits Marcus's direct ancestor.

HENRY CASSON, BORN 1604, PENDLE.

Marcus is the descendant of Henry Casson, the man who did his best to take everything from my family. The fury is unexpected, as if the memory of the injustice he inflicted upon us was coded into my DNA. Almost four hundred years shouldn't mean a thing between that man and the man whose house I'm standing in, but it does. So first I feel fury, and then, underneath it, I realise I'm afraid.

So Casson came from Pendle. He would have been a child of eight at the time of the hysteria of the witch trials, he could even have been one of the child accusers; at the very least he would have known the power that the terror of witchcraft could hold over a God-fearing population, power that he decided to use against Agnes, to punish her and silence her. And as for Marcus, I know now exactly why he was so interested in me, in my house.

'Ah, Trudy,' he says behind me as if I have conjured him from the air. 'There you are; right in the heart of my collection, just where you belong.'

CHAPTER FIFTY-FIVE

'Oh, Marcus!' I manage a laugh, my hand fluttering to my mouth, girlish and foolish. I'm going with that angle, which isn't at all like any behaviour that he's seen from me before, but maybe he will believe that I've been seduced by his marvels. 'Please forgive me. I was finishing up in the library and thought I'd just like to figure out how Will got back here; and, well, I couldn't resist climbing the steps – I mean, who could? And when I got here the door to this room was open, so ...'

Marcus smiles, leaning against the wall as he watches me. He produces his phone and holds it up for me to see.

'I get an alert to my phone every time someone attempts to log in. But credit to you, it didn't take you long to figure out my passcode. The truth is, I was rather hoping you would.'

'You are obviously a *huge* Emily Brontë fan; why on earth keep that under your hat?' I gesture at the books, glossing over my incursion. 'I mean, Marcus, these are incredible treasures. I'm totally blown away, really. I know I shouldn't have come in here without asking you, but I mean, *wow*. These are the sorts of things to make a girl's heart race.'

Marcus steps into the room, pushing the door shut behind him. I watch it thud to a close. Walking over to the empty cabinet, he stares at the vacant plinth within for a moment, before looking at me; a few seconds in which it just seems like a good idea to stroll a little closer to the shut, but unlocked, door.

'You know about Emily's second novel, don't you?' he says.

'Yes.' I admit it at once; what's the point of lying?

'What did you find in your house?' He turns to me, leaning towards me, intent on discovering what I know. 'When I was looking through the Ponden books, that's when I found those letters. I couldn't believe it, Tru. A new novel, a Brontë novel. A new *Emily* Brontë novel. And it felt like she meant it just for me. I searched every one of the other books from the Ponden library, but there was nothing else, so I figured that there must be more clues in Ponden itself. After all, that's where the books came from, where Emily spent a great deal of time.'

'I found more notes from Emily,' I tell him. 'And a buried strongbox – but it was empty. And I found out her inspiration for the novel. The story of a girl called Agnes. She lived at Ponden at the time of Henry Casson, your ancestor. It was her story that Emily was writing about, Agnes's, and what Casson did to her.'

Every sensible part of me rebels against what I'm telling him, and yet I can't resist sharing what I know with someone who will find it as incredible and exciting as I do.

'Emily's second novel was about my family?' Marcus shakes his head in amazement. 'I *knew*, I always knew that I had this special connection to her. I felt it. When I read *Wuthering Heights* for the first time, I felt it. She would have understood me, I know it.'

'Perhaps,' I say. 'Though I have to say that from what I know so far, Henry doesn't come out very well.'

'Legend has it that he was a bad 'un,' Marcus says and grins. 'Some even say he's the Greybeard that you people see when there's about to be a Heaton death. That he's doomed to haunt the people he can't have for eternity. But he can't be that bad; he let you Heatons get your property back, didn't he?'

'Yes,' I say carefully. Nothing about him is offensive, nothing is threatening; he's his usual jovial self, and yet I am terrified of him. 'Do you know why he did that? He could have argued about it in the courts for decades, but he didn't. He relented.'

'I don't know.' Marcus shrugs. 'Henry made a deal with Robert Heaton, but I don't know why, so Robert bought back his inheritance, and Henry – well, he vanished into thin air. Luckily, not before he'd done his duty in continuing the family line. Some thought Robert had paid him to leave, or even killed him himself, but we'll never know.'

I wouldn't be so sure of that.

'You'd never heard of Agnes before now?' I ask him. 'She came to Ponden with Casson from Pendle – you have some papers on her in your box files that I came across the other day.'

'Oh those!' Marcus grins. 'That was my dad's project, tracing the family history, etc. He's the one that had the family tree commissioned. Never really appealed to me. All I want is to find that novel. Imagine that, Trudy, to be the first people to set eyes on it, to read it, to hold it. To know what was in her mind before anyone else. It would be like … it would be like being as close to her as it's possible to be.'

'It certainly would have been a wonderful discovery to give to the world,' I say. 'And that's what I plan to do with the papers I've found, Marcus. But I've looked everywhere for her novel, everywhere there is to look. In the house and on what's left of our land. There's twenty more acres to search, but that doesn't belong to the Heatons any more. I think we have to accept that it's lost.'

'No, Tru, we don't.' Before I know it, Marcus has crossed to room and is holding my arms in his hands. 'You and I aren't the sort of people to give up on something like this, are we?'

I see the focus in his blue eyes, the determination and, yes, obsession.

'No, you're right. For now, though, I'd better get home to Will.'

'Will you let me help you look at Ponden again?' Marcus asks me. 'Let me search the house with my builder's eye. I could take it apart, brick by brick, and put it back together and you'd never even know.'

'No, honestly, Marcus, I swear to you it is not there.' I have to hold his gaze for several seconds before he seems to accept my word and lets me go. 'But thanks, we'll just have to keep looking and hoping for the best. And thanks for not going mad about me being up here. I'll call you tomorrow.'

'Trudy ...' Marcus steps in my path as I walk towards the door. 'I hope you don't think less of me, for my passions.'

'Of course I don't.' I make myself smile. 'I love her too, you know. We differ on what to do with treasures like these, but I understand you, Marcus, because I feel the same way that you do.'

'Then don't go now.' Marcus closes the space between us. 'I admit that when I first came to Ponden it was the manuscript I was interested in, that I was excited by being so close to a part of Casson history. But then I met you. I never expected to feel so drawn to you, Trudy. You excite me. A Heaton, a direct descendent of the family that took Ponden away from my ancestor, of the man who loved Emily Brontë. You are like a living artefact yourself – and I want you. If you were mine you could have my library, this room, all of these treasures, whenever you wanted them. I'd be kind to you, Trudy; I'd love you, take care of you – and it wouldn't matter if you never loved me in return, as long as

I had you. Together we'd reunite two families and Ponden would be back in the hands of both of its owners. Wouldn't that be something?'

'I have to go ...' But even as I say it, I know that he isn't just going to let me leave.

'Don't go, not yet.' Marcus holds my arms once again; I feel his hot breath on my cheek. 'Trudy, it feels like fate, doesn't it? Our families have always been entwined and now, here you are. I know it's soon, but maybe your husband wasn't the one you were meant for. Maybe it was me. It *is* me.'

He presses me against the cold wall and I feel his lips, gums and teeth on my mouth.

'No!' I push him away, and do all I can to keep the fear out of my voice. 'No, Marcus. That's not how I feel about you.'

It takes every ounce of composure I have to look into his eyes without showing him that his desire to collect me, and keep me, just as he has these precious books, makes me sick to my stomach.

'Marcus,' I say carefully, 'you are a great man, and this is an amazing house. I've told you before, in another life I can't see how I would have resisted you, but I love my husband – and the idea of being with a man who isn't him is impossible to me.'

'You don't have to love me back, Trudy,' he says, taking my chin between his finger and thumb. 'You just have to let me have you. Please.'

'No, I don't have to do anything, Marcus.' Oh, the great relief when he doesn't resist as I push him aside and make my way onto the staircase. But he doesn't simply let me walk away.

'Trudy, if you find the book I'll buy it from you. I'll pay ten times more than anyone else. I'll give you back the First Folio and *Birds*, if you'll sell to me.'

'If I find it,' I say, focusing on keeping my footing on the twisting stone steps. 'If I find it, I'm going to make sure it is protected and preserved in a place where anyone in the world can see and study it.'

'But that's not what she wanted!' Marcus grabs hold of my shoulder. 'She wanted it to be kept private, Trudy. Let me have it, give it to me. I'll pay you whatever you want.'

As I try to break free, his grip tightens and I stumble, feeling my feet slide, and I'm tumbling painfully down the stone stairs. The room sparkles and blurs and I taste blood. For a few seconds I stare, stunned, at the shadow above, and then I pull myself up into a sitting position. I'll be covered in bruises, but I don't think I lost consciousness.

'God, Trudy!' Marcus runs to my side. 'Please. I'm so sorry, I didn't mean for that to happen …'

'Just get away.' I stand up, a little unsteadily, grabbing my bag. 'Just leave me alone.'

'What will you say happened?' Marcus keeps asking me the same question as he follows me out to the car, which

I'm pretty sure I shouldn't be attempting to drive, but I don't care; I just have to get away from here.

'It was an accident,' I say. 'I just want to go home, Marcus, just let me go home.' But he takes the keys out of the ignition.

'Marcus!'

'Trudy, promise me you'll keep it to yourself – about my treasures room?'

As I stare at him, the world swims and sways a little. I should just say yes and get my keys back, but the words come before I can think of them.

'Marcus ... there's a stolen Gutenberg Bible in your treasures room. Everything else you have, maybe you acquired them legally, although you and I both know that all the Ponden books should be with my family. But I *know* that Bible is stolen – and I can't keep that a secret. Now give me my keys.'

'Wait,' he says. 'I've got something. I'll let you see it if you promise not to go to the police.'

'What is it?' I ask him impatiently. When I wipe my forehead with my fingers they come away tacky with drying blood.

'Henry Casson's confession,' Marcus tells me. 'The last thing he wrote before he vanished. If you keep quiet about the Bible, I'll let you have it.'

The moment he says it I know that I want it, and I also know that I will never have another chance like this again.

'Throw in all the Ponden books you have in the library. Return them to me and you have a deal.'

Tru and Abe

His hand had moved from the top of my thigh, over the curve of my hip, and settled in the nook of my waist, his eyes on mine as we lay, face to face, covered only with a sheet.

'I wish you didn't have to go,' I'd said softly. 'I miss you so much when you aren't here, Abe.'

'It's just for a few weeks. And you'll get full control of the TV back and all of the bed – you know how you like all of the bed.'

'I do like all of the bed,' I said. My hand had travelled up the curve of his bicep to his face, and he'd rubbed his stubbled cheek against my hand. 'But even after twenty years I like you more.'

'Good to know.' Abe nuzzled in closer to me. 'This will be the last time. I'm getting too old for humanitarian aid work. Who do I think I am, Captain America?'

'Captain Hackney, more like.' I had pressed my lips into his cheek. 'All that we've been through to get here, Abe. There have been times I thought we might not make it, but through it all we've stuck together. That means something, it means we're strong.'

'The strongest,' Abe had told me. 'Strong enough to last one more trip.'

'One last trip,' I'd sighed. 'Just be safe and come back to us.'

'No need to worry.' Abe had smiled as I'd rolled into the crook of his arm. 'Don't you know by now that what we have is unbreakable, Trudy? When we've come this far there isn't anything in the world that will keep us apart, I swear it. Twelve weeks and I'll be home again. Forever.'

'Promise?' I'd climbed on top of him. 'Promise you'll come straight home, that you won't be seduced by some young doctor, or the offer of another trip and a chance to bask in glory again?'

'I promise,' Abe had said. 'I love you, Trudy. There is nothing in the world that will ever keep me from you.'

'Or me from you,' I'd said.

CHAPTER FIFTY-SIX

'Bloody Hell!' Ma makes me sit down the moment I get through the door. 'What the Hell happened?' She narrows her eyes at Marcus as he follows me into the sitting room.

'She fell,' Marcus says as I collapse onto the sofa. 'Total accident. I drove her home – she wouldn't let me take her to a hospital.'

'They'll only tell you to keep an eye on me for forty-eight hours, and I'm fine now. I'm married to a doctor, remember?' I tell Ma.

'That's not the same as being a doctor, lass.' Ma observes me anxiously.

'I just need a rest and a cup of tea, Ma.' My head is pounding, but I'm not about to tell her that. I want Marcus to go as soon as possible, not find more excuses to hang around.

'Bring in those boxes,' I tell him, and at once he does my bidding.

'Where's Will?' I ask Ma.

'He met Jean's grandkids on the lane, and they took him back up to Jean's for a play. One's in his year, so I thought it'd be all right. I'll walk up and get him in a bit.'

I nod. 'Yes, that's good, I think.'

'What did you fall down to get a cut that nasty?' Ma narrows her eyes at the door Marcus has gone out. 'I'll kill him.'

'Will you put the kettle on? Cake might help, too.'

'I'll get some Dettol, clean you up,' she says, bustling into the kitchen.

'You can go now,' I tell Marcus when, several minutes later, he brings in the last boxes, setting them at my feet.

'All the Ponden books, except for the First Folio and *The Birds of America*.' Marcus repeats the terms of our deal, during the making of which I realised that I hadn't been that badly hurt at all, but there was no harm in exaggerating a little.

'And you'll lend the miniature book to the Parsonage for an indefinite period,' I say.

'And if you do find Emily's novel ...'

'I don't think I will find it, but if I do, you will be the fourth person I tell,' I promise him. 'I'll send out a cab and an extra driver to pick up my car tomorrow.'

'Do you think, one day, sometime in the future, you might feel differently about me, Trudy?' Marcus asks me.

'No.' I look him in the eye. 'No, I don't.'

And as I wouldn't put it past him to have kept some of the books back, I follow him out to his car, scanning the boot and the interior as he climbs in.

'I'll call about the restoration work,' he says. He really is unbelievable.

'Don't.' I shake my head. 'I think it's best if I find someone else.'

I walk a few steps down the hill, watching his car retreat, tracking it as it takes the narrow bridge across the reservoir, then it's out of sight.

As soon as he is gone I feel the stillness.

I see him as soon as I turn around, standing in the dark afternoon, staring at me, squat, ugly face lined with misery and hate, a grey beard. In his hand he is holding a lamp. Greybeard doesn't move even one fraction as I walk towards him, my heart quickening with every step. Never have I been so afraid, and never have I been so furious, so much so that I realise I am running at him.

'Leave my family alone!' I shout, in full charge and then—

There is nothing there. Not even a disturbance in the air. Nothing.

I touch my finger to my bruised head. He was there, *it* was there. But it was a knowing thing, a conscious thing. What I had seen was nothing more than a reflection, an echo of one moment that happened very long ago.

And yet my legs are trembling as I turn into the house.

Ma is standing in the doorway.

'This time he's come for me,' she says with a faint smile. 'I am so much a part of this place now that I'm a real Heaton ...'

CHAPTER FIFTY-SEVEN

'I found the lump the night before Jean came to tell me you'd called,' Ma says as I pour her tea, strong and sweet. 'Right big it is, too.'

She gestured to her right breast. 'I thought maybe it'd go away. I don't know how long it's been there, maybe months. I been trying to pluck up the courage to go to the doctor's, but what's the point, Trudy? I don't want those drugs that they give you, that radiation that makes you more sick than the cancer. I've been dreading it, wondering what the point would be. And then ... then you and the lad came home, and I knew I had to try. I wanted to try, I was just working up the courage.'

'Oh Ma, you must have been so scared.'

'Not now.' Her expression is one of resignation. 'Not now Greybeard's been for me, because now I know. Nowt doctors can do, is there?'

'Ma, are you serious?' I look at her. 'That ... *shade* or whatever it was out there, that *nothing*, doesn't determine whether you live or die. It could be anything, it could be a cyst.'

'Omens of death don't turn up for a cyst,' Ma says, taking my hand, and it hurts me to see how sad she looks, how defeated. 'Look, lass, I know all that's happened to you, and it's been an awful tragedy, but you mustn't feel sad about me. I'm only glad that Ponden called you back home when it did, for your sake and for me and the lad. To have you and our boy here, to feel like we've – we've made amends. It means the world to me. I can die happy, I can.'

'No, you can't.' I shake my head. 'Ma, do you think I'm going to let you die now? Now, when I need you more than I ever have? I always thought that Greybeard was a curse, that's what everyone told us, but what … what if he's a warning, Ma? And if he's a warning, then that means there's time to save you. We are going to the doctor first thing in the morning.'

Ma shakes her head, and a tear falls onto the table top; her fingers tighten around mine, her voice is tightly controlled.

'I'm right scared, lass.'

'You, scared?' I smile. 'There ain't nothing in this world that scares my ma.'

CHAPTER FIFTY-EIGHT

*A confession to Murder made this day on All Hallows' Eve
1659.*

*I am an evil man who has done wrong and am set to
burn in the fires of Hell. I write this confession, only hoping
that after my death, Hell is where my soul may reside, and
that it will not be those that I have wronged who will lay
claim to me.*

*It was I who murdered William Heaton and did hide his
body in a peat bog. I found him on the road, uninjured, and
returning home after the war. He told me of his land, his
wealth and his wife and child, and I that had none of this,
desired to take what was his. A small girl that I had bought
from a woman on the side of the road saw me do it, and though
I paid no mind to her, I was wrong not to.*

I married Heaton's widow, beat her and her son.

*I killed Agnes Bolton's baby, the same girl that I had
purchased years before, to keep her from exposing my crimes.*

*It were my actions that caused Agnes Bolton's death, and
I saw her buried in secret on unconsecrated land where she
will find no hope of rest.*

Now her revenant has found me and she will not leave me be. Not night nor day, not if I close my eyes, nor struggle to keep them open. I see her everywhere I look, head half drenched in her own blood, waiting for me.

Dear God, do not forgive me, I do not ask it, but let me burn in the sanctuary of Hell.

Dear God, do not let that woman take me.

At the very end of the confession, someone, perhaps Henry Casson himself, has drawn a portrait of a man and written his name underneath it, a crude sketch of an angry-looking man, wearing a furious scowl, with coal-black eyes and a long grey beard. It's the image of the man I saw less than an hour ago.

Is that what became of Henry Casson? Did he became tied to this house, somehow, doomed to spend eternity as a voiceless Gytrash?

'I'm going for a lie-down,' I call to Ma and Will as I head upstairs, but instead of turning into my room, I walk into Cathy's room, and I feel a little light-headed as I climb inside the box bed and draw the door shut.

'Did he kill you, Agnes?' I find myself muttering out loud as I look at the little square of night sky outside the window. 'Is that what happened? He killed you and put you somewhere and you can't be with your baby, is that is? And you, you bound him to this house, turned him into a wraith with no home or purpose except the foretelling of a death.

Is that what happened, Agnes? I wish you would show me. Show me where you are.'

It feels like a dream when I see a hand with slim white fingers and broken, bloody nails extend out of the darkness at the end of the bed and reach for my hand.

It almost feels like that, but it's not.

The whites of her eyes luminesce in the darkness, black at their centre as they stare at me.

'Come,' she whispers. 'I have been your ghost. Now you will be mine.'

CHAPTER FIFTY-NINE

Not in the dark of the box bed room any more, but in a dark that is so all-encompassing it feels like I have been swallowed whole by it, that I will be lost to it for evermore. I am curled against something, something rough and hard and freezing cold. Stone. A stone wall that, when I run my hands over it, is slick with moisture, and yet I cleave onto it, for at least it is solid, real. It reassures me that I am not lost in some dark eternity.

From somewhere else in the darkness I hear weeping, weeping that is almost silent. A drawing in of jagged breaths, a quiet, whimpered release. And then, behind me, I hear footsteps and the weeping ceases at once.

Bolts draw back, and a tall man enters, carrying a lantern before him, and as crude as the drawing was, I recognise him: Henry Casson – Greybeard himself. The room lights as I scramble up, backing against the wall in terror as he walks past me, setting the lantern on the butcher's block. And then I know where I am: I am in the cellar and it is Agnes crying silently in the corner.

'What do you cry for, Agnes?' the man asks her, leaning against the very wall that I am cowering against, as if I am not here. But of course I am not here, not for him. *I* am the ghost here. My vision swims violently, terror spreading through me at the thought that this might be the rest of my existence, trapped in one moment of misery forever more.

He leans forward, his face cruel and harsh behind his scraggy, filthy beard.

'What do you cry, Agnes? I saved you from the noose, didn't I?'

'I would have died with your name on my lips.' Agnes stands and I see her as she really was for the first time. A girl, hardly more than a child, thin, dressed only in a cotton shift, bruises covering almost every inch of her frail body. 'You took my baby from me, my child that had never done you harm, you took her from my arms and you ... and you ... and you ...' Her cries are gut-wrenching. 'God's mercy, please kill me now, Casson, I beg you, for I only want to die and be with her once more.'

'You would have killed the child one way or another,' Henry Casson says, licking his lips. 'I warned you. I told you to leave this place, but you did not. What I did was cruel, yes, and bloody. It gave me no pleasure, but it was necessary, Agnes. You made it so when you ceased to fear me.'

'Why did you not just let them hang me?' Agnes wails, darting forwards as far as the heavy chains around her ankles will let her. 'Why not let me be hanged?'

'Because you are mine.' Casson stalks across the room. 'I paid good money for you, remember? You are mine and I shall do with you what I please, for as long as it pleases me.'

Bile rises in my throat as I watch him looming over her, his pleasure in cruelty pouring off of him, radiating into the flickering lamp.

'You will not.' Another man stands in the doorway, younger, not much older than Agnes, and I know at once that this is my ancestor, Robert Heaton. He has my father's eyes.

'You will give her to me. And you will leave this place forever.'

'Why in God's name should I do that?' Casson turns on Robert.

'Because when Agnes told me that you had murdered my father, she also told me where. I have found his body, Casson, and I know she speaks the truth; many know it. Many have been too afraid to say it, except for this one woman that you brutalised and tortured. Whose precious child you took from her. You are a killer, Casson, and a thief, and I have witnesses up and down the county willing to say so. You will certainly hang unless you relinquish Agnes to me and write over my house, and all of my property, back into the Heaton name, removing yourself and your son from my sight at once.'

Agnes watches, her face rapt, her eyes shining in disbelief, as her beloved comes to rescue her after all. And it kills me to see the hope there, to see her belief in their love that can endure even this torture.

'And what? You'll put aside your pretty, rich wife, for this whore?' Casson's laugh is bitter.

'I will,' Robert says. 'For she is my true wife. And my true love. And though I am sorry for the hurt I have caused, I was not free to marry another.'

'Robert!' Agnes reaches out for him, but before Robert can reach her Casson strikes him hard in the gut, and it is only when Robert falls back at my feet do I see the punch delivered the blow of a blade.

But Robert is not finished. With almost superhuman determination he climbs to his feet, charging at Casson, whose head collides against the meat block, and he sprawls unconscious on the floor.

'Come, Agnes.' Robert hastily unlocks her chains, wraps her in his cloak. 'I'll take you far away from here, to somewhere you will be safe until this matter is sorted and Casson is finally gone.'

'He will never be gone.' It was Agnes who spoke, her voice as thin and as sparse as a single spider's silk floating in the morning air. 'He may leave Ponden Hall, but he will never be gone, I will not allow it. The moment death ends him, his soul will be brought back here to this place. To these halls and rooms that he coveted so. But he will never be allowed inside again, only stand outside as the centuries roll by, staring in at the life inside with

longing and misery that will never end. This the curse
I lay upon him.'

Robert starts at the sound of shouting from above.

'Come, before his men find him and the whole house is
awake.'

'Go fetch me some boots and a shawl.' Agnes presses her
lips to him. 'I am coming.'

As soon as he leaves the room she looks right at me and
reaches for my hand.

Oh, but it's cold, and the night is a bottomless pool of ice
black. It takes me a second to understand where I am, and
where I am not. I am not here in body, and yet I am here, on
the very brink of Ponden Kirk, the wind tearing and snatching
at whatever I am, doing its best to drag me into the wild air.

In the distance I hear the bark of hounds. I see the light
of torches and hear the thunder of hooves – and then I see
them, one black, moving shape against the night sky, Agnes
and Robert, running for their lives.

'They will be on us, Robert,' Agnes says as they grind
to a halt at the Kirk. 'We can't run any longer, my love; we
can't escape him this way.'

'We can,' Robert assures her. 'We will find a safe haven and
someone will take us in. I will protect you, Agnes, I swear it.'

Her face is luminescent as she stands there in the dark,
her eyes shining as she gazes up at him, as the torches and
the horses draw nearer.

'All I ever wanted was to know that you truly loved me,' Agnes says. 'And you do, you really love me, Robert, you really do.'

'More than my own heart,' Robert says, holding her to him. 'I wish I'd been a stronger man to know it before this moment, Agnes, but I loved you from the first, and I always shall until my last.'

Agnes pushes herself away from him.

'And I love you. But I am bad, Robert. I killed a man and cursed another. I'm not the girl you once knew, and I can't let you end your life for me.'

Her eyes meet mine, and there is one moment when we see each other so clearly it's like glimpsing all of time in one heartbeat.

My cry becomes the howling wind as I watch them part before she runs off the edge of the Kirk and flies into thin air, before falling, her body breaking hard on the boulder below, tumbling limply into the depths of the valley.

'No!' I hear Robert shout in anguish, feel the thunder of the horses' hoofs, the shouts of the men. And then there is nothing but quiet and dark, and her eyes.

And then ... nothing at all.

When I wake, I am standing in front of the closed bookcases in the library, and I know where Agnes's body is hidden.

CHAPTER SIXTY

The crest of dawn arrives over the reservoir as I head up to the Kirk, painting the sky with streaks of silvery violet, and I revel in the birdsong, the glittering frost that makes mirrors of puddles, the grass crunching under my boots.

Once I'm at the Kirk I stop and stare at the splendour of the rising sun, caught for a moment as our earth bows towards it, bathed in its powerful light.

As I half climb, half slip, down the hillside, I have no fear, no doubt. It doesn't take long for me to find the marriage hole and I rest my palm against it, remembering the day that Abe and I came here, and then I turn back to the craggy landscape, full of giant boulders, cleaved with deep fissures, and I begin to search for Agnes Heaton.

The minutes turn into a long, cold hour, but I don't stop, because I know that what's left of her earthly remains lie somewhere here. Of course, this is where Robert would have buried her, here at the place where she gave herself up for him – and Casson would have had no choice but to agree that with the men who surrounded him and had heard what Robert had to say. It would have been done in secret; there would have been no words of God for this poor girl, no chance of rest. Perhaps she followed her beloved home on that very first day, perhaps sometime later, but I know, as certainly as I know anything, that she is somewhere here.

Then, as I reach into the next narrow ravine, I touch a hand. A skeletal hand. Shining my torch in, I see she is laid out in a very deep crack in the rock bed, wrapped in a rotted cloak, the enclosing rock acting as her coffin. Shining my torch around the narrow enclose, I find what I am looking for, three words carved roughly into the hard rock.

Agnes Heaton, beloved.

'I've found you, Agnes,' I say into the wind. 'I've found you, and I'm going to bring you home. Thanks to you I have all the proof I need to find a way to have you and your baby rest together. And everyone will know your story, now; so no more searching, Agnes. No more looking for you or your baby; you can both have peace at last.'

Turning my head into the wind, I hear something wonderful, just for a few seconds, and then it gusts away into the sky.

I hear a baby's laughter, echoed by her mother's.

CHAPTER SIXTY-ONE

Will laughs as I chase him round the house.

Spring has rushed in, full throttle, and we have flung open every window to let in the sun. The builders are about to start on the roof, so we run and we race, enjoying our time together before Will starts back at school, and I return to Peru to search for his father. Ma insisted I go now, though I offered to wait a little longer, but although the lump she had found had been dangerous, they removed it early enough to be sure of her recovery, and she is feeling strong and optimistic about life again. I even found myself thanking old Greybeard for showing up when he did, if I really did see him. The more I think about it, the more I wonder if it wasn't just a trick of a light, and a very bruised head. At least, that's what I tell Ma when she asks me.

I'm nervous about going, and I don't want to leave my little boy, but he is nothing but optimistic, and since I told him that was what I was planning to do, he's never stopped smiling.

'You have to understand that I can only stay for a few weeks,' I told him. 'And then I have to come home to be with you, and to work on my book and get the exhibition ready at the Parsonage. I might not find anything this time, Will, or even the next time I go. And if I do, it might not be good news.'

'It will be good news,' Will reassured me, hugging me close. 'I know it will. Here, I want you to take this with you. It's important.'

'Darling ...' He'd taken his drawing of the brown snake thing down from the fridge and handed it to me.

'Mum, it's OK, I understand. Promise you'll pack the drawing?'

'OK, I'll do it right now.' He'd stood and watched me zip it into my pack, before throwing his arms around me.

Now Ma laughs as she watches us play. Will's disappearing in and out of doors; we hear him chuckle in one room one minute, and then another at the opposite end of the house the next, and it's full of delight.

If this moment should become impressed into the air as so many other Ponden moments have, I hope that when it replays, the people walking in these rooms in the years to come will feel how happy we were, how hopeful.

'I got you!' I hear Ma outside in the garden with Will, and I go into the library, to sit on my own for a moment, because before long this room will be gone and the library will be returned to the way it once was. And when the restoration is finished, I am going to put every single one of the Ponden books back on the shelves. Flopping back onto the bed, I drink it in, this room of mine, where so much of me still remains. And I suppose, even when it's gone, it will still be here, a version, at least, a trace that remains forever.

My phone rings, a novelty since we had a signal booster fitted, and I see Marcus's name on the screen. It looks as if he will escape a custodial sentence, which I'm glad about, if I'm honest. Marcus would not do very well in prison. And even though Ma sent the police to him moments after he left Ponden, he kept up his end of the bargain, and, perhaps as a way to show his good character, he gifted the miniature book to the Parsonage. I let him keep *The Birds of America* and the First Folio, and the last time we spoke I told him they were my gifts to him, as long as he never sold them, and as long as he wills them to my son, and gives me a copy of his will for safekeeping. Will's a Ponden Heaton, after all. Every now and then Marcus still asks me to dinner, though I never accept. That's the thing with a true collector: they never ever give up.

I reject his call and, as I do, I sense the gentle quiet in the room solidify into something else. Becoming perfectly still, I simply wait. It's been so long since there was trace of anything but warmth and peace in this house, that this atmosphere takes me off guard, but it isn't frightening. How can it be? It's Ponden.

There is the sound of a cracking to my right, and when I look I see its source – a thick waterfall of debris, tricking down from a narrow gap in the top of the casement window.

Slowly, I sit up, watching as the plaster dust continues to fall in a steady stream.

Reaching up, I touch the panel of wood that runs across the top of the window, pushing it slightly with my fingertips. It gives a little, moving in and springing outward. This is the only window in the house configured like this, with the panelling all around it. It's the only place I never looked.

Something shifts inside; a weight bowls down towards where I am standing and the panel gives way, delivering what was concealed into my arms in a shower of detritus that rains into my hair and face. Coughing and blinking, I sit down on the bed to see what it is I am holding.

It's a strongbox, exactly like the one I found under the pear tree stump, but this one isn't locked. Drawing in a deep breath, I clean my hands on the bedspread and slowly open the box. And there it is.

The House at Scar Gill by Emily Brontë.

A ream of pages, bound together with a faded black velvet ribbon. It might be all three volumes, it might not, but however much is here it is substantial. A substantial amount of new words by Emily Brontë. Catching my breath, I see that, resting beneath the central knot, there lies a faded and delicate pressed sprig of once-white flowers, some kind of blossom. This will be the first, and perhaps last, time that anyone touches these pages with bare hands in nearly two hundred years, and it goes against protocol, but I don't care. Leaning back against the wall, I hold the manuscript to my chest and feel its weight against my beating heart.

'Thank you,' I say, but now the air is empty of anything but dust and sunlight.

'Ma, Will!' I call out to them as I walk round the back, holding the strongbox, the novel safely within. 'I've found treasure! Where are you?'

'Here!' Will calls, and I see him begin to run up from his den at the bottom of the field; Ma, much slower, follows in his wake.

As I wait for them, a little flutter of white catches my eye low on the ground. Turning my head towards it, I see that the pear tree stump, planted by Robert for his beloved Emily and believed dead for so many years, has suddenly produced a single bloom.

A sprig of white blossom.

Tru and Abe

You never get used to the heat or the oppressive humidity in the air, that much I have learned. I do my best to tune it out, to think only of the vibrant green, the rising mountains and valley, the snaking, steady flow of the brown river. It's so different to home, but also somehow connected at its deepest roots, sharing the sun, sharing the earth, knitting together the world that we live on.

I'd begun in Peru, back at the medical centre where Abe had volunteered for so many years. I was greeted as a friend, as part of the family, and on my first night I wandered from room to room, looking at all the photos of him pinned around the building, even traces of his handwriting. Louis, the centre manager, gave me Abe's favourite bunk to sleep in, and folded up on his pillow was one the shirts he had left behind the morning he'd boarded that plane. It comforted me that night to realise he'd had a life here, he'd had friends. This wasn't a strange, alien land that he had been lost in; it was another place where he'd felt at home.

Louis set me up with a young man who had guided Abe when he went on treks into the forest to offer medical care to the tribes there. On the second day, Adao sat with me and showed me on his maps every inch of every square mile that had already been searched, that he had continued to search in his spare time. To know that Adao had never stopped looking touched me more than I could articulate. As he explained to me the areas he planned to cover next all I could do was to reach out and hug him with gratitude.

Adao smiled and shook his head.

'They were my friends on that plane,' he told me. 'I want to bring my friends home.'

I had been in Rosachina, a nearby town, at an outreach clinic, when I heard two Matsés women, the local people, talking. It was the first time on any of my visits here that I'd seen these truly indigenous people. Something in the animation of their voices drew me to them, and even though I had no idea what they were saying, I knew I'd heard their language before somewhere, and it was as if I could almost understand them. Their backs were to me and I couldn't see their faces, but I knew they were laughing and smiling, and for reasons I will never know I followed them a little way outside of the settlement until they came to the edge and were about to return into the depths of the jungle and to their families.

Then one of the women turned back to look at me.

And I recognised her.

Not her features, not her bright eyes, but her tribal body art.

When she turned to me, I could see that the lengths of her arms and the top half of her face were painted bright red. Just like the faces that Agnes had drawn, over and over again.

'Hello?' I said. 'Do you speak English?'

The women shook their heads.

'Spanish? Portuguese?'

They nodded, laughing as I beckoned them back to where Beatrice, the French volunteer who had brought me here, was working. I asked her to ask them to tell her what they had been talking about before as they'd walked into the forest.

'Trudy,' Beatrice warned me, 'these women aren't a sideshow, you know. You must treat them with respect.'

'I am, I am, I just ... *Please*,' I begged her, and relenting, she asked them the question.

They told their story to Beatrice, who translated it for me.

It was a story of the Korubo tribe who live across the border in Brazil, and were the mortal enemies of the Matsés. Beatrice explained that the Korubo tribe hadn't made contact with the modern world until 1996, and since then have only been seen perhaps twice. The women didn't like them. Beatrice didn't tell me this, but she didn't need to; I could see it in their expressions and gestures: the Korubo are their enemies. But that didn't matter, because they retold a story to Beatrice that had been whispered through the forest, whispers that have found their way to me. Tales of an injured man, who fell out of the sky and almost died, who would have died if the Korubo hadn't taken him in. A man who had been living with them while they healed him, and he healed them. A mad man who couldn't walk, his broken legs yet to heal, but who was crawling to the border anyway, even though he would surely die, because he must return home.

A European man of colour. A doctor.

It was hardly more than a fairy tale, not even really a rumour, born out of half-told facts but how could I not follow this thread through the forest?

Both Beatrice and Adao told me that I was mad to travel on my own into this world where outsiders are not welcome, or wanted, where the arrival of new people brings only destruction. But when I looked at the faces of the Matsés women, remembered the drawings that Agnes had made, remembered her description of a green inferno, I *knew* that I had been on a journey to meet these women all my life, perhaps since before I was even born. I knew now that Agnes had been trying to tell me where to look for Abe – four hundred years before he was born. I tried to explain all this to Beatrice, who shook her head and swore in French. She asked the women to show her where this man was supposed to be on a map.

The women bent over the map, following the line of the river with their fingers, and finally those fingers stopped on a small tributary branching off from the larger river. I caught my breath when I looked at it. And reaching into my bag I brought out the drawing that Will had made, and I realised that it wasn't a snake, it was a river. It matched the map *exactly*.

Beatrice was not interested in what I tried to show her, she brushed it away as superstition and coincidence, but nevertheless she brought me here; she wouldn't let me go alone.

So here I am, approaching the building in the centre of a clearing, where the team have set up temporary medical care for any of the surrounding people who may want it. As I stand there, I hear the call of a bird, louder for a moment than any of the other thousands. I've heard this call twice before, once when I was a little girl at Ponden Hall, sitting around a Halloween fire with my father, and once when my son was lost in a derelict house.

'What's that bird?' I ask Beatrice.

'Toucan,' she says. 'They are like the pigeons of the rainforest.'

And I know that I am in exactly the right place, at exactly the right time. Whatever I discover next, I know that it is meant to be.

Beatrice has gone on ahead; she is talking to a group of men by the door. And after a short conversation she looks at me with such astonishment that I can't discern what it can possibly mean. Reaching out for my hand, she leads me around the back of the building.

'Don't get your hopes up,' she says. 'I expect it's some kind of a mix-up. People get hurt in the rainforest all the time.'

'You mean ... ?' I look at her.

'There's a man on the reserve who may be your husband,' she tells me.

There's a makeshift bed in an open-sided room, covered in a mosquito net, obscured by a half-drawn curtain hung from the ceiling.

Beatrice holds my hand and nods in encouragement, ushering me forward.

It takes every ounce of courage I have to draw back the sheet and see the sleeping face on the other side of the net.

I never thought I would see the face of my husband again.

'Abe.' I fight with the netting to get to him, taking his hand in mine, and his eyes open at the sound of my voice.

'Tru, is it you? Is it really you?'

'It is really me,' I tell him, touching his face with my fingertips. 'Is it really you?'

'Trudy, I never stopped trying to get back to you and Will! I'm sorry it took so long ... my leg, I was injured and couldn't walk for months; there was no way to reach the outside world. But I—'

'You never gave up hope,' I say.

'No.' Abe's hand reaches up and I rest my cheek in the palm of his hand. 'I never gave up hope.'

'Neither did I,' I tell him. 'Neither did I.'

AUTHOR'S NOTE

In writing *The Girl at the Window* I have merged fact and
fiction to create a haunting love story. Ponden Hall is an
ancient home packed full of fascinating history in its own
right, so here are the things that are true.

Ponden was first built by the Heatons in 1541, and
added to in 1634 and 1801 to become the grand house
it is now. It was lived in by the Heaton family until 1898,
when the last Ponden Heaton died and their closest relative
Hannah Knowles Heaton sold the house soon afterwards,
together with the contents of the historic library. It is true
that the most valuable books from the collection, including
a Shakespeare First Folio and the Audubon *Birds of America*
went missing, but other than that the books were sold. We
know what was in the library thanks to a sales catalogue
drawn up by an auctioneer with help from a local teacher,
and all the Ponden books mentioned in the novel were in
the collection, so if you ever find a book with a Ponden
book plate in please let me know!

The Brontë Family were close to the Heatons for many
years. As children Emily, Anne and Branwell took refuge

from the Crow Hill Bog Burst – an explosive landslide that unleashed a deadly tsunami of mud – in the porch of the Ponden Peat Loft, which probably saved their lives. They all used to visit Ponden to use the library, and Emily probably sat in the oldest part of the house, the box-bed room, to read by the fire. In recent years, various house historians have pointed out where the original box bed would have been positioned in that room. We think that bed was still in situ as late as the 1940s, which is the last time it was recorded as being seen. (If you visit Ponden Hall now you can sleep in a reproduction box bed right next to the original Cathy window.) It does seem certain that Emily used that, and other aspects of Ponden's history, as inspiration for *Wuthering Heights*, including the interior of the house. It very probably inspired part of Thrushcross Grange and Anne Brontë's *Wildfell Hall* too.

There is a sketch drawn by Emily, aged ten, of a window, possibly the one in the box bed room, with the fist of a bearded man smashing through the glass, and it's fascinating to think that she might have been dreaming up *Wuthering Heights* even then. Emily was friends with Robert Heaton, who seemed to have had a deep affection for her, and did indeed plant a pear tree for her at Ponden Hall, the root of which can still be seen. As far as we know Emily never returned his affections, but we do know that Robert remained unmarried until his death.

Henry Casson is a real historical figure, who did indeed marry Michael Heaton's widow (and was rumoured to have murdered Michael), and is said to have badly mistreated Michael Heaton's son and heir Robert Heaton until as an adult he was able to buy back his inheritance. Many believe that Henry Casson was an early model for Heathcliff in *Wuthering Heights.*

Agnes Heaton is a fictional character, and both her ghost, and the ghost of the Ponden Child are my creations.

However, legend has it that Henry Casson did indeed return to Ponden Hall in the form of Greybeard, a gytrash, or evil spirit, said to haunt the Heatons by appearing every time a Heaton was about to die, although he hasn't been sighted since Hannah Knowles Heaton last saw him in 1898.

Today Ponden Hall is a thriving and lovingly cared for home and bed and breakfast, which you can go and visit and enjoy!

ACKNOWLEDGEMENTS

The greatest debt of thanks that I owe in the writing of this book is to Julie Akhurst, Steve Brown and their children Kizzy and Noah, who not only allowed me to set a novel in their home, but put up with my numerous (and continuing visits) and have become dear and life long friends. For nearly two years I lived in an imaginary version of their house, you could even say I haunted it. And thank you too to Ponden Hall itself, which is a bright and beautiful building, lovingly renovated and cared for by its owners and you can't tell me it won't know if I leave it out of the acknowledgements. When I first walked in the door I fell in love, and it is a love that is set to endure forever.

Thank you also to my brilliant editor Gillian Green who knows exactly the right balance to strike in amongst my whirlwind of ideas. She is kind, patient, clever and I'm always grateful for her insight. I'm so lucky to have such talented professionals on my side at Ebury Press, including Tess Henderson, Stephenie Naulls, Katie Seaman and Aslan Byrne, and I can never thank them enough for the hard work they all do on my behalf.

Thank you to my amazing agent Lizzy Kremer, who is literally super agent and a woman I admire and am inspired by in so many ways. And the whole team at David Higham, Georgina Ruffhead, Harriet Moore, Maddalena Cavaciuti, Alice Howe, Emily Randle, Margaux Vialleron, Emma Jamison, Johanna Clarke, Claire Morris and Emma Schouten.

Thank you to Sarah Laycock at the Bronte Parsonage who sat with me for a morning and explained to me the intricacies of her fascinating job, and to Ann Dinsdale, Lauren Livesey and the whole team at the Parsonage.

Thank you Flavio Marzo and Liz Rose who took me behind the scenes at the British Library and showed me how they preserve precious books and artefacts. That was a morning I will never forget!

An author's journey is a solitary one, but thank goodness for the community of writers who are out there cheering each other on, especially Julie Cohen, Tamsyn Murray, Kate Harrison, Miranda Dickinson, CL Taylor, Angela Clarke, Katie Fforde, Tammy Cohen, Callie Langridge, Katy Regan, Eve Chase, Carole Matthews, Milly Johnson, Rosie Walsh, Paul Burston, Janie Millman to name just a few. And also to the RNA for its continued community and support.

And to my friends who put up with my moaning and dropping out of dates at the last minute for book reasons; Kirstie Seaman, Catherine Rogers, Margi Harris, Harriet Ivory, Lucy Davies, and those I don't often see but never forget Jenny Matthews, Sarah Darby, Cathy Carter, and Rosie Wooley.

Without the support of readers this job would be pretty depressing. So thank you to the bookish cheerleaders who do such an invaluable job getting the word out, Tracy Fenton and the incomparable members of The Book Club. Anne Cater and the wonderful Book Connectors, Fanny Blake, Nina Pottell, and Isabelle Broom. Also Victoria Stone, Wendy Clarke, Meghan Gibbons and the The Fiction Cafe Bookclub.

In 2018 we lost Yasmin Selena But, a bright and beautiful woman and the founding member of The Bookshop Cafe and huge cheerleader of all books. So much love to you Selena, and all those who I know are missing you so much.

Finally my family, my husband Adam and my children who are so tolerant of me and my work, I love you guys with all my heart. And of course my darling Blossom and Bluebell, without whom I'd probably write books much quicker as I wouldn't be constantly getting up and down to let them out and then in again.

Read more uplifting stories from Rowan Coleman

ROWAN COLEMAN

the *Memory Book*

'Wonderfully uplifting'
LISA JEWELL

What would you do if your memory started to fade?

When Claire writes her Memory Book, she knows it will soon
be all her daughter and husband will have left of her.
But how can she hold onto her past when her future is
slipping through her fingers ...?

Stella Carey exists in a world of night. Married to an ex-soldier, she leaves the house every evening as Vincent locks himself away, along with the scars and the secrets he carries.

During her nursing shifts, Stella writes letters for her patients to their loved ones – some full of humour, love and practical advice, others steeped in regret or pain – and promises to post these messages after their deaths.

Until one night Stella writes the letter that could give her patient one last chance at redemption, if she delivers it in time ...

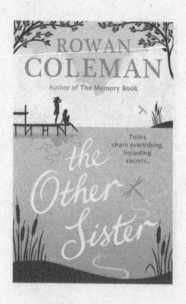

Every family has its secrets …

Willow and Holly are identical twins, as close as two sisters can be. But while Holly has gone through life being the 'good twin', Willow has always been the less than perfect one. Holly is happily married, Willow is divorced and almost twice her twin's size. And when she puts on a brave face to the world, Willow knows she's been hiding her unhappiness for far too long.

So when the past catches up with her, Willow realises it's finally time for her to face her fears, and – with her sister's help – finally deal with the secrets of their childhood before it's too late.

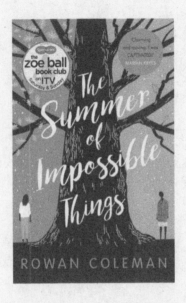

If you could change the past, would you?

How far would you go to save the person you love?

Luna is about to do everything she can to save
her mother's life.

Even if it means sacrificing her own.

Keep reading for a preview …

Watching my mother's face for the first time since the night she died, I am altered. I am unravelled and undone – in one instant becoming a stranger in my own skin.

There is a theory that just by looking at something you can transform the way it behaves; change the universe and how it works at quantum level, simply by seeing. The observer effect, we call it in physics, or the uncertainty principle. Of course the universe will do what the universe always does, whether we are watching or not, but these are the thoughts I can't shake out of my head as I watch my mother's fragile image, flickering as it's projected on the wall. That just by looking at this film of her, I have changed the fabric of everything I thought I knew.

Just seconds ago my mother told me and my sister that my dad – the man I grew up with, and whom I love – is not my biological father. Yes, the universe around me shifted and reformed for ever; and yet the second she said it I understood that I have always known it to be true, always felt my incongruity, in every beat of my heart and tilt of my head. In my outsider's blue eyes.

There is no choice now but to watch on: the course is set and I am travelling it. I have to see, no matter what, although looking will change everything. It's simple physics, the mystery of the universe encapsulated in these intimate, pivotal moments.

But there is no equation to express how I feel, looking at the face of the woman I have missed every second for the last eight months.

She sits in the Oxfordshire country garden of the house I grew up in. The same garden is in full and glorious bloom outside the creaking barn door now, the roses still bear the scars from her pruning, the azaleas she planted are still in bud. But the garden I am watching her sit in may as well be on Mars, so far away from me does she seem. She is so far away now, out of reach for good. A light-grey, cotton dress blows against her bare brown legs, her hair is streaked with silver, her eyes full of light. There's an old chair from the kitchen, its legs sinking slightly into the soft grass. This must have been recorded in late summer because the rose bushes are in bloom, their dark glossy leaves reflecting the sun. It was probably last summer, just after Dad got the all clear, after a few terrifying weeks in which we thought he might have bowel cancer. That means that as long ago as last summer, months and months before she died, she knew already what she was going to do. I experience this realisation as a physical pain in my chest, searing and hot.

'Although the watch keeps ticking on my wrist,' her captured image is saying, the breeze lifting the hair off her face, 'I am still trapped back there, at least part of me is. I'm pinned like a butterfly to one single minute, in one single hour, on the day that changed my life.'

There are tears in her eyes.

'To everyone around me it might have seemed that I kept walking and talking, appearing to be travelling through time at the allotted sixty seconds per minute, but actually I was static, caught in suspended animation, thinking, always thinking about that one act ... that one ... choice.'

Her fingers cover her face for a moment, perhaps trying to cover the threat of more tears; her throat moves, her chest stills. When her hands fall back down to her lap she is smiling. It's a smile I know well: it's her brave smile.

'I love you, my beautiful daughters.'

It's a phrase that she had said to us almost every day of our lives, and to hear her say it again, even over the thrum of the projector, is something like magic, and I want to catch it, hold it in the palm of my hand.

Leaning forward in her chair, her eyes search the lens, searching me out, and I find myself edging away from her, as if she might try to reach out and touch me.

'I made this film as my goodbye, because I don't know when – or if – I will have the courage to say it in person. It's my goodbye, and something else. It's a message for you, Luna.'

When she says my name, I can feel her breath on my neck as she speaks.

'The truth is, I don't know if I ever want you to see it, to see any of this. Perhaps you never will. Perhaps here, in this moment, in this way, is the only time I can tell you and Pia about my other life, the life I live alongside the one I have with you girls and your father, the life I live in a parallel universe, where the clock's second hand never moves forward. Yes, I think ... I think this is the only place I'm brave enough to tell you.' She shakes her head, tears glisten, whilst behind her head the ghosts of long-dead bees drone in and out of the foxgloves, collecting pollen over the brickwork of a derelict building.

'You see, once, a long time ago, something really, really bad happened to me, and I did something terrible in return. And ever since that moment, there has been a ghost at my shoulder, following me everywhere I go, waiting everywhere I look, stalking me. And I know, I know that one day I won't be able to outrun him any more. One day he will catch up with me. One day he will have his revenge. One day soon. If you are watching this—' her voice hooks into me '—then he already has me ...'

She draws so close to the lens that we can only see one unfocused quarter of her face; she lowers her voice to a whisper. 'Listen, if you look very hard and very carefully you'll find me in Brooklyn, in the place and the moment I never truly left. At our building, the place I grew up in, that's where you will find me, and the other films I made for you. Luna, if you look hard enough – if you want to look after you know what I did ... He wouldn't let me go, you see. Find me ... please.'